# ABOUT THE AUTHOR

B. D. Reeves is a Melbourne-based writer. His first novel *Jemma and the Raven* was published in 2023. When he is not reading and writing, B. D. Reeves teaches philosophy and literature. Loving to travel, he once camped in an old shepherd's hut on a remote Greek island where he discovered the remnants of ancient frescos, the secrets of bees, and the friendship of a goat who followed him wherever he went. He has since adored the concept of animals in fiction.

www.bdreeves.com

'Jemma and the Raven is a massive feat of storytelling, a work of fabulous imagination, a fantasy inspired by historical realities. It will convey its readers on an epic journey that will both captivate and exhilarate them.'
ARNOLD ZABLE

'The relationship between Jemma and Edgar is endearing...the pair's mutual loyalty never wavers. A compelling multi-species cast fuels a labyrinthine plot.'
KIRKUS REVIEWS

'This is a beautiful ride through memory, time and a lost world. Jemma and her raven buddy Edgar are characters to take to your heart.'
ROSE HARTLEY

# JEMMA AND THE RAVEN

## B. D. REEVES

Junedog Press

First paperback edition August 2023

*Cover art by Andrei Bat*

Paperback ISBN: 978-0-6456346-1-7
EBook ISBN: 978-0-6456346-0-0

Published by Junedog Press
www.bdreeves.com

*For my Family,*
*Sarah, Asher and Raphaelle.*

# A NOTE ON GEOGRAPHY AND PRONUNCIATION

This story takes place in one part of a memory-land, called Adocentyn. It is pronounced Ad-o-sen-tin, and is comprised of a great city (sometimes referred to as the City of Light, or the City of the Sun) and surrounding lands.

The Wharf is a small, insignificant sea-trading enclave on the edges of the lands of Adocentyn, far away from the city. This is where Jemma lives.

Unlike other parts of the memory-lands, Adocentyn has been shaped by the influence of a magician of sorts, a brilliant Memory Magus named Jiordano Bruno. It is protected by memory Keepers who can change between human and animal forms.

Adocentyn has an opposite - a Shadow city of dying or forgotten memory. These cities exist in different realms. It is possible to travel between realms - this requires the use of magic from the Book of Memory to create special passages, sometimes referred to as Ruptures. It takes much training and knowledge to become a passage-maker.

Behind the Wharf are the wild and jagged mountains of the Scarp, shaped by an older, mysterious type of memory magic. The Scarp once contained lavish and decadent memory palaces that have long since gone to ruin. There are forests in the valleys of the Scarp where Shadows dwell.

Further along the coast from the Wharf, yet closer to the city, are the Delphin Caves. On the other side of Adocentyn and across the sea are the Raven Halls, which hold a vast library of memory-scrolls protected by the Raven Scribes. Beyond the Raven Halls are the unformed lands that are, as yet, unexplored.

# CONTENTS

# PART I
# THE SCARP

## CHAPTER 1

# SOMETHING BIG THIS TIME

'You mustn't climb any further,' Edgar pleaded, 'it's going to be dark soon.'

'We aren't stopping now, not until we've seen what's over that rise. Then we'll turn back, I promise.'

Even Jemma knew this was a lie. She'd had a feeling, ever since they left the road – something was pulling her this way. Normally they wouldn't have taken a route this far to the East where the ruins were too scant, the pass too steep. They had never climbed this high into the Scarp.

From here they could see the road below, where an endless line of Caravanassi wagons was snaking into the valley. In the distance, the lights of Adocentyn glowed as a golden crown beyond the furthest hills, where a searchlight circled, pulsing and winking in the sky.

Jemma kept her eyes fixed on the highest peak. When the cliffs were this crumbly, she knew Edgar didn't like to fly ahead in case she lost her hold. The mere thought of her tumbling off a precipice was enough to keep him hovering just above, calling out instructions about where to place a hand, now a foot, when to slide left or right, to reach for a gap in the rock.

'You'll be late for the fight,' he urged again, 'Sharmenai will scold you like a boiling pot.'

'If we find something this time,' she shot back, 'I'll never have to work in that stinking pit again.'

By night Jemma worked in the wrestling dens, in the precinct of the old Wharf. By day she hunted ruins in the Scarp for the treasure that would buy her a passage to the great city of Adocentyn.

Now her arms ached and she was thirsty and needed to catch her breath. She grew dizzy looking down the sheer face of the cliff where she had spent the last hour bruising knees and scratching skin on thistle-weed. But nothing was going to stop her from reaching the top. Not when she'd already come this far.

From up here, the Wharf looked so small, jutting into the scanty harbour on the edges of the lands of Adocentyn. She could see the glow of the Caravanassi roasting fires and the lanterns of the trade ships blinking on the docks, and the white sails of the wrestling tents. And if she squinted, she could even see her own tiny room, stuck like a barnacle on the end of the Walrus shacks.

Already, the chinking sounds of hammers hitting the iron spikes echoed in the valley. They were securing the sides of the wrestling tents. She didn't have long.

She felt a prickling on her skin, the shiver of the biting Scarp-winds. She turned away from the valley and kept on climbing the rocky cliff, ignoring the sting of her cuts and bruises. Something was up there. She knew it. Something big this time.

For a moment, the clouds darkened. A flock of Sparrows passed swiftly overhead and formed a black hand sweeping across the sky.

Edgar swooped beside her.

'Hide. Quick!'

Jemma ducked beneath a ledge as Edgar flew into a hollow. She had seen these Sparrows before, changing into their human forms and swarming all over the Caravanassi camps, searching rooms, asking questions.

'Where have they come from?' Jemma said.

'The city. There's no one around here who could afford to pay for a Sparrow swarm.'

'What are they looking for?'

'I don't know,' Edgar said, watching the hand pass over them once again and then sweep down towards the forest. 'But they are almost certainly scouting ahead for Poachers. And if they're anywhere nearby, we don't want to be left out on the road.'

When Jemma finally reached the top, on the far side of the ridge, she could see something through the shifting mist. A shape arising from the ruins in the oncoming night. At first, she had to look very hard against the darkened sky. Now it was unmistakeable. It was the tower of a palace rising up above a ring of grey rocks at the end of the plateau.

She couldn't believe her eyes. The idea of ancient castles had always sparked wonder in her mind, but she had only ever seen them in her wild imaginings from the stories an old sea-trader had told her. Never had she dreamed that she would find an actual palace in the ruins.

'Didn't I tell you, Edgar – didn't I say we'd find something big this time?'

'I don't like this. I don't like it one little bit. We mustn't go anywhere near it.'

Jemma took off at once down the slope, running through the mountain grass swishing in the fierce gusts of wind funnelling through the Western gully. Edgar beat his wings to follow her.

'We don't know where it's come from. Who made it. Why it's here.'

'Just hurry up, Edgar.'

Didn't he know by now? This was *her* Scarp. These were *her* ruins. And if anyone was foolish enough to make a palace appear out of nowhere, then anything she found inside belonged to her. By *right*.

Already a plan swirled in her mind. She would raid every room, take every jewel, every golden goblet, every trinket she could find and carry it down to the trade ships of the Wharf. Then she would glory at the astonished faces of the Trade Masters when they saw their 'little Scarp rat' seated in the finest berth to Adocentyn!

'This is reckless,' Edgar implored, flying ahead of her.

The tower of the palace loomed up before them, made of the same grey stone as the Scarp.

'At least let's come back tomorrow. If we're caught up here in the dark...'

'Stop worrying,' Jemma said, feeling her way around the perimeter of the great stone wall, until she came to a thick wooden door with huge iron hinges.

'And help me find the latch. If you weren't a Raven, you'd be worse than an Arctic Gull.'

'Better a Gull than a prisoner. Trust me, we don't want to end up in a dungeon. You've heard the stories – there's magic in the Scarp. The mists can shift and change with your desires, only to trap you forever. What if we never come out again?'

'I'd rather be locked in a Scarp dungeon than spend the rest of my life in that fish-stinking Wharf. This is our ticket, Edgar, once and for all. Our ticket to Adocentyn.'

She found the latch and slowly opened the door.

'Come on,' she said.

Edgar flew inside and Jemma followed. Never before had her feet glided over such smooth shining white marble. She looked up and all around her at the panelled wooden walls with candles set in alcoves, disappearing like little stars into an astonishing vaulted ceiling.

Delicious aromas came drifting, rich and sweet, from somewhere in the palace.

Edgar landed on her shoulder. She could feel his trembling feathers tickling her cheek. Jemma's heart was thumping, more with a kind of thrilled desire than with fear.

'I hope you know where you're going,' Edgar whispered, 'and fast. What if someone's here?'

Jemma followed the enticing smells through a hallway veering off to the side, then curving sharply to the left. Up ahead they could see a crack of light beneath a wooden door.

'This must be the kitchen,' Jemma mused, 'and I'm starving.'

'Be careful,' Edgar said. 'That can only mean there must be a cook.'

She eased open the door and crept down an oak staircase. Lines of copper pots were gleaming above the kitchen fire. The hearth was made of stone and the ceiling was raised with smoother vaulted arches. In the centre was a long wooden table with two glass lamps hanging suspended from the turrets of the vaults. Over to the right there was a pantry built into the stone, containing bags of flour and potato sacks and jars of currants and spices.

The smells of cooling pies and loaves of bread filled their nostrils. A pot of ragout bubbled gently on the stove.

Jemma helped herself to a ladleful while Edgar scolded her. Apart from the hearty cooking, she was disappointed.

There was nothing here to sell. They might get something for those copper pots.

She tiptoed to the adjoining room and saw a beautiful dining table made of a dark shining wood with a fine grain. It must have been twelve feet long, but there were only two chairs, one at either end, which made the other spaces look both empty and quite absurd. Hanging above the table was a glittering three-tiered crystal chandelier that wasn't alight. Opposite the door was a mantlepiece of the same fine wood, supported by carved and gilded columns. To the right, there stood a cedar sideboard with brass handles and cutlery drawers.

On the dining table, Jemma spied two silver candelabras that splayed their polished wealth. She opened her bag.

'Don't even think about it.' Panic rose in Edgar's voice.

'Imagine how much we'll get for one of these in the city?'

'It's too risky. If they see they're missing, they'll know for certain someone's here.'

'Well, you can keep a look out while I search these drawers,' Jemma said.

'And what if someone sees *me*?' Edgar hopped along the dining table after her.

'They won't, because you're such a clever Raven aren't you.'

'Quite the opposite I can assure you,' Edgar said. 'Just don't take anything obvious. And listen out for my warning call.'

'I've never heard that before.'

'It goes like this,' Edgar said, as he flew towards the kitchen. '*Kraa, kra, ah, ah.*'

Edgar saw another door beside the pantry and landed firmly against the handle, releasing the latch. A cold silence emanated from the dark, and the smell of damp. He flew to the end of a hallway where several other corridors ran off in different directions. Along the winding passages were candle-lamps set into the walls.

The whispers of a draft made his feathers shiver. He could hear a faint murmuring from one of the passages ahead.

*I wonder what that is?* he thought. Now he was the one being reckless.

As he came closer, Edgar heard the low hum of chanting. He saw three hooded figures in long black robes sitting in meditation, each in front of a chamber door.

Edgar flew closer in the shadows. The doors were thick and made of a dark heavy wood, cladded at the hinges and around the lock and the peepholes with iron plates. From behind one of the door's grates he saw a bright flickering white. The chants grew louder, the incantations rising intensely as if they battled against whatever was inside, and then the flicker was gone.

Just then, the lamps blew out and the chamber went black. He heard the sound of walking on the marble floor above. Edgar took off down the passage. Someone was talking. He cursed himself for letting his curiosity get the better of him.

He turned right, but this only took him in a winding loop. He'd forgotten the scheme of the passages, and it was only a matter of luck that he saw a crack of light ahead.

He sped down the corridor and back through the kitchen, sweeping into the dining room with a *Kraa, kra, ah, ah.*

Jemma shut the drawer she was pilfering from and dashed towards Edgar, catching him on her arm.

'Voices. Coming right this way.'

She ducked into a servant passage, feeling claws grip her skin.

Edgar heard the jingle in her bag. 'What did you take?'

'Silver spoons – for my collection.'

'And what if they need them for dinner?'

Now she could hear the sound of a match striking light into the chandelier, followed by the clattering of dishes and cutlery, and the tinkling of a wine bottle on the tip of a glass. A deep, urgent voice sounded in the corridor and then the room.

'Did you see the Sparrows? It is only a matter of time now before they find us. You are sure she is safe?'

'She is. I watch her every day. And the Terns would never let a hair be harmed on her head. I'll not leave you either, Master.'

'I cannot risk taking you with me. Piera, I insist you leave first thing tomorrow. You must go and hide in the valley.'

'I'll do no such thing.'

'And if they find you? I'll not have you thrown into the dungeons of Adocentyn.'

'What do you think they're talking about?' Jemma whispered.

'I have no idea, and I don't like this at all. It sounds like big things they're speaking of. We need to get out of here, now.'

If only she'd been able to nab just one of those silver candelabras. 'We're not going anywhere,' Jemma said, 'until I've had a look upstairs.'

~

THEY TIPTOED THROUGH THE SERVANT'S DOOR AND BACK to the ground floor. A grand staircase led them to a long, curving corridor, eventually reaching the door to a study.

Jemma had never seen so many books. It was as if the walls themselves were leather spines etched with golden words reaching to the ceiling. A ladder to the highest shelves hung on a polished brass track. A fire burned in a grate opposite the door, filling Jemma with warmth.

In the centre, a luscious Persian rug was circled by divans and cushions. Jemma threw herself into the soft cocoon where a silver tray was set with fresh steaming tea and almond cakes.

Edgar landed on the mantelpiece. His feathers gleaming like oil in the firelight.

Jemma sank into the cushions and helped herself to some tea and cakes. She was starving after all that climbing.

'We mustn't stay long,' Edgar said, 'and don't even think about eating all of those cakes.'

Despite his warnings, Edgar seemed to be drawn by the surrounding comfort and warmth. He swooped to the other side of the room, where a book lay open on a reading table and began flicking through its pages.

While he was distracted, Jemma scanned the room and spied a crystal decanter full of brandy. There was nothing the traders wouldn't do for that. She slipped it into her satchel, along with a silver paperweight and a brass telescope she swiped off the desk.

Then she opened the desk drawer and took out a gleaming object, holding it out before her – a golden blade, shining with a strange brilliance that she could have mistaken for a ray of the sun.

All Jemma had ever wanted was to find a piece from the ruins, a jewel, a golden cup, whatever it was, she didn't care, just as long as it was enough to buy them a passage to

Adocentyn. The traders had told her of the fine cobbled roads and copper rooftops and a harbour that glittered golden with ships. The market sold the finest of everything in the land. There was a wrestling hall that was ten times the size of their little tent in the Wharf, and Jemma longed to have just one tiny glimpse of the giant tanks and the enormous crowds. All she wanted was a room in the city walls where she and Edgar could live. Where he would no longer be an exile, she an orphan.

Now it was as if she held it in her hands.

Jemma stashed the blade and went to Edgar. 'What are you looking at?'

The open pages of a manuscript held him enthralled.

'I've never seen anything so beautiful as this.'

With a flurry of wings he glided to the fireplace, taking a glowing stick to light an oil lamp on the desk. He peered with awe at a page of magnificent pictures encased in circles, letters and numbers like a combinatory wheel. There were images inside of stairs ascending through layers of symbols, to a brilliant gold-leafed sun.

'I've seen pages like this only once before, in the libraries of the Raven Scrolls.'

'You mean the ones you were forbidden to see?'

'You could say that.'

'Is that why you were banished?'

'It's a long story,' he said, 'and this isn't the time to tell it.'

Jemma saw his hackles flair and she let it go.

'What does it say, that writing?'

Edgar traced the words. 'It says this is the first Book of Memory, that shows the discovery of Ruptures.'

'What are they?'

'It says here they are like passages between lands of memory. And then it speaks of memory as a kind of matter itself – a dark matter – that can be shaped into real, visible forms with the powers of a Magus. A warning of the Shadow of memory, and the danger of its yearning for the light.'

Jemma touched the heavy parchment. She stared at a circle of pictures surrounding one of the wheels in the centre, images of animals changing into human form, just like she'd seen every day on the Wharf. Except they looked more like sketches, as if drawn from what the artist could see before them – Arctic Gulls and Terns, and the forms of the Delphin caught halfway in change between animal and human, frozen in transformation. They looked so vivid and real. She peered closer.

'What's that word,' she said, 'scribbled inside?'

Edgar traced out the letters of a faded text.

'It seems to be the name for all of the pictures in this layer of the circles. *The Keepers of Adocentyn.*'

'Keepers?'

Outside of the circles, Jemma noticed the sketches of other creatures. They, too, were drawn in sequences of change between animal and human form – Seals, Moths hiding in shadows, Sparrows and Finches. And there were the Walruses, their changing forms captured just like Jemma had seen a hundred times before in the wrestling dens. Then she noticed another creature. She looked up at Edgar.

'I wonder who could have drawn them?' Edgar said, adjusting the lamp to a brighter flame. 'Why are you looking at me like that?'

'Well...can you change? It's just that, there's pictures here too, of Ravens – changing into people.'

'I expect that if I could, I'd know about it, wouldn't I?'

Jemma caught the sharpness in his voice. 'Don't be like that,' she said.

'Like what?'

'You know *like what*. I wouldn't have to ask if you told me things.'

'You assume that I know far more than I do,' Edgar said. 'The lands surrounding the Scarp have greater mysteries than I could possibly have fathomed from the scraps I have stolen in the Scrolls. But here is something I do recognise. These lines passing through the circles.'

'They look like the spokes of a wheel,' Jemma said.

She traced a line with her finger.

'It seems to be a sort of map,' Edgar said. 'And here – it shows the figure of a Magus – some kind of magician – combining these pictures with other numbers, letters, symbols to build passages along the lines. It says the paths of memory are difficult to travel. But look.'

'What is it?'

'At the centre, inside the picture of the sun, is the City of Light.'

'That's another name for Adocentyn!' Jemma said. 'One of the sea-traders told me that.'

It was a beautiful, intricate map, and Jemma's eyes filled with brightness. No one had ever taught her respect for books. She'd only ever seen the grotty fish-stained ledgers in the Trade Hall, records of shipments, sales, debts and contracts.

In a single swipe she took hold of the page and sliced it clean away with the golden blade and put it inside her satchel.

Edgar looked horrified. 'You can't do that!'

'Why not?'

'This is quite possibly the most exquisite manuscript I've ever seen. What you've just done is criminal.'

'And I can't carry this lead-heavy thing down the Scarp.

We'll take what looks like the most important page. This map could be *worth* something.'

'You really are a Philistine, aren't you.'

'Whatever that means.'

Jemma turned away from the book and her eyes landed on another object across the room, a funny-looking contraption next to a chair. She felt an irresistible urge to find out what it was and went over to investigate. It was some kind of machine with two reels on the top, which were threaded with dusty, transparent tape. She ran her finger along the tape, it felt like the brittle papery wings of a butterfly. There was a small silvery handle below the reels. She turned it and a scratchy faded image began to flicker on the wall opposite. She could see a child appearing now, perhaps no more than three years old, playing in the shallows of the sand by the sea.

Jemma had never seen pictures like this before, projected from the bulb of a lantern-light. She had only ever seen her own shadow cast by the sun, but these images were moving and beautiful and they drew her in.

The child in the picture was trying to catch the waves with her hands...and then she picked up a fistful of sand and was just about to eat it.

Someone was rushing up to her. It was a woman and she was trying to stop the little child from eating the sand. She took hold of the girl's hand.

The woman's hair was long and full and wavy and Jemma had an intense desire to see her face.

Then something surprising happened.

The woman stood up.

She started to walk away from the little girl, along the sand.

'Wait –' the child cried after her. 'Don't leave me.'

'I never will,' she said to the child. 'I will always be with you. You will hear my voice in the whispers of the lights.'

The woman kept turning, and she was nearly looking back towards the girl.

Jemma was about to see her face. Her heart began to flutter.

But then. No. The film froze.

A black spot appeared on the screen.

'No!'

She let out a loud cry as the blackness expanded. The projector coil jammed and the bulb melted the film.

The heat engulfed the image and suddenly the film snapped and released the coil and flickered around and around the reel.

Jemma rushed forward and snatched the broken reel off the projector and held it with her trembling hands.

Edgar swooped towards her, gripping her vest with his claws. 'Quickly,' he whispered. 'Someone's coming!'

Jemma dashed towards the desk.

'This way.' Edgar sent her scurrying to a little cubicle between two of the bookcases, hidden behind a thick velvet curtain.

# CHAPTER 2

## A SHADOW CITY

'I told you we had to get out of here,' Edgar said.

'You were the one poring over that book.'

'And you were the one making such a racket with that old projector.'

'Is that what it's called?'

'Yes – I've seen them before in the Raven Halls. Images, captured on reels of film, displayed with light. Whatever made you cry out like that?'

'How am I supposed to know?' Jemma whispered crossly.

Two men walked into the room, deep in conversation.

'If your weakness grows any further...' The tone was accusing.

Jemma recognised the second voice from the dining room below.

'Don't waste your words. I'll never let her go.'

'You risk everything. The city itself. What next?'

'The city?' she whispered. 'Do they mean Adocentyn?'

The voices were dulled by the velvet curtains. Jemma parted them, ever so slightly, so she could catch a glimpse of their faces. The accusing voice belonged to a tall, broad-shouldered man with long, thick hair tied at the back. Raddahkin. He wore a leather vest and his fingers were covered in silver rings.

The other man leaned over the desk with his back to the door. He had dark, messy hair and Jemma had never seen eyes like that, fiery and alive even in the shadows.

'If they find her—'

'Perhaps they already have. At least, there have been reports. Except – I might as well say it – we have been watching. We know where she is.'

Raddahkin looked across the room to the gap in the curtain. Jemma jolted back. She could have sworn he was looking right at her.

'I recognise him from one of the great Councils,' Edgar whispered. 'And I've heard that name before.'

'I've seen him too,' Jemma said. 'He runs trading ships up and down the coast.'

'What if they notice the page is missing?' Edgar whispered.

'They won't. They're too busy talking. The sooner they leave, the sooner we can finish collecting.'

'You mean stealing?'

'These are *my* ruins.'

'But this isn't your palace. These are important people.'

'Well, they should have thought about that before they used *my* Scarp to make a palace appear. I'm not leaving here without enough to buy my way to Adocentyn, and some left over for my own little house in the Cobbler's walls. They can talk about whatever they like and they can be as important as the Delphin Queen for all I care.'

Now she had her eye on what else she could fleece. Those crystal glasses would fetch a good price, and those silver trays – just in case she decided to keep the blade for herself. There were sure to be gold trinkets in other drawers, maybe even jewels. And that brass-plated instrument – it looked like those navigation tools for measuring distances by the stars. She had seen them on the big trade ships. Must be worth a mint.

But then Jemma thought of the Cray fishermen at the Wharf, how they made a pretty penny trading knowledge of all the comings and goings of the shipping lanes. Hearing of a surplus catch could bring the fish prices tumbling down, along with a tidy commission for the Trade Masters.

If she listened, she might learn something even more valuable than gold – information.

'In any case, we need to get back to the Wharf,' Edgar said. 'Sharmenai will be cussing the moon by now.'

'Sshhh! I can't hear a thing they're saying.'

'We shouldn't be eavesdropping like this.'

'Just be quiet Edgar!'

Raddahkin turned his back to the fire. 'The Keepers are growing weaker every day.'

Jemma clutched the page from the Book of Memory. 'Do they mean these Keepers?'

'Who knows?' Edgar said. 'Just *you* be quiet.'

'They are putting all their faith in this prophecy of the Erigena: "She will come at the time of the fading of memory, when the Shadows will rise again" – this is what they are saying. And now we have lost the city of Adocentyn to an enemy who is as mysterious as the dark.'

'You must know where they have come from. Who they are,' the dark-haired man said irritably. 'You must have a theory, or you wouldn't be here. Do you care to share it?'

Raddahkin held up two fists, like two worlds held together, side by side. 'The lights of Adocentyn are being fuelled with a new source, like a sun, bright and black at the same time.'

He seemed to cast a glance towards the curtain. Jemma held her breath.

'And what is your point?'

Raddahkin held up his right hand. 'We believe there is another city.'

Bruno looked startled. 'What do you mean?'

'A Shadow city, existing in parallel – not made from memories of light, but memories of darkness, suffering, despair.'

The two worlds hovered before them.

'We believe it is from this dark city that one of your enemies have forged a passage to Adocentyn – using the power of the forgotten.'

Bruno steadied himself on the reading table.

'He looks like he's going to faint,' Jemma whispered.

'If he does,' Edgar said, 'let's make a run for it.'

Raddahkin collapsed his hands. Jemma watched with fascination, as if the two cities, one of light and one of darkness, vanished in the air.

'You have a choice Bruno. Her, or the preservation of this land, and all of its memory.'

Bruno stared forlornly into the fire.

Raddahkin thumped his fist on the table. Jemma's heart leaped inside her chest and she steadied herself against the wall behind.

'Do you sentence us to the doom of the Shadows?' Raddahkin said.

'The Keepers can defend themselves. They did once before.'

'Only because you fuelled them...and now?'

'What choice do I have?'

'Every choice.'

'Well, I know what my choice will be.'

Raddahkin threw up his arms. 'Then let us hope this

Erigena defies the foretelling of the Shadows, and somehow defeats this tyrant, and miraculously saves the Keepers.'

Jemma could hear the bitterness in his voice. Raddahkin looked again towards the curtain. 'And if they get to her first? Our only fortune is that none have ever seen her. They are ransacking the Wharf for every Caravanassi girl, every Arctic Gull child they can find. The Harpooners are hunting the waters everywhere. Can you imagine what they could do with the Erigena? She would be like a fuel of infinite potential. They are sending the Sparrow all over the Scarp. It's only a matter of time before they find you too.'

'I've made arrangements,' Bruno said.

Raddahkin laughed. 'And to where will you go? You're not the only one who can conjure a passage. There are plenty of charlatans who can do that. And even if you do escape, who knows where you could end up? Tell me, have you checked your palace lately?'

Jemma turned to Edgar and whispered, 'We've got to find this *Erigena*. If the Harpooners are hunting her, she must be worth a fortune. They don't come cheap. And that must be why the Sparrows are spying all over the Wharf. I've seen them, searching the Caravanassi camps. Even inside the Gull shacks. The question is, how much is a prophecy worth? And who would be willing to pay? You must know,' Jemma continued. 'What about the Raven – they'd want to have it, right?'

Edgar flared his wings and stepped away, disappearing into the dark edges of the cubicle.

'Edgar?' Jemma whispered. 'What's got into you?'

He flew up to her shoulder and she could feel the ripple of his feathers.

'It's nothing,' he said. 'Believe me, if there was a prophecy, the Raven would already know of it.'

Maybe she could talk to the Cray, except they'd never

give out their secrets. Treasure was more reliable. That was why she scoured the Scarp, for something she could hold on to. They could have their prophecy. If only they'd just stop *talking* and leave the room. Then she could pack her loot and get out of here.

'If what they're saying is true,' Edgar said, 'there might not be anywhere to sell your treasure in Adocentyn.'

'Sshhh,' Jemma shot across the dark. 'They're still speaking.'

'The Raven have abandoned you,' Raddahkin continued. 'They are taking matters into their own hands.'

'So, they have found this Shadow city? All the better. We will send someone after them, to destroy it.'

'And how do you destroy dark memory?'

Bruno fell silent.

'The more you seek to destroy, the more it will grow. But we have another theory.'

'Speak it then,' Bruno said. For a moment, he seemed to have regained himself.

'We think the Shadow city was made from the memories of your own past, from the time of your imprisonment in the dungeons of the Inquisition. When you escaped your own execution, you made a fool of the Authorities, and they have never forgotten. They will never forget. Not even for eternity.'

'That is impossible.'

'Is it? But I already know you feel it calling you. Beckoning for your return. Do you really think it is impossible? You are an even greater fool than I thought.'

'Go on then,' Bruno said. 'Tell your story.'

'This dark city was created not only to make a passage to Adocentyn. It is also a trap. A giant prison. Memory always seeks to remake itself, complete, so it can live. This dark city will draw you into its loop.'

'How? They do not have such powers at their disposal.'

Bruno reached for the book. He held it up, examining the pages, flicking backwards and forwards from where it had been left open. He peered up close, his gaze utterly still. Then he threw it on the desk and snatched up the lamp, pouring light into the crack of the spine. In the next instant he was riffling madly through the draw sending papers and quills flying about the room. Then he froze.

'You shouldn't have cut it out!' Edgar whispered.

Jemma clenched the golden blade. Something must have clicked in Bruno's brain. In an instant he flung the lamp into the fire where it shattered and blazed into a bright blue kerosene flame.

## CHAPTER 3

## RUN

Jemma held her breath. She reached along the panel behind them, feeling only the decorative trimmings along the surface of the wood. Then something caught her hand – it was a latch of some kind and she released it, tumbling backwards.

Edgar flew against the panel again and closed it shut, as the dark-haired man, Jiordano Bruno, tore open the curtain.

They were inside a small round chamber. At first, they sat still, not even daring to breathe. But the panel remained closed.

Surrounding them were other doors. And now, in the silence, they could both hear it, softly but distinctly.

'Singing. I hear singing,' Jemma whispered. 'It's coming from behind that door. It sounds like a song I've heard before.'

Jemma felt a longing to be closer to the beautiful singing and she reached out to the door handle.

'I would not advise that you open it.'

'I think I recognise that voice,' Jemma said.

'Are you sure?'

'Yes. I can't say why. But I remember it. I remember that song.'

'Perhaps you shouldn't open it, in any case.'

'But I want to see where it's coming from.'

'That's just what I mean,' Edgar said. 'There is magic in the Scarp, you know this. Something is pulling you to open that door.'

'I think it must be her, the woman with the dark hair. The one I saw in that film. She must have come back. And now she wants to see me.'

'You can't be sure. Yearnings are very powerful, very potent.'

Edgar heard the click of the handle, the creaking of the hinge. With desperate caution he flew up to her shoulder.

'Close it,' he said. 'It's not too late.'

But it was. The singing was louder now, clearer, more beautiful, and for a moment even Edgar found himself lost in the voice.

There was no furniture in the room, just floorboards and a single chair, where the woman was sitting with her back to the door, in the bay of a curtained window. Her hair looked untidy, as though she had only just raised her head from a pillow.

Jemma felt the same intense desire to see her face.

'Hello...' she said, reaching out, 'do you want to see me?'

Edgar flew up to the door. Perched, and ready. But for what?

The woman turned, not all the way, still singing. One of her hands gripped the back of the chair, and Edgar could see the strain on her wrist.

'Be careful,' he said. 'Don't get too close.'

Jemma went halfway across the room.

'What's your name? Do you live here? See, we're treasure hunters from the Wharf, and we climbed up here and found this palace in the Scarp, and maybe we shouldn't have, but we came inside, and – we don't mean any harm.'

The woman turned her head to the side, nodding gently in the dreamy rhythm of the song.

Then it seemed as if she was struggling against something, as if she wanted to turn but it wouldn't let her. The tendons on her neck strained and she gripped the chair so her knuckles were white.

Jemma stopped. 'What is it? Are you alright?'

The song hadn't changed but what they could see of her face was pained.

'Is there something the matter?'

Suddenly, as if she had just released herself from a terrible grasp, the woman called out to Jemma.

'Run –' she said, at first feebly, then stronger, louder. 'Run. Get out of here.'

Jemma hesitated – all of her wanted to stay, to rush forward and see the woman's face.

'I don't want to.'

'Go! Run! Now!'

Edgar took the back of Jemma's tunic in his claws, flapping wildly, pulling her towards the door.

A black hooded shape appeared from behind the bay window curtain and Edgar recognised one of the strange meditators he had seen in the chambers below.

Jemma saw the figure begin to move and she turned.

Running.

Edgar led the way back through the study, scuttling the two men who fell backwards, astonished, over a chair.

He rushed through the hallway, his black wings at full stretch beating and then gliding above the white marble floor.

Jemma sprinted trying to keep up and came to a sliding

halt as Edgar dipped down beneath the banister and landed in a flurry at the foot of the stairs.

'Come on,' Edgar said.

She stumbled after him.

'The door!'

Jemma opened it. Then leaped into the Scarp.

She could hear the woman's voice as if it had followed her, *hide in the rocks – beyond the tree.*

Running through the grass towards a flax tree, she felt a rushing wind behind her but she dared not look back until she had reached the trunk.

The palace was now just a fluid mass above the ruins, a dark screaming cloud filled with darker swirling shapes that seemed to pull into a void, eating and collapsing everything within.

'Edgar!' Jemma called out.

He had flown towards the dark cloud.

Peering around the tree, she saw the hooded man from the palace. Seeking her. The man wore heavy boots covered by a long black tunic roughly hewn from hessian. His steps were disciplined like those of a marching soldier.

*Hide* – the voice said.

'Where?'

*Use the Scarp.*

Jemma took off. Scrambling over the rocks. They were sharp and jagged and she fell, turning, seeing him already at the tree. Moving faster.

She rushed to the edge of the rocks and slid down to a ledge below, pushing her back against the stone, feeling like a hunted animal.

Now he was crawling on his hands and feet, leaning over the edge, reaching down to touch her.

A loud harsh *korr* came from above. The man raised his

head and cowered back as Edgar soared down, beating his wings in front of him.

*Hold out the blade.*

Jemma pulled it from her satchel. A glow of golden light pushed the man away. She climbed up the jagged rocks, holding the blade in front of her. With every step the hooded shape faltered back. In the glowing light she could see his eyes inside the hood, green and clear and sharp. His lip was turned up at the side and joined the edge of a scar along his cheek, set long ago, now clean and white.

She lunged with the blade and only then did he halter, turn and flee into the forest. The *swish swish* of Edgar's wings rushed after him. In less than a minute, she saw her companion vanish, a piercing *crooooaaak* disappearing over the edge of the Scarp towards the forest below.

Now she was alone. Her heart racing. She sat there, stunned. As still as a Scarp rock.

Nothing in her experience could make sense of any of this. She felt the golden blade in her hands and looked at the symbols carved into the handle, circles and lines like the ones she had seen in the Book of Memory.

Night was rapidly approaching.

Jemma stood, tucking the golden blade inside the vest beneath her tunic, feeling its warmth against her skin, like it belonged to her, always. The wind was gone and now an almost total silence settled on the mountain range. She listened to her own heart thumping inside her chest, and then she took off in the opposite direction, down the steep face of the Scarp.

The dusk lingered on and she had the strangest feeling that the blade held the light, that it resisted the coming of the dark. She could feel its radiance almost pulsing against her chest.

As the gully wind whisked through the valley, Jemma

looked towards the blinking lights of Adocentyn, always blazing from the great tower in the distance.

Something was different now. The lights seemed to be calling her. She could hear them faintly across the top of the Scarp every time they swept across the rocks, like voices so distant they were nothing but whispers on the edges of dreams. With every sweep of light they grew louder, and then quieter as the light passed away.

In the whispers, she could hear the woman's voice: *Hide amongst the wagons.*

Jemma scrambled down the Scarp-face and hitched to the side of a Caravanassi wagon. Never before had she felt such comfort, hearing the familiar clanging pots tied up on the backs of mules and the smells of clove-smoke drifting from the pipes of the drivers. She knew they were heading to the safety of the Wharf.

She scanned the skies, Edgar was nowhere to be seen. She felt a jolt in her stomach with every pothole on the road – where was he? Why did he follow that hooded man into the forest when he should be here with her?

A band of Caravanassi kids had once caught him in a net and pelted pebbles at him. She'd boxed the kids' ears and set him free. It suited her perfectly, wandering proudly through the market lanes with a Raven Scribe on her shoulder.

Only the thought of falling off the side of the wagon kept her mind focussed on her immediate concerns. How late was she? Had she already missed the wrestling match? Several times along the way she nearly lost her grip.

On any other evening she would have looked for her two

friends, Besh and Daria, a Caravanassi brother and sister who lived in one of the shanties. They would have made her a meal of hot flatbread cooked in the coal fires. Then, they would have run through the winding maze of lanes or tried to sneak into the gambling dens.

But Jemma's bag was now so heavy and her mind was running wild with everything she had seen and heard in the Scarp.

She felt almost naked without Edgar perched on her shoulder. Normally, she delighted in the superstitious fear that cleared her a path wherever she went, just as if she was a queen. The traders and stall holders didn't dare call her *Scarp rat* or *little wharf thief* when Edgar was around. He gave her glimpses of the world outside the Wharf, a world of high politics from which he had been forever banished.

When Jemma had asked him why, he said it was for 'overstepping the boundaries of my station,' whatever that meant. If she pressed him further, his feathers only trembled.

'What are you hiding from me?' she often asked.

This was Edgar's Scribe-knowledge. So much of it, he kept to himself.

She remembered his usual answer – 'Now isn't the time to explain. It's a long and difficult story.' Jemma didn't like long or difficult stories, and would always let it pass. As long as he helped her hunt the ruins, kept her company and gave her a status in the Wharf akin to royalty, she had been content. Now all she wanted was to hear his story. She felt cold and tired and stupid because it never occurred to her that she would find herself alone again. She had taken for granted that Edgar would always be there, perched on her shoulder, or scouting ahead while they hunted the ruins.

The wheels began to slow and she could see the smoke

of charred flatbread rising above the flames. Smells of cloved coffee wafted in from the gambling tents.

Edgar had been scouting the Caravanassi wagons ever since they had first appeared in droves along the road several months ago, jostling for room in the overcrowded camps on the edges of the Wharf. What Edgar had observed about them unsettled her. He had told her about his theory of the loops.

'You see that wagon?' he said one night, pointing to the road. 'The one with the swinging lantern? I've seen it before, several times now. The same people return along the same road. They don't seem to know what awaits them in the future – they must have experienced it many times and then forgotten it.'

'How could they forget?' Jemma said. She had never cared for details, except when it came to ruins.

'They're called memory loops,' Edgar said. 'Until now, I had only ever read about them in the Scrolls.'

Edgar noticed everything. In their little room at night he was constantly scribbling in his notebooks, an old habit of a Raven Scribe.

'These loops are quite fascinating,' he'd said. 'I have a whole list of observations, if you're interested. There is always a long story behind strange events. What we're left with is a feeling. And this is it. I don't know how, or why, but I am almost certain they're caught in this loop, and cannot release themselves. Indeed, they do not even seem to know they are prisoners.'

Back then, she didn't believe him. When she quizzed Besh and Daria, they only said – 'We came one month ago. Never before.' But if the Scarp-palaces were real, what if these loops were too? She didn't want to get stuck in one.

As soon as the wagon came to a halt, Jemma dashed into the shanty lanes, her satchel clanging with Scarp treasure.

She lost herself at once in the pungent crowds, rushing through the empty fish market where the stench of old guts and salty pickle brine shot into her nostrils. Lamplight swung along the Wharf, where the Trade Masters were inspecting crates from a night cargo hauled from a ship.

The Wharf was nothing more than a trading harbour, and Jemma knew all too well that what held all of this seeming chaos in order were the Trade Masters, who kept their eyes on everything. They took a commission from every transaction, recorded in ledgers that filled the Trade Hall with endless rows and stacks like a vast, dishevelled library.

Of course, Jemma knew that what was recorded in the ledgers resembled nothing of what actually changed hands. She watched all the secret backdoor deals right under the noses of the Masters. Graft was how things really worked. If a ship wanted the best mooring, that would cost them a barrel of cargo. If you wanted to unload in a hurry, you'd need to give the Dockers a crate of brandy, at the very least. The Cray fishermen would supply a juicy basket of catch to secure the best stall in the fish market. If you wanted to get ahead you didn't play by the rules.

Jemma passed behind the Trade Hall and went alongside the great white wrestling tent, where it was her job to collect the losing betting tokens thrown into the sawdust at the end of the fight before they were lost forever, stamped into the earth.

It was dirty work and that was why wharf rats were of a rank even lowlier than Arctic Gulls. An ironsmith from the smelting barges had once told her the Gulls had migrated from the icefields in the North and were the last of their kind in the lands of Adocentyn. They had been hunted by the Harpooners for their feathers, which they used to line their coats. Jemma listened to the ironsmith's story only because it gave her perfect cover to fleece an iron spike or two that she would use for digging in the Scarp.

In their human form, the Gull's eyes were sharp and suspicious. Their cheeks were thin and gaunt. She had always been fascinated by their constant changing. It was like they had a reflex in the back of their throat where all of a sudden they collapsed into the hollow of their chest above the collar bone. In some, this reflex was more pronounced than others and seemed to get worse at the slightest inkling of fear.

Once, Jemma decided she would try to change by throwing her shoulders forward and jerking her weight back into her chest. Nothing happened. She couldn't imagine what sort of animal she would have been, anyway, but she was jealous that she couldn't just change into a Tern or a Gull and fly to Adocentyn.

The other traders called the Gulls' ramshackle tangle of tin-rattling huts a 'slum', but to Jemma it was another maze of streets and alleys to explore and run amok in and, most importantly, it was a good place to hide if an ironsmith noticed two spikes were missing and he'd just been made a fool of.

For Jemma, only what was useful for seeking treasure in the Scarp was considered 'good' – everything else was irrelevant, though not forgotten. And in this way she had picked up an almost encyclopaedic knowledge of life in the Wharf.

Further along were the smelting barges where Jemma had first spoken to the sea-trader with plaited ash-grey hair. He had told her the stories of the palaces that once stood majestic in the Scarp, scattered in the hills, long since faded to ruin. They had once been great castles luring you inside with a shimmering magic. Rooms were filled with riches that would shift and change with your desires, only to trap you forever. They were stories of loss and disappearance. Everyone feared the strange allure of the Scarp.

But the trader told her how the myths were true. These palaces were made from memories, according to an ancient memory-craft. And if she searched these ruins, she would be sure to find treasure. He had known of the Scarp hunters from long ago who found such bounty there and were now wealthy merchants in the city.

'If you know so much about memory,' she had asked him, 'then tell me, who knows where my parents went? The day they left me on the Wharf. They must have found a passage on one of the trade ships, how else could they have got away? Who is the keeper of such memories. My memories? And where would I find them?'

'That is everyone's journey,' the old trader had said, 'to find who Keeps them. And none can discover it, except for you.'

'Well, all I know is – I've got no one to keep me, except myself.'

She had once broken into the Trade Hall and searched through the piles of ledgers for a record of that day. After hours of searching, she found a single entry.

> **Cargo:** cane-fleece basket with child.
>     Wharf 1.
> **Description:** girl. 3 years (approx). Brown
>     hair. Small mole on right cheek.
> **Quantity:** 1.
> **Vessel:** Navigator.
> **Commission:** 0.
> **Trader:** unknown.

Ten years later, she still didn't have any answers. What was the point of memory, if it couldn't even tell you where you came from? She knew you couldn't rely on the past. You couldn't breathe it in like air or feel it as a sharp edge as you pulled yourself up the rocky Scarp. Jemma knew that if she was ever going to get out of the dens and make it to the city, she'd have to find treasure.

Now she had a bag of it slung across her shoulder, and there was no one to share it with.

All the way home she looked into the skies for Edgar's black wings amidst the haze of the roasting fires. When she finally reached the Walrus shack, she breathed a sigh of relief.

At least Sharmenai wasn't standing in the doorway with a bucket of clams for her to open, scowling at her, making her feel like nothing more than a wharf rat.

But she would be sure to throw open the curtain any minute now.

Jemma snuck inside, went into her room adjoining the shack, closing the cloth door, and lay down on her bed.

There was no other furniture except for a driftwood table that she had found for Edgar to use as a desk. They had made pens out of fennel-stalks and ink from the berries of a forest tree. She wanted more than anything to see him there, scribbling about theories of loops in his notebooks.

Jemma felt restless. She went over to the desk and touched the cold stub of Edgar's candle, remembering the time when she had teased him with a list of superstitions that she had heard about Ravens.

'We are considered *bad omens*? Why is that?'

'Probably because your feathers are black.'

'Our feathers *are* black,' Edgar had said, 'that is a fact. But how do they move from this fact to the claim that we are...let me see...ah yes...*unlucky. Signs of misfortune. Messengers of death and darkness?*'

'How do I know?' Jemma had said. 'Maybe it's your voice as well.'

'My voice?'

'Not *your* voice, but a Raven's voice. The way you...crow.'

'*Crow?*' Edgar raised his beak.

'Yes,' Jemma had said. 'Your crow.'

'But I have never *crowed* in my life. We speak our own language. Not to mention our mastery of yours. It would be like you grunting in a cave. You *can* grunt, can't you?'

'It's just what they believe. It doesn't mean it's true.'

'Then why do they believe it?'

'I don't know Edgar, because they do.'

'Well, I simply cannot understand it,' the hackles stood up on his neck. 'And here is another one: *Ravens are malevolent, deceitful beings, who bring about destruction and desolation* — this is ludicrous!'

'What's *ludicrous* is you keeping me awake! If I'm too tired to go out digging in the Scarp...'

She felt terrible about being irritated with him then, because part of her was cross with him now. How would she sleep at all, if Edgar wasn't here?

She went over to his bed in the corner, a pile of seaweed and straw, and tried to make it for him, to make it soft and nice. He nestled himself into the middle of it, somehow. It wasn't like a nest, though. How did Edgar sleep? Jemma wanted him back if only to tell her this, and every other thing she didn't know because she was only ever thinking about hunting in the Scarp. What did treasure mean, now?

Beneath his bed was the hollowed-out hiding place for all the things she had found in the ruins. Jemma took out her bag and inspected the treasure — a flask of brandy and a silver paper weight. One brass telescope. Five silver spoons. A map. And the golden blade. Surely the telescope, alone, was enough to buy herself a passage on a trader to the city harbour. But what was the point, if Edgar wasn't here?

She poured over the map, gazing at the circle of the sun and the drawings of the city she knew was Adocentyn, with its beautiful tower at the centre.

The lovely stone walls and winding cobbled roads descended in tiers to a harbour strewn with ships. If the map was true, the city was a place where other worlds opened up and converged, where passages led to even greater mysteries than the lights that now seemed to beckon her.

Jemma wondered at the flickering images she had seen on the wall in the Scarp-palace. The ocean washing the shores of a beach, a girl playing in the sand. Why did they feel so alive? It was like they were inside of her, like memories. And yet from somewhere far away. A different place. She wished she could have seen further into the film. She wanted to hear the woman's gentle voice again, and she didn't know why she wanted to hear it so much, that it hurt.

She took out the golden blade. She had never felt herself to have a destiny but there was something about the metal itself, the strange lustre of the gold. She knew that she could never sell this radiant treasure.

When she hovered the blade above the map, the picture of Adocentyn seemed to glow with a golden hue. She could see the light so clearly, as if it was coming right out of the page.

But then, something else.

A shadow, beside.

It looked like another city, appearing on the map. Just like Raddahkin said!

She could see the outlines of buildings, and canals, and little bridges. There were many spires and steeples that looked sharp and jagged, unwelcoming.

All the roads and canals seemed to lead to a high, dark tower, surrounded by a shining black moat.

When she took the blade away, the Shadow city was gone.

Jemma felt a quiver along her arms, like the stroke of an invisible hand.

Two cities – one of light and one of darkness.

How could such a thing exist? The traveller had made the city of Adocentyn sound so beautiful. But this picture of another world was even more unthinkable. How could a city be made of dark memory?

In a strange way, it made sense. Jemma remembered every cut and every bruise she'd ever got from the Scarp. She remembered the scorn of Sharmenai that day she'd come home after dark. As a punishment, she was made to dig in the freezing winter sea and fill ten buckets with clams. She remembered this pain and misery far more than she ever remembered being happy.

It made it all the more remarkable, and strange, that a city could be made of memory at all.

Jemma placed the map and the blade and all her treasure beneath the hollow straw of Edgar's bed.

Every time she blinked, she saw images of the Scarp.

She saw again the dazzling cloud engulf the palace. And the hooded man with green eyes and a white scar, who recoiled at the sight of the blade. What if he was on his way to find her in the Wharf. What then?

Jemma went to the fire stove. She blew into the ash hoping for an ember, but nothing came. Edgar had rigged up an elaborate contraption – a kettle on a chain, on the end of a swinging pole. When they returned home exhausted from the Scarp, he would always say: 'I've just made a pot of tea. It's black and strong but not bitter. The secret is a sprinkle of cinnamon. It neutralises the tartness and gives the brew a delightful aroma, don't you think?'

She couldn't bear the thought of him returning to a room that was dark and lonely and cold. Jemma knelt and flicked a spark from a flintstone into a handful of cane-fleece. She put a peat log onto the little flame and fanned until it smouldered and glowed, then ladled water into the kettle from a bucket they kept by the door hanging from a pole. Then she placed two mugs on the hearthstone beside a tin of black leaf tea, and a little jar of cinnamon.

## CHAPTER 5

## FACE OF A SEAL

Edgar followed the hooded man into the forest, flying through the branches of the pines.

The figure paused now and again, slowed by a bag slung over his shoulder. He went along the path of a stream until he came to a rocky ledge where the water trickled into a ravine. It would have been easy to jump the stream but instead he trod along its bank, heaving the bag over the edge before climbing down the rocky face to a pool below, beside the entrance to a cave.

Edgar waited above.

The man crouched by the pool and took off his hood and glanced from side to side. Then he splashed water over his face and cupped his hands to drink. He had light brown, almost reddish hair and freckly skin. Edgar saw the white scar along his cheek. It was not an altogether unfriendly face. He seemed deep in thought, as if he was barely feeling the water. Then he looked around him once again.

There were no sounds in the forest other than the running water and the wind in the pine-tips. There were no cries of animals. No bird calls in the trees.

The man stood up and looked directly above him, as if to catch something by surprise. His eyes were a deep green and Edgar knew he did not want to meet those eyes.

Edgar crept along the branch towards the trunk, not daring even to breathe. He sensed an awareness tuned even to the slightest parting of air.

The man sat down beside the pool, assuming the same posture of meditation Edgar had seen in the dungeons of the Scarp-palace. He began chanting the same chant, his voice humming through the valley where the pine trees merged with enormous trunks of ash.

While the man was lost in his trance, Edgar noticed a hollow knot in the side of a tree and flew swiftly, diving in head first.

From inside he had a clearer view of the pool. He saw the man had placed his bag just outside the entrance to the cave.

*What are you up to?* he thought.

The man continued to meditate. His face and palms were turned up towards the waterfall as if he were receiving its cooling flow.

Edgar stayed in his hollow. He was thirsty and hungry but he dare not move. There was a deep silence inside the tree and also the smell of burnt wood. Edgar noticed that nearly all the trunks were black and seared and the bark was peeling away, revealing a white and fleshy layer that looked like streaks of ghosts.

A fog was forming in the distance, as if released from the trees. He did not want to be stuck in the hollow when the fog came creeping through. But to lose sight of him – this could only put Jemma in danger.

Still chanting, eyes closed, the man waded into the pool and washed his face and then slowly pulled himself out of the water. He lay on the rock as if the effort of chanting had exhausted him.

*Good*, Edgar thought, *something must have weakened him. But I wonder what, and for how long?* Edgar began to worry – just how long would it take the man to recover his strength? By Edgar's calculations, at a steady walk it would take half a day to reach the Wharf. Though Edgar ached to find Jemma, he knew he could not leave his vigil.

The man lay there long enough for the tips of the fog to creep almost to the rocks. Then he went over to the bag, reached in and began to sprinkle handfuls of a course white powder into the pool. It looked to Edgar like salt. The man tasted the water, put in one more handful, tasted again. Then he dived into the pool.

To Edgar's surprise, what appeared again out of the water was not the form of a man. It was the face of a Seal.

~

NIGHT WAS APPROACHING. THE FOG HAD NOW SETTLED over the pool, enough for Edgar to perch on the edge of the knothole without fear of being seen. The sleepy, inert shape of the Seal had not moved for several hours. The white fog had erased part of the forest, and Edgar thought he saw Shadows lurking.

His eyes were fixed on the Seal, who had almost disappeared completely into the greyness. He grew anxious. The Shadows came closer. It was as if the trees were now floating in the fog. He wanted so desperately to fly over to the rocks and quench his thirst.

As the Shadows closed in he could see they were like charred ghosts drifting towards the tree. He tried to fly off, but his wings wouldn't move. The Shadows were swarming around the base of the trunk, reaching up to him, clamouring over each other to get to him. Several of the Shadow-shapes broke free from the swarm, gripped the bark and stretched up to touch him.

He let out a *kraah* – it penetrated the fog like an arrow in the silence. The Shadows fled. Edgar retreated into the hollow of the tree, his heart hammering inside him. A moment later he heard the cracking of twigs coming from below. The Seal must have changed into his human form. His footsteps receded into the forest.

Edgar darted to a ledge above the rocks and found a gap to land in. He knew the Seal would return because he had left his bag in the entrance to the cave unguarded.

Taking a chance, he swept down and looked inside the bag, where he saw a thick coil of chain the colour of tarnished gold. Then he returned to the rock ledge.

In the fading light he longed for his notebook and fennel-stalk pen. He could have made a sketching of this peculiar chain. Written down his questions. There was always a pattern, he knew, however hidden away.

He wanted more than anything to be reading at his desk and drinking tea, with Jemma lying beside him on her bed. But he knew that he could not leave the Seal, who was gaining his strength. When it returned he would seek to find her. This Edgar could sense with the clearest intuition.

The human Seal returned with some wood and kindling and set out a fire. Edgar felt a surge of desire for their own hearth stove in their little room. What if Jemma thought he had abandoned her? He couldn't bear to think of it.

The Seal now toasted a piece of bread in the flames and Edgar felt the pangs of his own ravenous hunger. He watched the Seal eat the bread with strips of smoked fish, before curling himself around the last of the glowing coals.

Edgar wished for sleep, but could not risk the possibility of losing the Seal. Already, he cursed himself for letting out that ridiculous, primitive crow – how could he have been so foolish? He set himself to thinking, but the fog had surrounded the cave and seemed to fill his mind with an empty cloud. Nothing would come.

The fire smouldered into embers. He felt his own exhaustion, the irresistible heaviness of his wings. A weight-lessness overcame him and then nothing but the white fog, which seemed to erase all the images in his mind. Edgar drifted into sleep.

HE WOKE TO THE SOUND OF SPLITTING BRANCHES, AND the clearest sense that he had forgotten something. How long had he slept? It was still night. He could not say what it was. The fog seemed to have made a gap, like a cube of empty space inside of him. It was a feeling that something was now lost and could not be recovered. He could not see it anywhere, no matter how he tried to search inside his memory.

A loud cracking noise came from above, the sound of breaking splintering wood and a terrible screech.

The Seal woke immediately and fled with the bag into the cave. A large white shape was falling and flapping through the trees. It twisted and flayed about, desperately trying to break its fall but unable to gather enough resis-tance. The white-winged thing fell to the bottom of the ravine and then disappeared into the cave, as if it had been drawn inside against its will.

Edgar flew back to the knothole of the tree. In the fire's half-light it was almost impossible to make out what the thing was. At first he could only see bright twitching wings and the glinting of a chain. He knew it was still alive, flickering with the same white light he had seen in the Scarp-palace. It was obvious that whatever had escaped from Bruno's dungeons had been summoned here by the Seal with his chants, and now he chained it up inside the cave.

The Seal emerged, pacing along the rock. Edgar darted out of the hole and landed on a small, stunted branch higher up.

He could not see in front of the Seal, who had now kneeled down beside the fire and seemed to be constructing something out of wooden pieces that he was taking, one by one, out of the pocket of his tunic.

When he had finished, he reached through his hood and took off what looked like a piece of string from around his neck.

Edgar swept to the next tree, not quite above him, but close enough.

The Seal turned and in a single movement he took a shot from the cross bow. The arrow brushed Edgar's wing. The Seal loaded another, so fast that Edgar could barely react. The second arrow passed through his tail. He darted through the trees as a third struck the trunk. He flew up high into the canopies and broke through and went higher still, as high as he imagined an arrow could pass.

Now he had lost the Seal, and the trees hid all in darkness below.

*Jemma*...he thought. He flew towards the Wharf, aware of a gap between his tail feathers and the right tip of his wing. It was enough to unsteady him. Feeling for a current, he glided and held his balance as best he could above the road below, where the steady lines of the Caravanassi wagons trailed their lanterns towards the smoke of the roasting fires in the distant camps. Edgar felt it now, a danger and a fear that seized him – somewhere below, amidst the maze of alleys and tents, was his friend. The Seal was on his way.

All he knew was, he would have to get to her first.

## CHAPTER 6

## SORENSTAR

'Where have you been?'

Sharmenai appeared in the doorway to Jemma's room. Her straight, dark hair covered half her face and gathered about her large, round shoulders, strong from carrying clam buckets. She might have held a regal beauty, if not for the permanent scowl she thrust upon a world that had made her live beneath her station.

'I've been nowhere,' Jemma said.

'Scavenging in the Scarp, empty handed, I can see. A bet collector you are, a little wharf rat you'll always be.'

Her harsh and husky, mocking voice cut like the shells of clams. Her eyes scoured the room for Edgar.

Jemma was fuming at the taunt. She was desperate to say it: *I did find something, so rare and golden and beautiful it must be worth a fortune. And I'll be living in the finest palace in the city, while you're stuck here in this stinking Walrus shack.*

But she didn't. She followed Sharmenai into the adjoining room, where a familiar figure was standing beside the peat stove. He was a big man, with long red hair and a ginger coloured moustache that grew down past his chin and formed two points like Walrus tusks. His cloth pants and tunic resembled a butcher's, covered with the muck of working all day on the Wharf. At night, he was a wrestler. Soren.

Sharmenai pointed to a bucket of clams. 'It's food and board for work, not for being late,' she said.

Jemma cursed as she opened the clams, cracking her nails on the shells.

'You'll be picking up useless scraps, anyway. Ask him, when did he last win a fight? How about *never*. And he says you're supposed to be his "luck"?'

'I will not listen to this,' Soren said.

'Oh, come on, let's see you angry! Let's see you want to fight, instead of die.'

'I will not fight for you. I will save that for the crowd.'

'Then take this basket of fennel-weed,' she threw it at Jemma's feet. 'You'll need it to score his thousand wounds.'

He seemed to ignore this last insult.

Sharmenai stomped through the door to fetch some herbs. Soren sat down at the table next to Jemma.

'You look weary, Scarp hunter,' he said in a gentle voice. Then he paused, as if he were obliged once again to explain. 'She was not always this bitter. When my luck comes back, then we will see.'

Sharmenai returned and caught the last of his words.

'Tell me, have you seen the odds? Am I forbidden to bet against you? A strange betrayal in this house, when loyalty is to starve!'

'That is when I will surely win,' Soren said. 'The day you bet against me.'

'Spoken like a true warrior. What courage! But now I see your blubber has turned to bile. Spite is the last refuge of the vanquished.'

Soren stood up and, as if containing an immense wave of emotion, released his two clenched fists. He sat back down.

'And yet I still eat like a prince,' he said with contempt.

Sharmenai ordered Jemma to take the bowls to the table.

Soren held his bowl with two hands and slurped. Jemma raised a spoonful to her lips. The soup had a slimy texture from the seaweed. It was a strong, salty, leathery taste that was only rarely relieved by the texture of a clam, whose flesh was sweet at first, then awfully gritty with sand. Jemma forced herself not to think of Edgar, feeling a hard knot in her throat and the bitterness of the weed. Outside, she could hear rowdy laughter from the beach, the preparations for the wrestling match. There were beating drums and music and the tinking of hammers on iron spikes.

Soren finished his bowl and stood in the doorway. Jemma joined him and looked at the Seal, his regular wrestling opponent, processing along the beach.

'There was a time when he would have faced them as they passed. Cursed them to the stars,' Sharmenai said.

All three of them watched the Seal's parade. He was carried aloft in a tank of water by ten burly men. As part of his challenge to Soren, he leapt up and changed between Seal and human forms and dived back into the tank. A display of power and prowess.

'See how he can change,' Sharmenai said. 'What vigour!'

'Only fools waste their energy,' Soren replied.

'At least a fool has something to waste.'

'It is the luck that is gone. It will return.'

'No,' Sharmenai said. 'Our luck will be the day that Raven has gone for good, and never shall return.'

'His name's Edgar, actually,' Jemma said. 'And he'll be back tonight! You wait!'

She saw the smirk on Sharmenai's face and forced

herself not to take the bait. She slammed her bowl on the table and stormed out of the hut.

ON THE BEACH THE OTHER WALRUSES, CHANGED INTO their human forms, stopped eating and stared as she passed.

'Hey, Scarp rat!' one of them called. 'Here is some real flesh! Why don't you come and take some of your "winnings"! Better than clams, eh?' Bellows of laughter followed.

'At least I don't lie around like a piece of lard!' Jemma said.

'Come here and say that, why don't you?'

She walked on. The white canvas sails of the wrestling tents loomed before her. The Trade Masters stood below in their long cloth gowns and velvet hats, counting and recording every token distributed to those entering the tents. Beyond them, she could hear the wailing songs of the Caravanassi drifting across the water to the barges of the Terns, whose fires lit up the surface of the sea.

Jemma entered Soren's dressing room, waiting for him. It was nothing more than a canvas bed, a few stools and a table. Fresh sawdust spread on the ground was the only attempt at glamour. A barrel of water stood in the corner.

Through the canvas wall, there was an eruption of cheering and laughter as the Seal entered the ring. Jemma peeped through into the main tent. The wrestling pit was a shallow pool, deep enough to dive into from one of the platforms on either side, about waist deep to stand. Ropes held back the jostling crowd while all around were rough wooden scaffolds tied together with basket weave. The pit was lit by a large ring of tallow lamps.

Jemma closed the canvas. She sat down at the table and lit a candle. Her thoughts fixed on Edgar. She refused to believe that anyone would dare to harm her Raven Scribe, and since that concept was impossible, she imagined him flying to their room, pulling on the chain, swinging the kettle out of the flames and making himself a cinnamon tea. But even if he did return, how could she leave Soren?

She remembered all the times he laughed when he saw her scamper from the fish markets covered in slime with a bucketful of guts to bargain with the Gulls.

Once, when a trader accused Jemma of stealing a skein of basket cane and held her up by the scruff of the neck, her feet dangling in the air, Soren marched across the Wharf. The trader was shaking as he saw what was coming towards him. Without speaking, Soren gently let her down and threw the trader headlong into a fish basket and had him winched onto a Tern ship, headed for god knows where. It had taken the trader two weeks to return to his stall. All his produce had rotted and moulded. No one dared lay a finger on her ever since.

She remembered what he had told her: that day when he found her on the Wharf in a bundle of cane-fleece, he thought she was a token, that she would bring him back the luck. Then he could restore his honour name, Sorenstar, the title of the Prince.

But everyone knew his luck wouldn't come tonight, or any other night. His luck would never return. When Soren entered the dressing room, Jemma could see the fate written in his eyes.

He sat down at the table. The candle flickered his shadow on the wall. He looked like a giant sitting at a children's play set. Behind him, long strips of sea-fennel hung from the rafters. Later they would use them to soothe his wounds.

'Open the flask,' he said.

Jemma poured him a cup of aniseed spirit.

He savoured the smell, breathing in the fumes. Then he threw it back.

'Give me some of this again after the fight, so I do not pass out.'

He stretched his arm out along the table and unwrapped the old fennel that was bandaging his latest wound. Jemma saw the lines of scars. There was more scarred than unscarred flesh. He pulled a fresh piece of fennel from the rafter, stripped away the outer skin and lay the wet side on the wound. Then he wrapped it with the second piece, the opposite way, to draw out the mucus. Jemma could see that it must have stung badly, but the Walrus-wrestler did not flinch.

Ever since Edgar had told her about the memory loops of the Caravanassi, Jemma was asking questions: why did Soren suffer the same terrible fate, night after night, like a film caught on a reel?

'There are always patterns if you look for them,' Edgar had said. 'And once you find one, you cast a prediction out into the future and then see if it comes true. If it does, ask – what does it mean?'

Edgar wasn't the only one who was clever enough to come up with a theory. As she watched Soren, she was forming one of her own. If this was her last night in the Wharf, she had to tell him.

Soren cast an immense shadow on the wall, its movement in the flickering flames at odds with his stillness. The scars on his back were like the lines of a map, with contours and mountains and valleys and the deep gashing gorges of rivers.

Another loud cheer erupted from the tent.

He rose now from the stool with a heaviness upon him.

'Come, we had better finish the preparations. There is some more bandage over here.'

'Wait...' Jemma hovered by the table. It had been so clear just before, but now she wasn't sure if she could put her theory into words. 'Can I ask you something?'

'Of course.' He sat down again.

She could not hide from herself the fact that she felt a deep devotion to Soren, and to leave him now would be to scatter a part of her heart like the ruins in the Scarp. At least before she left, she had to try to make sense of all this. Maybe, to set him free.

'Do you remember when you came to the wrestling games?'

'It seems so long ago,' he said. 'So long ago I – cannot remember.'

'And you can't even remember the last time you won?'

'It is not my right to, since I live in shame.'

'But haven't you ever wondered why? I mean, why you *never* win a fight?'

'It is the luck,' he said.

'But I think I know why – why it is you *always* lose.'

'And how can you possibly know this? It is only the luck that knows.'

Jemma shook her head. 'It's something else,' she said. 'Each night, there are things that are different, but there's things that are the same. That's what got me thinking – why does it happen again and again, night after night? The same Seal? And the fight itself, it's like you're broken, all broken up and cut. And the cuts, they might be different, but it's the same wounds, over and over.'

'That is just what it brings,' he said. 'It is fate.'

'– and then *she* comes in and she dresses your wounds. And then it's like the end is cut off. When Sharmenai lays you on the bed. Before, I never noticed. But...it's like you're caught in a circle. And now I think I know.' Jemma's voice softened. 'It's just like Edgar said. You must have a sort of –

Keeper. Someone who Keeps you in a loop, going over and over.'

Soren stood and looked at her. Jemma saw the moment he came to understand. It was as if the answer to a riddle hidden in the night had quickened from the light of a star. A bitterness came over his face.

He clenched his hands and the scars on his arms shifted and tightened.

'Who is this Keeper?' he said. 'The one who remembers, who keeps me here? You have to tell me.'

'I don't know, for certain. Maybe someone who wouldn't let you go.'

Soren's gaze fixed upon the candle flame burning with the clear, pure brightness of the tallow.

'I am supposed to die on this stretcher. I know I am,' he said. 'Each night I feel it, the life rushing out of me. And then, each day, I wake. Reborn. It must be her. It must be Sharmenai.'

He sat down on the stretcher. Jemma saw a pain greater than his body's in his eyes.

'It is time,' he said. 'We will test this theory of yours. Tonight. If I am caught in a spell, then I will break it!'

~

THE SEAL SPUN AROUND AND PERFORMED A BACKFLIP into the pool, changing form in the water, then back again to human on the opposite side where he worked the crowd into a frenzied chant.

Jemma felt a shot of adrenaline as she pushed herself through the crowd, surging like a hungry beast. Another roar of cheers erupted. Soren must have taken his place on the stage. But Jemma could not see him, she was too busy pushing through the stalls, forced to get down onto her hands and knees and crawl – shoving at legs or ankles, anything that would give her a passage through.

The sawdust sent up clouds into her face and she coughed, desperate to see the fight. She heard the slap of skin on water, the cracking thud of wood and the roaring of the crowd. Something big must have happened. Another cheer erupted, with fists thrown into the air waving the silver-coloured tokens of the Seal.

Jemma scrambled up to the stalls and squeezed through until she finally found a gap between two rafters. She dreaded what was coming next but she hoped with all her heart that Soren was right. That he would break the spell. That she would see his red tokens thrust into the air. Usually, this was the time when she would cover her eyes. Now she forced herself to look.

The great Walrus tumbled into the water. He did not seem to have the energy to change and stood up on the opposite platform in his human form, where the Seal tore into the flesh of his arms, then scratched terribly into the sides of his stomach, causing him to keel over. Soren managed to push him away.

The Seal slipped back into the water. With one last gasp of energy, Soren in his human form, dived after him into the bloody pool, his body curling into the shape of a mighty Walrus with fierce tusks bared, to the tremendous cheering of the crowd who threw their fists into the air, clutching their red betting tokens for the triumphant Prince.

Jemma cheered as the Walrus held the Seal under the water with awesome strength. The Seal took a savage cut from Soren's tusks, which looked red and menacing, dripping with water and blood and mucus. But then he broke free and leapt right over Soren's head, landing behind him in human form. He grabbed the Walrus by the tusks, one in each hand, and from there, took one jab at a time with alternating fists into Soren's neck and ribs and even his eyes.

Jemma gasped at the ferocity of the strikes and turned away. But something made her look again. Soren was writhing in agony. She leaped from the stalls, pushed through the crowd towards him, but then the fight was called.

The attendants prised the Seal apart from the Walrus and held up his arm in victory. Then they dragged the losing hulk from the bloodied pool onto the platform.

At first, Soren was not moving at all. Jemma kept pushing but then, with furious gestures, the losing tokens were being thrown into the dust.

It was her job to pick them up before they were lost forever, stamped into the dirt. She shoved her way through, oblivious to the jostling limbs that flung her around and jabbed, stomped and kicked.

Jemma gave as good as she got, scrabbling for every token she could find, then scampering under the stalls where she collected all that were thrown down between the rafters. But then, unable to bear it any longer, she pushed her way through to the stage.

At first she could not look at him. Tears welled up in her eyes. Her theory meant nothing. There was only the pain. It was not the revulsion of his blood, of the torn and mangled skin that shocked her. It was the woundedness of his heart.

The two attendants rolled the defeated Walrus onto a canvas cloth and were preparing to carry him outside when Sharmenai came rushing over, pushing them away.

'Don't you dare touch him, you filthy draggards.'

She kneeled beside Soren and began to kiss and stroke him with such tenderness, at once gazing over his wretched body and then holding him in her arms against her lips.

Taking out strips of sea-fennel, she gently wrapped the

wounds. Was it more for her own sake? As if to ease her own suffering or guilt, or both?

For a while Sharmenai held him, quivering in her arms. Then she stood and called for the attendants, who carried him outside, dropping him onto the beach.

Already the sea-fennel must have soothed his wounds enough for him to open his eyes.

'Push me into the water,' he said.

'Come on,' Sharmenai snapped at Jemma. 'You heard him. Push!'

Jemma heaved, but she could not budge him. Then, with both of them taking hold of the canvas cloth, they were able to roll him still in his Walrus form down the slope of the beach.

For a while he lay in the shallow lapping waves while Sharmenai scooped up handfuls of water to soothe his face. Then, with a final lunge, he at last found the weightlessness of the sea.

Jemma watched as Sharmenai changed before her eyes into the same Walrus form as Soren, two shapes swimming together not far from the edge of the sand.

She followed them, until she saw them emerge from the water's edge further up the beach, their skin extending into limbs in the shallows. Sharmenai helped Soren to stand. In their human forms they walked together past the fire. None of the other Walruses jeered this time. Soren limped badly and held himself against Sharmenai, who looked at the luminous faces with flashing eyes.

'It used to be that when the fighter returned, all would change form, out of respect.'

Then she spat into the flames a searing contempt.

Jemma came behind them into the hut. Sharmenai laid him gently on the canvas bed and now dabbed at his bruises with aniseed ointment, whispering something sweetly into his ear.

Jemma closed over the cloth door and went into her room. 'Edgar?' The fire-stove no longer glowed and the kettle hadn't been touched. In the dark outside she could hear crashing waves, triumphant cheers, the cries of an Arctic Gull drunken in the night, and in the room next door, the laboured breaths of Sorenstar.

She lay on her bed and wiped away the wetness in her eyes, wishing she had Edgar beside her. Wishing she had the power to release Soren. Maybe if she could find this Erigena, then she'd be able to help him. Didn't Raddahkin say – *the Erigena will come at the time of the fading of Memory... when the Shadows will rise again* – but what did this mean? Is that what would happen to Sharmenai and Soren if they weren't together in this loop – they'd somehow turn into Shadows?

If *she* was Sharmenai, could she have ever let Soren go? Wouldn't she too want to hold him in a memory forever? Still, it wasn't fair. And even when Sharmenai kissed Soren to sleep, Jemma saw it for what it was, the cruelty of a selfish love. But if Jemma was leaving tomorrow, wasn't that the most selfish thing of all?

To be an orphan was to think of nothing but your own advantage, what you could fleece, buy or sell to secure your own survival. Never before did Jemma have the slightest care for memory. But the Scarp-palace had released something inside her. It was like an ache that seemed to never end, a missing memory that took on the form of a vast ravine where nothing but the echo of a voice sounded in the dark: *Run.*

Jemma closed her eyes. Exhaustion took hold and she found herself drifting into a dream where she was inside this vast ravine. In the darkness, she could see the whole sequence of the night – Soren's fate – projected in a circle, painted in pictures like the ones she had seen in the book they had found in the palace. Jemma was standing in the darkness, holding out the blade. Its golden light set the images moving and she wanted them to stop but they played over and over – Soren and Sharmenai's bitter rows, the Walruses who insulted her by the fire, the cheering crowds, the entrance of the Seal, the image of Soren so weakened, battered and bruised at the end of the fight. How could she bear to see it, even once more? Jemma flicked the golden blade. One of the images, as if responding, disappeared. She did this again, one by one, until all she could see surrounding her was a bright circle of light with no beginning or end. It was hovering and pulsing in the dark. Jemma stepped forward, a surge of energy rushing through her body into the tendons of her arms. She held the blade above her head, her fingers tingling and alive. And with a single stroke, she cut the loop.

A wailing cry. Jemma opened her eyes. Sat bolt upright. The blade was in her hand, no longer glowing with light. She rushed to the door where a gust of wind struck her face and a crash of waves thudded on the shore. A flock of Gulls circled and shrieked above her. Jemma retreated, tucking the blade into her vest and huddling into the corner of the darkened room. In the wind, she could hear the voice again, but it came from far away.

'Who are you?' she said. 'Where will I find you?'

Jemma held her breath, counting the beats of the crashing waves. When she closed her eyes, she thought she could hear a whisper in the dark.

*I am with you. Follow the lights.*

## CHAPTER 7

# BESH AND DARIA

Whim Jemma woke, her plans were simple. Find a berth on a trade ship to Adocentyn and say goodbye to Besh and Daria, her two Caravanassi friends.

In the light of day, the events of the night before seemed like another world, nothing but the strange effects of the Scarp's strange magic. What worried her the most was how that magic nearly got inside her, nearly fooled her into thinking she had memories from other lands – that's just how the Scarp could work its ways. The trader had said, 'You have to know what's real, and what's not, or you can lose yourself in the ruins.'

Jemma knew she couldn't afford to care for the past, to believe in illusions of memories or strange, whispering voices that drifted in her mind, so insubstantially. There was only now, and the future. No spell would keep her stuck in this stinking Wharf.

She put the map and the blade inside her vest, opened the cloth door and went into the adjoining room. The stove fire was cold. Sharmenai must have left early to swim for sea-fennel. Soren was sleeping and would remain so until work began on the docks.

Just because she had wanted him to be free and dreamed she had cut a pulsing loop of light, didn't mean he *was* free. Jemma had dreamed of falling through a ravine in the Scarp, like a fissure made by an earthquake. Every time she grabbed hold of a ledge the walls would flatten out and send her falling again. Did this mean she *was* falling?

She had told Soren the truth, if it was the truth, and now he'd have to fend for himself, just like she did. But it didn't feel right to leave without saying goodbye. Jemma went over and, without waking him, hugged Soren and whispered in his ear, 'I'm going. I'll never forget you.'

Then she ran outside, pushing her tears away, telling herself she wasn't going to wait for anyone, not even Edgar, who should have been here by now. Where was he? Why had he taken so long? What was the use of waiting in the Wharf when she could be making a new life for them in Adocentyn?

Even if the Scarp had played its tricks, at least her treasure was real. She could feel the blade inside her vest, but it wasn't glowing warm anymore. It felt cold. If she had to flog the golden blade to get a berth on a trade ship, so be it. For the right price, she'd sell it in a flash.

Jemma decided to wander through the docks, hoping to eavesdrop amongst the traders and find out who was scuppering a load of cane-fleece. If worse came to worst, she could at least try to stow away in a cargo hull, sleeping in the crates filled with the soft threads of weave they used to make fine cushions in the city. But she felt it in her heart – what would be the use, if Edgar wasn't with her?

Careful not to be seen by the Masters, she knocked against the back of a trade ship until an irritated voice emerged on the deck.

'What do *you* want?'

'I got treasure,' she called up. 'Real treasure this time.'

The burley trader smirked and would have picked her up by the ankles if the thought of Soren hadn't crossed his mind.

'And what would I want with a handful of Scarp rocks weighing in my pockets?'

'I got silver and a crystal flask of brandy.'

Now he was listening. He leaned over the stern, his stomach bulging over the side and his pudgy eyes squinting in the morning sun.

'Go on. Show us then.'

Further up the docks, one of the Trade Masters was eyeing her with suspicion. Jemma spoke quickly, 'It's in my cabin. You give me a berth and I'll bring it with me.'

'You think I'm gonna trust a wharf rat? Or even worse, a little scavenging bet collector.' He shooed her away.

Jemma felt the fury rise within her. She took out the blade and it glowed with the same fierce wave of emotion. She thrust it into the air, 'And I found this too, and you aren't ever going to get it.'

For a second the trader froze with curiosity. The slits of his eyes opened in surprise. Then he let out a bellowing laugh.

'What would I want with a rusty knife that wouldn't even scale a fish!'

Jemma heard the trail of laughter echo as he disappeared, howling, into the bows of the ship.

In an instant she swept her arm across the back of the boat and sliced off the rudder, a clean line cutting right through the smelter's steel.

'You'll wish you helped me. You'll wish you never called me a rat!' she hollered.

What was left of the rudder fluttered like a wind chime

in the breeze. She ran down the Wharf, past the corn stalls, looking back to see if anyone had noticed. Luckily, a cargo ship docking further up had stolen the attention of the Master, who would now be caught for hours checking off items in his ledger. In any case, she had cut the rudder just below the water line and they'd never even realise until they tried to steer a path away from the Terns, who would sink them with a hail of tar-fire before they let a trade ship strike their barge.

Jemma took off again, feeling almost frightened of the blade itself. *A rusted knife that wouldn't even scale a fish.* How could it cut through smelter steel? How come he didn't see it shimmering golden, like her?

Less than ten minutes ago, she was ready to sell it to the highest bidder. But now she felt that to lose the blade would be to wrench away a very part of her soul.

She could always sell the brass instrument, but she would need a navigation ship for that, and they anchored out beyond the Tern ships. She would have to waste a whole silver cup to hire a schooner, and there was no guarantee they wouldn't rather starve than help a little wharf rat.

Jemma scurried through the markets, taking a short cut under the counters of the gutting blocks where the chop chop of cleavers sent fish muck flying everywhere. She passed a haggle of Gulls squawking in frenzied battle for the juicy entrails and kept going towards the Caravanassi roasting fires, to find Besh and Daria.

Saying goodbye wasn't the only thing. If she was really leaving this time, then she had to warn her two friends, just like she did for Soren, about Edgar's theory of the memory loops.

~

When Daria had first approached her several months ago, Jemma was suspicious – she'd seen what those Caravanassi kids did to Edgar. But she and her brother, Besh, had only come to give her some of their stew wrapped in flatbread, dripping and hot.

Daria and Besh had taught her how to dance, at first clapping their feet and their hands until she had found the rhythm of the song. It was like knowing another language but without any words, as if thoughts could be written in the air.

In return, Jemma had taught them how to dive for sea-fennel. You had to hold on to the end of a thick mooring rope and wait for the swell to come all the way in and then suck out to sea, and only in that instant could you swing down to the rocks below and pull out a handful of the slippery weed.

The first time Besh was nearly swept away and the others had to pull him in, laughing as he bobbed in the water like a fishing float. But then, determined, he tried again and grabbed several of the biggest slimy weeds, which he proudly gave to Jemma to put in her satchel for the evening fight.

They had guided her through the shanties, where the wagons and tents made streets and alleys winding in all directions. They weaved through the lines of coloured washing and the cooking fires, where women stood beside the flames holding out long pans of flatbread baking in the coals. All around there were chickens and mules and the shanty stores and the smoke-house smells of cloves and boiling coffee.

They would sneak inside the gambling tent with its dark, thick rugs and walls of deep-red woven curtains that formed little hidden chambers. Jemma could hardly breathe at first with the pipe smoke and the steam of the coffee in scillioned pots, their spouts shaped like the heads of peacocks. The pipes emerged from elaborate metal beacons carved with intricate swirls and patterns that sat in the middle of the table, where groups of smokers gambled with dice carved out of bone.

But there was a section of the tent where they could not go. Where the Caravanassi stood around, guarding it, except you weren't supposed to notice that.

Jemma had tried as best she could to look inside but Daria had shaken her head. She seemed to have picked up the eyes of the Caravanassi men and Jemma had seen, then, how suddenly afraid her friend had become. Daria pulled on her arm to leave.

Jemma had the feeling of being watched, but there was something different too. In the middle of the tent, the curtains became very thick and formed circular corridors, almost like the passages of an intricate maze. And from somewhere inside, the music of an accordion could be heard.

It sounded to Jemma like another substance, as tangible as the smoke and the steam. The music drew her into a longing she could not name, and she did not want to leave.

~

STANDING ON THE EDGE OF THE CAMPS, JEMMA COULD hear the same music drifting from the gambling tents. A curtain of pipe-smoke hung in the entrance.

Daria had spotted her and came running over, calling out, 'Sister! Sister!'

Besh came after her, laughing.

'You have the peacock's face,' he said, holding out a piece of flatbread dripping with gravy. She guzzled it down, still keeping her eye on the trade boats in the harbour.

Out of pure habit, they went over to the stalls along the docks and shared a round of their favourite corn cakes.

'I've come to say goodbye,' Jemma said, after devouring hers in less than a minute.

'And we are going, too —' Besh said. 'Our parents, they only told us yesterday.'

'We didn't know if we get to see you before we leave,' Daria said.

'Before *you* leave, but...' Jemma turned to look at the docks once more. Thinking about her own departure, she hadn't noticed the wooden hull of a cargo ship, filling with Caravanassi.

She saw that Besh and Daria's caravan wasn't there anymore — it was standing in the line.

Customs officials, dressed like soldiers, were checking papers and slowing the whole train down. They had appeared at the Wharf along with the Caravanassi and wore high black boots and long grey coats that reached to their knees and bell-shaped hats. A brown belt circled their waists and crossed over their chests and shoulders. They each carried a long stick they used for pointing ahead or whacking animals that came too close to the edge of the planks as the Caravanassi boarded the ships.

Jemma felt frightened, not for herself but for her friends. She thought of Soren's memory loop. Edgar's theory of the Caravanassi, how they kept returning, again and again.

Daria's eyes were full of life, excitement, anticipation.

Besh looked anxious and his feet wouldn't stand still. Jemma noticed they were dressed in their finest clothes.

Daria held a doll in her arms, the ones she had stuffed and sewed with her mother and sold in the market.

Maybe Edgar was wrong. Maybe things would be different this time. Maybe they wouldn't come back in their caravans, returning along the road. 'We go now,' Daria said, and held out the doll. 'For you.'

'Where are you going?' Jemma said, as she held the gift.

'Ask no questions,' Besh said. 'Better place. Where are *you* going?'

'I don't know,' she said. And she didn't know what to do. Should she tell them about the loop? What if she caused them worry for nothing? Stole this moment from their hope. Wouldn't they always remember her, as the one who cast a shadow over the sun?

'Thanks for the doll.' This was all she could say. She felt bad having nothing to give Daria in return.

Besh held out his hand and Jemma shook it.

'Good friend,' he said. 'Farewell.'

Jemma nearly blurted everything out, but didn't. She felt like a coward. Hadn't she taught them how to dive for sea-fennel?

She watched them join their parents, sitting on the back of the caravan, waving. Besh was pulling faces. Daria looked as if only now had some emotion struck her. Jemma watched them until they had passed through the trade gates onto the Wharf and disappeared from view.

Her heart raced with indecision and then, in a flash, she went after them, pushing through all the bags and sacks and cooking pots bundled together.

A line of soldiers stood at the gates. If she couldn't get through, she'd never catch them. She crossed to the other side of the line and crept beside a caravan. She ran until she found them.

Daria immediately took Jemma in her arms and Besh tried a smile, but his eyes were worried. Something was older in his face, as if he had lived and suffered many lives. She hadn't seen it before. Now she did.

'You don't know where you're going?' Jemma asked again.

Besh shook his head. She saw him grow confused, as if he half-remembered something. His eyes were set deep with fear, but he could not say what it was. Instead, he took his sister's hand.

'We go now.'

'Wait,' Jemma said. 'You've got to listen to me. You don't know where you're going because maybe you don't remember, but you have to believe me. You're caught in a loop. You'll just keep returning to these camps. My friend, Edgar, he's clever, see, and he worked it out. It's like some kind of trap. You have to try to get away. Try to escape.'

They made it to the gate. The second line of soldiers called out and Jemma could only watch as they handed over their papers.

'Come,' Besh said to his sister, and Daria let go of Jemma's hand as they went through to the landing. With her other hand, she was clutching the little cloth doll to her chest.

'Remember what I said.' Jemma ran to the fence. 'You've got to try. When you get a chance. Run. Get away.'

And then she lost them in the crowd. All she could hear was the clanging of the bells. They disappeared onto the ship.

## CHAPTER 8

## I GIVE YOU THIS TO KEEP

Now everyone was gone. Edgar. Besh and Daria. She couldn't bear to think of Soren, and if Sharmenai knew what she'd told him, she'd never be able to go back to the hut again. All she had was a stupid blade and no one to take her to Adocentyn.

So much for the whispering lights to keep her company. Jemma couldn't hear any voices telling her where to go, just when she needed someone. Anyone.

Maybe she would never see any of them again. Maybe she'd be stuck in the Wharf forever. Jemma felt a flash of resentment for the ones who'd abandoned her in a bundle of cane-fleece rags. She couldn't even call them her parents, because you had to have a memory for that, and she had nothing but a bottomless ravine inside her.

That's why an orphan had to look after herself. If you cared for others, they'd just leave you all alone and then what? You'd be left with nothing but useless *feelings*.

Already she'd been stupid enough to wave the golden blade about in front of that ugly trader. Now she held it firmly strapped beneath her vest, along with the map she had torn from the book. If she could learn how to read those lines and pictures and symbols, maybe then she could make her own way to Adocentyn. Why stop there? She could follow paths to who knows where and travel forever and ever and never stop. Except she couldn't even begin to know how.

As Jemma walked towards the market, she saw a jittery Gull woman by the fish stalls peering into the sky. A fierce gully wind swept into the Wharf. The woman stumbled backwards, breathing rapidly, and then Jemma saw it too – a flock of Sparrows darting in the sky, that same shadow of a hand, scouting ahead for Poachers.

The Arctic Gull changed and flew to her children who scurried in from the Wharf. They changed again to their human forms and ran towards the shacks. Panic erupted in the camps. Pots and pans clanged wildly in warning and the Caravanassi who had just arrived at the camps scampered to the tents.

Jemma hurried into the laneways, not knowing which way to turn. She heard the shrill cry of an old, silver-feathered Arctic Gull and followed it down a narrow passage. It seemed to beckon her. She had the clearest sense that it wanted her to follow and now it led her through a maze of tin and seaweed and old frayed baskets piled into higgledy towers or strewn into the dead ends of alleys, where the smell of rotting fish was overwhelming. Jemma had to keep her sleeve pulled over her mouth.

As she hurried through the twists and turns, she caught glimpses of faces in the windows or the sudden emergence of a rushing train of children. In the midst of this flurry she lost sight of the old Gull, but then she heard again the same persistent call and she followed it through winding tangled passages. The Sparrows darted overhead.

The silvery Gull let out one last cry at the entrance of a

dishevelled shack held up with layers of rusted sheeted iron and the frayed remains of basket weave. The tin rattled in the gully wind and there was smoke drifting from a stove pipe attached to one of the walls.

When Jemma stepped inside, the Arctic Gull had changed into an old woman sitting by the fire stirring a pot of soup. She did not yet look up. It was not an unpleasant smell, a rich stock of fish heads and onions and something else Jemma could not name, a spice that she recognised from the Caravanassi kitchens. There were twisting stalks of garlic hanging between the black iron pots and many jars of leaves and herbs.

'Saffron,' the woman muttered. 'Come.' She motioned Jemma to sit beside the pot.

Jemma looked into the Gull-woman's clouded eyes. They were blind yet seemed to stare at her. The woman's hair was a patchwork of feather-tangled strands, silvery grey and white. When she breathed, the place in her throat seemed to stick and she gagged intermittently with the sound of a *thuok*. Jemma would have found this revolting, if it wasn't for the Gull-woman's hands that brushed Jemma's face with gentle strokes, as if she was tracing its outline with a feather.

The old woman let go of Jemma. She held the red threads of the spice in her palm and took a small pinch – releasing a sweet pungent odour – and dropped it into the pot.

In the steam of the soup, images seemed to float all around Jemma. She felt disoriented and shivery. She was back in her room in the hut but she was also standing in the cold of dawn. She could see the dark glow of a city. The Shadow city. Yes, she could see it so clearly, the black lines of the canals, the bridges, the pointed steeples. And then she saw the vision of a man, not Raddahkin, but the one she had seen in the palace with the wild black hair. Bruno. He was huddled by a window, shivering in the cold. A single candle burned low, the wax had dwindled and the flame was struggling against the encroaching dark. She could see herself, walking up a narrow staircase into the room, gently placing a blanket across his shoulders. The vision had the quality of a waking dream. She held the candle up to his face. His eyes looked like the turrets of a palace in the wintry snow. Flecks of ice melted down his cheeks. Then everything went black.

The images dissolved and a strange afterglow pulsed in her vision.

'And what did she see?' the woman inquired.

'Nothing,' Jemma said. 'A dream. That's all. But now it's gone.'

'Yes,' the old woman nodded. 'I have been watching.'

Her hands brushed Jemma's face again, as if she was mesmerised by its shape. For some time the Gull woman swayed in a trance.

'Too old to Keep, can't keep it any more. Now they are coming ...'

'Who?' Jemma said. 'Who is coming?'

'Poachers from the city. Hunting us. Too weak to fly.' She held Jemma's temples in her hands. 'You must be their Keeper now.'

'Whose Keeper?' Jemma said. 'Please – I don't understand.'

'Tell no one,' the old woman whispered. '*I give you this to Keep –*'

At first, Jemma saw the image of a single Arctic Gull flying from a great distance across the ice wastes and the sea, no more than a speck on the horizon. It seemed a long time that it flew, but as it came closer she could see that it was not one bird. There were many thousands, each flying and scrapping and pecking at each other with their beaks and claws, fighting to be seen. And then they swarmed about her with a frightened cry. A rushing torrent of time entered that ravine in her mind and the images of another world of memory swirled inside her eyes.

The Keeper released her hands.

Jemma felt as though she was drowning, gasping for breath, as if something alien and alive was inside her. Then a feeling of nausea filled the back of her throat.

'Please,' Jemma said, still gasping. 'I don't want it. Take it away.'

'You are their Keeper now. Have to save them. Or they'll fall into the dark and become Shadows.'

'But how? I don't want to!'

'Have to keep them deep inside you. Tell no one. Do not resist. If it's strange within you, it will consume you.'

Then all Jemma could hear was the shrieking of a Gull. The old Keeper had changed and her cry was desperate, threatening as she lurched forward, flaying her wings.

Jemma backed away. Through the window, she could see the dark robes and heavy boots of Poachers. A line of carriers held the box of a carriage, where she saw a face that she would never forget. It was pale, like a furnace-hardened stone. The man's eyes seemed to burrow into her skin. A jolt of pure fear ran through her and released in her mind images of the Arctic Gulls fleeing in the sky, screeching above her with the same piercing cry.

She took off out of the shack, struggling against the wind, the Gull woman's cry fading behind her. When she turned, she saw the Poachers holding the screeching Gull in a cage. A hand appeared from the carriage, glinting with golden rings, and then the Gull Keeper was taken inside.

Jemma stopped in her tracks. She didn't know whether to hide or to do something, anything. Shouldn't she try to set the old Gull free? It was then she heard the voice come whispering again, *run to the Tern ships. Now.*

She pushed through a gap in the tin and found herself back in the maze of alleys, stumbling over the tangled baskets. Jemma ran until she could no longer hear that awful screeching in her ears.

When she reached the edges of the Wharf a weariness came over her. It was like an invisible weight of memory pulling her into that dark ravine, and even if she had wanted to, she couldn't shake herself free. What would they do with the silver-haired Gull? The Keeper?

A cloud of Sparrows flew above, circling in the air.

Jemma looked around for Soren, but the baskets had already been cleared and stacked onto the trade ships. For a moment there was stillness – the howling wind had ceased.

If she could just make it to the wrestling tents, maybe Soren would be hiding inside. She made herself move, and as she did, all around her Arctic Gulls on the Wharf began to change, taking their bird forms and flying up in a sudden frenzy. They were circling the boats and surrounding her, driving the Sparrows away.

She cast her eyes towards the caravans where the Caravanassi men stood watching the Sparrows from the camps.

As she hurried along the shore, a swarm of Sparrows swooped down. Jemma tried to dodge them but they flocked around her in a cloud. The Arctic Gulls attacked, squawking and shrieking as they hurled the swarm away. Inside the Caravanassi camps, a loud commotion had started, the banging of cooking pots, the waving of burning sticks. The Gulls formed a protective circle around her, squawking and screeching at the crowd.

In the midst of this flurry she felt claws digging into her shoulder, wings against her cheek.

'Don't look behind. Go straight to the loading dock.'

'Edgar! Where have you been?' She felt the gap in his wing as it brushed her cheek. 'What's happened to your feathers?'

'I don't have time to explain. You have to hurry.'

He flew back towards the crowd, drawing it towards the entrance of the jetty. It seemed to be working – they were blocking the way.

Then Jemma caught sight of the hooded man she'd seen in the Scarp, pushing through the Caravanassi. She saw a glimpse of his eyes and felt a terrible doubt, as if a different voice inside was commanding her to stop. She fought against it, running towards the Tern ships.

Right above, the Sparrows circled as a band of Arctic Gulls beat them off. But a volley of Poacher's arrows reigned down from the rooftops of the market stalls – the Gulls were falling! She could feel it as her own pain and she sprinted towards the docks. A stinging sensation came into her chest like nothing she had ever felt before.

All around her the skies lit up with swirling tar-fire that blazed into the market and scattered the crowd, catching the wings of Sparrows, who plummeted like burning embers into the sea.

The last thing she heard was a whooshing in the air. A net, thrown from above, engulfed her as she toppled over. Suddenly she was weightless, her cheek pressed against a harsh material that scratched her arms as she flailed in every direction. Until the great thud of her body on wood sent her spiralling into blackness.

# PART II
# THE SHADOW CITY

# CHAPTER 9

## BETRAYAL

S oren lay on a bench near the table. There were no candles in the cabin, but in the starlight, in the pale glow filtering through the window, Jemma could see his terrible cuts still raw. Sharmenai was sitting beside him, stroking his face. Something was different about her body – it was fading.

At first, the shadowy figure did not speak or look beyond her task. She was dressing her beloved's wounds.

'Why did you take him from me?' she sighed, the gentleness of her voice almost forsaking the accusation.

It was only in the manner of her movements, the way she reached above for the aniseed flask, the gentle cleansing application of the healing weed, that Jemma realised they were back in the hut. It was after the fight, the smell of stove wood drifting in the smoky air.

'Give him to me,' Sharmenai said, without turning, her gaze fixed upon the wounds. 'Give him back.'

'I...can't...I don't even know how,' Jemma said.

Sharmenai turned. Her face was menacing now. She stood glaring, then she lunged. Jemma stumbled back into the corner of the *bunk, screamed and held out the golden blade. Its halo of light cast out a shroud of blackness at the edges. The Shadow was gone.*

Edgar swept into the room, scouring every corner.

'You're awake! Thank goodness. I've been so worried.'

Jemma felt the wood surrounding her, the beauty of its polished grain gleaming in the candle light. The bed where she had slept was soft with cushions and cane-fleece blankets.

'That's not the first time you've had this dream. You always cry out, and then you hold up that blade like you're driving something away.'

'What's going on, Edgar?'

'Tell me what you see in the dream.'

'It was her,' Jemma pointed to the corner, 'Sharmenai. She was right there, except it was like we were back in the night, when she dresses Soren's wounds. That's always the time when I leave them. Edgar, where am I?'

'You are safe, on one of the Tern ships,' he said. 'Thank the Scarp. But only just. There's so much we need to tell you. So much you need to hear. Come this way. There's someone who wants to speak with you.'

He led her through a maze of dark passages, the air thick with the smell of salty wood and wax smoke, then into a windowless chamber where an oil lamp burned on a table. A man, tall and broad-shouldered, with long thick hair tied at the back, stood over a coal stove against the wall. He wore a leather vest and Jemma could see in the glowing fire that his fingers were covered in silver rings. She recognised Raddahkin at once.

'Please, sit.' His voice was startling in the deep quiet, gentle and rough and welcoming all at the same time.

Jemma took a place at the table. Raddahkin ordered a servant boy to bring over the steaming pot of tea. But it was a gentle, tender order. The boy had a look that she recognised.

'You like the black leaf?' he asked.

She nodded.

The boy brought over the pot and, shaking, he poured her a cup. He was a Caravanassi and Jemma thought he looked a bit like Besh, except he was thinner in the cheeks and his eyes were more skittish.

But it was Raddahkin's face that surprised her. Even though she remembered it from that glimpse in the Scarp-palace, up close he brimmed with the vastness of oceans, with a will that must have protected and fought and loved, and never lost. He looked neither old nor young. It was a face of the sea, sun-coloured and stubbled and wind-swept.

'You must be hungry,' he said, and gestured again to the Caravanassi boy, whose arms trembled as he gave her a bowl of soup.

Jemma greedily drank up the salty brew and hoed into a thick crust of bread. It wasn't until she had scooped up the last spoonful that Raddahkin spoke.

'You've been sleeping for two days now. I must apologise for the rough landing – it was all that we could do under the circumstances.'

A wild array of images swirled in Jemma's mind. The frenzy of the Gulls and the Sparrows burning with tar-fire and arrows reigning down. Those green eyes that seemed to burrow into her soul and chase her into darkness. She felt the nausea in the back of her throat when the old Gull had released her hands. She pushed her bowl away.

'I want to know what's going on.'

'Let's start with the dream,' Raddahkin said. 'Do you know why you're having it?'

'It's something to do with Soren,' Jemma said, 'after I told him he was caught in a loop.'

'You did more than tell him,' Raddahkin smiled through the tea-steam and turned his rings, 'you released him. Do you think just anyone can set another free in these lands?'

'I never thought about it,' Jemma said.

'There is a cost. You have severed a bond. You have freed him, but you have also taken Sharmenai's memory. She will haunt you, while she still can, to get her beloved back. She will be very dangerous now that she is turning into a Shadow.'

'I didn't mean that to happen.'

'How could you have known?' Raddahkin looked at her with pitying eyes. 'As I said, that is the price for setting another free. You must be careful. This land itself is made of memories that are very much alive. Think of it like a tapestry of silk, woven by the Keepers, its pattern finely balanced.'

'Are you a Keeper?' Jemma asked.

Raddahkin nodded. 'I am the Keeper of the Terns.'

'Is Sharmenai?'

'No, she is not. She has some powers, but they are limited. She belongs to those who hold a single memory that they can never let go of – in her case, the death of her lover. She created a loop around this event. You have seen this many times over. But without a memory to hold, she will fade. That is why she will try to weaken you whenever she can. Tempt you, draw you as a stray thread into her dying memory loop, so she can pull you in and pit her will against you and take back what she so desires. Beware of her. She will seek revenge on you, until she turns completely into a Shadow.'

Jemma stood so quickly, she skittled her chair. 'I don't want to know,' she said, going to the door. 'I don't want to hear any more.'

Edgar flew up to her shoulder.

The door would not budge. She turned, sending Edgar flurrying back to the table.

'I'm not as clever as a Raven Scribe, but I'm guessing I'm some sort of prisoner.'

'You are not,' Raddahkin said. 'You are here for your own protection.'

'I don't need protecting,' she said. 'I need to get out of here, so me and my Raven can find our way to Adocentyn. Unless you're planning on taking us there. But you're not having my blade. I got treasure stashed away and I'll tell you where to find it once we reach the harbour.'

Raddahkin didn't hide his amusement.

'And what do you expect to find in this City of the Sun?'

'That's none of your business.'

'Have you ever wondered why the lights of Adocentyn burn so very brightly?' Raddahkin leaned back in his chair.

Jemma was growing irritated by these questions. She felt suffocated, hemmed in. And why was Edgar so quiet?

'I will tell you what we know,' Raddahkin said, 'but first, the boy. Ask him his name.'

Jemma looked again at the wispy figure by the stove. 'What's...your name, then?' she asked, feeling foolish.

The boy did not speak, but his eyes were shimmering and Jemma felt she might have drowned in them if she stared for too long.

'You see it too,' Raddahkin said, 'the terror in his face. He does not speak. We found him, half-drowned in the water. He came from one of the ships.'

'I've seen them,' Jemma said. 'Old cargo ships, packed with Caravanassi.' She thought of Besh, Daria. 'Tell me, where do they go?'

Raddahkin lit a candle-lamp and traced a line along the table.

'We followed them all the way past the city harbour, and

beyond, to another hidden port, where they send the Cara-vanassi walking towards the mountains. From there, we do not know what happens to them, until they return along the road. At first, we thought they were sent to work in the old Moth caves. Then, we began to piece together more ques-tions, from the scraps of nightmares he calls out in his sleep.'

'What does he say?'

'Are you sure you want to know?'

'Yes,' Jemma said. She felt ashamed. Here she was, worrying about herself, when Besh and Daria were probably inside the tunnels by now, headed for god knows where. 'I got Caravanassi friends.'

Raddahkin took a sip of tea, its steam spiralling in the candle light. He gestured to her and Jemma took her seat again. Edgar perched on the chair beside her and listened.

'You have already heard of the dark presence that has come into the city, because you were hiding behind the curtain, were you not?'

Jemma felt the colour flush in her cheeks. So he *had* known she was there, inside the palace. She nodded.

'The lights of Adocentyn were once fuelled with whale oil. Now the Whales are being hunted, and a brighter substance burns. You've seen it yourself, the search light that circles from the highest tower, like a menacing eye. What makes the light so beautiful? What do you suppose it is searching for? The old oil glowed with a softer yellow hue – this is like phosphorous streaked with flame. It seems to cast a darkness all around, cutting itself out from the black-ness of the night.'

Jemma almost said it – *those lights, they call to me* – but it seemed too personal to share. She didn't know if she should trust Raddahkin, even if she sensed the goodness in him.

If Raddahkin noticed her hesitation, he chose to ignore it.

'We believe it has something to do with the Caravanassi, and this "loop".'

'I know of it,' Jemma said. 'Edgar, he worked it out, the Caravanassi, returning again and again. You tell him...' she gestured to Edgar. But Raddahkin cut in.

'It's all very well to give it a name,' Raddahkin said, 'but what does it mean? And how is it fuelling the lights? That is the more difficult question. And the one who we need to answer it has disappeared from this land.'

Jemma's heart thumped.

'You mean the man in the Scarp-palace – Bruno? He said they were coming for him, that he was going to make a passage. Maybe that's what he did, and he got away.'

'That would be nice to believe, if it wasn't for one thing.'

'And what's that?'

'You.'

'What d'you mean, *me*?'

Raddahkin clasped his hands. His rings gleamed in the stove light.

'There are many things you heard behind that curtain. And I am glad that you did, for they concern not only yourself but the fate of things you cannot even yet imagine.'

'Wait –' Jemma stood again. 'I'm not this *Erigena*. Ask Edgar. We're only Scarp hunters and all we took was a decanter of brandy and a telescope, I swear.'

'And not a golden blade, or a map, by any chance?'

She felt a wave of prickles on her skin.

Raddahkin stood and seemed immensely tall.

'You stole from the Book of Memory – but you know this already, for you are hiding, at this very moment, its most important page. How did you expect that Bruno could have made a passage without it?'

'I don't pretend to know anything,' Jemma snapped, 'except what I need and what belongs to me by *right*. And that includes anything I find in the Scarp.'

He planted his hands on either side of the candle-lamp, so his face grew suddenly bright.

'Regardless of the consequences?'

Jemma took out the map and the golden blade and threw them on the table.

'Here, take them back, then. I don't want them anyway. I don't want anything from you or anyone.'

Raddahkin thumped his fist on the map so the blade leapt into the air and the Caravanassi boy cowered in the corner.

'Whether you like it or not, you have played a part in the banishment of Jiordano Bruno. You have helped to put the lands of Adocentyn in terrible danger! Have you never thought to question why you don't belong to anyone? Why you run so wild and free? Why this blade glows with bright light at your touch? Calling you to find it? You know it's true, because you feel it too. I saw it with my own eyes, when the Arctic Gulls came to you, fought for your life. When the Keeper gave their memory to you before they disappeared as Shadows.'

Jemma felt the queasy, swirling shapes within her. 'Well, they can take it all back. I don't want it, *any* of it!'

Raddahkin fell into the chair, the same look of despair in his eyes that Jemma had seen inside the palace when he'd stared into the fire.

'How could you have helped it,' his voice grew gentle, resigned, 'when the prophecy is already coming true. And you heard that too, didn't you?'

'*The Erigena will come at the time of the fading of memory, when the Shadows will rise again* – that's what it said, right? A stupid prophecy you couldn't even sell to a Cray.'

Raddahkin raised his head. 'That is only the first part. There is more you did not hear. But now I think it is time for your Raven to tell you what he knows. For he is the one who first discovered the foretelling in the Scrolls. And he is the one who found you.'

Edgar stepped forward into the light.

'What are you talking about? I'm the one who saved *him* from being pelted to death by those Caravanassi kids.'

'Tell her Raven. I think she'll want to hear this story.'

JEMMA CROSSED HER ARMS. 'WHAT IS IT, EDGAR? WHAT have you been hiding from me?' Her stare burrowed into his feathers and he shifted from side to side.

'You already know that I was banished from the Raven Scribes.'

'Except you never told me *why*. You knew about this prophecy, all along? That I'm supposed to be this *Erigena*, and you didn't even tell me? I want the *truth*, Edgar, or I'll hoist you up a Cray pole myself.'

Edgar paced along the table. If he had hands, it would have looked as if they were clasped behind his back.

'What Raddahkin has said is true. There had been talk in the circles of high politics for some time, rumours of this foretelling. I only confirmed what we already knew. Something weakened Bruno. Many traders now entered the city, from where – we could not say. Poachers searching the towns. Harpooners hunting the waters all the way from the ice wastes in the North. Yet the Raven feared this prophecy more than any others, because they feared that the Shadows were themselves, that the stories telling of their darker nature were true. Suspicion swept through the Raven Halls, of who might be seeking to awaken the power of the forgotten. A great Council was convened and it was decided that the only way to end this speculation, this chaos – and to restore the Scribes to their place as the protectors of the light of the memory-lands – was to find the Erigena and shut her in a Raven tomb. I was sent on the mission to find this Erigena. And I found her.'

Jemma stood and gripped the back of her chair. 'How could you!'

'Of course I couldn't.' Edgar raised his beak, as if he was about to fly up to Jemma's shoulder. Then he bowed his head.

Raddahkin spoke between them.

'Before you cast judgement, girl, listen to me. Edgar was that intelligence. He was their spy, their scout, watching you for all those weeks. And when he refused to reveal your whereabouts, he was branded a traitor, an exile. One day, you will come to understand the magnitude of his sacrifice. He was the most brilliant interpreter of Scrolls I have ever known – that is why I trust his way. That is why we must work together, and quickly.'

Jemma turned to Edgar, feeling her cheeks blazing with the hurt that held back her tears.

'Why didn't you tell me?'

'Do you really think you would have listened? Far better to keep you safe.'

'What! From dreaming stupid dreams of Adocentyn, which doesn't even exist anymore? Except the light that searches for this – Erigena. And that's supposed to be me? Except now I'm stuck here on this stinking Tern ship. I thought you wanted to be with me. A Scarp hunter. Because you *cared*. Because you're my *friend*.'

'I know you're angry with me, but listen—'

'You should have just taken me to that tomb yourself. It would have been better than *this*.'

'*Please* listen.'

'What, then? You might as well say it. I'm *not* listening, by the way.'

'Very well,' Edgar said. He paced along the table, gathering his thoughts. 'I will just talk, as if to myself. I will tell a story, in fact, about a girl, and a Raven who was sent on a mission to find her. But what he saw, who she was, changed everything. He didn't believe what others believed about the prophecy. She gave him faith in another way. She was wilful and fierce and brave and audaciously foolish. She could mete out justice to miserly Wharf traders. She could defy the dusk, climbing the sharpest rocks. She could see across the tops of mountains to the lights of the city and dream good things. I saw in you different words, a different story. I took my oath in exile, for a friend.'

'Well, I never asked for *that*.'

With those final words, Jemma forced open the door, hearing Raddahkin's voice as she slammed it shut:

'Leave her, Raven. Let her be alone.'

# CHAPTER 10

## THE ERIGENA

In the dull light of the cabin Jemma threw herself onto the bed. No one had followed her. She was terribly cold and wrapped herself in a cane-fleece blanket. She could hear the silence in her ears, the pulse of her heart. Why should she care for the world, when it never cared for her? This destiny felt like the biggest disappointment of her life. All she had known was how to look after herself, and she was good at it too – digging through the ruins to find trinkets, relics, scraps of silver, scampering through a thousand angry stamping feet in the wrestling dens without getting so much as a scratch.

Before, she knew exactly what she needed to do: search the ruins, find a piece of treasure, travel to Adocentyn. Now she had a priceless blade she never wanted to part with and the image of a land that seemed to travel in endless circles of time, like Jemma's thoughts, spinning around and around. Before, she knew who she was. Where she was going. Now...who was she?

Jemma dug herself deeper into the cane-fleece, cursing

the day she was left abandoned on the Wharf. Wishing for her simple dream once again. Thief. Scarp hunter. Adocentyn. She would even welcome being called a 'wharf rat' – scurrying under the market stalls for a spaghetti handful of guts or fish heads, whatever she could grab to trade with the Gull kids in exchange for digging up her quota of clams. She'd nearly lost her finger once with the swift chop of a cleaver – even this would have been worth it, if it had given her more time in the ruins. It was a fair deal. A bucket of fish-muck for a bucket of clams. But *this* wasn't fair. She couldn't *do* anything. What did it matter if she ran away, or lay here forever, waiting for *fate* to take its course? For the first time in her life she felt an intolerable lack of direction. Like someone had sliced off her rudder with a golden blade and left her drifting at sea.

Desperate for air, Jemma ventured outside. The smoke of the broth pots billowed in the air, and the tar-fires, which she'd only ever seen from the shore, blazed on the long flat decks of the Tern ships. A spiral of twenty boats encircled the Keeper's vessel, their masts towering like a forest in the sea. The Terns who worked the decks in their human forms, scurried about in their loose-fitting fishermen's pants and open-necked shirts, scaling the masts, folding sails, or resting in lines along the rails with their feet dangling over the edge, guzzling bowls of broth. It was difficult to separate the men from the women with their long hair tied at the back or curled up in buns.

She watched a group of Terns stoking the tar-fires and setting the catapults, the ones who must have launched those blazing balls of fire against the Sparrows. They were covered in soot, with moon-like circles around their eyes. All this time, they had been watching her from these very decks. Even now, the other Terns lined up on the rails had stopped eating and looked at Jemma through the steam of their bowls. They had always kept their distance, but they had always been waiting with tar-fire for the day when someone might be coming for her. Jemma felt a strange kind of honour that she had never really been alone. All this time, they had been protecting her.

How could they have deserved this task? She'd once led a pack of little Arctic Gulls to topple a tower of Tern baskets stacked on the Wharf – a whole day's labour ruined. Even Soren had scolded her then.

When she saw herself through their eyes, she saw where she belonged – pestering smelters for a spare bit of iron to make a digging tool for the Scarp, running with the Cara-vanassi kids through the shanties and the roasting fires and the tin shacks of the Gulls. If the Terns knew about the prophecy, what a lousy Erigena they must think her.

Even if she had wanted to, where could she go? Not even the Scarp was safe, especially if the Poachers had caught a glimpse of her face. It would take much less than a bag of silver for the traders to paint a picture – 'that little wharf thief, I'll tell you exactly what she looks like.'

As Jemma walked along the deck, the Terns froze and stared at her, star-struck and fearful to see this girl. The Erigena. She had never felt so awkward. So embarrassed of herself. They would not start their work again until she left. *Keep out of sight*, they seemed to urge in silence. *I'm not what you think I am*, Jemma wanted to say, as if to give them an answer. But they had never asked her a question. The plain fact of her existence was not a curiosity, but a burden she could see they carried without hesitation. The least she could do was to keep herself out of sight. And with this thought, she hurried back to the cabin below.

EDGER TAPPED GENTLY AGAINST THE DOOR. IT WAS NOT fully closed and he opened it easily, stepping into the darkened cabin. He flew up to the bunk and paced along the edge, catching the lamp's soft light in his feathers.

'I know that you think I have betrayed your trust. But let me explain.'

Jemma sat in the corner with her arms curled around her knees. 'What's the point?' she said. 'It won't make any difference anyway.'

'I think it will make all the difference in the world.'

'How come they never sent someone to follow you?'

'Because at first I did not leave the outskirts of the Raven Halls. I wandered the boundaries, the wastes outside the walls, calling all through the days and nights until they grew so tired of my constant wailing. They drove me away, happy at last to be rid of me. I knew, otherwise, they would have followed. They needed to feel power over me. They needed to see me helpless and pathetic. A nobody. Someone who it no longer mattered if they lived or died. An exile. When I came back to find you, I was starving. That was when those orphans caught me scavenging for food on the edges of the camp. That was when you saved *me*.'

Jemma remembered the feeling of Edgar trembling in her arms as she carried him back to the hut. How carefully she had unpicked his feathers caught in the net so she did not hurt his wings. How she loved to see him taking his first sip of tea, raising his beak in the air as if he was about to sing. His manners – *thank you...this is too kind* – had melted her heart. Was it all spoiled now? She had felt so alone when Edgar disappeared into the forest. Jemma knew, then, that she never wanted to be apart from him again. She wasn't sure if this could be true, any more.

'Never think you are just a mission to me,' he continued,

'try to understand – doctrines turn people into fictions, prophecies into illusions. Neither see what is real and unique, and that is why doctrines and prophecies are lies. Believe me, I've read them all. Fate – now that's another matter. There is no question about your fate. Look what has already come to pass. But fate is no less uncertain. That is why we need knowledge, of who has taken over Adocentyn.'

To join Edgar in his search for knowledge could only mean she had to forgive him. Right now, in this airless heavy room thick with the smell of salt and wood. Right now, she couldn't. She folded her arms. Remained silent.

Edgar moved towards the door.

'I know this isn't easy. There's so much to take in, and all at once. But I must speak to Raddahkin. Come, if you are ready. You know where to find us.'

~

JEMMA TIPTOED AFTER EDGAR, LETTING HIM DISAPPEAR through the splinter of light into Raddahkin's room. In the Wharf, she always hovered in doorways and hatches, or lingered at the market stalls listening out for information about the trade ships. Who was carrying a load of iron spikes that she could use for a digging tool in the Scarp? When were the smelting barges coming through so she could sell them a piece of silver? So much more is told to those who are not supposed to hear.

She listened. Edgar was speaking.

'If Bruno has been cast into this Shadow city, we must find a way to make a passage there.'

'How?' Raddahkin said. 'You are now an enemy of the Raven. You have no access to their Scrolls.'

'I may be able to disguise myself. Break into the great library.'

'And risk getting caught? That is ridiculous. Even if you could find your way to this dark city, how would you know where they were keeping him? How would you ever bring him back?'

'The map,' Edgar said. 'We take him this page. And then we find out who has made the passage here. We find who has taken over Adocentyn.'

'But how?'

'This Shadow city is built around the events of Bruno's trial in the Inquisition. The Authorities must have confiscated the Book of Memory – how else could they have made a passage to Adocentyn? They would have used it as evidence to charge him with heresy, to justify the order for his execution. This time, they will make sure he doesn't escape his fate.'

'Wouldn't they have burned the Book?' Raddahkin said.

'If there is one thing we know about inquisitors, they are hypocrites. They will always make a show of destroying heretical works – throwing them on the execution fires – but only after they have made a copy.'

*They're going to burn him*, Jemma thought, and she felt a wave of heat on her body. *What if it is my fault?*

'Perhaps this could work,' Raddahkin said. 'Inside the Shadow city, you find the scribe who makes this copy, and follow the trail.'

'Not quite,' Edgar said. 'What if we let them make the copy, except for one thing. It is missing a page. A very important page.'

'I do not follow,' Raddahkin said.

'Like all memory loops, the Shadow city turns. Over and over. If we cut out this very same page, before the scribe copies it, they will have a book full of useless knowledge – for it will contain no co-ordinates, no map. No records of the memory-paths.'

'A promising idea. It may work, except for one thing.'

'What is that?' Edgar said.

'Whoever has taken over Adocentyn must have used another copy of Bruno's book. Even if you do escape alive, you would then have to find where they have hidden it, here, in the city. You would have to steal this last complete copy.'

Jemma heard Raddahkin let out a little laugh.

'Of course, I see it now. This was your plan all along. You are cleverer than I ever imagined, Raven.'

'And if we do manage to steal it back,' Edgar continued, 'they will be forced to return to their own Shadow city to retrieve our tampered manuscript. Then, we will seal the Rupture. Without this map, they will never be able to decipher the secrets of the codes. They will never be able to return to Adocentyn.'

'Trapped in their own dark city of foul memory – I daresay this would torment them for eternity. But you are forgetting one thing.'

'And what is that?' Edgar asked.

'We have no way of actually finding a passage to this city of Shadows. Without co-ordinates, I'm afraid your great plan is doomed from the beginning.'

Jemma felt a presence behind her. The Caravanassi boy hovered in the passage, his figure ghostly in the stagnant air. She saw a hollowness in his eyes, as if they were hiding secrets impossible to tell. He had been watching her and she felt unsettled by him. Exposed. His expression was not accusing. More like pleading. He reached out his hand and waited until Jemma did the same.

At first she hesitated. Then she slowly raised her arm. The tips of their fingers were touching and Jemma could see images forming in that dark ravine inside her. She was under water, seeing through his eyes, a memory. He reached forward and clutched her arms and then she felt his grip releasing.

She was floating beneath the water, looking up at the wavering sky, her lungs bursting for breath, her eyes bulging like bulbs of salt-weed. Panic rose in Jemma's chest as she couldn't breathe. She was drowning, drowning under the sea. She lunged to the floor choking and wheezing for breath.

The boy turned white, as if the memory he had given her, momentarily releasing him, had leapt with all its terror into his eyes. He scrambled up the ladder and through the hatch.

'Wait!' Jemma called, still desperately catching her breath. She chased after him, but he was gone. The decks were clear. It was approaching night in the West and the Terns had retreated to their cabins below. Only the tar-fires glowed, casting out trickles of light between the nestling, knocking ships. The sea and the Scarp were dark, allowing images of the Shadow city to float in her mind.

She sat on the wooden deck and curled her knees up to her chin. She hadn't asked for any of this. How was it her fault that the Keepers were being hunted? That some kind of memory magician, who she had seen only one time in the Scarp-palace, was now a prisoner, trapped in another dark city? Waiting for the Authorities to...she couldn't bear to think.

An icy wind cut through her vest and chilled her. For the first time in her life she could not hear the sharp chinks of the iron spikes hammering down the sides of the wrestling tents at sunset. She desperately missed Soren and all the times they walked together to the tents, telling stories of their days. What would become of him now?

Most of all, she didn't want to be this Erigena. She didn't want to hold a Keeper's memory. She didn't want the golden blade to glow whenever she held it in her hands, and yet she felt so drawn to it. She didn't want to remember what it revealed when she held it hovering above the map, because that might mean she would have to help them. And then what? There'd be no turning back. Not ever.

She thought of her dream again. What did she think she would even find, once she got to Adocentyn? What would she have done in the city anyway, if she couldn't escape into the wild lands of jagged stone and mysterious ruins that sparked her mind to see, imagine, hope? She had never thought about her actual life, once she had made her fortune and set herself up in one of the Cobbler's houses in the city walls. Would she have just sat there all day, twiddling her thumbs? Edgar would no doubt have scoured the libraries and the bookstores and lived a life completely separate from hers, an invisible life of books, in word-spun visions of knowledge.

But Jemma did not have the patience or the inclination to sit still for long. How sorry would she have been, surrounded by pretty buildings, longing again for her old life in the ruins.

Perhaps the idea of destiny was nothing more than the simple avoidance of a life that would send you mad with boredom. But it was more than that. The Scarp had given her a feeling of something vast and mysterious and beyond herself. How could she even begin to understand the foretelling that conspired to surround her with events beyond her control, and for which she would be responsible? How could a little Scarp-thief matter at all? And how many times had she run this all in her mind, only to find no answers.

Even if she had wanted to, she could never return to

that old dream. It was no longer in the future, but in the past. And even there, everything ran in circles.

Jemma cast her gaze into the distance. The lights of Adocentyn blinked across the jagged Scarp. A ladder on the side of the ship lead to a platform below. She climbed down, smelling the salt and feeling the wind. As her fingers touched the cool water, she heard the sound. Distant at first, an echo beneath the sea. It seemed to rise from somewhere deep below and come cascading towards the surface. It was the call of a Whale, a single longing note. She felt its aching song right in her heart. It called to her, and her alone, the kind of sorrow that could pull you under. She could feel that the Whale was in great distress – that it was calling to her, like the whispers from the lights dimpling across the sea, the whisper growing clearer and more urgent with every pulse of light – *hurry hurry hurry hurry*.

Jemma leapt to her feet and climbed up to the railing.

'What do you mean, hurry?' she shouted into the night.

But the whispers disappeared into the wind. It was as if they were waiting for her to speak again.

Jemma gripped the rail.

It was as if the whole land stood still, watching, listening. As if everything hinged on these next uttered words: 'All right,' she called back. 'All right, then. I'm coming!'

SHE FLEW DOWN THE STAIRS AND BARGED INTO THE ROOM below, startling Raddahkin and Edgar.

'Wait!' She rushed up to the table and leaned over the map. Lantern smoke drifted, filling the air with the smell of kerosene. 'I think I know a way.'

Edgar flew up to her shoulder, nuzzling his beak into her hair. 'I knew you would come.'

Raddahkin looked at her with great adoration. 'You have arrived just in time. Our questions only lead us into circles. Do you have something you wish to share?'

Jemma picked up the golden blade.

'I've seen where he is. When the Gull Keeper gave me that memory to hold – before that – she opened up a vision of the Shadow city. It's filled with dark streets of buildings and canals. Bruno's locked inside some kind of attic. I saw him, shivering by a window. There were stairs. A house, on the edge of a canal, a big house, next to a bridge. I remember a name on the door – Mocenigo.'

Edgar dropped to the table in a flurry of wings. 'Why have I heard that name before? Perhaps from one of the Scrolls.'

They all huddled around the lantern light.

'The city of Shadows,' Jemma said. 'It's on this map.'

'That would be quite impossible,' Raddahkin said.

'Then take a look at this.'

Jemma picked up the golden blade and hovered it above the images on the page. 'What do you see?'

Raddahkin peered as best he could. 'Only what I could already see before.'

'Look at the picture of Adocentyn. Now loosen your focus. Try to gaze at the sun that surrounds it.'

Edgar stared into the centre. 'The city of Adocentyn... appears to be glowing.'

'What else?' Jemma said.

'I see a halo of light...but wait. There is something forming, on the edges.'

'What is it?' Raddahkin's voice was quivering. 'What do you see?'

'There's a shadow,' Edgar said. 'But that's not all. It looks like another city. This is incredible. How come I couldn't see it before?'

The dark city appeared again like a black reflection of the glowing Adocentyn, and even Raddahkin could now perceive the etchings of canals and spires. A high tower appeared, surrounded by a black moat.

He placed a finger on the map. 'The golden blade has chosen you, girl, for this mission. And now, Raven, it looks like you have your co-ordinates. Come,' he said, 'we do not have a moment to waste.'

He led them to a small door, beside the coal stove, where the Caravanassi boy stood holding it open with trembling arms.

'A Keeper can open the doors of memory, but only you can make the path you need to travel. The Raven was trained in the art of passage-making,' he turned to Edgar, 'and now you have everything you need to craft your tunnel.'

'Only for a little while,' Edgar said, pacing along the edge of the map. 'And I never completed my training.'

'It is time to put what little knowledge you have to the test.'

'I'm not even sure if the passage I make will hold. Or where exactly it will take us. The co-ordinates are nowhere near as reliable as—'

Raddahkin handed Jemma a white cloak with a black hooded cape. 'This was a gift, once left by a traveller in return for our hospitality. Now you will need it, if you wish to enter the dungeons of the Black Moat, unnoticed. And also, to conceal the Raven. They are not well liked in the realms of memory.'

'The Black Moat,' Jemma said. 'Why there?'

'Where else but such a foul looking place would you find the court of the Inquisition itself?'

'What is this – Inquisition?' Jemma put on the cloak. 'Before we go anywhere, I want to know.'

'There is little time to explain,' Raddahkin said. 'But while the Raven is crafting his passage, I will tell you as much as I can.'

## CHAPTER 11

# NEW ALCHEMY

E dgar scribbled furiously into the margins of the map. Jemma watched as combinations of letters and numbers descended from the point he had marked on the page. Raddahkin began to speak.

'Imagine if you could use your memories of lands and mountains, of trees and skies and animals, all that you had ever seen or heard, use them as the raw materials to make another world? That is the power of a Magus. During the time of the Inquisition, it was called the New Alchemy, and any who practiced this forbidden art were considered enemies of the Authority. They were put to death for heresy.

'Before Bruno, Alchemists had tried to turn base metals into gold. But he believed they had always misunderstood its true meaning. Gold was not a metal. It was the sun. All memory is derived from matter through our lived experience. It exists in shadow, until it is brought to life with light. The New Alchemists believed that if they could discover the memory of the first rays of the sun, this was the elixir to make matter again from shadow, to create new worlds from the substance of memory itself. Worlds nothing like the one they wanted to escape, where time ran in a line, filled with repression and death and misery, where minds were shackled by the chains of the Authority. Bruno had discovered in an ancient manuscript the blueprint for Adocentyn, the formula for a city made from the matter of memory. It was known by the Alchemists as the City of the Sun – a place where time would not run in lines, but in endless circles of rejuvenation.

'There were others who practiced this New Alchemy, who tried to decipher the elixir. But none were as brilliant as Bruno. Some lands, formed by charlatans, their elements mis-combined, gave rise to barren wastes. That is why they are called the unformed lands, and they are very dangerous. Others, like the Shadow city, cohere around the memory of a single, great event. Within these places, dark memory could take hold.'

Jemma thought of the time her fingers turned blue, having to dig for clams in the icy sea. 'I heard you in the Scarp-palace. Dark memory is made of pain. Misery...'

'Indeed, the execution of heretics is cruelty and suffering on a grand scale. I must warn you, such events attract Shadows. They are the forgotten who yearn for light, who will seek out the execution fires. There are also many small tyrants who sustain their existence through the memory of the cruelty they inflict on others, who become their slaves.'

'What sustains Adocentyn, then?' Jemma asked. But she already knew. She touched the circle of images on the map. 'The Keepers...'

Raddahkin smiled. 'It is a beautiful world, is it not? Animals had always been used by the Alchemists as totems of memory. Bruno created hybrids – Keepers who could take both animal and human form, so they could thrive in the lands of Adocentyn, and also protect them. They are part of its very fabric. Over many cycles, the radiant sun of Adocentyn has attracted other paths and Ruptures where travellers, traders, wanderers, or those like Sharmenai seeking to sustain a single memory, have found their way in. The land grows and changes. In Adocentyn, memory and matter mingle together, as one.'

Edgar continued scribbling. Jemma was glad to have these last few minutes. She pressed for more.

'Why do the Keepers have this power, to change?'

'We might need to, if the land is threatened. We might need to fly, or swim, or strike between forms, because there has always been a risk that someone from the past will come to find us, as they have done before. I am not the first Keeper of the Terns. There have been many before me who have fought for the land. And this memory is also a part of what sustains us.'

Edgar was speaking into the dark passage he had made, reciting the lines he had scribbled on the map. It was a language Jemma had never heard before. The words had a rhythm that could put you into a trance. She remembered the first Scarp-wind of winter howling through the frosted gully. It seemed to whirl and whistle in the ravine inside her, whispering with the voice that mingled with her own thought: *only you can bring Bruno home.*

'I think it's finished.' Edgar stood on the threshold of the passage. 'At least, I hope so.'

Jemma wasn't ready to leave. She wanted to hear more.

'What if I'm from another place? You said it before – the City of the Sun could call to others, opening Ruptures from different lands. Other paths. You said I don't belong here. I just *run wild and free.*'

'I have said many things,' Raddahkin said, 'in the heat of

anger. But listen: could someone ever take away the Scarp from inside your very being? Your heart?'

'I have other places, inside me.'

She didn't know why she told Raddahkin this. It made the ravine seem even more real. And terrifying. A look of compassion mixed with sorrow came into his face.

'I know,' he said. 'You are the Erigena...'

'But what does that mean?'

'If only I had more time to give you the answers that you seek. I do not have them all, but I promise – when you return – I will tell you everything I can.'

Jemma stood beside Edgar, peering into the dark.

'How will we know where to go?'

'Use the images the Gull Keeper gave to you. They will lead you to Frater Jiordano – that is the name he was once known by. And he will not remember this land. That is what happens when you are forced against your will, through a Rupture. But perhaps you will awaken a memory of his future.'

Jemma tucked the map and the golden blade inside her vest.

'There is no more time,' Raddahkin said. 'You have the co-ordinates. The Shadow city turns,' he handed Jemma a candle-lamp, 'and if you do not go soon, you may be too late. The execution may have already begun.'

'Wait,' she said. 'There's one more thing I want to know: you never told us how you escaped the Scarp-palace. When it collapsed through that Rupture, why weren't you sent to the Shadow city too?'

'I steered a path to the Tern ships. Our memory will always call us home. Bruno had no defences. It was another memory that took him – not one of his creation, but one of his own past. And the past, none of us can control, for it does not belong to us alone.'

Jemma had forgotten about the Caravanassi boy, hiding beside the coal stove. She held out her hand, like he had done before, and waited. At first, he cowered into the corner, but then he slowly raised his hand towards her, his fingers trembling in the air between them.

'I've seen what you've seen,' she said. She touched her chest, as if to show him where she held his memory inside. The terror had gone from his eyes, but little tears were glistening down his cheeks in the lantern light. 'And when I come back, I'll find out what happened to you.'

Raddahkin knelt down and held Jemma's shoulders. 'Soon as I saw you moving behind that curtain in the Scarp, I knew something extraordinary was going to happen. I've seen you running rackets on the Wharf, pinching iron spikes. Even the day you toppled our Tern baskets, you made me curse. But I saw your spirit, too. I have my faith in you girl, and the Raven.'

He handed her a little tin on a string and put it around her neck. 'This is a flint box, so you can make a spark of light if ever you find yourself in the dark.' Raddahkin stood and made room. 'The boy has something for you as well.'

The Caravanassi boy stepped forward, clutching a brown satchel to his chest. He gave it to Jemma.

'Look inside,' Raddahkin said.

Jemma could already smell the smoky sweetness. 'Corn cakes!'

'We know how much you love them,' Raddahkin grinned. 'And there's a little tin bowl full of black leaf tea. I wouldn't count on finding much to eat or drink in a city of Shadows.'

The boy released a half-formed smile quivering in the corners of his mouth.

Raddahkin went to the passage door.

'While you and Edgar are gone, I will travel to the

Raven Court and find out what I can about the Caravanassi. When I return, we will be waiting for you. Now go,' he said, 'and for Scarp sake – be safe.'

## CHAPTER 12

## DARK KEEPERS

Jemma held out the candle-lamp to the tunnel, which disappeared into pure blackness.

Edgar huddled on her shoulder.

'It's a good thing we have this cloak,' he said. 'We must try to avoid drawing any kind of attention to ourselves.'

'Ouch – you need to trim your claws.'

'I'm not a pet,' Edgar said. 'Besides, our claws are weapons. You never know when you might need them.' He shifted beneath the cloak. 'How's that.'

'Better.'

Jemma studied the wooden scaffolds running along the walls, testing the spongy planks beneath her feet.

'Are you sure this passage will hold me?' She tried to peer further into the dark but it was impossible to see anything beyond the little flickering flame.

'We'll soon find out.'

'And you don't know where *exactly* we're going to end up?'

'I'm afraid not.'

'So we might be lost before we even begin.' She thought of what Raddahkin had said about the Shadows. What would happen if they touched you? She imagined it would feel like an icy Scarp-wind shivering through your bones. The realisation struck her of what she was actually stepping into – the echo of inquisitions, Bruno's past, full of Shadows and strange loops and dying memories.

'No, not lost,' Edgar said. 'We have your vision, remember. Or was it a dream?'

'All I saw was a house, by a canal. That could be anywhere. How close do you think we are?'

'Not far, I hope.'

Jemma scuttled along the flimsy scaffold, keeping Edgar tucked inside the folds of her hood. 'Raddahkin said there were Shadows. And prisoners of memory. Do you know about them, too?'

'Only from what I have read in the Scrolls,' Edgar said. 'In Shadow cities there are Dark Keepers, who are only interested in protecting themselves against becoming a Shadow. They are the very opposite of the Keepers of Adocentyn. Rather than sustaining life, they instead enslave their victims, who will always remember them for their cruelty. Memories of suffering and misery will never forget their masters.'

'That's horrible,' Jemma said. Even in the wrestling tent, Jemma couldn't stand the feeling of being trapped beneath the stalls. 'Can't these prisoners just escape?'

'It is a choice between enslavement or becoming a Shadow. This city will be filled with dying memories. Just don't venture into any alleyways. And stay away from the fog.'

The passage narrowed and then curved gently to the left. The candle flame flickered in the dark.

'How did you make this tunnel, anyway?' Jemma said. 'I

saw you writing on the map, and then you spoke those strange words.'

She felt Edgar's feathers tickling her cheek.

'There are many old, dead languages that Bruno used and brought to life in the Book of Memory. I learned bits and pieces as a scholar in the Raven Halls. Ancient scripts all woven together. It is said they are the words of the first memories. But only Bruno knows how to speak the elixir that recalls the memory of the sun. If I knew these words, I would be able to make my own Rupture and craft a passage to a land all of my own.'

'Would you want to?'

'There are already so many lands to explore, why would I desire to make another? I can see the allure of such an idea. But these powers are difficult to master. I can barely make direction, even with the aid of Bruno's map. It is not the words by themselves that make a passage.'

'What do you mean?'

'You must also use other sources within yourself. That is why it takes many years to become a master. It seems to help if you've...lost something.'

'How?'

'It gives the passage a certain depth, dimension. It's very difficult to explain.'

'Have you − lost someone?'

'We've all lost someone, or something, haven't we? Even if we don't know it yet.'

'I never knew my parents,' Jemma said. 'But I can't really say I've lost them, because I never really had them. And loss is a feeling, right?'

'I suppose that is so. But there is no point thinking of that now,' Edgar shifted his wings. 'We must keep focused on our mission. We should hurry. This candle won't last much longer.'

The wood stopped and the tunnel became stone, damp stone. Finally, they came to a thick iron grate where a salty breeze came through, and the stagnant smell of sea. Beyond it was an alley.

'I am sorry,' Edgar said, 'that the very first journey you have ever taken outside the Wharf is to this foul place.'

Edgar peered through the grate. Jemma could feel his feathers trembling. It was night time, and only the faint light of an oil lamp penetrated the darkness.

'You will need to try to remember your vision of that house. Only you can find the place where they are keeping Frater Jiordano.'

She couldn't imagine what it would be like, to be imprisoned in your own past – a past you had already escaped.

Jemma tried to open the grate.

'It's stuck.' She went to give it a good kick.

'Wait,' Edgar flew to the cold floor. 'We don't want to be sending metal grates rattling down the street. You might as well stand on the rooftops and shout, "We're here!"'

'What am I supposed to do then? Unless you plan on opening it with your beak.'

'Try wiggling it. Loosen the mortar.'

Jemma gripped the bars and wiggled, but nothing gave.

'It's not working.'

'Keep trying. Put some grunt into it.'

'Alright for you to say.'

She placed her feet on the wall, grabbed hold of the bars and jiggled back and forth. With one last shove the grate pulled free and sent her tumbling backwards into a putrid puddle.

'Nicely done,' Edgar said.

Jemma brushed off the water and smelled her hands. 'This stinks.'

'Didn't I tell you. A foul city indeed.'

They peered into the alley. To the right was a dead end. To the left, they could see the edge of a canal. The waterway looked perfectly normal, and yet it wasn't. Plumes of fog rose up from its black waters and lines of ghostly gondolas were floating at its banks.

'At least we've only got one way to follow,' Jemma said.

Edgar stood in the hollow of the grate. 'Before we go, I must warn you again. Stay away from the fog.'

'Why?' Jemma folded her arms. 'Don't tell me, fog isn't really fog.'

'Exactly.'

'What is it, then?'

'You could call it – an unintended substance.'

'And what do you mean by *that*?'

'Alchemy always produces some sort of by-product. The New Alchemy was no exception. I first read about it in the Scrolls. Fog is an unintended substance of all the memory-lands. In Adocentyn, it only lingers in forests, ravines, canyons and caves. In dark cities, it is everywhere.'

'What does it do?'

'In theory, it is the opposite substance to the sun. Perhaps according to a principle of balance. The fog does not sustain memory, but obliterates it. I only understood what this really meant when I was in the forest.'

'What happened to you?' Jemma crouched down, so she was closer to Edgar.

'I fell asleep and the fog surrounded me. It must have touched my wing. When I woke, I knew that I had lost something. But it wasn't just forgetting. It was like I had a perfect square of nothing inside of me. If I'd had my note-book, I could have drawn its co-ordinates. I could have held it in a box. And yet, I knew that I would never know what was inside. What I had forgotten was gone. Forever.'

Jemma swept Edgar into her arms and stroked his feathers.

'Why didn't you tell me?'

She held him perched on her hand.

'Because you were being attacked by Sparrows, and Poachers, and a Seal was after you, and volleys of tar-fire were flying all around. Not to mention the Caravanassi waving burning sticks at me. And then, of course – your crisis.'

'What d'you mean, my *crisis*?'

'You know, about my betrayal, and you being the Erigena. I could see it was a lot to process.'

'I wasn't *processing*. I was *angry*. And you did betray me.'

'I protected you.'

'You lied to me.'

'I never lied. I just withheld the truth.'

'That's the same thing, isn't it?'

'Not exactly...but I fear we could be caught in a lengthy debate if we continue. In any case, have you forgiven me?'

'I don't know,' Jemma said.

'How could you not know?'

'Because I don't. I thought we were meant to be together. As Scarp hunters. Forever.'

'But that's exactly what we *are*,' Edgar said. 'Except now we're hunting the ruins of Bruno's past, for a book. The most powerful, beautiful book that we could ever see, or know.'

'Then what about knowing *my* past?'

'Perhaps we will find that too. And then, from these ruins, we'll make everything whole again. Isn't that the greatest treasure of all?'

Jemma could see her breath streaming in the cold air.

'Maybe...except for one thing.'

'And what's that?'

'All the things you're keeping from me. All the secrets and sacrifices you still haven't told me.'

'About what?'

'About your past. The Raven Scribes. What you've left behind. The mysteries of the memory-lands, as you always called them. Just to name a few.'

'You used to find all of this boring.'

'Not if we're hunting for treasure again.'

She smiled. Edgar flew up and nestled on her shoulder, inside the folds of her cloak. Jemma could feel his warmth. She could hear his beating heart.

'Then I will tell you,' he said. 'Not now, of course. But when the time is right. I promise.'

THEY CREPT ALONG THE ALLEY TO THE EDGE OF A CANAL where fog plumes thickened in the black waters.

'We'll keep walking,' Jemma said, 'towards that bridge. I think I recognise it,' but she couldn't be sure. Further up, there was another one that looked almost exactly the same.

The fog began to drift between the floating gondolas. It seemed to contain voices, echoing and disembodied, that searched and reached into Jemma's mind, as if they were trying to find a room in which to live and take form. It was nothing like the voices in the lights.

'That whispering,' Jemma said, 'do you hear it too?'

'Try to ignore it.'

'I can't.' She felt a yearning to truly hear the voices, to decipher what each was saying. It was like they were trying to creep into that ravine inside her. She tried to close her mind against them.

'Don't be alarmed,' Edgar said. 'For some reason you seem to be attracting beggars.'

There were four of them, arms outstretched, reaching from the gutters of the street. All with hollow cheeks and fading eyes. None were as solid as her, but they weren't Shadows either.

'What do they want?' she said. 'I don't have any money.'

'They are not begging for money. But for a Keeper, someone to hold them as memories before they fade completely into Shadows. Don't look at them. Follow the edge of the water.'

'What about the fog?'

'Well, yes, avoid that too.'

They crossed the bridge, passing the light of a baker's shop. A noise came from within, then its door burst open behind them, as a boy scuttled into the street and fell onto the pavement. Jemma caught a glimpse of a man in a white apron, covered in flour, who followed the boy and began to beat him savagely, kicking and cursing as his victim cowered into a ball, whimpering.

'Hide!' Edgar said. 'Now.'

Jemma backed into a doorway, her face concealed from the spilling light.

Yet the boy looked up at her as if he knew she was there.

'Help me.' He mouthed the words.

Jemma took a step.

'No,' Edgar said firmly. 'Don't move.'

'We have to help him.'

'Whatever we do, we must not alter the memory.'

'We *have* to do something.'

'I'm afraid there's nothing we can do,' Edgar whispered, 'at least not without drawing a great deal of attention to ourselves. This is how a Dark Keeper sustains his existence – through the longing of a memory to escape these terrible moments that can never be forgotten. Turn your eyes. If you pull him towards you, his master will sense it.'

Jemma unlocked her gaze, but she felt an overwhelming desire to Keep the boy, just as she felt the hateful will of the baker who held him prisoner. She felt the tugging lines between them, as if this Dark Keeper had wrapped the boy in invisible strings of elastic.

'There must be a way to set him free.'

'Only a very powerful Keeper could possibly free another from such a terrible bond,' Edgar whispered, 'and then you would have to know how to fight him. You would draw in a torrent of Shadows. Let's move on.'

Jemma let the string of the boy's hope snap.

'You never told me about *this*.'

'I'm sorry,' Edgar said, 'but the last thing we need are Shadows chasing us. You must never enter a dark city without having a mission and sticking to it. Or you would never escape.'

The streets opened up and the canals grew wider. She could see outlines of pointed steeples set against the darkened clouds and, in the far distance, there was the building she had seen in the vision – the spires of the Inquisition, rising up above the others like the jagged points in the Scarp. Except they weren't natural and beautiful – they filled her with dread instead of awe.

They walked along the edges of a large open square. 'Be careful here. Do not step into any doorways,' Edgar said. She could feel his claws gripping her shoulder. 'This place will soon be crawling with Shadows. Look.'

In the centre of the square, a lamp hung from a high pole where drifts of fog diffused a murky orange light. Beneath, Jemma could see a criss-cross of logs and branches covered with black pitch and straw piled onto a wooden structure.

'They have already built the pyre,' Edgar said. 'This must be the public square where they intend to execute Bruno. Shadows will come and bathe in the light of the fire. While the fire burns, they will not be Shadows any longer. Brought to life by the memory of this despicable act, they will dance around the flames – but as the flames go down, they will throw themselves on every dying ember. They will rage and howl and attack any in their path as they become Shadows again.'

Jemma's eyes searched. Every crevice seemed alive with dark shapes shifting, sleeking in the sewer grates, flickering between the columns of the palazzo. The canal's stench now smelt to her like charred burned flesh and she felt a sickness rising in her stomach. But she refused to imagine Bruno on the pyre, with gleeful Shadows dancing all around.

'How can it be a memory, if they never burned him. If Bruno escaped?'

'They executed another in his place,' Edgar said. 'An old inquisitor's trick. That is why the form of the memory still holds. This time, they will try to make their false history, true. Who knows what ramifications that could have?'

~

JEMMA WALKED THROUGH THE OPEN SQUARE THEN followed a trail of sickly light down the middle of a laneway, avoiding the dark edges. The lane took them to the magnificent façade of another palazzo above the canal, its ornate stone-carved windows and marble stairs descending to a beautiful wooden gondola moored at the front. The gondolier was sitting lazily in the cushioned seat, staring into the void of fog.

'This is it,' Jemma said. 'I remember those stairs, and

the canal. Up there,' she pointed, 'that's the attic. And there's the name, over the door. Mocenigo.'

'We cannot enter from the front,' Edgar said. 'We'll have to use the servant's entrance.'

They walked along the side of the palazzo, down a narrow cobbled lane. Up ahead, a crack of light came from beneath a wooden door. Jemma opened it, slipping into a delivery room. Through a gap in the shutters, was the warm glow of the Mocenigo kitchen. A cooking fire blazed in the hearth, and iron pots hung above the flames.

The cook was a large, bawdy-looking women with unkempt orange hair spilling from a scarf, her arms covered with soot.

Jemma noticed an old tea towel hanging on a hook above the door. She quickly took off her hood and tied the tea towel around her head.

Edgar shifted on Jemma's shoulder, nestling himself in the remaining folds of the cloak. 'Good thinking,' he said.

A surly-looking maid, perhaps the daughter of the cook, walked out of the pantry with a jar of currents. She handed it to the cook, who ignored her. The maid sat down at a long wooden table.

'Why do I have to carry trays all the way up them stairs. Why don't they put 'im in the basement?'

The cook turned from the hearth: 'Because you aren't what's important round here. Anyhow, it won't be for much longer. Rumour has it, he's headed for the Black Moat. And if what they're saying is true, there's going to be an execution in the square.'

'Execution? What for?'

'It's all about them books of his and all the papers he's left strewn about. They're full of diabolical magic. That's what for.'

The maid shrugged and seemed not to give it another thought.

'Still, I gotta carry *that* all the way up again?' She pointed to a large wooden tray set for a meal.

'You do what you're told, less you'd rather be out begging in the street. Now fetch the chutney pot for his tray and be quick about it.'

The maid skulked off back into the pantry and the cook turned to the fire, stirring her pots. This was Jemma's chance. She scuttled across the kitchen and climbed the staircase. She slipped through the servant door and found herself in an alcove at the stop of the stairs, before it joined the main hallway.

'What are you doing?' Edgar released his wings from the cloak.

'Waiting,' Jemma said. 'Get back inside the hood.'

'More like a straitjacket. My feathers are itchy.'

Jemma stroked Edgar's wings and then made room in the folds of the cloak. 'I'll tell the maid that I'll take the tray up to Bruno. I don't think she'll complain.'

'Brilliant,' Edgar said. 'But how will we find the attic? This place is huge.'

'I'll recognise the stairs, if I see them.'

The maid appeared with the tray, her expression surly and resigned to climbing the passages all the way up to the attic.

'Is that the tray set for Frater Jiordano?' Jemma asked.

'Dunno,' the girl replied, leaning against the door.

'You are taking this to the attic, yes?'

The girl sighed. 'All the way up them stairs.'

'Mocenigo has sent me to take the tray. You've got to wait until I return.'

'Here?' she pouted.

There was a chair beside the door.

'Yes, here. You can sit and wait.'

'I'll not argue with that.' The girl smiled and handed Jemma the tray.

'Now show me the...usual passage.'

The girl pointed to a plain door further down the hall. 'Through there an' all the way up.'

Jemma took the tray and headed down the gaudy hallway, which was filled with grand family portraits in the finest fashions of the day, staring down at them through generations.

'This Mocenigo must have been the one who handed Bruno over to the Inquisition,' Edgar was peeking through the hood, studying the paintings on the walls.

Jemma heard a noise and ducked into the servants' passage, a narrow corridor leading onto a staircase. She climbed the stairs, ascending several floors. Then the stairs came to an end, but not in an attic.

'There must be another way,' Edgar said. 'Let's be careful.'

Jemma opened the door at the top of the stairs and followed a hallway, the floorboards creaking beneath her feet. She heard the sound of china clinking on a tray. A maid stepped out of a room ahead and Jemma slipped behind a cabinet against the wall. The maid came towards them. Jemma pressed against the wooden panel, putting her tray on the floor. The maid suddenly stopped and turned at the sound of a harsh voice behind her, 'You were late for the service.'

The maid's arms were shaking as the Master servant came up close. Jemma could see his black shoes through the legs of the cabinet.

'I were waiting for the milk to boil, Master. You know how Sir likes it hot with his coffee.'

'Watch yourself, or you'll be out in the streets, begging for the light.'

'Yes, Master. It won't happen again.'

Jemma covered her face with the black hood. If the maid had looked down she would have seen them, but she was too concerned with settling the coffee pot and scuttling away.

The Master servant stood still. Listening. Jemma heard the girl clomping down the stairs. Edgar's feathers itched her cheek. She didn't make a sound. The servant took a step towards them. One. Two. Three. Jemma braced herself, ready to spring up and run. He stopped. His heavy breathing filled the corridor. Then he went back the way he had come.

'What a nasty piece of work,' Edgar said. 'Let's be careful.'

Jemma picked up the tray and crept further along the hallway. To the right was an open door. A wonderful candelabra hung over a large desk, which was cluttered with beakers, crucibles and strange burners of all different shapes and sizes. A space had been cleared at the front of the desk where a large leather-bound book lay open, revealing pictures of beautiful geometry, the image of a sun blazing in the centre.

'This is it!' Jemma let Edgar out of the hood.

'Judging by those paintings below, the Mocenigo family once made their fortune in perfumes,' he said. 'This must have been where Bruno was working, in the old distillery, before they locked him in the attic.'

'This is the page,' she whispered excitedly, taking out the blade from beneath her cloak. She raised her hand, just about to swipe.

'No!' Edgar called out too loudly.

The blade hovered in the air.

'Not until we find out who makes the copy, remember?'

Someone was opening the door. Edgar burrowed himself into the folds of Jemma's cloak. 'We must wait to see where it goes.'

'What are *you* doing in *here*?'

Jemma's body stiffened at the low, harsh voice. She turned and saw the severe, pale face of the Master servant.

'I am looking for Frater Jiordano, to give him his supper.'

'He has been moved to the attic. Who are you?'

Jemma's pulse rushed. She felt a sharp flick of Edgar's beak against her ear. 'Tell him you were sent from the Black Moat.'

'I have...come here from the Black Moat. Sent as a gift from the inquisitors.'

'Very convincing,' Edgar whispered.

The Master servant winced at the mention of the inquisitors. He turned almost white, then cast a look of contempt at being out flanked by a lowly maid. Jemma knew she had to hold his gaze and not flinch. She had to burn with an immovable faith – it was her will to save Bruno from the savage dancing Shadows.

'Very well,' he said.

'I will tell them you have been helpful,' Jemma replied.

'Leave at once.'

'Will you point the way.'

He gestured to a servant's door across the room.

Jemma picked up the tray and walked out, feeling the suspicious eyes of the Master servant follow her.

They came to a staircase. 'I recognise this from my dream,' Jemma said. 'These stairs lead to the attic. I know it for sure. What should we do?'

'Give Bruno his supper, of course, and find out what he knows. Remember what Raddahkin said – we may be able to stir a memory of his future. But we don't have much time. If that servant talks to Mocenigo about a strange maid from the Black Moat, we may be in trouble.'

Edgar shook himself from the hood and flew to the door handle. Jemma slid open a large bolt, knocked, and walked in. Edgar hid again in her cloak.

The room was sparse with only a fire, a chair and a small desk by the window. Frater Jiordano stood in the shadows, leaning on the mantelpiece. He signalled her to come in.

Jemma was struck by the same look she had seen before in the palace, his eyes fiery and alive even in the shadows. She had never felt so suddenly present to another. It was as if she had just been lifted up into adoring arms. It was obvious a great passion stirred in him, a fullness of being that made her feel almost afraid.

'You may put the tray on the table.'

Jemma did as she was asked, scanning the sheets of paper strewn on the desk with the same strange symbols as the Book of Memory.

'I have not seen you here before,' Bruno said.

'I have only just come into the house of Mocenigo, Sir.'

'Step forward,' he said. 'Let me see you in the light.'

Jemma left the tray and walked towards the fire.

'You seem...not of this place.'

Jemma did not know what to say, so she curtsied. It was enough to make Bruno laugh.

'Manners,' he said. 'What are manners to the light of a sun?'

'I don't know, Sir.'

'That fool, Mocenigo, wants my secrets,' Bruno said. 'I would rather divulge them to a maid than to a patron who is an imbecile. Tell me, have you ever heard the saying, "You will not be poor, for you will share in the treasures of memory?"'

Jemma shook her head.

He peered at her again. 'Why do I think I have seen you before?'

She could hear stomping on the staircases below.

'They are coming for me.' He went to the desk draw and took out a scroll, wrapped in a fine silk cloth. 'Here,' he said, 'before they come, let me show you what I have just completed.'

He opened the scroll to reveal a picture of her blade, beautifully coloured with gold-leaf paint, dazzling in the firelight.

'It is an image of the Blade of Adocentyn, composed from the memory of the first rays of the sun.' He smiled. 'One day, I will craft this blade. And from the same source I will make a city, once described in the ancient manuscripts. Adocentyn. The City of the Sun.'

Jemma wanted to say it – *You will make it. One day I'll see the city too. And I can even show you the blade. It's right here, inside this vest.* She reached for it.

'Wait,' Edgar whispered. 'Remember, we cannot give him the map until they have put him in the dungeon. Otherwise, when they search him, it will be discovered.'

The heavy clomping grew closer.

Jemma pointed to another image on the page.

'Is that a – Keeper?'

Bruno was startled.

'What do you know, of the Keepers?'

'Only what I have imagined, from this page.'

'I will tell you what a Keeper is,' he said. 'They are the ones who burn with memory itself. They are like a torch. All memory is Shadow, unless summoned, nurtured, cared for by a Keeper. One day, I will bring the memory Keepers to life, like an artist of lost forms, painting what is remembered with light. That is why memory never dies. But when it is forgotten for too long, it becomes a Shadow. Dark memory. I have been tempted. I have seen the power of the forgotten. If the Shadows should rise again...'

Bruno touched her cheek. 'Now you will always remember what I have told you – for what is extraordinary can never be forgotten.'

Five servants burst in, their sleeves rolled up as if ready for a fight. Each took hold of Bruno's arms, dragging him out of the room. But he was silent.

## CHAPTER 13

# THE SHADOWS OR THE FOG?

'Hurry,' Edgar said. 'We have to follow that book.'
Jemma ran down the stairs and inched along the side of the corridor. Hearing voices inside the perfumery, she peeped around the door. A finely dressed man was gazing with adoration at the open page of the circles around the sun of Adocentyn. Beside him stood the Master servant.

'That must be Mocenigo,' Edgar whispered. 'I recognise him from the paintings below. Look at him yearning for Bruno's secrets. The jealousy for genius has inspired more acts of treachery than you can imagine.'

'Have you prepared the gondola?' There was a quiver in Mocenigo's voice.

'Yes, Sire.'

Mocenigo wrapped the book in a velvet cloth, barely able to bring himself to cover it. Then he flung it at the Master servant.

'Let's go.'

Jemma waited until they had disappeared down the main staircase and then sprinted along the hallway to the servants' passage, taking it all the way down to the kitchen, where the maid and the cook were kneading dough for the morning's bread. She rushed past, hearing the cook bellow after her, 'Oi...where's my tray?'

The fog had now drifted into the streets, hovering in the air above them, heavy and oppressive and menacing. Across the canal they could just make out Mocenigo in the gondola – the Master servant was holding a lamp – then the boat disappeared completely into the fog. A line of beggars moved towards them from the shadow of the wall and held out their hands to her.

'Come on,' Edgar said, ignoring the beggars. 'We cannot lose them.'

Jemma ran along the canal to a ragged gondola tied up on the bank.

'You keep an eye on them while I undo this.' She struggled with the knot until she realised she could just uncoil the rope from the boat itself.

She grabbed hold of the oar and pushed off, fighting back the beggars, who were grasping at the boat. She placed the oar in the groove at the back and began to stroke against the current.

'Hurry,' Edgar said.

'You try paddling one of these.' Jemma was already panting.

'Even if I could, I admit, compared to you, I'd be hopeless.'

Jemma took long sweeps of the heavy oar.

'Too rough for your soft scholar's hands?'

'That's not entirely fair. But I think you'd be the one to struggle with a quill.'

'So it's true, you did hold a quill in your hands? That means you must have changed forms. Why won't you change now?'

'Do you really think this is the time to explain?'

They kept their eyes on the faint light ahead drifting in and out of the fog. 'Is that why no one likes Ravens in the memory-lands – because you let everyone else do the work?'

'If only it were that simple,' Edgar said. 'The short answer is, we are spies. We keep our eyes on everything. We meddle in other people's business.'

'What's the long answer? You said you'd tell me things.'

'Because we are the protectors of memory. We always have been and we always will be. At every battle ever recorded in history, isn't there always a Raven lurking in the background, "feasting" on the carrion? Records of ghastly scenes etched into our Scrolls. The Ravens have always been the scribes, in our black robes, from the very first writings, recording, sketching, witnessing. Just think about it – haven't we always been there? In the trees and on the rooftops. At every birth and every death, we have been watching...'

'That's kind of creepy,' Jemma said. The light ahead grew faint in the fog. She paddled harder.

'You can be sure there'll be Raven spies hiding some-where in the Black Moat. We must be careful of them, too.'

They emerged from the narrow waterway into the grand canal. Drips of sweat prickled Jemma's brow. It was almost impossible to tell if they were gaining on them, or if the light was moving further away.

'I've just noticed something that I've never noticed before,' Edgar said.

'And what's that?'

'Where there is fog, there are Shadow people. The ques-tion is, what comes first, the Shadows or the fog?'

'What's it matter? They're getting away.'

'Because behind us there is a plume of fog following, and

it seems to be attracting the Shadows and – you seem to be attracting the fog.'

Through the shroud of fog Jemma could see shadowy airborne figures, their limbs clamouring over each other as if they were fighting their way towards her.

'What should we do?'

'I would paddle faster if I were you. Much faster.'

The fog was closing in. Jemma did not want this misty substance touching her. It seemed to have its own intentions, creeping up behind and then parting and rushing past them as if it was seeking to form a circle and trap them inside.

'Faster,' Edgar called.

He flew towards the Shadow-figures.

'I'm trying!' Jemma desperately worked the oar. She felt a sudden weakness in her arms. Bile was rising in her throat.

Edgar swooped in front of the fog, *Kraaah Kraaah Kraaah*. The Shadows scattered, but there were too many behind who surged to take their place.

'You must paddle faster.'

'I can't!' A thousand desperate voices hissing inside her mind – *take me keep me hold me me me me me Erigena Erigena Erigena...*

'Don't listen to them,' Edgar said. 'They are trying to take hold inside you. Drive them out.'

'How?'

'I don't know!'

Jemma remembered the Gulls – fighting, scratching, clamouring to reach that ravine inside. She called and they released. With a surge of anger the Gulls flew up and swirled around her, dispersing the fog and clearing a way. Then they vanished.

The light of the lamp was just ahead, disappearing into

the small black vein of another canal between two high buildings.

Jemma could see the Shadow-figures clearly now, reaching for the boat. They were like the beggars, except their forms were almost completely faded. The closer ones were held back by the others, who clawed at them to get in front, only to be ripped away by another Shadow.

Edgar flew up and then swooped down and let out a last almighty *Kraahhh* that sent them scattering from the boat.

Jemma regained her focus. She steered them into the long, narrow canal, only just wide enough for a gondola. She swept the oar with a strength she didn't know she had. An immense determination was rippling through her body, a fierce desire to outrun the Shadows, to reach the canal.

They shot through like an arrow, Jemma throwing herself to the floor of the gondola as a last plume of fog swept over the boat. Edgar crouched beside her.

The fog rose up in a tower behind them. It was filled with the floating Shadows, who writhed in the air like slithering eels, the water on the other side keeping them at bay.

'What on earth was that?' Jemma asked.

'I have to admit,' Edgar said, 'I've never actually seen anything like it before.'

'They were trying to grab hold of me, Edgar – they were reaching out to touch me. To live inside me. I could feel it.'

'Yes, I saw that too. I did warn you it would be dangerous. Wherever did those Arctic Gulls come from?'

'I don't know,' Jemma said. She really couldn't explain.

'That was extraordinary. If you could do that more often, it could come in very handy.'

Jemma didn't think it was extraordinary. All she had felt was a wave of nausea. Whatever had happened, she was at its mercy. She couldn't control it, any more so than a torrent of fear that erupts all on its own and disappears. She felt the

Gull memory as something rifling in her soul, where it didn't belong. And yet it had come, when she needed it. Fuelled with anger.

'We will investigate this properly when we return,' Edgar said. 'Right now, we have to follow the Book.'

The lamp of Mocenigo's gondola was ahead, the air clear. Behind them the fog had collided with the majestic buildings, rearing up like a vast grey pillar. She could hear the Shadows screeching.

'Pull in before that bridge,' Edgar said. He flew to Jemma's shoulder and hid inside her hood.

'Where are we?' she said. But she already knew the answer. They had reached the shores of the Black Moat.

Jemma scrambled out of the gondola, the hem of her cloak drenched with foul-smelling water, and joined the entourage of servants behind Mocenigo.

~

As SOON AS THEY PASSED THROUGH THE GATES OF THE Black Moat, the house of the Inquisition, Jemma peeled off to a cloister on the side. She and Edgar watched Mocenigo go into a room.

'This place is almost certainly the realm of a Dark Keeper,' Edgar said. 'Once we find who copied the Book and swipe that page, we have to get out of here. The sooner the better.'

A voice was coming from the room. The power of its conviction penetrating the freezing walls of stone.

Jemma eased open the door, peering inside a cold grey chamber. An Inquisitor in a severe black cloak sat on a raised wooden chair, looking down on Mocenigo and his entourage, who were seated along a sparse table. The Book of Memory was in front of them. Her heart beat double when she saw Bruno, over to the side.

She was shocked at how calm he was. Two robed figures held each of his shoulders. Sitting upright, so still, he looked like he was cast in bronze.

'You would not want to keep this book in your possession now, would you, Mocenigo, for fear that suspicion may fall upon you.'

Mocenigo's voice followed. He did not once look at Bruno.

'If it may please Your Excellency, I offer not only this book, but the testimony of a true witness,' his body twitched, 'Frater Bruno spoke of the existence of multiple worlds. Infinite suns. Cities of light. The transformations of matter to memory and of beasts into human forms.'

A chorus of robed judges on either side of the Inquisitor let out affected gasps. Their gestures were mannered, as if they were actors in a play.

'A direct assault on the very doctrines of creation, of the immovable earth, of the humble mind that dares not summon the power of gods.' The Inquisitor spoke with a hollow authority, growing impatient. He seemed to loathe wealthy merchants as much as he did heretics.

'I'm sure you'll tell no one of the whereabouts of this forbidden volume.'

'Of course not,' Mocenigo held up his hands in a gesture of innocence, and to perhaps shield himself from Bruno's gaze. 'I wished only to confirm my suspicions—'

'You may rest assured they have been confirmed. With your testimony, we may in good faith proceed tomorrow with the execution of your heinous teacher. Thankfully, you have not been corrupted. You may go without the taint of guilt upon your soul. I have signed the deposition. This book of diabolical magic will be destroyed, burned no less, along with its maker, their ashes thrown into the grand canal, dispersed by the Graedian currents, into the Seven Seas.'

'I thank you,' Mocenigo said, bowing and grovelling at once.

'Traitor,' Jemma whispered.

'Indeed, they call such men "flatterers"' Edgar said. 'They stand for nothing but their own pathetic preservation.'

'Shouldn't we try to free Bruno while we can? I could throw those oil lamps into the curtains. Make a distraction. While they're beating down the flames, we'll get Bruno to the boat.'

'And paddle right back into a torrent of Shadows?'

'You heard – they're going to execute him. Tomorrow!'

'Remember, we must not draw attention to ourselves, no matter how tempting it may be. All we can do is wait until they take him to the dungeon so we can give him the map.'

As Edgar was speaking, two monks took Bruno to the centre of the courtroom to stand in front of the main Inquisitor, who held up the Book of Memory.

'You may repent,' he said.

Bruno raised his head: 'You pronounce this sentence against me with greater fear than I receive it.'

The Inquisitor signed the deposition with a stroke of his quill. 'When the flames burst your eyes – oh, how you'll see fear. Take him.'

The monks ushered Bruno out of the courtroom, past Jemma and Edgar still hiding in the cloister. Mocenigo cowered behind his servant. A younger monk in a black Frater's robe entered the chamber.

'Your excellency, I was sent from the scriptorium to collect the Book.'

'Here it is.' The Inquisitor met the Frater at the door,

lowering his voice so Mocenigo could not hear. 'I want the best scribe working on this.'

'Of course.'

Jemma and Edgar waited. The courtroom door closed.

'Now...' Edgar said.

They followed the young Frater down a cold stone hall-way, his shadow looming above them as he passed the wall lamps. He descended a spiral staircase for what seemed like eternity. At the bottom of the stairs was a long passageway with chambers on one side. Up ahead, they could see Bruno being shoved into his cell.

'These chambers must have once housed the novice monks,' Edgar said as the Frater went through a door at the end. 'Now they are the prisons of the Inquisition.'

Jemma gazed at the hideous images painted on the walls opposite the cells.

'This is one of the corridors of vice,' Edgar said. 'These images were designed to be seared into the memory of the novice monks, so they would never forget their sins. They are the dark shadow-images of what is good and virtuous.'

Edgar pointed to a picture of a banquet, where insect-creatures with the claws of crabs stuffed the mouths of bursting sinners. Jemma traced the image of a creature with thick feathers and talons, the head of a gargoyle and serpent tongues lashing between its razor-sharp teeth, its wings outstretched in black flames, devouring the light with shadow. Another creature, a White Moth, magnificent and hideous all at once, sent its spawn into the skies in a great cloud and blotted out the sun.

Peering through the bars of each chamber, Jemma cursed those who must have wanted Bruno to look upon these images, his last vision before they sent him to the pyre.

They found Bruno in the final cell huddled on the

floor. His knees were curled into his chest. They had shaved off his hair and stripped him of his robes so he shivered and seemed naked and cold in his garments of white cloth.

Jemma took out the map and pushed it through the bars.

Bruno's eyes flashed in the dark. He rose from the floor and gripped the page.

'It's *you*,' he said.

'That's right,' Jemma said. 'It's me, and you've got to listen. You've got to take this map and use it to escape. Get back to Adocentyn. There's co-ordinates written out. Look on the page. Edgar worked it out. It's true. It's all true. It'll take you home. You've got to remember. You're caught in a loop.'

Then she couldn't breathe. Someone held her in a grip and was trying to pull her into another dark passageway.

Jemma could only see the arms of a black cloak. A hand covering her mouth.

'What are *you* doing here, *Edgar*, you *stupid* Raven.'

The voice was sharp, accusing.

'I'm in the middle of a very delicate operation.'

'A fine time for meddling. Are you insane? Who authorised you to enter the city? I thought you had been banished.'

'I have all the authority I need to solve any mystery that threatens the lands of Adocentyn.'

'But not to threaten it yourself. You put us all in danger. If you should be caught – one disturbance and you'll have these corridors swarming with Shadows. And I hope this isn't who I think it is.'

'Let her go,' Edgar commanded.

The grip released. Jemma panted for breath. She could not see the face inside the black hood.

'I'll be having words with the Council over this. I am supposed to collect the Book.'

'And I'm sure that you will,' Edgar said. 'Except someone makes a copy before you do, and we need to know who made it. I'm sure the *Council* would love to hear the story of how their incompetent spy, Haegar, managed to let a copy of the Book of Memory escape. Now if you'll excuse us, we have a mission to complete.'

What Edgar had said changed Haegar's tune and he turned, still furious: 'Very well, I will take you to the scriptorium where they keep all the heretical works, on one condition.'

'And what is that?'

'You find who is making the copy and then you leave at once. I'll have nothing to do with your defiance. You've heard the prophecy. This is on your shoulders. Not mine. Now follow me,' he said to Jemma as he went down the hall, 'and keep Edgar out of sight.'

Bruno called to Jemma through the grate. 'Who are you? Where are you from?'

She went to him. 'I'm from Adocentyn...' she didn't know what to say, 'just wait until you see it. It's more beautiful than you could ever imagine. There's a wrestling tent ten times the size of the one in the Wharf. And the land, it's all filled with life. The Arctic Gulls and the Terns. The Seals and the Walruses changing and flying and trading and fighting. There's the Whales and the Delphin too, the Keepers, just like you said. And the lights of Adocentyn, they shine so bright all the way to the Scarp. I've seen them and I've heard a voice, calling me. And maybe she'll call to you too. Help you to make a passage. Bring you home. But you've got to hurry.'

Bruno looked at the page. She could see something click in his mind. He held up the map to the pale light coming through the grate. There were cuts on his scalp where they had sheared away his hair. He looked more like a boy than a man. He held out his hand and Jemma took it.

'Thank you,' he said.

She let go and felt a knot in her throat for all the good-byes. Soren. Raddahkin. The Caravanassi boy. Daria and Besh. What if she never saw them again?

Edgar emerged from her hood as she ran to Haegar. 'What you described was beautiful. I could almost believe you had seen the city itself. I take it back, what I said about the quill. One day, you will write your own scroll.'

'Not likely,' Jemma said. She followed after the Raven spy, trying to mimic his walk, keeping her hands folded in the manner of a novice monk.

~

THEY PASSED THROUGH MANY CORRIDORS UNTIL THEY came to a vast scriptorium filled with rows of desks set between grand pillars of stone reaching to the vaulted ceiling. Before them, many scribes were working by candle-light, no more than boys. Every now and then two old wardens whipped their backs with wooden rods, the sharp cracks echoing through the pillars. Jemma saw the red bruised welts on the skin of a boy's neck. Across the hall, another one raised his head and looked at her with the same pleading eyes as the baker boy, *save me*. Jemma shook her head but it was too late. One of the wardens rushed over and dealt him three savage strikes. Jemma winced at the boy's pain.

Edgar must have sensed her body tense. 'Stay focused,' he said. 'There is nothing we can do. All we need is a name. We take the page, and we get out of here.'

The Raven spy handed Jemma a scroll and a quill and spoke with barely a sound.

'The scribe you are seeking is on the other side of that pillar. Speech is not permitted here. Ask no questions.'

Then he disappeared.

Jemma sat down at the empty desk and stole a glimpse of the scribe who copied the Book of Memory. He was older and occupied a special desk. His angular face looked severe in concentration and his forehead was glistening with sweat. His eyes did not blink. They seemed fixed with an angry patience that did not show a love for his work, rather an envious desire. It was a mean, ungracious face, Jemma knew this for certain. And it made her task seem impossible.

'What are we going to do?'

'Improvise,' Edgar whispered beneath the sounds of scratching ink on parchment.

Jemma peered around the pillar again, this time focusing on the Book of Memory open upon the desk.

'It's funny,' she whispered. 'Now that I know so much about it, I don't want to cut out anything, not even a single page.'

'Sometimes I can't work you out at all,' Edgar said. 'Just when I need you to be rash, you're cautious. I hope we haven't changed you too much. That would be our loss.'

It was then she noticed a novice scribe across the hall, whose job it was to collect and replace the little pots of ink. Now she had an idea.

She took the full pot from her desk, walked around to the other side of the pillar and put it down beside the scribe, who did not look up. Then she reached across his page for the pot he had only just used to dip his quill. A startled, angry gesture knocked it out of her hands, spraying ink across the desk.

The scribe gripped Jemma's wrist and flung it to the side. She acted with penance, as the scribe stood back in silent fury, accepting her humility and letting her clean up the mess.

There was a letter on the desk, signed with a name.

'Gaspar Scoppius,' Edgar said from beneath the cloak. 'Now strike the page and let's get out of here.'

Across the room, the ink boy was pointing her out to one of the wardens. Jemma leant over the desk so the scribe couldn't see. Without the slightest hesitation, in almost the blink of an eye, she took out the blade and turned to the map, cutting the page clean away with a single stroke. Then she returned the manuscript to the place where it had first been open.

Jemma gathered the pots and looked at the scribe once more – his hatred burrowed into her spine as she turned and swept behind the pillar.

The two wardens were coming, a flurry of black robes moving right towards them. She went along the outer wall, pressing into the shadow.

'There,' Edgar said, 'take that door.'

She entered a dark passage, running now as the wardens followed. Then she felt someone pull her into another doorway. A harsh grip dragged her up endless spiral stairs, until they came to a chamber at the top of a tower.

The Raven spy shoved her inside.

## CHAPTER 14

# THE RAVEN SPY

Edgar flew out of Jemma's hood and landed on the mantelpiece.

'I hope you don't mind if we borrow one of your passages,' he said to Haegar. 'We need to get back to the Scarp.'

Jemma could hear footsteps down below, on the stairs. The sounds of doors opening and closing.

'You wait until the Council hears of this.' Haegar was pacing the stone floor.

Even with his hood down, his eyes were as dark as his hair, like perfect pools of night. His face seemed too wide and pointed at the chin, which was swathed with black stubble. Is this how Edgar would look if he changed? She had assumed that his hair would be black, but Edgar was a beautiful raven. She imagined him more handsome, his face slender and pale and smooth. His eyes? Dark blue or emerald green.

'I never would have guessed, Haegar,' Edgar said, 'that you would have risen to the rank of a spy. They must be sadly lacking in talent in the Raven Court. Tell me, who did you have to grovel to?'

Haegar crooked his head, 'Thankfully one of my chief competitors managed to exile themselves – and here you are.'

'Yes. Here I am.'

'If you had any sense at all,' Haegar said, 'you would bring her with me, to the Raven tomb, and end this before it begins.'

'I'm afraid it has already begun,' Edgar said.

'Do you have any idea of the destruction she will cause?'

'I have read the prophecy.'

'Alas, Edgar, you did not read far enough into that forbidden Scroll. I am not talking about the rising Shadows. I am speaking of the third prophecy.'

Jemma saw a flash in Edgar's eyes. She had never seen him with another Raven. Even in exile, he seemed in every way above Haegar in rank. Jemma could see the tremors in Haegar's face.

'What prophecy?' she said, stepping forward.

'Ignore him,' Edgar said. 'He is just trying to frighten you.'

'I want to hear it.' She spoke with a forcefulness that surprised them both.

Haegar sat down at his desk. He adjusted the wick inside a candle-lamp. Then he leaned forward, casting Edgar another scowl.

'Do you think a Magus as powerful as Jiordano Bruno would have been content only with the secrets of the light? He meddled in the dark of memory, too. Once he had completed the city of Adocentyn, he knew he needed a way to protect it from his enemies. A way to protect his Keepers.

'Perhaps he had stared for too long at those hideous

images outside of his cell. He discovered the incantations and learned to conjure the nightmares and monsters of memory from the dark. They are called the Sigilli. He had wanted to use them for his own protection.

'But then Bruno realised he could not control the creatures he'd summoned. If anyone should ever use this knowledge, they would unleash such a devastating power. And, so, for each of the Sigilli that he had awakened, he assigned a special Seal.'

'What do you mean, "special"?' Jemma demanded.

'The Seals once came from the wrestling dens. Bruno trained three of them, to suppress and control the creature entrusted to them. The Seals are fierce warriors and skilful in memory magic. In order to protect the land, they can craft powerful illusions, release and channel memories, use them as raw materials to manipulate and control. For the most part, they practice a constant meditation, muttering the incantations that keep the Sigilli prisoners.'

He paused and looked across the room at Jemma, who was standing beside the smouldering fire.

'Tell me, did your "friend" happen to inform you, poor child, that one of these Seals has been pursuing you?'

Edgar swept across the room, forcing Haegar against the wall. 'You've said enough.'

'But what's this got to do with the prophecy? Edgar – I want to know. Let him speak!'

For the first time, Haegar seemed to have gained the upper hand. 'It says that you will unleash the Sigilli.'

Jemma clutched her hands. 'How?'

'No one knows exactly,' Haegar continued. 'But for as long as you threaten the lands of Adocentyn, the Seals will stop at nothing to hunt you down.'

Jemma stormed up to him.

'Are you saying that's what's been chasing me? One of those Seals?'

'Believe me,' Haegar pressed himself further against the wall. 'You would be better off in a Raven tomb, than to have a Seal chasing you.'

Edgar lashed at Haegar, 'Don't you *ever* say that.'

'Then tell me how what you are doing is not a crueller fate?'

'Because I know who she is,' Edgar said.

Haegar cowered at the vehemence in Edgar's voice.

'And by the way, I'll be needing your scroll,' Edgar continued. 'Everything you have collected about the scribe below. This Gaspar Scoppius, and all his descendants. Now.'

'Not a chance.'

Edgar flew up to the mantlepiece, taking the measure of the Raven spy.

'Give me your scroll,' he commanded. 'You owe me this, at least.'

Haegar was clearly wavering, but he straightened his back. 'I will not.'

Edgar flew against him. Jemma had never known Edgar to be so fierce. She saw the fear in Haegar's eyes as he changed and flew across the room.

In the stand-off, Jemma noticed Edgar was the bigger Raven, his feathers refined and silky compared to the short, rough feathers of Haegar. Edgar's beak was slender and elegant. Haegar's was thick and curved.

The next instant they flew against each other, entwined and flapping madly in the air like a single beast until Edgar, gripping Haegar's neck, forced him down and pinned him to the desk. Edgar's claws were like talons and for a moment, Jemma could not imagine they had ever held a quill. Haegar's claws were curled up in defeat, his hackles flattened in submission while Edgar's were bristling.

When Edgar released him, Haegar changed into his human form, holding himself in pain. He slouched forward and Jemma could see the gashes on his neck. He reached into a chest beneath the desk.

'Give it to her,' Edgar said.

Jemma put the scroll in her satchel.

'When the Council hears of this—'

'One day,' Edgar said, 'all may hear of it. Your deeds will be written in the Scrolls. As will mine. As will hers. This is the day you made your choice.'

The Raven spy opened a small trapdoor in the wall and stepped away. Edgar flew to the opening.

'The pleasure was all mine.' Edgar fluttered his wings. 'Let's go,' he said to Jemma.

She could hardly squeeze herself inside the passage. As the door thumped angrily behind her, she heard the last words of Haegar: 'Do you even remember your home? Arlia still waits. She still pines for you, did you know?'

And then Jemma heard it, the sound of a sorrow in Edgar's crow — *aahh ahh ahh...aahh ahhhhh*.

# PART III
# DELPHIN CAVES

## CHAPTER 15

# SIGILLI

'Where will this tunnel take us?'

'We are following one of the ancient memory-paths. It will lead us back to the Scarp. The Raven have always used them,' Edgar said. 'They are somehow connected to the ruins of the memory palaces you once found so fascinating.'

Jemma slowed her pace. Had she come all this way, only to end up where she started?

A faint glow of light ahead of them. The passage widened and Jemma could almost stand up. Her legs aching with cramps, she felt along the sides of grotty stone until they emerged at the ruins of an ancient palace, nestled in a ring of grey rocks on the Eastern plateau. She was hungry and cold. It was strange, to not even feel the desire to search for treasure. There was only the ghost of herself, digging in the ruins.

Edgar flew above her, scouting in the skies.

The Scarp was a heavy place filled with fog and cold that gripped her face. She had not noticed this before. It was a lonely, desolate waste. There was more emptiness here than she had ever known. It was like the mirror of that ravine inside her.

Hunger took hold. Her stomach gurgled and she remembered the corn cakes and the flint box and the little tin cups! Raddahkin had even left a ball of cane-fleece.

Jemma set to work lighting a fire. She found a clump of flax leaves and instructed Edgar to fly to the cliff and collect some twigs of thistle-weed. She struck the flint and the cane-fleece smoked then burst with flame. She filled their cups from snow patches and stirred in the tea leaves when the water had boiled. Then she toasted the corn cake to a golden crust, smelling the smoky sweetness, and gave half to Edgar.

Jemma took delight in watching Edgar pecking at the corn cake, raising his beak and swallowing with the grace of a king. He plucked out the juicy bits of corn and then devoured the fluffy steaming cake.

'I wasn't hungry at all in that awful place, but I'm starving now,' he said. 'We mustn't stay for long. We cannot have this fire going when it's dark. And that will be upon us soon.'

Clutching her warm tea, Jemma felt the cold air of the Scarp in her lungs. It was comforting after all to see the arid stones and the wastes of grass. Already in the haze of late evening she could see the sweeping beams of Adocentyn glowing on the horizon. She had almost forgotten that their mission had only just begun. How would they ever reach that tower flashing in the distance, so far away? How would they get inside to steal the last Book of Memory?

If Raddahkin had gone to see the Raven, he couldn't help them now. Whatever faith he had in her, Jemma knew the truth. At heart, she was only a Scarp hunter. A two-bit wharf thief who stole useless scraps from half-drunk traders. How would they even know where to begin?

Now she wasn't hungry. She felt the Scarp-wind in her bones and huddled into her cloak. She forced herself to eat.

'Is it true what Haegar said? Am I going to release those horrible creatures, the Sigilli, Edgar?'

'I don't know,' he said. 'That is the truth. I don't know. But even if you do, there is nothing to say what will happen after that.'

'It doesn't help when you keep hiding things from me.'

'I said I would tell you everything, when the time is right...'

'I heard your cry in the tunnel,' Jemma said, 'it was like something was killing you. Like you were bleeding inside. I've only ever seen that in Soren's wounds. Something tearing you up. Arlia – that's her name isn't it. You've left someone behind, haven't you? And you didn't tell me that either.'

Jemma threw the crust of her corn cake into the fire and sent up a coil of embers.

'All I can say is, she would believe in what I am doing. She would believe in you too. I will tell you about her – yes – when the time is right. You must forgive me for needing some time. I was expecting to see Shadows and nasty Dark Keepers and beggars and fog. But I never expected to receive Haegar's blow. You know there is magic in the Scarp. To dwell in memory is dangerous here. The Seal will be hunting us, and that is why we must leave before nightfall.'

'Not until you tell me what you know about the Sigilli,' Jemma said. 'And don't tell me it's not the right time.'

'Very well,' Edgar said. He settled close to the fire, puffing his feathers against the cold. 'Remember when we found Bruno's palace and you were stealing those silver spoons from the dining room? I flew into the kitchen and followed another passage leading to a dungeon. Three Seals were sitting in meditation, each of them facing a thick wooden door. Through the grate of the first door I saw something flicker inside. A creature. I couldn't see its shape, only a bright white light. The Seal's chanting grew louder, suppressing a surge of energy. What Haegar said is true – the Seals were controlling the Sigilli. Keeping them prisoners, locked away inside those chambers.'

'What happened when the palace collapsed? Where did they go?'

'You know that I followed one of them into the forest. He lured his creature into a cave and used the incantations Haegar spoke of to keep it chained as a prisoner inside. I can only suppose that is true for the others too.'

Jemma stood, restless, feeling an urgency to move. But the prophecy felt like an invisible cage. It didn't matter where she went. What she did. She was caught. She paced in front of the fire.

'What are we supposed to do now?'

'We go to Adocentyn. We steal the Book. We follow the plan.'

'Even if every step takes us closer to releasing one of those hideous things? Not to mention the Seal that's hunting me!'

Edgar flew up to a raised stone plinth. It could have once been an old statue, or perhaps a forgotten sundial.

'As far as we know, nothing has yet been released. Nothing has happened. And until it does, we cannot even begin to know what we will do. The only thing we can be certain of is that we cannot stay here, exposed in the Scarp. Yes, the Seal is hunting us. We must hurry. It is far too dangerous to linger here. If we can at least make it to the road, we can hitch a ride in one of the Caravanassi wagons. Then we can find a berth with a Cray fisherman. It will be much safer out at sea.'

'Why can't we just walk across the mountains?'

Edgar fluttered to the other side of the fire, closer to Jemma.

'The Seal will have sensed our return through the Scarp passage. There is no way that we could ever outrun a Seal along these tracks. He would spin us illusions, lead us willingly to pathways only to trap us, as surely as a spider snares a fly. You heard what Haegar said, there is nothing these Seals won't do once they have you in their sights. But containing the Sigilli has weakened him. He barely had the energy to change, let alone swim great distances. Our best chance is to travel by boat. If the Cray can take us to the Delphin Caves, that is the safest way to reach Adocentyn. It is a risk, to be sure, but it is the only choice, as far as I can tell.'

Shadows of clouds passed over the ruins and Jemma scattered the fire coals. She started walking. 'What are we waiting for?'

Just when she thought she had forgiven Edgar, now she felt that cry of pain as a burden in her heart. How much more would she have to carry of his past?

Edgar circled ahead, scouting for the Seal.

The Scarp was a heavy trudge. There was a long walk ahead of them to the road. Whispers came with a flash of light from the tower of Adocentyn, but they were weaker. She could not hear what they were saying, only a desperate murmur in the wind. She covered her ears, wanting nothing but the silence.

Perhaps that was why no one ever came to the Scarp. They must have known of the sense of loss pervading the very mountain air. All these absent palaces. All these ruins.

'Do not let the magic weigh you down,' Edgar flew back and hovered at her shoulder. 'I know, after all that's happened, it is a different place, now, from what it was. I know that. And I am sorry. Though I wish we could live one more happy day together, digging in the ruins.'

'You sound like the magic has got you too,' Jemma said. 'How about we hurry? My legs are getting heavier and heavier.'

Edgar flew up high, keeping watch.

Jemma knew these paths so well, every step of the way, even as the night set in. After several hours, they came to the edge of the valley. The long trek had made her bones ache and she wasn't expecting a sudden rush of feathers at her cheek.

'Keep moving,' Edgar said. 'I'm afraid the Seal is coming.'

Jemma felt Edgar's words ignite her from the strange trance of the Scarp. She took off down the rocky ledge.

'Let me hide in the cloak.' He fluttered to a space inside the hood as Jemma stumbled in the darkness down the rocky ledge. 'If we ride in the back of a Caravanassi wagon, we will have a much better chance.'

Jemma kept going until they came to the road and joined the long procession of the Caravanassi, whose wagons swung with lanterns. They were too caught up in their own misery to notice anything, except for the children walking on the road, who surrounded her and held up their tins and tugged on her clothes.

She cut to the side behind a wagon, where cooking pots clanged and banged as the wheels jarred along the potholed road.

Jemma held up their cups and the tin of tea and knocked on the back of the wagon.

'Are you sure we won't need them later?' Edgar said.

'Of course not, but we've got nothing else to trade. The Caravanassi won't let you ride in their wagons for nothing.'

A hand, coming through a gap in the cloth, waved to

her. A head poked through, wrapped in a coloured scarf. A woman reached out and took Jemma's offerings and pulled her into the caravan.

She peered into a big round face that reminded her of a wooden doll with red and chubby cheeks, except the woman's skin looked rough and weathered. A pipe hung from the corner of her mouth. The smoke was sweet like the smell of cloves from the Gull Keeper's kitchen.

Jemma's eyes scanned the children in the back of the caravan, who all stared at their feet. There were nine of them. None looked up at the woman or at each other.

The woman gave her a cup of water and gestured for her to drink, then turned and disappeared behind a curtain to the front of the carriage.

The children had the same dusty faces as the orphans outside. They continued to stare down at the floor of the wagon as if they were afraid to make any disturbance or risk being thrown again onto the road.

One of the boys sitting in the corner looked at her, his eyes wispy and dazed. Jemma sipped the water and peered over the rim of the wooden cup, trying to look back but also to avoid his eyes. She wanted to ask him, *where have you been? What have you seen?* He had the same startled expression as the boy in Raddahkin's ship.

Edgar shifted in the cloak. Jemma noticed, through a gap in the shutters, a dark human shape standing up on the ridge in the moonlight, peering down. He was scouring every caravan. Edgar must have sensed her go still.

'What is it?'

'The Seal. I can see him up there, in the Scarp. He's searching for us.'

Whispers came to her again, as if drifting in from the valley, and then the guiding voice: *get out of the caravan.*

Jemma felt a surge of panic in her chest. She looked to

the back of the carriage for a way out, but the woman had closed the grate. The whispers grew louder, but now they sounded different than before. The voice was deeper. Too close. Coming from the opposite way. Something wasn't right. And then she knew it must be the Seal. Trying to trick her.

*I'm not that stupid*, she thought.

'We must find a way to get off the shore,' Edgar said. 'When you reach the Cray fishermen, tell them you are a friend of the Delphin. Don't show them you are afraid – the Cray don't like trouble.'

The rattling wheels began to slow and there were voices in front, and in the distance the sounds of music and beating drums. The woman returned from behind the curtain. As soon as the carriage stopped, Jemma shot up from her seat and kicked open the grate. She ran as fast as she could, hearing the woman shrieking at the sight of Edgar and banging against her pots.

Jemma disappeared into the crowds of mules and wagons and cooking fires, pushing and jostling her way towards the docks. A group of Gull kids changed before her eyes, running and then leaping into fluttering wings that lifted them over the Tern baskets, where they swirled in circles, pecking at bits of guts dangling in the weave. They swooped down, changed into their human form and wrestled and scuttled the tower of baskets. A trader holding a lantern shooed them away but one of the Gulls had stolen a fish head. The trader yelled and waved a fist and they took off again into the night air squawking in a twirl of feathers fighting for the prize.

'Wait here,' Edgar said. He was jittery now, trying to see through the baskets. 'There's a Cray boat moored over there. Do you see its light?'

'Yes.'

'That could be our only chance. Tell him you are a friend of the Delphin. Remember, don't show any fear. You're a friend and you have a message for them. Say it will be worth his while. I will create a diversion just like before. At the mere sight of me a crowd will erupt upon the Wharf.'

Jemma could see the older Arctic Gulls watching her, as if they were ready to fly into a swarm on her behalf. 'I give you this to Keep...' − she remembered the words of the silver-haired Gull. She had not seen the wonder of it before. The Gull Keepers' memory had felt so alien, so separate from her being − 'If it's strange within you, it will consume you.' Right now, it wasn't strange. It was already here, and it always had been. All she had to do was to join it with the life of the Wharf, swirling with energy around her. The Seal was trying to make her weak, afraid, filled with doubts. But the Wharf made her feel alive. Strong. Bursting. If that was what the Erigena had to do − to hold the land if the Keepers couldn't − for the first time she believed she could do it. All she would need was to think of that fish head flying through the air, a gang of Gull kids squawking and changing and fighting and free.

But then she glanced at the frayed, empty wrestling tent, the canvas flapping in the wind. A wave of regret and sorrow washed over her. A rush of worry for Soren. Where was he? Another memory burned inside her. Soren's. She felt his aching wounds. That could only mean he was alive. That she somehow held him too. *I'll find you.*

'As soon as these baskets are loaded up,' Edgar returned, 'cut through to the jetty. Come on!'

Jemma pushed through a gap in the baskets. She saw the alarm in Edgar's eyes. He shot up into the air, the Wharf erupting all at once into a panic of superstition.

Just then a winch line tightened and lifted the pile of baskets onto a long night trawler. A commotion had started.

She could hear the pots banging, see the waving of burning sticks. The Gulls flew around her, forming a circle and squawking and screeching at the crowd. In the midst of this flurry she heard the woman's voice again – *Don't look behind. Go straight to the Cray boats.*

She didn't know if she could trust it any more.

Edgar flew towards the crowd, pulling the ruckus towards the entrance of the jetty.

Jemma couldn't help it. She turned and caught a glimpse of the Seal behind her, pushing through the Caravanassi. Her pulse throbbed in every vein but she fought against it and held her breath steady – she couldn't approach the Cray unless she appeared to be calm.

Ahead of her the boat was ready to leave for the night. She knew not to look over her shoulder again or else she would give away her fear. All she wanted to do was run and never stop running.

'Excuse me,' she said to the Cray leaning over the engine. 'I am a friend of the Delphin. Can you take me to them?'

At first he ignored her as he tinkered with a spanner and then closed the engine case. Jemma could not help it. She cast a look behind and saw the dark figure of the Seal stepping onto the jetty. For a moment his eyes fixed on hers and she heard that almost-same voice in her head, *step away from the boat.* She turned with all her will towards the Cray.

'I have a message.'

'I don't take passengers out to sea.'

'I can work. Pay my way. I'll cook. Scrub your pots.'

He held a lantern to her face. Looked her up and down. She tried as best she could to hide the surging panic rising up inside.

'We fish tonight. If you work, I'll pass that way tomorrow.'

'Yes, please. I mean, that would be fine.'

'Very well. Watch the aft deck, it's slippery with oil.'

She stepped on board. He started the engine and untied the mooring rope. The boat chugged out of the holding dock towards a streak of stars appearing on the night's horizon.

Out of the corner of her eye she could see the black-cloaked figure of the human Seal running towards the Cray boat. Jemma held her breath. She dare not turn around in case the Cray grew suspicious. *Kraa Kraa Kraaah* – it was Edgar's warning call. But what was he saying? Had the Seal changed? Was he swimming right behind them? Her heart leapt in her chest and she gripped the rail. Where will Edgar go? How far can a Raven fly across a darkening sea? She didn't want to be on her own. Not again. Friends stay together no matter what. They should have sworn this to each other in the Scarp instead of feeling the weight of its sad, forgotten ruins. She should have made him an oath, that she would never doubt him again.

Jemma looked into the skies, and mouthed her words into the wind – 'I trust you, Edgar. Always and forever.'

*Kraa Kraa aaah aaah.*

## CHAPTER 16

# THIS IS HOW A RAVEN SLEEPS

The Cray stood crookedly, twisting his hardened gaze around the gunwales of the boat where the baskets lay piled, waiting to be thrown into the sea. There were deep grooves in his cheeks, an almost permanent scowl. He chewed a piece of basket cane constantly in the corner of his mouth. He did not once look at her. He was so deep in concentration that Jemma could look right at his eyes without him seeming to notice. She had the uncanny sense that he was not just looking but reading the elements around him – the sea, the sky, the fading points of land, the first stars appearing in the sky. Aligning, calculating, navigating as if by some ancient craft.

And when his eyes returned from those vast spaces to the mundane cabin of the boat, he seemed annoyed to find Jemma there. She was busy peering over the edge of the rail at the whitewash trailing away from the hull and sparkling into the ocean's dark. She searched for Edgar everywhere in the skies, desperate to see him, but knew that she could not appear to be anxious or the Cray would grow suspicious.

'We are out fishing tonight,' he said. 'We are out deep at sea. There is mussels and onions for soup, and there is bread for you to prepare. Then you may sleep. Then you will be woken to help clear the baskets. I will take you to the Delphin Caves by the evening tomorrow.'

He paused, expecting no reply, and pointed to a wooden door.

'Down there you'll find a peat stove,' he said, 'and some wick grass you can light with the flint box. All the requirements for the stew are in the bucket beside the pot. Fresh water's in the barrel above.'

Jemma nodded and without any fuss made her way through the hatch and down the stairs to the cabin.

She hadn't used a flint box like this before and didn't realise that you had to twist the top piece like a pepper grinder to make some powder from the flintstone. Then, separating the pieces altogether, you would strike them swiftly against each other to make a spark. She had almost given up when, finally, a flame caught. Jemma lit the wick of a candle-lamp, happy for the light because by then it was almost pitch black in the cabin. She could see only the most basic stove and a small wooden table with benches on either side.

Jemma used the candle to light the peat logs then closed the stove door, careful to leave the vent open to fan the flames. She filled the heavy iron pot with water and heaved it back over to the stove. Inside the bucket there were mussels and clams and beside them, potatoes and onions.

She peeled the vegetables first and placed them in the pot. Only when they were soft, did she add the rest to make a chowder. With a dash of salt and pepper and some other dried spices that she did not recognise, she closed the stove vent and left the pot to simmer with its lid on. Then, ravenous more with curiosity than with hunger, she took up the candle and opened the hatch to the left of the stove.

Inside, there was nothing but a crude bunk and a bucket with a shaving mirror. She closed it and tried the other. This room was different. It looked as if it had been carefully decorated. There were shelves and small tables displaying smooth and delicate pieces of driftwood, crayfish claws, shells, and old buoys covered in woven hessian ropes. On one of the shelves were balls of weed stalks, rolled so tightly they looked like exquisite eggs born of the sea. There were jars of different coloured stones that looked like gems, and lovely pieces of glass, their edges rolled smooth by the currents of the sea, shining in the light of the candle.

Jemma reached out to touch one of the stones, but then stopped. She became aware that someone was standing behind her in the doorway. She turned and held up the candle. It was a boy. He looked to be a few years older than her, fourteen or so. He was tall, obviously the son of the Cray, though in his face there was nothing surly at all. It was a kind face, she knew that right away, but there was something almost desperate in his eyes that held other emotions too – longing, trepidation. He just stood there, silent, staring.

'Hello,' she said. 'I'm Jemma. What's your name, then?'

At first, he did not say anything. His body twitched and his mouth seemed to open in an attempt to speak. But he froze. And then, looking both bewildered and embarrassed, he ran back through the cabin and up to the deck.

She could hear his heavy clomps above and then a hollow thud where she imagined he had thrown himself down amongst the craypots.

Jemma finished preparing the meal. She cut the hard stale bread into chunks and then put on a smaller pot of black leaf tea. Soon the Cray came down and, seeing the table empty, called out, 'Boy!' and then sat down.

The boy emerged, at first looking down at his feet and then at his black tin bowl. They ate in silence, using the empty mussel shells as spoons and soaking up the broth with the stale bread, making it soft and tasty.

When the Cray had finished, giving no indication of whether he was pleased or disappointed with the meal, he wiped his mouth with his sleeve, packed himself a pipe from a tin kept in his pocket and then took his mug of tea up to the deck.

Jemma cleared the plates and put them in the bucket. The boy hovered near the stairs. She gently refilled their tea. Jemma watched him reach out and take the mug in both of his hands as if he was shivering.

'So, do you like being a fisherman?' she asked.

'S-s-s...al-right, I guess,' he said, without looking at her eyes, 's-s-s...what I am.'

'Your fingers must get cold and blistered.'

'Ssssswhy I g-g-grow them c-c-calluses on me h-hands.'

Jemma understood at once the reason for his shyness.

'And how do you know where to drop the baskets, all the way out here?'

'Used to f-f-follow the Whale-lines.'

'What do you mean, the "Whale-lines?"'

'Sss-how we f-find the cray fields.'

'You mean, the Whales help you find them?'

'We r-r-read the s-stars, and the Whale-lines. Tells us where we are, sss-like a memory map, but the Whales aren't there and the m-memory's gone.'

'Where are they? Did someone take them? Hunters? Whalers?'

'N-n-not Whalers. Other's come. They're called H-Harpooners. Come and trap the Whales 'n t-t-take 'em to the city, alive, half d-dead, maybe, wrapped in wet cloth. They try to k-k-keep 'em alive.'

'But why would someone want to harpoon a Whale and keep them alive?'

'D-d-don't know.'

Jemma took another sip of tea.

'I'm sorry,' she said. 'I'm asking you all these questions, when I don't even know your name.'

'Arlen.'

'Arlen. That's a nice name.' Jemma smiled. 'And you didn't even stutter when you said it.'

A radiance lifted his face.

'They say a name is like a destiny. Where does Arlen come from, then?'

'N-n-name of a Cray warrior from the l-l-long past. That's all I know.'

'Maybe you'll be a warrior one day?'

Arlen smiled, though his cheeks were flushing.

'Can you tell me something else,' she asked.

The boy shrugged and nodded, while reaching for the stair rail.

'Do you know what happens to the boats? The ones filled up with all those Caravanassi?'

'We do not ask and we do not want to know.'

Jemma was taken aback by the deep, clear voice from above. The Cray stood in the stairway.

'They is none of our business. Now see to the dishes. I give you passage to work, not to ask questions. You'll sleep in the front, past his room, another door. And you,' he told his son. 'Get to work.'

~

Jemma finished up the dishes, turned out the peat stove, and went through the boy's room to the cabin at the front of the boat. It was no more than a cubicle for a bed. Above, in the ceiling, there was a hatch for air, and she opened it. Just enough for Edgar to poke through his beak.

'A little more,' he said.

'Edgar!' Jemma caught him in her hands. 'Where've you been?'

'Hiding in the craypots.'

'I couldn't see you anywhere. I thought you were lost.'

'Well, yes, I suppose there was always a risk.'

'What if you were lost? What if you never came back?'

'I did, though.'

'I'd be left here on my own. Don't ever do it again. You've got to swear we'll stay together.'

'I cannot say I won't, so long as that Seal is following.'

'Say it...'

'Very well, I swear, for both our sakes. At least the Seal has not yet taken to the water. My suspicions were right – he is still too weak to change. But he is following along the cliffs.'

Edgar flew around the cabin trying to find a place to perch, but there were no ledges to speak of and so he came to rest on the bunk itself.

'Not much room in here,' he said.

'Sshhh, you've got to be quiet. I think the old Cray's watching me. I was asking too many questions.'

'The Cray don't like questions, never mind how many. If he thinks you're worth anything, he will sell that information to the highest bidder.'

'He got angry with his son for talking to me. The boy was telling me things, like the Whales being hunted, but not killed, kept alive, taken somewhere. And he was just about to tell me about the Caravanassi boats.'

Edgar began to pace. 'In any case, we need to find out more about that scribe, Gaspar Scoppius.'

'The scroll –' Jemma took it out of her satchel and stretched it out along the bunk. It was a long continuous sheet of Haegar's writings.

She held up the candle as Edgar pored over every word.

'Let's see: began working in the scriptorium of the Inquisition. Copier of heretical works. This is interesting.' Edgar looked up from the page.

'What is it?'

'It says here, he hunted down other practitioners of the New Alchemy, using particularly brutal methods.'

'He was nasty alright,' Jemma said. 'Look what he did to my wrist after I spilled that ink.'

Edgar read through the reams of notes.

'It documents how Bruno escaped from his cell, through a passage he had created, before they could carry out the execution. That must have been the path to Adocentyn. It seems that after the escape, Scoppius requested to command the army who followed after Bruno through the passage. This was denied. Scoppius was instead held personally accountable for the escape and expelled from the scriptorium. What follows are the chronicles of the first wars against the Keepers, where Scoppius is not mentioned.'

'He must have hated Bruno,' Jemma said.

'For more reasons than one. Frater Jiordano's ideas alone gave him many enemies, but very few people like to be made a fool of. Especially someone with the obvious ambitions of Gaspar Scoppius.'

Jemma adjusted the candle.

'What happened to him after that?'

'According to these last recorded notes, he went on to start an orphanage, a puritanical school of some kind. I feel sorry for the poor wretches who must have suffered under the blows to Scoppius's pride.'

Edgar froze in thought for a moment, his neck craned, his beak pointing upwards. The boat rolled over a wave and still he didn't move. Jemma heard the craypot's hollow whistling in the wind outside. The wooden cabin creaked and groaned.

'What is it?' Jemma said.

Edgar leaped onto her arm.

'I can't believe I didn't see it before! I am almost certain that Scoppius is the one who made that terrible city – the Shadow of Adocentyn. As a copier of heretical works, he must have known of the other side of Alchemy. How to become a Dark Keeper and live off the pain of others. The question is, how? Now I have half the answer.'

Jemma sat up and sent Edgar scuttling across the cabin.

'Tell me.'

Edgar settled in front of her. 'Scoppius must have used the orphan's memory of his cruelty. You saw those poor novices in the scriptorium, chained and beaten. There would be no better way to sustain your existence in a Shadow city than to sear yourself into the minds of frightened orphans.'

Jemma still winced at the warden's savage blows.

'While the dark city turned and turned, he gave himself all the time he needed to scribble away in his scriptorium, working on the codes to the Book of Memory, until he finally made a passage to Adocentyn.'

'You said half the story. What's the other half?'

'I don't know.'

'What d' you mean, you don't know?'

'We are missing something. I cannot put my claw on it. A gap in the Scrolls. Obviously, Scoppius could never leave the Shadow city...'

'Why not?'

'Because he is the one who holds it all together. Its Dark Keeper. But he could not have acted on his own.'

'He sent someone else to Adocentyn?'

'Precisely. And this leads to the greatest puzzle of all – what else helped to create such a powerful dark city? The misery of orphans could never have fuelled such a vortex of hatred on its own.'

When Edgar unravelled the bottom of the scroll, Jemma got the shock of her life. The Raven spy had made a sketching of the execution, a man burning in the flames. His face was twisted in agony, but Jemma would never forget those eyes.

'Wait...' She took a closer look, and then she was certain, 'I've seen him before. When the Poachers came and took the Gull Keeper, that man was sitting in the carriage. I know it was him.' She remembered his shining gold ring when he held up the cage. The shrill screech of the Keeper. His gaze that burrowed into her skin and made her run away with the fearful cries of the Arctic Gulls.

Edgar peered again at the contorted image. 'I fear it is no coincidence that when he appeared in the lands, so too did the Caravanassi. But look here, there's a name.' Edgar crooked his head to read Haegar's scrawl beside the sketching. 'Boldevar Ramus.'

'Who is he? Have you heard of him?'

'Not in anything that I have read. We need to find out more. There is no mention of him anywhere else in this scroll. We have reached a dead end. Except we know one thing.'

'What's that?'

'He is the one hunting the Keepers, sending out the Sparrow swarms, searching for a girl all over the lands. He knows about the Erigena.'

'About me?'

'Not about you. Not yet. Thank the Scarp you are nothing but a "wharf rat". But who knows how long our cover will last. We must be careful. The Harpooners will be searching these waters.'

Jemma heard the old Cray coming and rolled up the scroll, stashing it inside her cloak. Edgar whispered: 'Find out more from the Cray boy, if you can. I have a feeling that if we follow the trail of the Caravanassi, this will somehow lead us to Boldevar Ramus.'

'Hide,' Jemma said, opening the hood. 'In here.'

The hatch flew open.

'Who were you talking to?'

Jemma jolted back. 'No one,' she said.

'I heard you. Voices.'

'I was...imagining talking to my...'

'Sh-sh-she were talking t-t-to me, only she didn't want you to know, cause I h-haven't f-f-finished cl-cl-cleaning out the c-c-crayp-pots.'

Arlen stepped into the tiny cabin. His father regarded him with contempt and said nothing, pushing past him on his way out.

The boy stood at the door.

'Thanks,' Jemma said.

'Sss okay.'

'Why does he always look at you like that?'

'S-s-spose he d-d-doesn't like my s-s-s-stutter.'

Arlen's eyes flicked to where Edgar was hiding in her hood.

'Did you hear us talking?' Jemma asked. 'Don't tell, you promise? You know what Cray do to Raven.'

'Sss okay,' he said.

Arlen smiled as Edgar leaped onto Jemma's shoulder.

'Edgar, this is Arlen.'

'Can you help us?' Edgar said. 'We have to get to the city of Adocentyn and we don't have much time. Are the waters safe?'

'H-harpooners are r-raiding every boat, l-looking for something.'

'What about the Caravanassi? Do you know anything about what happens to them?'

The boy went back into his room and they heard the sound of something heavy being dragged across the floor.

'C-c-come in here,' Arlen said. 'W-want to sh-show you this.'

In the middle of the room there was a large wooden chest. Arlen took a key from around his neck, unlocked it, and opened the lid. He stood back and let them look. Inside, there were coloured scarves and porcelain coffee cups, like the ones she had seen in the Caravanassi tents, painted with gold swirling patterns. There were silver bracelets and a little wooden box with a pair of dice inside, the ones she had seen carved from bone. And there was a line of dolls, fastened to the lid of the box.

'Where did you get these?' Jemma asked.

'F-f-f-found 'em in the craypots. I'm not a K-Keeper but I keep these. S'like I'm a Keeper too. S'my way to k-keep.'

'So, you pulled them up from the bottom of the sea?' Edgar said.

'S-s-spose.'

Jemma selected one of the tea cups and held it up for Edgar to see, feeling its fragility, the gold-leaf paint flaking off in her hands.

'I have a kind of trinket too,' she said, and took the blade from her cloak, having nothing else to share. Arlen reached out and held it up against the candlelight.

'That's v-v-very fine,' he said. 'C-c-carving's very intricate, very b-beautiful. I would like to have f-found this in my pots.'

Jemma had not admired the golden blade like this since that first night alone in her hut. The circles carved into the handle were in the same patterns she had seen in the Book of Memory. There were drawings inside them, too, but she would need a magnifying glass to make out what they were.

She tucked it back inside her vest and picked up one of the dolls.

'That's like the one my Caravanassi friend made. Her name's Daria.'

'All these things, they're from the boats, aren't they?' Edgar said. 'The boats, filled with the Caravanassi.'

Arlen nodded.

'Where do they go?' Edgar asked.

'They t-travel out p-past the Delphin waters, towards the city h-harbours. That's all I know.'

Arlen looked up. Jemma heard them too – the Cray's footsteps above them. She saw a sadness come into Arlen's eyes, or perhaps it was a fear. He gently took the doll from Jemma's hands and placed it back where it belonged. Then he closed the lid, locked it again with his key and pushed the chest away under his bed.

'You s-s-sleep now. G-gotta get up early to raise the pots. We can f-find out more if we're careful.'

He gave Jemma his candle, led her back to the bunk and closed the door after her.

SHE PLACED THE CANDLE IN A HOLDER BESIDE HER PILLOW and lay down beneath the blanket, making room for Edgar beside her. In the hut, that time when he had disappeared into the forest, Jemma had wondered how a Raven sleeps.

He nestled into the side of the pillow and relaxed his wings so they puffed and looked like a feathery cushion.

In the silence they could hear the chest slide out again. The boy must be gazing once more at his collection. Perhaps it was his ritual.

A wind blew in and rocked the boat and whispered in the craypots.

'Edgar, why don't you ever – change? Is it because you can't, or you won't?'

'Both,' he said, 'and the longer you remain in one form, the quicker you forget the other. And then you start believing you never could change, until it feels impossible. Just as if I asked you, now, to fly. Could you do it?'

Jemma turned on her side. She knew that she could never even think of trying. Not seriously. Not as any kind of real possibility. But then she thought of the time when she had released the memory of the Gulls against the Shadows. The anger she had felt, that she couldn't control. If you have a power, you have to know how to use it. Or else it might start using you.

'Is that what Raddahkin meant – what you gave up for me?'

'I suppose it is,' Edgar said.

'It's not fair. I never asked you to. I never would have. Now I've got to carry that too.'

'You don't.'

'But I do. It's like – when I was out hunting in the Scarp – I remember when I started feeling someone was watching me. The feeling was always there. I caught a glimpse of you behind the rocks.'

'I remember that too,' Edgar said, 'but you only saw a flicker of my wings. After that, I was more careful. I liked to watch you turning over those ruins. Every clod and every stone, digging with no more than a makeshift pick or a stone tied to a stick. You always had this look of determination and contentment all at once. And when you found that silver cup, you didn't stop digging in that spot for days. I knew, then, which way the prophecy would go. I fought the Council, and when I refused to give you up, it was decided by vote of the cast-stone that I would be derobed and exiled. That I would lose my powers to change.'

'Well you shouldn't've done it. I never would've asked you to.'

'And I would never have given you the choice. It was only mine to make. I saw who you were. I knew that to lock you in the tombs – that would be a crime. It is the right of an exile to be granted one last request, and so their own punishment turned against them. I demanded that they never touch you, and I took a vow of protection over you. That is only mine to give. Two laws they are forbidden to break.'

'Still, you had no right.'

'And then, where would you be? They would have followed you to the Scarp. No one would have been there to see. Who would have missed a wharf thief? A bet collector? A ruin hunter, taken in the night?'

'How do you know they'll keep their word?'

Edgar shifted his wings.

'One day, I fear the time will come when the Raven will break their own laws. That will be the day I return to face them.'

'But what about your vow to me?'

'That will never be broken,' Edgar said. 'That is a law of the heart.'

She touched his wing gently, reached up and blew out the candle. Then she rolled onto her back and stared into the dark. Something else was bothering her.

'But *could* you change, if you tried. Right now?'

'Even if I wanted to, the truth is, I am so far out of practice. It would be very painful, like stretching every muscle beyond their limits in every direction all at once. Without a long process of preparation it would be near impossible, much less dangerous. Imagine trying to do a backflip without first lying down and learning how to arch your back?'

'How did you learn in the first place?'

'We are born Raven, and if we are chosen to be Scribes, we are taken through a great ritual. We must make a crown from our feathers by plucking them one by one out of our own wings – a bit like pulling out your hair.'

'Ouch! Why would they make you do that?'

'It is the crown that we will wear in our Scribe form. It is supposed to symbolise the transformation of our powers of flight to our minds, to the soaring heights of knowledge. Our devotion to the Scrolls. There are some who cannot bring themselves to do it, and they remain Raven. This is the first test.'

'What happens after that?'

'A long process of training. We must first learn to conquer the pain of change through will, concentration, meditation. We must then learn how to hold our new form. At first, there is a constant yearning to change back. To fly. This desire they call our "weakness". This is why, once we can remain for a time in our human form, we must undergo tests. Trials. It is through fear, longing, nostalgia and other weaknesses that we are tempted back to our first forms.'

'So Haegar must have been frightened of you, to change like that?'

'They would say that he had not, yet, mastered his fear.'

'And because you wanted to save me, they thought you were weak, so they made you change back?'

'It was the greatest dishonour they could inflict upon me. But it is no dishonour at all.'

'Why?'

'Because I can fly. That is a Scribe's constant yearning, to return to their wings. They make up a whole lot of nonsense about honour, temptation and weakness to hide the fact of what is lost. Honour is how the powerful make you believe in sacrifice. The Scribes have always needed to blend in. We have perfected the "art of transformation", as it is called. But it only serves the purposes of the Scrolls, not ourselves. Better to stay fixed in one form than to risk exposing yourself. There have been reformers in the past who have challenged this doctrine, saying Scribes should be free to change as they please. The more radical have said we should never have changed from our pure, true form at all.'

'It sounds complicated.'

'It is just politics. Scribes pride themselves on their vast knowledge, but really, they are the most pedantic and political of all.'

'Which form do you prefer – honestly?'

'This one.'

'Really?'

'Yes, really. I can do anything I could before. I can read and hold a quill...'

'You make good tea.'

'And I can fly. That is my greatest pleasure – to see from the heights. To soar and glide and tumble.'

'You can tumble?'

'Haven't I shown you? Think of the Gull kids at the Wharf. Then think of me like them, as a child, darting through the forest, playing "spies" with my friends, daring ourselves to plummet down the Black Gorge and turn up only just in time. A bit like you used to do collecting sea-fennel in the swell. I held the record for the highest number of tumbles in one go. This is the form I want to be. And what's more – I can stay much closer to you.'

As Edgar nestled into the nape of her neck, Jemma felt the airy lightness of his wings released. She kept herself awake until he had long drifted off, feeling the rising and falling of his feathers tickling her cheek as he breathed. She marvelled at her new knowledge – this is how a Raven sleeps.

## CHAPTER 17

# THE HARPOONERS

*S**he reaches over the side of the boat, her fingers rippling in the water. A sound, distant at first, like an echo beneath the sea. It rises from somewhere deep below, cascading towards the surface, a call, a song, a single longing note. She can feel in the voice a great distress – it is calling to her, like the whispers in the lights. She sees pictures in the water, like clouds of floating memories, lines of Whales striking the rocks, changing and emerging as giants. Terror in the faces of their enemies, who wear the same black robes as the Inquisitors in the Shadow city. 'The army of the Keepers,' she whispers. And wakes...*

Jemma shook off her dream, opened the hatch above her to see walls of towering black-shale cliffs. And there was Edgar, circling high above. She waved him back, annoyed that he had risked being seen. Why hadn't they woken her to help clean out the pots?

She ducked down again through the hatch, startled by Arlen standing in the doorway. Had he been watching her sleeping?

'G-g-good m-morning,' he said, 'I've made some t-t-tea.'

A flush of pink came into his cheeks as Jemma smiled

and climbed out from her bed. She followed him into the cabin.

'You should have woken me up. I was supposed to help you with the pots.'

'S-sorry,' he said. 'You looked like you n-needed the sleep. D-didn't take me long.'

While the old Cray tended to the engine, Edgar darted through the hatch and into the cabin.

Arlen poured Edgar some tea. He took a sip and then flew up to Jemma's shoulder, looking directly at the Cray boy so he could not turn away.

'Who were those men in the other boat last night? The one with those harpoons. Were they Whale hunters?'

'D-d-don't know,' he said.

Arlen flinched. Jemma took Edgar down onto her arm.

'What are you talking about?' She didn't like being left in the dark.

'While you were sleeping,' Edgar said, 'another boat pulled up beside us. It was big. There must have been a dozen crew on board. I couldn't see them very well in the dark, except I could tell they were short and stocky and wore thick jackets of fur and hide. Mounted on the front of the boat were the tips of two nasty-looking harpoons. One of the men handed over a bag of coins to your father,' he pointed his beak at Arlen – 'what was the old Cray selling them?'

Arlen cupped the tea in his hands and stared into his lap.

'D-don't know.'

'And then he was pointing at the sky,' Edgar continued. 'He was pointing, like he was showing them something, on a map.'

'Sh-sh-shouldn't have b-been l-looking out the hatch.'

Arlen shifted in his chair. 'N-n-not good to be n-nosey,' he said. 'Anyways, g-g-got to prepare the p-p-pots.'

The dawn sun glowed red on the horizon, the sea still smoky and dark against the cliffs. The Cray started the engine while Arlen and Jemma moved to the bow, picking out the remaining weeds from the craypots. Edgar hid inside Jemma's cloak.

'And what was that pattern the Cray was laying out on the cabin-top?' Edgar said. 'The one with the grass and the stones?'

'S-s-s'like a m-map of the stars and the W-Whale-lines, and the ghost islands.'

'The ghost islands?'

'It's what we use to navigate when we're out at s-sea. We n-need land-points to make our co-ordinates, so we have the ghost islands l-like imaginary points in the sea. Ghost islands is like our m-memory from the long past.'

'You mean, like the co-ordinates of a map?'

Arlen nodded, then returned to picking weed.

'Wait,' Jemma said, 'I heard one of the Whales. Now I remember, in my dream last night. But it wasn't just a dream, it was real. A song. It was calling me. But it was faint, more like an echo. It was filled with sadness, like it needed our help. Why would your father sell co-ordinates to the Whale hunters if you need them for finding your fishing grounds?'

'D-d-don't know. Don't ask questions. N-n-not good to ask questions.'

'All I sells is information, pure and simple.'

The Cray's harsh voice startled them, as it had before. The boy cowered against the pots and Jemma felt her heart leap and burn. She faced him.

'And that is simply what they buy – not curiosity, nor

nothing else that is foreign to me, like other people's business. My business is my own, that is my rule. Is it not, boy?'

'Y-y-yes f-f-f...'

'Come on, out with it!'

'F-f-father.'

The Cray looked at Jemma.

'They say Ravens is bad omens, yet none of memory here has ever borne one to the Cray boats.'

'S-s-strange things b-been happening.'

'Not this strange. Prophecies and Shadows. You hold your tongue – boy!'

'N-n-not "boy",' Arlen said, and raised himself up to stand before his father. He threw a handful of the weed into the sea. 'D-don't call me "boy". I am Arlen!'

The Cray stepped back. 'And who bestowed you such an honour? What right have you to a warrior's name?'

Jemma stood up and took her place beside Arlen. 'More than you, who cares for nothing but those coins in your pocket!'

The Cray backed away. 'You want to get on in these parts, you'll mind your own business too.'

'Even if you threaten the Whale Keepers?' Jemma said.

'My secrets are my code. And this is my honour, when a man keeps his own worth. I see what is to come.'

The Cray retreated to the stern and steered the boat along the cliffs where the dark shadows looked like streaks of charcoal smudging out the shoreline.

Jemma touched Arlen's arm. He had not yet released his silent fury and threw himself back into the task of clearing pots. She went to the rail and leaned over the side, calming herself by losing time watching the boat's wake and the endless walls of shale.

'I heard the song, Edgar,' he had come to land on her shoulder. 'That must mean the Keeper is alive. If it's got anything to do with those lights, we have to get to Adocentyn.'

'Those lights are very strange,' Edgar said. 'But right now, I think we may have some others to worry about.'

Edgar flew up to the mast head. A light was shimmering in the distance. It looked as though one of the stars had fallen from the sky and was floating in the sea. But now it was coming closer. Arlen had seen it too. He went to the side of the boat and peered into the distance.

'What is that, coming towards us?' Edgar said.

Arlen sprang from the railing, rushing for Jemma.

'G-g-got to get d-down, out of s-sight.'

Already the Cray had changed course. He was searching for positions of fading star points with the same distant gaze Jemma remembered from the night before. But his eyes were different too. She sensed his fear this time.

The boat steered abruptly away from the coastline.

The light was gaining on them. Jemma stood in the main hatch, as Arlen piled craypots along the edges of the boat, as if to make a defensive wall on each side. Then she saw two more shimmering points beneath the brighter light, moving towards them at great speed. She knew they were the points of two harpoons.

'G-g-get down,' Arlen said.

Jemma scurried through the cabin with Edgar to the smaller hatch. She tried to push it up, but it was locked from above.

The boat lurched to the right then swung wildly to the left, throwing her against the cabin walls and sending Edgar scuttling to the floor.

She could hardly hear herself breathe with the roaring of the engine at full throttle. Then she felt an enormous thud as something glanced off the side of the boat. She knew it must have been one of the harpoons.

'Edgar – over here, ' she called out, as she felt the force of the Cray boat swinging around again just as another harpoon hit its side. This time she heard it pierce right through the metal skin.

She crawled forward to a little hatch leading to the hollows of the bow and looked through. The huge harpoon had driven itself in, above the water line, its tip opening up like a claw.

'What do we do?' Edgar said.

'Keep watch for any leaks.' Jemma ran to the kitchen. Sounds of the boat splitting and groaning. She took hold of a knife. Back to the bow, she began to saw at the rope attached to the end of the harpoon. It was thick and crusted with a hard layer of sand and shells and she made no impression at all.

*The blade*, she thought, and took it from her vest, but she was thrown back. The Cray boat was being pulled against the throttle, the roar of the engine straining now in reverse. They were losing ground, the screeching sound of a winch in the distance, holding them like a marlin on a fishing line.

Regaining her balance, Jemma struck the thick layers of twine with the golden blade. The rope stretched and heaved and then snapped itself free.

Edgar flew up through the hatch to take a look and circled back.

'You did it!'

'What happened?'

'The rope whipped back. The Harpooners are all scuttling across the decks, shouting in chaos.'

At full throttle the Cray boat sped forward and swung around once more. One final jolt sent her flying against the wall. And then, suddenly, everything was still.

Jemma rushed through the main hatch with Edgar on

her shoulder, and up to the deck, where Arlen and the Cray were staring at the massive stern of the Whale breaker, its harpoons reloaded, slowly scanning the waters.

A fascination gripped her as the breaker glided past them. She could see the Harpooners clearly, their stubbled faces, their still bodies. They were squinting and staring intently at the ocean with the look of hunters. But it was like they were looking right through them. Then she realised.

'Why can't they see us?' Jemma crept up to Arlen.

'Sshhh,' Arlen said, 'they can s-s-still hear us. We're in a ghost island.'

She watched the breaker circling them. Its engines had been cut and the great hulk was now only drifting. The silence was almost unbearable. Arlen put his finger to his lips. The Cray held the boat steady. For a minute or so, for what seemed more like a year, she dared not move or even breathe. It would take only a single falling craypot to give themselves away.

If she had wanted to, she could have reached out and touched the side of the Harpooner. She looked up at the fur-hooded figures, at least ten of them, lined up along the deck. The almost endless metal side of the breaker glided past and then she heard an order from the rear to fire the engines. The sounds of clamouring crew, of grinding winches and chains filled the sea.

As soon as the ship had gone, the Cray turned to Jemma.

'That's what yer get for sticking yer head out of hatches into other people's business. What price have they got, to want you for their bounty? Why is there such a profit on your head? Well?'

'I don't know,' Jemma shot back. 'I just need to get to the Delphin Caves.'

'The sooner we get there, the better. We don't need no more trouble from *you*, or I'll be throwin' you out with the craypots.'

He stomped to the bow, shaking his head as he inspected the damage. Jemma sat down and huddled herself to her knees. She couldn't deny all the trouble she had caused.

'They weren't just Harpooners on that boat,' Edgar said. 'Who were the others?'

'P-p-poachers,' Arlen said. 'That means s-s-someone's p-paying them to c-catch you. Someone with l-lots of m-money, cause Poachers d-don't come cheap.'

'But how come they couldn't see us?' Jemma said.

'G-g-ghost islands make us hidden,' Arlen said. 'Only the C-cray can s-see them.'

Already the old Cray had re-started the engines. Arlen looked as if he wanted to say more, but a sharp look from his father sent him to the baskets, which he took apart and strapped into place. He hung one over the side, covering the damage to the boat. And Jemma knew why. The Cray don't like questions.

~

THEY CAME IN CLOSER TO THE SHORE, RIDING IN THE shadows of the cliffs as the sun arced high in the sky, dazzling the ocean. They continued on through the afternoon and into the evening when the sea, reflected in the rocks, sent her into a dreamy trance. Many hours had passed when her thoughts were interrupted by a watery shape moving in the wake.

She had only ever seen the Delphin far from the shores of the Wharf, seizing an illegal trade ship. They had formed in perfect lines on either side of the vessel, changing to their human forms with the precision of a ritual dance as they rose into the air and landed on the decks. Who knows what happened to that ship? All she remembered was the beautiful assault, and how she had imagined what it would be like to be so revered, respected, feared. She had always scoffed at any who thought they were above her, but when she had seen the pure majesty of the Delphin guard, she had never felt smaller, more insignificant, more like the drowned little wharf rat laughed at by the same traders who now bowed to the Delphin's might.

Back then, she would never have dared to cross the Delphin waters. She would never have dreamed of entering their caves.

Arlen stood at the bow, looking back to his father, making him aware of the lines of swimming Delphin, and pointing. The Cray steered the boat towards an enormous cave, where the stone walls changed from blackened shale to the colour of golden sand.

Jemma called to Edgar, who fluttered to her shoulder. 'You better hide,' she said, making space inside her hood.

Now there were more of them, darting in the waves of the bow. Jemma could see the Delphin turning their eyes towards her as they passed with quizzical, radiant smiles that seemed both friendly and fierce. They wore thick leather vests of armour around their chests. And then, to her amazement, one of them leaped out of the water and changed form, looking right into her eyes before diving down again into his watery shape. His human form was slender, the same vest covering his torso but not his arms, which stretched out in front and glistened with water as he dived into the crest of a wave.

The Cray kept his word and did not speak to Jemma or even look at her. He steered the boat into the mouth of the cave, where a jetty spanned the entrance and helped to frame a vast architrave carved into the cave itself, with panels of wondrous images chiselled into the stone.

The Delphin, who'd been swimming behind in the silence of the wake, passed them with incredible speed. They leaped out of the water, changing in the air, and with a military precision, stood in a perfect line along the wall. Two of them fell out of line and took hold of the mooring ropes. The Cray let go of his wheel and slowly lit his pipe.

'What business do you have here?' one of the Delphin said.

'I come to bring this friend of yours.'

The Delphin looked her up and down. 'She is no friend of ours.'

'She calls herself one.'

'Who are you, stranger?'

'It's true,' Jemma said. 'I am a stranger. But I've come to seek your help.'

The one who had spoken whispered to another, who seemed of a higher command. Then he stepped forward.

'Very well, you may come.'

Jemma nodded and scampered down into the cabin. Arlen stood waiting below, holding her leather satchel in his hands and a package wrapped in brown paper tied up with string.

'Here,' he said, 't-t-take these. Supplies. We g-got more than we need. F-filled up your tea tin. Some t-tin cups too. B-bread. Sugar. Some c-couscous and sweet potato. N-not much, but enough for a meal.'

Jemma couldn't find anything to give him in return, except for the flintstone she found in her bag.

'N-n-no...' Arlen curled her fingers closed. 'K-keep it. You'll need it.' He gave her a handful of wick grass. 'N-never know when you m-might find yourself in the dark and need some light.'

Jemma unwrapped the little parcel. It was one of his sea-eggs.

'Arlen, you can't. It's from your collection...'

It was no bigger than a quail's egg, exquisitely sculpted from the finest wispy weed stalks coiling, entangling, knitting themselves together in the motions of the sea.

'It's l-like a memory,' he said. 'S-something to remember me by.'

'I wouldn't ever forget you,' Jemma said, holding it close. She could smell the ocean's brine, the chalk of tiny corals and shells, the musty weedy stalks that took her back to their room in the Wharf, to the smells of Edgar's wings when he had been soaring in the sea winds.

'Where will you go?'

'D-don't know. Wherever we f-find cray.'

'Just be careful.'

'S-sounds like you're the one who n-needs to be careful. I'll l-look out for you, everywhere. F-find me if you need me.'

'I hope to see you again. I know I will.'

'Might do, n-never know.'

Edgar poked his head through Jemma's hood. 'Well, it's been a pleasure to meet a Cray who doesn't think I'm an agent of darkness and misfortune.'

'N-nice to meet a r-real Raven too,' Arlen looked at Jemma. 'You're l-lucky to have a friend on your shoulder.'

'You have one too,' Jemma said. 'Just imagine I'm standing behind you when you're pulling out weeds from the craypots.'

'And you can imagine me,' Edgar said, 'swooping on your father every time he cusses you.'

'I've seen Edgar's talons,' Jemma said. 'He'd better watch himself!'

Tears welled in Arlen's green eyes. Jemma had her own,

and hugged him before they spilled, feeling the warmth of his cheeks.

'Good bye,' she said.

'G-good bye. I'll m-miss you.'

Jemma climbed up onto the deck. Composed herself.

'You need to be quiet,' she whispered to Edgar.

If she had been a second earlier, she would have seen another leather coin bag changing hands.

The Cray stepped back from the soldiers when he saw her approach.

Jemma eyed him with suspicion. 'Well, thanks, I suppose,' she said.

'I keep my word,' he said, 'that is my honour.' Then he turned and fired the engine, sending the Cray boat chugging and rattling out of the cave towards the first faint star in the sky.

## CHAPTER 18

# A GREAT DISCONTENT

The guard who had spoken to the Cray stood waiting. Jemma hurried to catch him, her eyes drawn up to the marvellous carvings on the walls, as he led her towards a grand entrance in the cave.

At the end of the passage a gate opened out to a vast dome ceiling, polished smooth and dancing with the reflected light of a pool below. Pieces of the dome had fallen away and crumbled into little piles here and there upon the floor, as if someone had forgotten to sweep them away.

The guard led Jemma down a darker passage that smelt of salt and damp. He stopped at a door and put her in the charge of an attendant who stood outside, holding out a towel and some clothes for her to bathe and change before she was presented to the Delphin Queen.

Inside, there was a pool of mineral waters that flowed from a pipe in the rocks above. The old attendant limped across the room, placed the clothes and towel on a bed in the corner, and left without speaking, as if he were disturbing her own private room.

Edgar wriggled out of the hood and flew up to the opening of the water pipe.

'I think they'll suit you,' he said, gesturing to the Delphin clothes. 'You'll look like a fine young warrior. In any case, you'll blend in much better around here.'

'And what will you do?' she said.

'While you're living it up in the banquet hall, I'll be crawling through these water pipes like a miserable rat.'

'Well you can start by turning around,' she told Edgar, preparing herself for the bath.

If Edgar could have rolled his eyes, he would have. 'Really,' he muttered, 'so easily embarrassed.'

Jemma peeled off her cloak and her old Wharf clothes. She climbed into the soothing waters of the bath, warm and heavy with salt. When she had finished, she dried herself and put on the clothes she had been given – a long tunic beneath an outer layer of leather armour and sandals with special guards that covered over her shins.

She looked at herself in the still pool. She had not seen her own image for such a long time. If her hair had been tangled before, her face all white and drained with fear, the mineral pool had released its waves and curls and restored the colour in her cheeks. She admired the vest especially – it gave her a feeling of strength, protection, grace.

She lay on the water bed, feeling that a blissful sleep could descend on her like a shower of rain.

Edgar settled beside her.

'I must warn you,' he said. 'There have been rumours for some time of a great discontent in the Delphin Court. Their Keeper is withering away. There is much brooding in the passageways. I have heard reports – you saw it yourself – parts of the caves crumbling. That can only mean their Keeper is terribly weakened. Though we are not enemies, we must be careful here. Find out what you can, but give little away.'

'How will I know what to say? Can I trust them?'

'You cannot trust anyone. If there is one piece of advice I can give you, it is this: with the Delphin you can never know where you stand. And if you find yourself feeling comfortable, that is when you should start to worry.'

'What else do I need to know?'

Edgar flew up to a shelf carved into the wall of the cave.

'I once met a Delphin ambassador. He had come in search of a scroll.'

'What about?'

'The succession of Keepers. They must have already felt a weakness growing. He said the caves were crumbling. And in the dark forgotten realms – their caves are vast – he feared the Shadows had begun to find their way in. The Delphin had started to wall up passages long since gone to ruin. He told me that the Keeper's heir had fled to Adocentyn.'

'Why?'

'It is not an easy thing, to be a Keeper, as you already know. The Delphin Prince rebelled against his fate, and became dissolute, eking out a living as a performer in the wrestling games. That is the greatest shame, for a Delphin.'

The burden of the Erigena helped her understand. Jemma always felt it, like a sickness within. If she'd ever had the choice, she would have escaped too. Though to think of the Delphin Prince in a wrestling tent, power and grace with no discipline, unleashed. That would be something to see.

'To pass through the Delphin Caves, you must first be a guest. Prove you are a friend, not an enemy. And the way they test this is with hospitality. The banquet will dazzle and disarm you. Careful what you disclose, but find out what you can. The Delphin waters stretch almost to the harbours of Adocentyn. There is little they do not know of what happens along these shores. You must be polite. Not too inquisitive, but not too dull. The Queen will seek to test you with all her charm. Above all, be wary of those who surround her – the Advisors – they will not speak to you directly, but they will be watching every move. Listening to every word you say. So long as you are no threat to them, so long as you are "friend", they will not only let you pass, they will help you too.'

Jemma stood beside Edgar, putting the golden blade inside her satchel and slinging it over her shoulder.

'But how can we be their enemy? I never took anything from the Delphin, I swear. Not unless that trader I cut from the wharf was meant for them. But they deserved it, with what they did to me.'

Edgar let out a laugh. 'You have nothing to worry about there. The antics of a wharf rat are of no concern to the Delphin. Their caves are deep, majestic, intricate structures of memory. Their caverns are like fathomless palaces. As long as you are nothing but a guest seeking passage to Adocentyn, they will let you pass. But if they have heard of the disturbance in the Scarp. If they have any intelligence of our mission, of the Erigena—'

'Then what?'

'It is impossible to say what might happen.'

Voices sounded in the passage outside.

'Remember,' Edgar said, 'no matter what happens, our object is to find a way through the caves. Keep a look out for doors, tunnels. Listen for any talk about a Seal on the cliffs. If the Delphin capture him, this may give us a chance.'

'Wait,' Jemma said. 'Where are you going?'

'To find a way out, just in case. If anything happens, call into the pipes and I'll hear you.'

~

SHE FOLLOWED HER HOBBLING ATTENDANT DOWN THE lighted passage until they reached a wall of curtains hanging in giant, velvety folds. Jemma struggled to push herself through, standing in awe at the vision before her – the splendour of the Delphin hall.

An emerald pool marked the centre of intense activity, a dazzling acrobatics of leaps and spins in glittering transformations Jemma could barely follow. All around, candle-lamps burned in little hollows in the walls, hundreds of them, so the stone itself was like a hive of flickering, molten bees, their flames the colour of honey.

Raised above the pool was a platform of stone, with a long banquet table and a throne carved from the stone itself. There sat a figure of stark and radiant beauty. She appeared in neither one form nor the other, but both at once, the curves of a Dolphin melding into a human frame, her dress glittering like the sea.

Jemma could not pull her eyes away as she was led to the table and seated to the left of the Queen. At first, the radiant figure did not look at her, but whispered into the ear of her Advisor, who sat on her right. A servant and a special attendant stood behind.

The Delphin Queen herself did not eat. The Advisor had a pale, thin face and lines of worry on his brow. He gestured towards a vast platter of food laid out on the table, crayfish and mussels and clams and oysters. The servant filled Jemma's glass with aniseed wine.

Only when Jemma had eaten all that she could and filled her glass again did the Queen turn to her and speak. 'I am

Queen Amara. It is tradition for a stranger to tell the story of their journey. How came you to the Delphinian Caves?'

Jemma looked up, at first almost speechless.

'My name's Jemma and I came from the Wharf. You know, where the Cray live, and the Gulls, and there's a big wrestling tent.'

Amara whispered something to her Advisor, who nodded. Then she turned again to her guest.

'We have heard something of a disturbance in this direction, and you have just come from there?'

Jemma paused, not knowing how much she should give away.

'Before that, I had a job, collecting bets.'

'What kind of bets?' the Queen asked, not seeming to notice that Jemma hadn't answered her question.

'In the wrestling tents, for a great Walrus. His name was Sorenstar. And he's a prince.'

Jemma felt the pang of something lost and hollow in her chest. The dizziness of being so far out of her depth.

'And where is this "Sorenstar"?'

'He...had to run away. A Seal came into the town, looking for him. Maybe he owed him something. I don't know. But he found out I was his friend, and now he's after *me*.'

Many rings glinted on the Queen's hands. Shimmering mother-of-pearl. 'Is this Seal still following you?'

'I don't know,' Jemma said, unsure if she should proceed. 'I think so. At least, I saw him, running along the cliffs.'

'Unusual that you should be pursued by a Seal. I have not heard of one in these parts for a very long time.'

The Queen watched Jemma closely. Edgar was right. It was impossible to tell how much the Queen knew. How much she was testing Jemma.

'To pursue you can only mean that you somehow

threaten him. Seals are very dangerous. You should remain with us. We will send out some scouts. You will be safe here.'

This time she motioned to a guard, the same commander Jemma had seen at the entrance to the caves. She gave him instructions and he left immediately.

'Thanks,' Jemma said.

In her vest of armour and the splendour of the hall, she had never felt more invincible.

'But he might be swimming, too,' she added. 'Except Edgar – I mean, someone in the Wharf – told me the Seals can only swim and change if they're strong, like the wrestlers. But something might have weakened him. So it's most likely if he's following, he'll be walking over the cliffs. And he wears a black tunic, and a hood. And he's got a white scar right here, just above his lip. That's all I know.'

Amara whispered to her Advisor again. He looked at Jemma, rather than the Queen, as he listened. Jemma felt her stomach dip.

'And where do you plan to go?' the Queen asked her.

'To Adocentyn, to make my fortune. I'll work as hard as I can and buy a little place in the old Cobbler's walls.'

Amara gestured for her to eat and drink and again Jemma could not resist the sumptuous feast laid out before her.

'There is one who may be able to help you,' the Queen said. 'An interesting man by the name of Pico Camillo. He lives in the old quarter of the city, sells relics of one kind or another. If I recall, he once explored the Scarp mountains near your Wharf, and wrote a book about the ruins. He may be able to give you some work. He is known to be fond of Finches and street urchins if they will save him a few hours of labour.'

This time, she sent her attendant out of the hall. He

returned several minutes later with a scroll. Amara took hold of a quill he presented, leaned forward and wrote a message that filled the page. Jemma could not see what she wrote, and neither could the Advisor, who was trying to peer over her shoulder. She sealed the scroll and handed back the quill.

'Tomorrow, we will give you passage to the port of Adocentyn. In return, there is someone I would like you to find. One of the Delphin, who makes his living in the wrestling pits.'

'I've always wanted to see them,' Jemma said. 'I've heard their tanks are huge, a hundred times bigger than ours.'

'To our great shame, there are some of us who have lowered themselves to such a level. You must be warned – when a Delphin lives for too long out of water, they become raffish. Careful when you look for him. He will be drunk and aggressive. But because you are in possession of this letter, he will not harm you.'

Jemma tucked the scroll inside her vest, overhearing the guard, who had returned and was whispering to his Queen: 'It was only a Raven, stalking the entrance. I tried to capture him, but he flew away. No Seals in the hills, or on the rocks.'

Amara spoke again. 'Do you know of a Raven?'

Jemma shook her head, irritated by the news. What was Edgar doing? Why didn't he just stay in the room and let her do the talking? She was doing well.

'If you see it again, catch it,' the Queen said to her guard. 'The Raven have no business spying in our court.'

Jemma almost smiled. To think they could catch her Edgar. Still, what on earth was he doing? Then she remembered, wasn't she supposed to be finding things out?

She took another sip of the sweet aniseed wine. It was warming her, right down to her toes.

'Do you know how they light the city?' she asked.

The Queen, who was still whispering to her Advisor, stopped and turned abruptly.

'You ask unusual questions, for a mere bet collector.'

'It's just, they don't use the sea tallow any more, do they?'

The Advisor seemed agitated now, but Jemma could not hear what he was saying. She looked around at the great hall and the radiant flames that were flickering in the walls. Except some of the hollows were now black, and as Jemma watched, another little fire suddenly extinguished itself and did not come back.

The Delphin Queen gestured her Advisor away dismissively. He stood, folded his arms and walked towards the darkened spaces in the wall.

'We had thought,' said Amara, 'when the Harpooners came to take the Whales again, things had returned to the old ways. They used to slaughter them for their oil to light the city's lamps. But now they use a different source. From where it comes I do not know, but the lights are brighter now. At night you can see its glow from here. Brighter than a star.'

Jemma had not expected this. Beneath the splendour, she sensed a lurking fear taking hold.

Noticing the Queen's rising emotion, the Advisor returned. Now Amara's voice sounded further away, as if she was speaking into the distance, into the dark corners of the cave.

'These lands are sustained by the old Keepers, but the darkness is coming. The Whales are vanishing. Another power has come into Adocentyn, and they are clearing out the lands.'

The Advisor took hold of the Queen's hand and looked at Jemma sharply.

'Perhaps that is enough for tonight my Lady,' he said, trying to encourage her to her feet. She seemed to have retreated even further into the dark. 'Already you grow weary.'

Jemma, sensing the hostility of the Advisor, took her last chance to find out more.

'Is that why there's all these migrations? Like the Caravanassi?'

Amara pulled her hand away from the Advisor.

'Ever since this darkness has come to Adocentyn, the forests have been filling with Shadows. We have seen the Caravanassi boats travelling past our sea lines and we have followed them beyond the city ports, to the chalk caves, where they are loaded into the old tunnels of the Moth. What happens to them from there, we do not know. But it is something terrible, we fear.'

'It is time, my Lady. Please.'

'Who's taking the Caravanassi to those caves? Who are the Moth?'

But the Queen did not answer. Her eyes drifted even further away, and she held out her hand to the attendant behind, who steadied her. Still, she would not let him lead her away.

'The first maker of the city, the Great Magus. He is gone. Vanished from the land itself. There is nothing to sustain the Keepers now. It is the old wars that are brewing, and they are coming closer.'

Though a weight pressed on the Queen's brow, still she had a majesty more splendid than anything Jemma had ever seen, a bearing she could perceive echoed in the soldiers, who now stood wary along the walls.

Suddenly, there was a splash in the pool. One of the acrobats had fallen, clumsily, out of place.

With a mighty will, Queen Amara rose to her feet. 'Must I put up with this...travesty in front of a guest?'

Almost immediately a stillness fell upon the pool and a tremor seemed to flee into the darkest corners of the cave. Jemma could see the strain in Amara's face. From deep inside a chamber there came the hollow crack of rock and the *drip drip drip* of trickling water.

'Is it not enough the caves should crumble? That you should debase this hall!'

Then she turned to her attendant and gently touched Jemma's hand.

'Bring her to the temple.'

❧

THEY LED HER TO A ROOM DEEP INSIDE THE CAVES. A passage with so many twists and turns that, even if she had wanted to, Jemma could not have found her way out. Amara stood before her, peering into a turquoise pool.

'Our Keeper is weak. He is fading,' she said. 'Come forward.'

At the surface of the pool was a white Porpoise, not swimming, barely moving at all. The trance that Jemma had seen before upon the Queen came over her again as she reached out to touch the water. The same deep anguish was present in her eyes.

'Put your hand in,' she said. Jemma wasn't sure if she should obey.

'Don't worry, he won't hurt you.'

Jemma knelt beside the Queen. The water was warm and it tingled against her palm.

Then Amara stood back, observing her. Jemma felt nervous. She rose to her feet, stepping back from the turquoise water. But already the Porpoise had moved.

'You will leave us now,' she said to her attendant. 'I wish to speak to the girl alone.'

'Your Majesty,' he said, and bowed, leaving at once.

'Perhaps I have told you too much, already,' Amara said, touching Jemma's cheek. 'And yet it feels right that I should reveal such things. There is something special about you. What is it? What could it be?'

'I...don't know,' Jemma said. She remembered Edgar's words: *with the Delphin you can never be sure where you stand.* Was Amara friend or foe? Jemma had played the Delphin for fools but now – was she the fool trapped in a cave? And yet Amara's soothing voice made her feel safe. Protected. Secure. *And if you find yourself feeling comfortable, that is when you should start to worry.*

'There was once a story, that my grandfather told me,' Amara spoke softly. 'It was about a Keeper who would come, the greatest Keeper of all, at a time of the fading of memory. They call her the Erigena. And we are in that time. Our Keeper is sick. He is dying. The caves are crumbling. And the one who refuses to accept his burden, the inheritor, my son, has fled to the city. But look,' she motioned to the pool, 'he beckons you. Do not be afraid.'

Jemma looked into the pool. The Porpoise was moving towards her. With a sudden rush, he leapt out of the water and changed, falling to his hands and knees on the floor of the cave.

Amara sprang forward and helped him to a stone chair, but he could not support his own weight. His body collapsed over his knees and he could hold himself up only by a withered arm. His hair was pure white and so long that it covered his face. When he managed to straighten, his eyes were cloudy skies, like she remembered the eyes of the Gull.

He reached out for Jemma.

'Come,' Amara said. 'Do not be afraid.'

She went to him willingly and the Keeper touched her face. Then he held her temples in his hands and Jemma could feel it, like before, the memories rushing in. After a time, they slowed and cohered around the single image of a boy, staring up at the walls of the stone, the carvings that Jemma had seen in the entrance to the caves. Except now the carvings were alive. And she was seeing through the eyes of the boy, feeling his gestures as he mimicked the actions of the warriors. The pool was dazzling, radiant. Then the Keeper let go.

Jemma stepped back as he slumped once more.

She went to speak but Amara held up her hand.

'Don't tell me,' the Queen said, as she helped the old Keeper back into the pool, where he changed again, floating still, as if all his strength had gone.

'It was a gift to you. A vision we call a memory seed. He sees all that is us. What we cannot see. Even what is dark and hidden deep inside the caves, absorbing thought. What he has revealed is for you alone. Show no one, until the time is right. You will know when to uncover it. Now come,' she said. 'I have something too.'

Her voice was sweet like the honey of the caves. She took a pendant from around her neck. The stone was more beautiful than anything Jemma had ever seen, as if it contained the sea itself, glittering with all the days of the sun.

'If I had a daughter, I would imagine her just like you. And since I have only a son, I give it to you.'

The Queen placed the pendant around Jemma's neck, warm and nestling against her skin. It felt like another sense with which to perceive the world.

'I want to know,' Jemma said, 'do all the Keepers go blind?'

'When they themselves grow old, their vision of memory gives them no need for earthly site. That is his greatest power – when he can summon the ancients from the past, to defend us. Now, he is barely able to sustain the caves – and that time is past. Something terrible weakens him. But I have faith that another will come. Before it is too late.'

Amara glanced at the pitiful Keeper and then at Jemma. 'Perhaps she is already here.'

Jemma backed away. Every part of her wanted to flee with the swift sickness of being caught, like the time the dockers saw her pinching an iron spike from the Wharf. But there was no exit. She knew, now, she was out of her depth. Where was Edgar? She'd never wanted him so much.

'Please. You don't understand. I don't know who I'm meant to be. What I'm meant to do.'

'It is already too late,' said the Queen. 'The Poachers are coming for us. If only we had more time. My Advisors have lost faith in me – the absence of my son. You have seen the lights extinguishing in the hall. The drips of the dying caves. I have been driven to erratic authority – my outbursts are like my own last breaths. This has only fuelled their cowardly revolt. I know it moves them to drastic measures...just as I know all that has befallen you, Erigena.'

'How could you?' Jemma said, feeling the stone warm against her skin.

'The caves listen and the Keeper echoes all to me that I must hear. But the other Delphin know it too. The Crays trade in such information – did you not see the little sack of money changing hands?'

Jemma cursed at the Cray's betrayal.

'They wish to imprison you, so that you will absorb our Keeper's memory and sustain us. Do you know? The silver-haired Gull is already dead. But the Gulls are still alive. She put her faith in you, and so shall I.'

'No,' Jemma said. 'Please. I have to get to Adocentyn.'

The Delphin Queen's gaze fell distant. 'Let me tell you how it is: there are no windows in our cells. When the door slams behind you, it will be the echo to a silence deeper than you have ever known. It will be the terror of an absence so final it will seem to eat away at your ears, your eyes. The blackness will smother your senses. At first, you will feel as if you are floating there, weightless, bodiless, unable to perceive which way is up or down, left or right. And then, as if the dark of memory itself has merged with the black of the cave, the images will swarm all around, changing as if with your very limbs and bones, inhabiting your flesh and the hollow of your throat and sending you gagging and choking and heaving onto the floor. There you will Keep us, locked away until you grow old and wasted and wither away, until your very body dissolves into the dark, to the very pit of your being.'

Jemma backed herself into the furthest corner of the cave, wishing for Edgar. The silence broke. There was shouting outside and now banging on the door.

'Do not enter!' the Queen bellowed through the stone. 'You will give us one minute more.'

'We are not like the Arctic Gulls.' She came to Jemma again. 'We have an intricate past. The very structure of the caves themselves would exhaust you. You would become our wretched creature, our creature of memory and darkness, to preserve us.'

Jemma didn't move. Amara waited. There was a focus in her eyes, a clearness like the glint of light in the stone.

'Believe me, it is not my intention to imprison you, but to set you free. Come. We must hurry – they are nearly here. Now I must play my part, and you must play yours, if you wish to escape.'

She led her towards a closed door behind the pool.

'Listen carefully. You must trust me,' Amara knelt and held Jemma's shoulders. 'They will shut you in this cell. Climb through the water shaft. Take the passage to the right. Do it quickly, before they suspect what I have done and send water rushing down the pipes to flush you out. When you reach the clifftops, crawl through the bracken until you find a path along the ridge, it will take you to Adocentyn. Go straight to Camillo. He has a shop in the old city walls. Be sure to give him the letter. You will be safe there.'

'What about you?'

She stood and gently stroked Jemma's cheek.

'I can defend myself. But you must escape from here. When they shut you in – hurry.'

The Advisor and his soldiers rushed in.

'It is true,' the Queen glanced at the Advisor and pointed to Jemma. 'She is the Erigena.'

The Advisor stepped forward, pursing his lips as Jemma pressed her body against the cell door.

'If she is, as the prophecy says, my Lady, we must begin at once,' he said gravely.

'No,' the Queen commanded. 'We will wait. Even this has exhausted him.' She gestured to the Keeper floating almost lifeless in the pool.

'We must leave him to recover. We will try again later.'

'And the girl?'

The Queen looked at Jemma. 'Lock her in the cell, until we need her again.'

'But my Lady, if she is who the prophecy says, how can we defy it? We must do it now.'

'We do not defy what must be. If she has the gift, she will become our Keeper.'

'Wait,' Jemma said, trembling with indecision. She no longer knew if she had been fooled. If she was willingly walking into a trap.

A soldier had taken hold of her arms. With every trick she had ever learned in the wrestling pits, Jemma wrenched and bit and kicked herself free of the soldier's grip and ran towards the open door behind the guards, who slammed it shut. Two others grabbed her. The solider opened the door to the cell.

'Please, you have to listen!' Jemma cried.

'This is not a risk we can afford,' Amara said.

'What do you mean?'

'I am sorry,' the Queen's voice sounded pitiless. 'I cannot stand by and watch my people fade – fade away into the shadows of the weeds like hidden creatures of the deep. Already the caves crumble around us. The lights, extinguishing to nothing. I have no choice. I must secure what is necessary for us to live. Take her.'

'Don't do this,' Jemma said, digging her heels into the stone, sure now the Queen had betrayed her, that she would find no escape from the cell. 'You don't need to. I promise to help you!'

'Take her,' Queen Amara said again, and swept from the room.

## CHAPTER 19

# THE LAST PLATEAU

There were no windows in the cell. When the door slammed behind her Jemma crawled to the corner. She pulled herself up, kicking the wall until the realisation of helplessness descended in a wave of drowsiness, and she slid down to the floor and lay on the freezing stone, hugging her satchel to her chest. She wanted to cry, to shout, but what was the use?

*Follow the water.*

Jemma listened. The sound of a trickling drain, coming from somewhere in the opposite corner of the cell. She traced along the walls until she felt the first patches of damp. And then a vein seemed to glitter on the walls. The Queen spoke true. The stone glowed, and Jemma saw what it revealed – a trail of water.

Above her was the opening where the pipe came into the cave. She could see it clearly now. The surface of the wall was rough and grooved, enough for her to get a purchase with the tips of her nails, but her feet kept slipping down. Then she found a deeper ledge and pulled herself through to the opening of the pipe, pushing her satchel out in front. It was as far as she could go.

'Edgar!' she called as loudly as she could. Her voice echoed through the tunnels. She called again, 'Edgar!' and heard something up ahead, the flutter of wings.

'Where are you?' It was Edgar's voice.

'Here! This way – hurry!'

Then she saw his shadow. He flew along the water pipe.

'I am sorry,' he said. 'I've led you not to safety, but to danger. I've been tearing my feathers out searching these tunnels.'

'I think they're coming,' Jemma said.

Gripping the edges of the pipe, she tried to slide in.

'Yes, they are certainly coming. I can hear them in the passage. Hurry.' Edgar pulled on the strap of her bag. 'They are going to flush the pipes.'

'I can't move.'

'You must.'

'It's no use. I can't!'

He pecked her on the hand and the short, sharp pain produced a final burst of energy. She reached again into the tunnel, clawing at the rock. There were muffled shouts coming from the passage behind. If the Queen had deceived her Advisors, it had not been for long. Jemma pulled with all her might, boring her fingers into the stone. She was nearly there, heaving and wriggling, when the cell door opened and, a moment later, someone grabbed hold of her foot. Edgar took the strap in his beak, this time hooking it over a sharp ledge.

'Pull on the bag!' he said.

Jemma took hold, kicking wildly, feeling a crack of bone against her heel. It was enough to release her foot and she scrambled up the passage.

Edgar led the way into the darkness as a hollow, gurgling sound came from somewhere up above.

'They've released the water,' Edgar said. 'This way. Quickly!'

He went ahead but Jemma remembered: 'Go to the right.'

They turned, just as a jet of water came gushing past.

'Don't stop,' Edgar said. 'We must be getting close.'

They climbed vertically through the jagged tunnel, until they reached an opening to the caves in the cliff top. Jemma scrambled up and over the shelf of rocks. They pushed through the low lying scrub, the bracken scratching Jemma's vest, until they came to a clearing. The last plateau. Beneath their feet were the Delphin Caves, the ocean lay behind them, and the land stretched far away along the ridge before them. Even from here, in the light of early evening, they could see the glow of Adocentyn on the horizon.

Edgar scouted ahead. He could see a shape moving on the opposite ridge – the Seal.

Jemma heard a thundering of water through the caves below.

'You need to start walking,' Edgar said.

'We have to help her.' Jemma held her ground. 'They must know she helped us escape. We have to do something!'

'There is nothing we can do.'

Edgar gestured to the Seal, moving along the ridge.

'There is only the valley between us now. That will give us just enough time to reach the city. We must make haste.' He flapped his wings towards the distant glow.

The Delphin had climbed out of the caves, holding the Queen Amara as their prisoner.

Jemma locked her gaze on the Advisor who had whispered and schemed. He ordered the soldiers to follow after

Jemma, but Amara, pushing her captor away, raised up her arm.

'Leave the girl!' Her voice boomed over the rocks. 'Do not follow them.'

The soldiers stopped, and turned to her, wracked with indecision.

'You will let her go.'

Jemma held the pendant, still warm against her skin.

'I'll come back,' she called. 'I promise.'

'Be sure to give my son the letter,' Amara said. 'Don't forget.'

Jemma turned away and walked on, feeling a bitter shard in her throat, the rush of terror delayed, a great sadness for the white Keeper whose touch still tingled in her temples. The vest of armour settled on her body, hardened against her heart.

Edgar landed on her shoulder.

'In a few hours it will be dark. We can use the lights of Adocentyn to guide us to the city. But we need to leave now,' he said. 'Or we'll never outrun the Seal.'

# PART IV
# THE COLLECTOR'S EMPYREAN

## CHAPTER 20

# A CONSTANT PRESENCE

They travelled into the night. The ridge was exposed and presented a waste of scattered rocks and tundra grass. Jemma felt her feet giving way. There were no caves or hollows around them. After a few hours, she simply lay down where she stood, thankful for the bread that Arlen had given her in the satchel. She broke a piece for Edgar who refused it, insisting she eat every crumb.

'You'll need your strength,' he said. 'We still have a long way to go.'

Jemma was aware of the constant presence following along the opposite ridge. When they stopped, he stopped. When they moved, he moved.

While Jemma slept, Edgar kept vigil all through the night until the Seal's distant silhouette seemed to rise as a shadow with the Eastern sun.

They set off again, not resting even as the midday heat beat down from the zenith of the sky, the Seal's dark shape moving with a strange menace across the other ridge top.

Ash woods filled the valley between them, and the sounds of trickling waterfalls descended from little streams running through the crevices of the ridge. They quenched their thirst at these streams along the way.

The sun passed into the West and they could see the glowing outline of Adocentyn still far off, yet not as far. The valley had narrowed and the Seal's shape was closer now. Jemma imagined the white scar on his cheek and his green eyes shining beneath his hood. She was thankful that she could not hear his voice whispering inside her head.

The Seal stopped and removed his hood to drink at the bank of a stream. He sat down on the rocky ledge, where the water disappeared into the misty valley, and seemed to form a pose of meditation.

Edgar flew up to the branch of a dying, overhanging pine tree clinging to the edge of the ravine. '*What are you up to?*' he thought. He hopped from branch to branch, trying to find a better angle.

Below him, Jemma became engrossed with a wooden chest she saw nestled in the rocks. Once, she'd found an old cellar in the Scarp, filled with abandoned chests just like this one. They were made of thick bark wood and strips of iron, and fastened with enormous locks. She had tried to break the locks with a rock but even after the first strike she knew they would never break. She was left with this intolerable mystery – what if they were filled with treasure? It was three days before she could get back there with her iron spike to have another go at the locks. The chests were gone. Ever since then, she had been filled with an intense desire to open it. To see what was inside. To solve the intolerable mystery. She picked up a rock...

Only when he heard the sharp chinks of stone on the metal lock did Edgar see what was happening. 'Stay away from that,' he called to Jemma.

The Seal was walking again.

He dare not move from the branch in case he lost sight of the Seal, whose eyes were fixed on the sheer cliff below.

Edgar felt a panic rising in his chest – what was the Seal doing?

*Chink. Chink. Chink.*

Jemma's hammering became more frequent, louder and louder.

The Seal stepped into the stream and peered over the edge of the rushing waterfall, deep in concentration, as though he was following the path of a single drop all the way down to the pool below.

*I know your trick*, Edgar thought.

The drop seemed to fall forever.

Edgar could hear his own heart, the constant chinks of stone on metal. He could feel the blood in his veins and a slight itchiness in his feathers. And he wanted more than anything to fly to Jemma. 'Stop!' he yelled.

*Chink. Chink. Chink.*

He remembered the effects of the singing in the Scarp-palace. Edgar recognised she was in the same trance and he was torn between releasing her, and not letting the Seal out of his sight.

It was then he saw the Seal turn, drop face-down onto the rock and slide feet first over the edge. In a second he was gone.

Edgar followed after him, pulling in his wings, darting through the huge canopies of the trees.

He tore through fern leaves to the waterfall, feeling its coolness in his feathers. An arrow brushed his wing. The Seal was waiting and loaded again while Edgar took cover behind a great Ash trunk, flying up as another arrow struck a branch. He crashed through the upper leaves into the sky.

He rushed to where Jemma was kneeling in front of the chest.

'You must stop. Let it go.'

'But I know there's something inside – it's from the Scarp.'

'How can it be from the Scarp if we're not in the Scarp?'

'Because I know every rock and every crevice and I've seen this ruin before and I want to see inside.'

She lifted the stone again, glowing turquoise in her palm. Edgar *kawed* at her, *kaw kaw kaw*. It was helpless.

'We have to move. The Seal is coming. He knows you yearn for this. It is a trick, to slow us down.'

Jemma struck the lock, this time with the golden blade. Sparks flashed and lit up her face and Edgar could see her clenched teeth and the frenzy in her eyes.

In utter desperation he pecked at her fingers, drawing blood, and Jemma let out a cry of pain. It was enough to jolt her out of the trance. She stood back from the chest. The Blade of Adocentyn was glowing in her hand.

'I'm sorry –' she was shaking. She could feel the yearning releasing from her chest like blood draining from her heart. 'I don't know what came over me.'

'The blade is warning us,' Edgar said. 'We have to go, now. As fast as you can run.'

Jemma took off, trying to shake this desperate longing. But nothing could take away the feeling that something had been wrenched from her. The constant urge to turn back, to open the locks. The feeling that something would be forever lost and missing in her life. She shuddered at this power of the Seal, ashamed of the weakness he had found within her.

'Keep running,' Edgar said, scouting for the Seal.

At last, as the ridge descended, the walled city of Adocentyn rose before them in a vision of astounding beauty. All of Jemma's dreams in the wastes of the Scarp could not have prepared her for the sight of the shimmering rings of cobbled roads and golden sandstone glowing in the brilliant rays of light projected from a vast tower upon the hill. She could see the stark-white billowing sails of the wrestling tents, the copper spires of majestic buildings glittering like harbour ships in the sweeping lights. How could such a place be filled with darkness? The tower itself, so high and splendid, concealed beneath its beams the shadows of a grand palace and the lush green of its manicured gardens.

Edgar flew high and then came to rest on Jemma's shoulder. 'Look down there,' he said. 'The valley leads right up to the Southern gate. The Seal may have already passed through. He may be waiting for us. Is there another way in?'

'There were three other gates on the map,' Jemma said. 'But I remember one of them glowed when I held out the blade – the Western gate.'

'You're brilliant!' Edgar said.

'If we follow the city walls, that's where Amara said we'd find Camillo's shop.'

Jemma stashed the blade in her satchel. Edgar flew ahead, and then called back, 'You still need to pick up the pace.'

She ran until they reached the Western wall. Two guards stood in front of the high bronze gate wearing the same black robes as the Scribes of the Black Moat.

'What are we going to do?' Jemma said.

'Climb.'

'Climb?'

'Just imagine this is the Scarp,' Edgar said. 'And you're searching for treasure.'

'As long as you're not going to peck my hand this time,' Jemma said. 'It hurts!'

'That's the whole point,' Edgar said.

She slung her satchel over her shoulder and lifted her body by the tips of her fingers in the grooves of stone.

Edgar hovered above her, 'Not that way, the stone is too smooth. Go left. Now reach up.'

Jemma felt the tingling in her toes. She felt her strength and lightness returning and the pleasure of mastering the climb. With Edgar guiding her she was not afraid. She never looked down.

When they reached the top, Jemma slithered across the rampart and went feet first down the other side of the wall to the road below. It was dark by now, and the great beams swept across the copper crowns of turrets and spires.

'This way,' Edgar flew to Jemma's shoulder. 'Keep to the shadows.'

~

IT FELT LIKE A SEEKING EYE ON THE HILL, SCOURING THE streets with every sweep of light. Jemma could hear the whispers again, growing louder the closer they came. *Hurry hurry hurry hurry*.

A figure in a black robe walked towards them and she crouched against the wall, heart thumping. But it was not the Seal. The man disappeared with his shadow into a narrow alleyway and the streets were empty again, except for the Finches chirping and fluttering on the rooftops.

Edgar flew up to a ledge above and Jemma, completely recovered, hissed at him.

'Get down,' she said. 'Here comes the search light.'

The whispering beam cut through the dark again with brilliant clarity.

'The Seal must have realised we have taken another way,' Edgar said. 'If he is not here now, he will be very soon. We must hurry and find this Camillo.'

They followed the dark ridges of the wall, peering in every window, examining every door. Edgar crouched on Jemma's shoulder and kept his eyes on the lane behind.

'Do you see anything?'

'Wait,' Jemma stopped. 'Amara told me Camillo traded relics and old junk. She called him a tinkerer. Can you read that sign?'

'"Fix Here,"' Edgar said. 'That must be it.'

Jemma approached cautiously. She waited for the light to pass then lifted the heavy iron ring and banged three times against the rusted metal plate. After a while, she heard heavy clomping towards the door.

'Knock knock knock, who's there? Stealers of peace who cannot let an old man sleep?'

Jemma looked once more down the lane. 'It's clear,' Edgar said, settling on her shoulder.

'"Fix Here" the sign says, "to the daylight hours" it should have read. I'll fix no relics now. Let it stay broke till the morning.'

The door swung open.

'Three shekels he wants for a broken harp to sing, and five she cries for a broken ring, he pays me ten to fix a ding, this hour is priceless, do you hear!' The ragged looking man stood in the narrow frame, stooping under the lintel. 'Now what do you want?'

'I'm sorry, to disturb you, but we are looking for one called Pico. Pico Camillo.'

'And who is "we"?'

'My name is Jemma and this is Edgar,' she felt claws digging into her shoulder – 'I mean, my pet Raven.'

He looked them slowly up and down.

'I see you have no broken relics. You are lodgers, I surmise, much to my surprise. I have not had a lodger here for many years. "Fix Here", they do not get the double meaning, you see, or not see.'

He stared curiously at Edgar. 'Is he house-trained?'

'Ah, yes. Of course.'

'Jemma and the Raven, eh? I suppose you may enter.'

In the dim light he shuffled to a counter, grasping at the edges for support, pulling himself around to the other side. Jemma cast her eyes once more at the cobbled lane.

'Come on,' Edgar whispered.

'What if he's seen us?'

'He will if we stand here.'

Jemma closed the door as Camillo struck a flint and set a candle burning with a sudden, radiant glow. The windows of the shopfront were frosted – would that be enough to hide them?

'Get down,' said Jemma, 'out of the light.'

Edgar flew from her shoulder and rested on the darkest edge of the counter amidst a pile of broken ornaments. There were dented urns and broken tallow lamps, some of them in pieces as if they had once been taken apart and never put back together. Coils of rusted harp strings wound through the pile of junk.

Edgar was fascinated by a box filled with keys of all different shapes and sizes. Keys to where? Who could say. Behind the counter there were shelves of little compartments reaching all the way to the ceiling where a ladder would once have run on a track, its bearings long since rusted to the frame.

Edgar flew to the highest shelf and looked inside a little box that was filled with broken pieces of amber resin. In others there were gold and silver knobs and clasps of brass, porcelain chips and a white substance that looked like the powder you would use to make plaster. There were nails and screws and coils of copper wire.

Jemma cast him a furious glance and he quickly flew back down to her shoulder.

'I'm very sorry to have woken you,' she said, stepping over a pile of matted rugs on the floor.

'I do not sleep in any case,' Camillo said. 'Please excuse my grumbling. It is a very old habit of mine.'

When he turned, Jemma saw that his hair was long and tied back in a messy tangle. He wore a gown of brown velvet, stained with plaster dust and oil and even splotches of paint.

She could not take her eyes from a pair of wings hanging from the rafters. They were made of canvas stretched over a wooden frame with intricate joints like those of a real bird.

Camillo placed a large leather-bound book on the counter.

'You see the dust on this old ledger? So long has it been since I've had a lodger. You may have the upstairs room. It has a fire, at least. Boy!'

Jemma heard the pitter patter of feet above and then a thumping down the stairs. It was indeed a boy who emerged, skinny and wiry, wearing an old-fashioned cap, a brown shirt, pants held up with bracers and high leather boots. He had the sharp, darting eyes of a Finch.

'What d'you want, then?'

'Take the girl's bag up to her room and set the fire and make the bed. Quickly!'

'Alright. Alright. But I'll need the key.'

Camillo rifled inside a box. 'Here,' he said, 'take it, and don't forget to give it back, you hear?'

'You won't get no shenanigans from me.'

'I'd better not.' He turned to Jemma. 'They come in off the street. Finches. Do anything for a coin. One day he'll be off, and another will replace him.'

'Me? Be off? I'm a loyal one, I am. A stayer an' all.'

'Well, you can start by stoking the fire and heating the kettle. I'm assuming you drink tea?' he said to Jemma.

'Yes. It's been a long walk. We've come all the way from the Delphin Caves.'

Camillo led the way to the adjoining room, a workshop filled with even more clutter, the worn frames of broken instruments and statues and relics of ancient crafts she had never seen before. Magnificent machines with pulleys and pendulums filled the space, and flying contraptions hung in tangles from the ceiling. In the middle of it all was what looked like a merry-go-round, with carved panels at the sides folded to the centre, like the closed petals of a flower. Jemma longed to know what was hidden inside.

Edgar was examining the array of suspended, concentric circles made of metal and wire. They were like the pictures in Bruno's book, brought to life in mechanical reproduction.

'Odd, that you should travel so late,' Camillo said, 'given Delphin hospitality.'

The fire was still only smouldering.

'I said light the fire, not smother it!' he yelled. But the boy had already gone upstairs to prepare the room.

Camillo shuffled over to a copper tub and clasped a piece of wood, swinging it stiffly into the fire. The embers stirred and sparked a flame. Then he lit a candle on the mantelpiece and another hanging down from the ceiling above.

'Sit,' he said, pointing to one of the two enormous armchairs. He settled himself into the other with a groan. He stirred a pot of black leaf tea sitting over a small burner, and poured them both a cup.

'My Raven, I have trained him to drink tea. Can he have some too?'

'Unusual,' Camillo said. He poured another cup.

Edgar whispered into Jemma's ear, 'Ask him some questions. Get him talking.' Then he hopped down to the arm of the chair where Jemma had placed his tea.

'Do you know the Queen?' she asked. 'The Delphin Queen?'

Camillo leaned back, shifting and groaning in the chair until he had found a bearable position.

'The Delphin Queen Amara. Yes,' he said. 'We were acquainted many years ago. She asked me to help persuade her son to leave the wrestling games. I tried, he refused. He was a very wilful boy, determined to destroy himself. Beyond salvation, as they say. There was nothing to be done.'

'It's just, she asked us to deliver a message to him. And told us that we should come and see you. That you might know about the palaces, that used to appear on the Scarp. I used to be a Scarp hunter see, and I once found treasure in those ruins. Now I want to know where they came from.'

'A Scarp hunter, eh?' Camillo took another sip of tea. 'Yes, I have known them to appear, these castles of memory, more frequently in the long past. I had thought the ruins on the Scarp were almost completely scavenged, now. When I first began to explore them, some still had rooms and chambers, though their gardens had long since withered. I have not heard of one for a long time. But then, I have not explored those parts for many years. They were Ruptures formed by an ancient art of memory, their practitioners long since perished, leaving only ruins. I once recorded my observations in a book, with pictures too, if I remember correctly. It was an esoteric topic, of academic interest really. They tended to appear in the stable regions.'

'What do you mean, in the "stable regions"?'

'Where the lands have been settled, formed. There are

some parts outside of Adocentyn that are very volatile, very dangerous.'

Jemma remembered what Raddahkin had told her, about the charlatans of the New Alchemy and their half-formed, distorted lands of memory. 'Do you still have this book about the palaces?'

'I only restore things now,' said Camillo. 'There is another in the city who collects such things. He goes by the name of Sir Francis Gilbert. I sold him my old books many years ago, an act I will forever regret. You will have to go to his palace if you want to see him. Though I cannot say if he will show you. I would not trust him, anyway.'

'Now ask about Bruno,' Edgar whispered.

Camillo let out a gentle laugh.

'I may be old, but I am not deaf,' he said. 'If your Raven has intelligence, let him speak for himself.'

Edgar fluttered his wings, more with embarrassment than with pride.

'Very well,' he said. 'We are seeking another book, that you may have heard mentioned by this "collector". Or perhaps by another, who has come into the city.'

'How can I know unless you provide me with its title.'

'It is called the Book of Memory.'

'Have I heard of his book? Of course.' Camillo looked into the fire with a distant gaze. 'I have not thought of Frater Jiordano for a very long time. You are speaking of his memory magic. I am merely a tinkerer compared to his genius. Though it has taken my own growing decrepitude to reach such a level of humility.'

'Did you know him?' Jemma asked.

The flames crackled and sparked and sent a trail of embers flying into the chimney.

'Too many questions,' Camillo snapped. His voice grew

harsh. 'I do not like to indulge in remembrance. And for some reason, you seem to be leading me into the past, a place I do not wish to go. Even to think of Jiordano Bruno has filled my heart with a heaviness that weighs upon me and fills my mind with images of the long past I do not wish to see, and yet, in your presence, I see them. Why? Who are you?'

'I am from a long way away,' Jemma said, feeling the discomfort of his sudden change of mood, 'and I just want to get home.'

'Well, the sooner you go, the better for my peace. You may stay tonight, but tomorrow you must leave.'

'That's all we ask for,' Jemma said, 'to stay one night.'

'A night can be filled with terrors if memories become mingled with dreams. Let us hope my night is short and black. I am merely a recluse who fixes things. I have no interest in the world outside this workshop. Now, where is he? Boy!'

'Coming!' Jemma heard the Finch's feet skitter down the stairs. He stepped into the room. 'That's that then,' he said. 'Nice 'n cosy 'n warm, like a proper inn, now, don't you think?'

Camillo ignored his cheerful tone, reaching into his pocket and then fumbling with a silver coin that he promptly launched blindly over his shoulder into the air. The boy caught it deftly.

'Right'eeo, I'll be off. See you tomorrow, then.'

'Will we?' said Camillo.

'A course,' he said. 'I'm a stayer, aren't I?'

The boy dipped his hat and then he changed into a Finch and flew off, through the shop window, with the coin in his beak.

Jemma looked at Edgar, who took a sip of tea in the awkward silence. But Camillo's face had already softened.

'I am sorry for my outburst,' he said. 'You must please forgive me. Joint pain is the enemy of civility.'

Edgar flew up to the mantelpiece and looked directly at Camillo. 'What if I was to tell you, they are killing the Keepers?'

The old Fixer jolted forward in his chair. 'What do you mean, "they"? Speak again, Raven!'

Jemma stood up. 'The Delphin Queen, she said it was the old wars, returning. And we've discovered a name, Bold-evar Ramus. Have you heard of him?'

'Indeed I have,' Camillo said, indignantly. 'But what has he got to do with the Keepers?'

'He's already captured the Arctic Gull. And the white Porpoise in the Delphin Caves is sick, dying. And some-one's taking the Caravanassi and putting them in this memory loop. And these Harpooners, they caught the Whale Keeper. And something's happening with the city lights – why do they glow so bright?'

Camillo sunk back again into his chair. Jemma could see a sorrow come into his eyes.

'I have long suspected that some evil has come into the city. Looking into the lights of Adocentyn is like looking into a black sun, bright and black at the same time.'

Edgar began pacing the mantelpiece. 'And what if I was to tell you that Bruno was banished to a Shadow city.'

'I would say that was impossible. There are none in this land who could possess such powers. None but Bruno himself.'

'We've seen it,' Jemma said. 'It's filled with Shadows and fog that makes you forget everything, and Dark Keepers, all built around the memory of Bruno's past. We need to know about a scribe called Gaspar Scoppius. Have you heard of him? His name leads to the last one written in the Raven Scroll – Boldevar Ramus.'

Camillo held his hands together, his knuckles clicking.

'Gaspar Scoppius was the cruellest torturer to have ever walked the chambers of the Inquisition, second only to Boldevar Ramus.'

'But how do you know of them?'

'Because I, too, was considered a heretical Magus at that time. A mere amateur in the New Alchemy, compared to Bruno. I had made memory machines and theatres, contraptions with mirrors and tricks of illusion that I could use to conjure half-formed images of memory-lands – the refuse of other charlatans. As one who was skating too close to "magic", I was forced by the Authorities to renounce myself. I was never as brave as Frater Jiordano. After my arrest, they used me to try and draw out Bruno's confession. Thankfully, I was too late. When I stepped inside the cell, I discovered the passage he had made. And I followed him, before he had time to close it.

'When I saw the city of Adocentyn, I couldn't believe my eyes. What was once merely a utopian description in an ancient text, Bruno had brought majestically to life. But it was also written: *the city of light will cast a shadow*. I can only imagine that to harness the shadow of Adocentyn would require the will of a very Dark Keeper, almost as powerful as Bruno himself, fuelled by its absolute opposite – malice, hatred, suffering and despair.'

Edgar swooped to Jemma's chair. 'After Bruno escaped, they had to perform his execution. Pretend that he was...'

'Yes...' Camillo shook his head. 'Another old Inquisitors trick. Let me guess, they burned Ramus in Bruno's place.'

Edgar shifted to Jemma's shoulder. 'We believe Ramus had to suffer this execution over and over, in an endless memory loop, to fuel the Shadow city until Scoppius could decipher the codes and open the Rupture. Now Ramus is taking his revenge, by drawing Bruno into the Shadow city. And destroying the Keepers.'

Camillo shoved a poker into the fire and released a flame. 'Ramus was an arrogant brute who would have threatened the other Inquisitors as much as Scoppius did. To have burned him after Bruno's escape would have been the perfect way to get rid of him. Alas for the world, that he survived in the matter of dark memory. This Collector has been scouring the lands in search of something. He has collected every relic and ravaged every library there is to find. If you are right, if Ramus has indeed taken over the tower of Adocentyn, working alongside Sir Francis Gilbert – we are all in great danger.'

Edgar returned to the mantelpiece.

'Somehow, we have to break in. Steal the last remaining copy of the Book of Memory. Will you help us?'

Camillo held himself up against the mantelpiece, skittling Edgar to the side.

'I sold my manuscripts to that Collector on condition that I could copy pages if and when I needed them. And I happen to know that Sir Francis made a passage directly to the underground vaults, where the chalk caves run beneath the tower of lights.'

'How do you know of these vaults?' Edgar asked.

'Because Sir Francis once commissioned me to design a huge machine that crushes chalk into fine powder.'

Camillo rifled through a draw and returned, spreading out an architectural drawing on the table. 'As you can see, I never throw anything away. Sir Francis gave me a map of the chalk caves so I could take the measurements for my design. But this map also displayed the vast caverns beneath his palace.'

He pointed to the plans. 'There are two doors that lead to what we might now call "the vaults of Ramus": this one passes through the chalk caves, the other, here, can only be reached via this labyrinth of passages and rooms filled with all the treasures he has collected. Sir Francis thinks of himself as a sort of Magus, but he is even worse than a charlatan. Stay away from these caverns, if you can – who knows what he keeps lurking in there.'

'But how will we break in?' Jemma said.

Camillo smiled. 'Through the front door. I will send you on an errand. Sir Francis will not think it strange, at first, for me to request access to my old notebooks. He will not know who you are. And for as long as he is ignorant, you may be able to acquire some information, search his "museum", sneak into the vaults of Ramus. But you must be careful. Say nothing of your identity. Tell him you are hired in the workshop of Pico Camillo. You seek the use of his library to copy pages from my drawings of inventions, that I so foolishly sold to him in a time of melancholic need. Can you scribe?'

'Edgar has much better writing than me,' Jemma said.

'Good, then tell him the Raven has been trained as a scribe, but lacks comprehension, only mimicry with a pen. He will believe you. He knows of my penchant for such trickery with machines. And is an animal nothing more than a biological machine?'

'I beg your pardon!' Edgar said.

'I am giving your friend some arguments. Calm yourself, Raven. If he suspects you have intelligence, he will exploit it, believe me. As one of my "machines" he will think you merely quaint, but not collectable. If Sir Francis Gilbert should ever desire to collect you, then you will never escape his palace. That, I can assure you. He is very curious. Perhaps the most inquisitive person I have ever met. And if he disarms you, he will have you disclosing all sorts of things you never meant to say. Already, a Raven Scribe is quite a novelty in these parts. But he must never suspect you are unique. Well, are you?'

He looked at Jemma.

'What?' she said.

'Unique.'

'I...don't know.'

'Good. Because of all things, you must be ordinary. And that is why I have given you this identity – an errand girl of Camillo. That is *all* you are. And you must believe it too, or he will see through you.

'Already, what you are doing is very brave, and very foolish, though not impossible. The Raven's scribing will only give you cover for a few days. By the way, the book you are seeking was also known by another name: *Ruptures*. You should know this, just in case.'

Camillo paused. 'I must warn you.' The thought seemed to have only just crossed his mind. 'You may never come out of there again. Let us rest and think it over carefully. I am tired beyond my wits. Now it is time for us to sleep.'

He led the way upstairs and showed the lodgers into a room empty but for a simple bed, Jemma's bag and a fire flickering in the corner.

'How will we know where to go?' Jemma asked.

'I will have my boy show you the way tomorrow. Now, if you will excuse me,' Camillo said, shuffling towards the door, 'I must retire to my insomnia. The fire should keep you warm enough. Just be sure to shut the grate. Oh, and one more thing,' he turned once again, 'keep away from the window. I heard you whispering about a Seal. If he is still following, if in any way you threaten his secrets, he will stop at nothing to protect them. If there is any comfort, at least in Gilbert's palace you will be safe from your pursuer.' Camillo closed the door and shuffled down the hall.

Jemma dulled the lamp and Edgar landed on the mantel-piece, seeing before him a look that he recognised so well.

'What is it?' he said.

Jemma lay down on the bed and gazed into the glowing fire. 'If everyone's got a Keeper,' she said, 'I must have one too. And I want to find her.'

'How do you know it's a "her"?'

'I just know. It's like a voice inside me. That must be what a Keeper is. A voice inside you, so you're not alone.'

'Perhaps it is,' Edgar said. 'I am not an expert in the laws of the Keepers. That is the kind of knowledge only a great Magus like Bruno attained and, no doubt, Ramus so desires.'

'If he hurts my Keeper,' Jemma said, 'if I ever lost the voice, I'd...'

'It doesn't bear thinking about now,' Edgar looked into her eyes. 'Promise me you'll hold on to what you have. Hold on and never let go. Then you'll never fall, and be lost, as a Shadow.'

For a while Jemma watched the dancing flames, thinking of Edgar's words. Then she picked up her bag and reached inside. She threw it onto the bed, fumbling in every corner. For a second, she froze.

'What's the matter?' Edgar swooped to the bed.

Jemma dropped to her knees, rifling madly inside her satchel. 'After I tried to open the chest, I put it in here. I know I did. The golden blade – it's gone.'

## CHAPTER 21

# SIR FRANCIS GILBERT

The Finch stood eagerly at the gate. Jemma waited a little way behind him, with Edgar on her shoulder.

'He has it. I know he does,' she said to Edgar.

'No doubt,' he said. 'It's better that he thinks we don't know, then we can see what he tries to do with it.'

A lush vine covered the wall and the Finch was about to ring the bell again when a face appeared in the trap door, severe and pale and hollow in the cheeks.

'What do *you* want?'

'I've got some guests, for the Collector.'

'Come back tomorrow.'

'Tell him it'll be worth his while.'

'It had better be,' the butler said, closing the little door and opening up the gate.

He signalled to Jemma, who followed the Finch up a winding path lined with tapering hedges. Through little carved windows in the hedge she could see manicured gardens and sparkling fountains and rows of fruit trees in the distance.

Before her, loomed a vast palace with a towering hexagonal spire casting a long shadow in the sunlight.

The butler took them in to a parlour. 'Wait here,' he said, and went through a connecting door, marking the beginning to a long, dark hallway. Just inside the hall, Jemma saw there were two rooms immediately opposite. At the far end, the entrance to a library. On the left, she could make out several other passages and doors, and the opening to a grand staircase.

The Finch kept his back to her, shifting nervously from one foot to the other.

After a minute the butler returned and gestured for the Finch to take the door on the right. Then he ushered Jemma and Edgar to the room on the left. It was some kind of sorting room for a collection, filled with ornaments, books and artefacts haphazardly arranged. In the centre was a large emerald table displaying an array of burners and crucibles.

The butler departed and Jemma stood in the semi-open door where she could hear voices in the room opposite. The hallway was empty.

'I have the feeling we are being treated like specimens,' Edgar said.

'Sshhh,' Jemma whispered. 'If we're quiet, I can hear what they're saying.'

She leaned half out of the room and peered through a gap in the opposite door, which the butler had left part open. Edgar flew to her shoulder, keeping watch over the parlour and the hall. Through the gap she could see a man in a long frock coat sitting in a velvet armchair. His hair, carefully oiled and combed, framed a face as refined and delicate as his clothes – sharp, angular, narrow in the cheeks. Behind him was a shelf with gold-spined books, delicate vases, a cabinet filled with crystal.

The Finch nervously placed the little sword on the arm of the chair and then stood watching the man examine the object. Jemma squeezed a fist.

'Calm yourself,' Edgar whispered. 'This may be our ticket inside.'

'What if he takes it? What if I lose it forever?'

'Let's wait and see.'

Sir Francis Gilbert held the golden blade up to a tallow light, frowning, examining, peering occasionally at the bony Finch before him with an expression that clearly unsettled the boy.

The sweet music of a piano could be heard from a distant room.

'I come from the Fixer's shop,' the Finch said. 'A girl's come in, with her pet Raven an' all. Camillo's sent her over to copy pages from one of them books he sold yer. I found this little knife,' he continued, looking over his shoulder. 'It were in her bag. Except it's more like a sword, a little golden sword.'

'Have I not eyes?' Sir Francis said. 'Though one may wish to ask, is this all you see?'

'Never had much imaginashun. You know what it is?'

The Collector sighed and put the object down on the cabinet. He walked over to the shelf, selected one of the gold bound books and placed it on an old reading stand. Then he began to flick through the pages.

'You say it was brought to the Fixer's shop by this girl.'

'Like I said, it were in 'er bag.'

'If you should be lying, I'll have you taken to the chalk mines, do you hear me?'

The Finch inched his way back towards the door.

'What's it do, anyway?'

Sir Francis closed the pages of the book and sat down again. 'If it was genuine, and not the forgery that you have brought me, it could have cut through Halogaic glass. It is a copy of the Blade of Adocentyn. These are a dime a dozen in the Harbour market.'

'But—'

'Never mind. Where did she come from. This girl?'

'Dunno. Some orphan off the street, maybe. Probly stole it to get some grub an' all. Except, if you give me another coin, I could tell you more.'

Sir Francis smiled and returned to his examination of the blade.

'Tell me first, then I will deduce its worth.'

'I were listening outside the door. They were talking about a book of Camillo. The old fool said they should come here and see you, for what it's worth. He's given 'er a job to scribe some pages, on the codger's advice.'

'And what is the name of this book?'

'It were something about inventshuns. I couldn't hear exactly. I heard the Fixer say: "I sold it to him, many years ago. An act I will forever regret".'

Sir Francis put the blade down. Then he reached into his pocket. 'This knife is quite worthless, by the way, a mere relic of little consequence. But here is a coin for your trouble, another for your fact. The last is for your intrigue. I do so love a mystery – you have left me, literally, on the edge of my seat.'

The boy jingled the coins in his hand.

'Shall I go back for more? The old fool's got some golden cups an' all. I saw them in his cabinet?'

'No. What you have already brought is sufficient. Anything unusual is of interest to me. At least, I have never heard of a girl who travels with a Raven. Now go and count your coins – a mystery never bought shall eat the soul.'

Jemma stepped away before the Finch skipped out of

the room, through the hall and into the parlour. Only Edgar held her back from grabbing him by the scruff of the neck.

The butler returned with a tray of tea, kicking the Finch out of the front door before taking it in to the Collector.

Jemma listened again. The sweet scent of apple blossoms filled the corridor and hovered about the parlour.

'Take this relic into the sorting room,' Sir Francis said. 'I will follow shortly.'

Jemma retreated as the butler came in and placed the blade onto the emerald table, then promptly departed.

Jemma resisted snatching it back. She had the feeling they were testing her. While they waited, Edgar feasted on the volumes of books. Some had already been shelved, others were piled in corners waiting to be sorted. He searched for anything with an old and dusty cover while Jemma stood looking at a strange furnace, a crucible with a burner below and the remnants of an ashen paste still sitting in the tray. It looked like a funny egg with the top cut off. Then she couldn't help it. She picked up her golden blade.

'May I try to tell you what it is?'

Jemma, taken by surprise, turned towards the sweet, soft voice.

'I'm sorry,' she said, 'I was just—'

'Don't be,' said the girl, who looked as fresh as the spring in her lilac dress, her cheeks slightly flushed.

She took the blade from Jemma's hands and held it up to the light. Then she turned it around to reveal the handle.

'It is very beautiful,' she said.

'Do you know what it is?' Another voice came into the room, refined and smooth, like wine. Sir Francis Gilbert walked over to the table, closing the pages of a book he had left out on a stand. 'See if you can guess,' he told the girl. 'I'm sure our guests will be very impressed.'

'I cannot imagine,' the girl said.

'Have I not trained your eye? More shame on me.'

The girl had a delicacy of touch, a refinement in her poise that seemed to please Sir Francis greatly.

'Well, then, Father, it is very old. Finely crafted. It is made of gold, I would say.'

'Gold? Perhaps I have made you too eager with your judgement. It is plainly nothing more than tarnished brass. Now look closer.'

'There is another marking. Circles and lines. A picture of the sun. So it is supposed to be mneumonic gold, is it not?'

'You are very clever,' Sir Francis said, reclaiming the object and looking pointedly at Jemma. 'You have guessed perfectly. Even these copies are valuable.'

Jemma again contained her urge to take it back, silently cursing that little Finch.

The girl looked at Edgar. 'Is this your pet Raven?' she asked, stepping towards Edgar, who flew to Jemma's shoulder. 'He has very fine feathers.'

'Does he talk?' Sir Francis inquired.

Edgar shook his head, ever so slightly.

'No,' said Jemma, 'he can only scribe. Camillo has trained him. We have come with his request to copy the pages of a book.'

Jemma held out an envelope and Sir Francis read the note.

'I'm surprised,' he said, coming closer to admire Edgar, who raised his beak and looked away.

'Why would you train a bird to scribe and not to talk?'

'You'll have to ask Camillo,' Jemma said. 'I am just his messenger.'

'I beg your pardon, of course. How rude of me. Who am I to judge the whims of a Fixer. Would he like some tea? Or perhaps, a bowl of water?' He turned to the butler, who was hovering by the door, 'Eugene, please fetch our friend, here, some water.'

'At once, Sir.'

'I did not mean to pry,' he went on, picking up the blade again. 'Yet I see you have exquisite taste. An eye for fine ornaments, don't you agree?'

He watched her directly, and Jemma thought, *he's testing me alright*. She resisted the urge to spit it out – *that's mine you thief*.

'We have already told her of its provenance, Father,' the girl said, with a hint of embarrassment.

Eugene entered with a bowl of water and placed it in the corner of the room.

'I do not like him,' Edgar whispered softly in Jemma's ear. 'Let us be careful.'

Sir Francis stared at Edgar as he spoke and he stopped, letting out a crow, flying over to the water and taking a drink.

'A very fine specimen,' he said. 'Very fine indeed.'

He stood beside the emerald table.

'Now, let us settle the terms of our hospitality. It is very rare that we have guests appear, so suddenly, as if out of the blue. Won't you stay for tea? I will, of course, set a place for the Raven. And, to be sure, my generosity extends still further – already the afternoon wears on. In the evening we will dine. Supper will be served. By then, well, the night is no place to be wandering in a city such as this, so deceptively pretty by day, yet in the cover of darkness things have been known to prowl. No, you will rest here tonight. I will settle it now: Eugene!'

'Sir Francis?'

'Have Mrs Hurley make up a bed for our guest, and a "perch", I suppose. Tell me, how is it that a Raven sleeps?'

*With open eyes*, Edgar thought. He flapped his wings.

'Very well,' Sir Francis said, looking unsurprised. 'Pretence can so rarely be prolonged. You will enjoy the menu, I hope. Now, to our afternoon repose. Will you take your little friend out to the garden, my Angel – you may pick some flowers.'

'Thank you, Father,' the girl said, taking both his arms and lifting him from the chair. 'May we choose from all the colours?'

'Of course, my Sweet One. Whatever fills your heart, but your joy, let it be impulse.'

'I have always trusted it, Father.'

'And so have I, through you, my Purity.'

'I think they will be yellow and red.'

'Then why not choose the orange ones, since that is their combination?'

'For, then, there would be fewer flowers to pick, therefore less joy.'

'Very well then. Off you go. I will set the Raven to work in the library.'

The girl came over to Jemma and took hold of her hand. 'Come,' she said, 'this way,' and led her out of the door.

## CHAPTER 22

# ANOTHER VISITOR

They ran along the tapered hedge to a wooden door opening into the garden. For a moment Jemma was lost in the sweeping vista of the orchard in the distance and the rising hill of olive trees. But before them were swathes of beautiful flowers and beguiling paths. The girl followed one of the paths and paused before a fountain, whose gentle stream of water dispersed into a crystal curtain in the breeze.

Jemma noticed the girl could not take her eyes off her. If they were cast shyly, her glances were also eager, hungry.

'Is it true, about the night?' Jemma asked.

'I do not know,' said the girl. 'I have never been out in it. But my father never speaks false. I have heard noises, though, through my window.'

'Like what?'

'Screeches, like thirsty bats. I have heard screams, long in the night, and cries sometimes. And in the distance cheers of great crowds, and music and drumming, and the sounds of hoofs and carriages. And other times, the ringing of bells, or of thuds like hammers beneath the earth.'

They wandered through the maze of flowers.

'Haven't you ever been curious to explore it?'

'I would not dare,' the girl said.

'Why not?'

'My father would not allow it.'

'Do you always do what he says?' Jemma asked.

'Yes. Father is very attentive. Do you?'

Jemma stopped. 'I never knew my father.'

'And your mother?'

Jemma shook her head.

'We have that in common then,' the girl said, and smiled, at first forlornly, then with a sweetness that was almost gladness. 'I, too, have no memory of my mother. But I am lucky to have a father. And I am sorry to hear you are something of an orphan.'

She bent down and picked a flower.

'Here is a nice yellow one. They are very beautiful but they have no smell. These red ones are not quite so pretty, but smell delightful. Here...'

Jemma crouched to breathe in the sweet aroma.

'So, which do you prefer?' the girl asked, 'sight or smell?'

'Smell, I think,' Jemma said. She missed the salty stench of the fish markets and the wafting sweetness of corn cakes and the Caravanassi roasting fires.

'So it is with me!' the girl said. 'What I told you before was not quite true. I remember my mother through this smell, but I don't remember her face.'

She blushed and then recoiled, as if she had given too much away.

'Well, since I'm here,' Jemma said, 'I'd better ask you your name.'

A strange look came across the girl's face. It was an expression at once quizzical and surprised.

'My father calls me many names,' the girl said. 'Like Sweet One, Purity and Grace. My Cherish is another.'

'But what's your real name?'

'I do not know,' she said. 'I have not really thought about it before.'

*How odd*, Jemma thought. *I wonder what Edgar would make of this?* 'What should I call you, then?'

'I've always loved another name. I don't know why. Perhaps I heard it once, or read it in a book. Adeline.'

'I like that,' Jemma replied. 'So that is what I'll call you.'

The girl stared into the flower. 'But how very rude of me. I haven't even asked who you are and where you've come from.' She looked ready to soak up every word.

'My name is Jemma and I've come from across the land. You get to it by sea, past the Delphin Caves.'

'I wondered why you were wearing Delphin clothes,' Adeline said. 'And your pendant is very beautiful.'

Jemma kicked herself for not hiding it better, but she didn't mind showing it.

'Here,' she held it out from her neck. 'You can touch it, if you like.'

Adeline held the jewel in her palm and Jemma only noticed then that her eyes were green, almost the colour of jade.

'It's very beautiful. Warm, like it's alive. And look how it sparkles and changes its hue in the light. Was it a gift?' Adeline pushed.

And Jemma sensed that it was daring of her, audacious. They had walked to the edge of the garden, nearly to the olive grove.

'I'm sorry.' Adeline blushed. 'I should not probe. Come, I'll show you a secret.'

The girl, as if to test the limits of her lilac dress, pulled herself up into the branches of an olive tree near the boundary wall. Jemma scrambled up beside her. The girl grasped hold of her hands.

'I have a confession,' she said. 'I was sitting here before, when I saw you coming up the road with that little Finch. And I wished you would knock on the gate. And then you did! It was me who sent for Eugene. I ran back to the house, pretending I had not been waiting.' Adeline blushed again, then changed the subject, gesturing beyond her property. 'Over there, you can see the only library left in the city, outside of my father's.'

'What do you mean, the only one left?'

'There used to be an Academy, an Academy of something. I don't remember. Or maybe I never knew? But then it closed, and so my father collected all the books. Well, most of them, anyway. He collects things.'

'What kind of things? I mean, besides books?'

'All kinds of things. Like that golden blade. When we go back to the house, I will show you more.'

Jemma smiled at the girl. 'Does he have books on memory?'

'Memory?'

'Old-looking books, you know.'

'He must. He has books on everything. I will ask him.'

'No,' said Jemma. 'I mean, don't worry. I don't want to trouble him.'

'He is always busy with his collection, that is true. He is always buying something. People come from all over the land to sell him things.'

Jemma had a thought – what if one of those measly traders came in from the Wharf? They'd pick her a mile away.

'But it will be no trouble,' Adeline went on. 'It will even please him, to help.'

Jemma looked over the wall – who was that? A man

had come to the gate, wearing clothes that she recognised, like one of those Harpooners she had seen from the Cray boat. He was wearing the same thick jacket of fur and hide.

'Who is the man coming now?' Jemma asked.

'I expect it is someone coming to sell my father something or other.'

Jemma watched him as he passed through the gate. He carried a box on his shoulder, an old wooden crate.

'Come,' said Adeline, 'let's make some tea. We can pick some fresh mint from the garden, or some camomile, whatever you prefer. I will show you the herbarium, and the greenhouse, where Father grows his exotic plants. He collects them, too. And over here, this is where he keeps the seeds.'

~

EDGAR FLEW UP TO THE HIGHEST SHELF OF THE SORTING room and looked for Bruno's name on the spines. So far, he had found nothing.

'I see you are a lover of books.' Sir Francis put down the golden blade and turned towards Edgar, who had now perched himself on the book stand.

He let out a *kraa*.

'And what do you think of my emerald table?' he asked, running his hand along its immaculate shining surface. 'There are none like it anywhere in the city.'

Edgar looked at the crucible in the centre.

'Ah, my egg-shaped vessel – do you like it? I have hundreds, and yet there are many more that I desire. I dabble in the "arts", but I am no magician, I can assure you. May I?'

He reached up and plucked a feather from Edgar's wing.

'*Arrrh!*' Edgar cried, flying across the room, landing on a silk-lined chair near the door.

'A Raven feather – it is just what I have needed to add to the mix.'

The Collector lit the flame beneath the egg-shaped vessel, putting several other powders from little dishes into the crucible. They began to bubble and smoke in the heat. He studied the reaction.

'Alas,' he said, after a while, 'it has only melted and deformed. There is no resurrection, merely ash from a process they call "putrefaction". Not impressed? I can tell you are a sceptic. Perhaps, indeed, the world is disenchanted. Perhaps there are no prophecies, no magic.'

He blew out the flame, went over to one of the shelves, and began to search for something.

'In any case, this is a very old furnace. My collection of them I call my "boiler room". The larger ones make excellent heaters in the winter when filled with peat logs.'

He found the volume he was looking for and placed it on the reading stand.

'I have a book here on the Ravens. You thirst to know, I can feel it.'

The butler knocked on the door and poked his slender nose into the room.

'Excuse me, Sir Francis. Another visitor.'

'Show him into the study.'

'At once.'

'You must excuse me, Raven. I will leave the book open for you in the library to browse at your leisure, along with Camillo's book. Perhaps I will see you there, shortly. You may follow me, if you wish. Please make yourself at home.'

He followed the Collector down the hallway, past the heavy staircase and through the library door. It was carved with geometric symbols Edgar could not discern in the dull light of the wall lamp. The library was in the shape of a hexagon, the lines of shelves all running diagonally from the centre of the room, where a desk stood. It was also hexagonal, each of its six sides in perfect symmetry with the walls.

'Here we are.' Sir Francis left the two manuscripts open on the desk and then disappeared down one of the corridors of books.

Edgar entered the library cautiously. He could hear the muffled clatter of a kitchen below. About him there was a stuffy silence. He swooped through the lines of shelves, admiring the room's extraordinary geometry. Above the central desk, there was a vast hexagonal spire with strange symbols painted on each of its panels. A candle-lamp was burning near where the Collector had left the books. Feathered quills sat beside an inkwell.

Edgar flew to the table at once and turned the cover of the first book, *A History of the Ravens*, running his eyes down the list of chapters: '1. Kings and Queens, 2. Wars, 3. Legends, 4. Prophecies, 5. Science of Transformation'. He turned to the last chapter, which had drawings of anatomy, the process of change itself, pictures of Ravens in transformation. His eyes scanned the images with an almost nostalgic fascination. He felt a burning desire to read every word – perhaps to do so would recover his own powers to change. Then he looked away.

*It is a trick*, he thought, *a test of some kind. He is trying to distract me.*

He closed the cover against his deepest yearning. Then he flew along the shelves, searching for the Book of Memory.

'Where to begin?' All he could do was to start with the obvious. He searched for the name itself, finding a line of books that were shelved in alphabetical order. But there was nothing under the 'Bs' for 'Book' or 'Bruno'. It was not in the 'Ms' for 'Memory'.

*Ruptures*, he thought. *Camillo called it Ruptures.*

He flew up and down the aisles, working his way along until he had found the R section. His heart jumped when he saw the word, and he pulled with his claws at the spine, flapping hard against the shelves, his wings sending up a plume of dust. He pulled it out at an angle, enough to open the cover and look inside. Someone was coming. He could hear footsteps near the door. His heart pounded as he scanned the title, but it said only *Raptures: a History of Seraphic Music.*

'Damn,' he whispered. The steps were coming closer. They were in the aisle behind.

Edgar pushed the book back into place as best he could. The sound of his flapping wings echoed into the spire above. The steps were faster now, almost running as they turned into the row. Edgar flew in the other direction, towards the table, then swooped over to the opposite wall and hid in a little gap behind a high row of books.

Eugene came out of the aisle and stood before the book of Ravens at the table. His face even more severe in the tallow light, he scanned all the shelves and the walls assiduously. Then he picked up the book and placed it back in the shelves, leaving only Camillo's book and the blank scroll.

Edgar watched him until he had left the library. Then he heard voices behind. The bookcase was also a secret door to another room. It was Sir Francis, and another voice, husky and harsh. In the wall of Edgar's hiding place was a little crack, and Edgar could just peek through, enough to see the Harpooner lift a wooden chest from inside a crate and place it on the desk.

'And what have you done with this Cray?'

'We were told to take him to Ramus. We found this in the boat – worth anything?'

The Collector examined the chest with the same intensity he had shown with the blade.

'It is rather crude,' he said, 'but a genuine craft of the Cray.'

He ran his fingers over each of the surfaces and then he tried to lift the lid.

'It is locked. Do you have the key?'

The Harpooner shook his head. Edgar could not see his face, only his long matted hair and the stubble on his cheeks.

'Thief,' Edgar muttered and cursed. He knew right away it was Arlen's chest, the one he had shown them on their first night on the Cray boat, filled with treasures of the Caravanassi. Edgar remembered the porcelain cups painted with swirling strokes of gold, the dice carved from the whitest bone, the gorgeous dolls fastened to the lid of the box and gentle Arlen, his gaze like an adoring lover's beholding his collection. Edgar tried not to think of what might have happened to him. To the old Cray.

'That will affect the price.'

'Why not just break it open?'

'Do I look like a vandal? I'll give you forty.'

'Sixty.'

'Very well, fifty it is, if I may cut to the chase.'

Sir Francis disappeared from view and returned with a small leather sack. The Harpooner counted the coins, and then, without saying a word, left through another door leading out to the garden.

Edgar watched with a feeling of disgust as the Collector gazed at his new possession, examining each of its details, touching its features again, delicately, one by one, as if to discern every stroke of craft. His expression was both rapturous and precise. Then, with a sudden movement, he stood and went to the door.

Edgar struggled quickly to free himself and flew to the table just as the two girls came into the library. He flew at once to Jemma's shoulder.

Sir Francis stepped inside. He looked at them, smiling.

'I see you have been reunited with your faithful pet. And, yet, you have not come back with any flowers?'

'It is all my fault,' Adeline said, taking Jemma's hand. 'We have not been able to stop ourselves talking. And we have so much in common already, it seems.'

She released her hand from Jemma's and took hold of her father's arm.

'I'm sorry, Father, but I boasted – I told her of your library, and now I have come to show her. You see,' she smiled at Jemma. 'He has books on everything, the biggest collection in the land.'

Sir Francis cast his eyes down the aisle where Edgar had been looking.

'What is true is not boastful, my Sweet One,' he said, 'and you have spoken no untruth. Indeed, we have many volumes here, some on the most arcane of topics. But perhaps let us view the collection tomorrow.'

'Couldn't I show some of it now. Please?'

'Very well. You may take your friend through one of the upper rooms.'

'Thank you, Father!' The girl turned to Jemma. 'And maybe tomorrow we will show you all the other ones. There is more than you could imagine.'

'Now be at your leisure, and please excuse me,' Sir Francis said. 'I have some business to attend to.'

When he had gone, Edgar, still perched on Jemma's shoulder, whispered: 'This isn't exactly going to plan. The Book of Memory could be anywhere. You might as well look upstairs, but be careful. See what else the girl knows. I have some exploring to do myself. I'm going to look for that secret entrance to the vaults of Ramus.'

'Be careful too – remember what Camillo said about those passages.'

'We made it through a Shadow city, didn't we?' Edgar whispered. 'I think we can handle the dungeons of a charlatan collector.'

He took to the air, determined not to let Sir Francis out of his sight.

## CHAPTER 23

# SPECIMENS

Adeline climbed the stairs.

'Wait,' Jemma said. 'Your father, he said these were the upper rooms. Does that mean there are more below?'

'Yes, but we are not supposed to go down there. Father has forbidden it. They are his special rooms.'

'Aren't you curious?'

'I'm not allowed to be.'

'I didn't mean if you're allowed to be. I mean – what about you?'

Adeline blushed. 'Well, a little. Once, I tried the door beyond the library. Of course, it didn't open. End of curiosity. Except I know of another way. At least, I followed the butler once.'

'Where?'

'It was through the kitchen. At the end of the pantry, there is a cellar. I only went a little way. It led down a passage, to a dark chamber below. I dared not go in.'

'Can't you just show me that door?' Jemma said, leading

Adeline down the stairs. 'I love a secret passage. I used to be a Scarp hunter, see.'

'A Scarp hunter? What's that?'

'It's like being an explorer – don't you want to try it?'

Adeline huddled her arms together. 'If Father ever caught me, it would disappoint him greatly.'

'But he's never told you not to explore a little bit, has he?'

'It's like he knows I never would.'

'And if he doesn't know, what harm can it do?'

'I suppose we could just have a quick look,' she said. 'I have never called it "exploring". But we mustn't go too far along the passage.'

They ran down the stairs to the kitchen, hearing clattering pots and slamming cupboards and smelling something delicious to eat. Jemma's mouth watered.

Adeline put her finger to her lips and peered through a crack in the door. Jemma leaned over her shoulder.

They could see the cook seeming to float in a fog of steam and stirring pots. In less than a second she had opened the oven and sent a tray of golden potatoes sliding along the centre table, then dashed across the slippery floor to scrub a pot.

That was when they took their chance, sneaking along the side of the table amidst the potato peels. Jemma, ravished with hunger, reached up and grabbed the most perfect potato she could find. Then she put another in her satchel.

Adeline, at first shocked, followed suit, reaching up just as the cook turned, her face like a pudgy pudding as her eyes squeezed into slits of fury.

'Get your hands orf!' she yelled.

The girls ran, half-petrified, through the pantry door at the opposite end of the kitchen. Adeline was giggling like a schoolgirl, as they both ducked to safety behind a sack of flour. Too busy even to curse, the cook continued with her angry clatter.

'I've never done anything like this before,' said Adeline, still grinning as she lead Jemma to the back of the pantry. 'Here it is – this is the door.'

Jemma reached out to try the handle. 'But it's locked.'

'I have a key,' Adeline said.

'Why do you have a key, if you're not supposed to come here?'

'I can't say, exactly. I've always kept it on this silver chain around my neck. Sometimes, I have a feeling, and I don't know why, that Father gave it to me, to test me. Or maybe for me to guard it, and keep it safe. We mustn't stay long. Promise we won't! It would be so easy to get lost down here.'

'We won't,' Jemma said. 'We'll just have a quick look. And we'll leave a trail of crumbs, like in that fairy tale, you know, except this time, it'll be little bits of potato.'

'I have never heard of that tale. Perhaps you can tell it to me.'

'It goes like this,' Jemma said, taking the second potato from her satchel. 'Two kids went exploring, and they didn't want to get lost, so they left these crumbs on the ground, so they could always find their way back.'

'What a funny story,' Adeline said.

～

THEY FOLLOWED A NARROW PASSAGE, EVENTUALLY coming to a wider chamber. To the right was the base of a staircase. On the left they could see the outline of a door. Jemma tried the latch and it was open.

'We mustn't.' Adeline stopped. She pulled on Jemma's arm. 'Please.'

'Just a quick look,' Jemma said. 'We won't do any harm.'

Together they stepped into a vast cavern like an underground warehouse, the air stagnant and smelling of damp. When her eyes adjusted to the dulled light, Jemma took note of another door on the opposite wall, signifying another passage.

They could just make out a series of containers in the centre of the room. As they moved towards them, she could see they were large glass tanks. Thick curtains were draped behind and between them, giving the impression of four cubicles. At the back of the curtained area, blank glass plates rested on frames like artists easels.

In the first container, something hung in a cloudy liquid, suspended and luminous, helpless and immense, its size almost unfathomable. And then, as if the dark itself revealed its secret, Jemma saw it was a white Whale. She nearly let out a cry.

'It is magnificent,' said Adeline. 'I have never seen such a wonderful creature as this.'

For a moment, Jemma stood in horror and in awe at its mighty frame. Was it dead or alive? She felt the warmth of her pendant and she knew it was alive, but the stone's glow was weak. She stepped forward and touched the glass, feeling her pulse in the tips of her fingers. She tapped the stone gently against the glass to try and wake the Whale up. But its eye was closed. She knew it was the Keeper.

'Here's another one,' Adeline said, standing next to a second smaller tank. 'But it's empty. I wonder what creature this once held?'

Beside it there stood another container with a strange specimen inside. It looked half-bird, half-human. And then Jemma could see. It was an Arctic Gull, somehow caught in the act of transformation, preserved as if it had been turned inside out, deformed, grotesque, abysmal.

She felt a sudden trembling come over her and then the urge to smash the glass, because she knew it was the silver-haired Keeper, who had brushed Jemma's face with her fingertips and helped her escape the Poachers and given her all their memory to Keep. And now she was dead. Frozen in the liquid.

'Father is especially fascinated with the power of trans-formation,' Adeline said, touching the glass. 'He must have had this specimen frozen in ice, excavated all the way from the wastes of the North. I am told this was the original home of the Arctic Gull.'

Jemma walked into the shadows, fighting back the bile in her throat. She gripped her pendant and felt its chill. If she'd had her blade, she would have sliced open the glass and released the Keeper and given her a dignified burial, if only she knew the proper ritual. In the Shadow city she had expected terrible things. They had survived worse than she had even imagined. But Edgar was wrong – she had never seen anything as horrible as this.

'Are you not feeling well,' Adeline said, touching Jemma's arm. Jemma pulled away.

'I'm sorry,' Adeline said, 'perhaps I am used to such specimens. I can see that they are also quite ugly.' Then she paled, a look of trembling guilt on her face, as if she had failed at something so terribly there was nothing, ever, to be done.

Jemma did everything she could to hide her surging emotions. She forced herself to say: 'You're right, it's prob-ably just a shock. To see such strange creatures.' Then she took hold of her companion's hand, gripping it tightly, seeing Adeline's face unburdened at her affection.

Beneath the easel, there was a box containing photographic plates. Taking one of them out, Jemma held it up but it was difficult to see. She could only just make out an image, a face she thought she recognised. She put it in her satchel.

In the final tank was a boy floating in the strange liquid. He looked like the Finch in Camillo's workshop, except he had only half-changed into his human form; the feathers of a Sparrow ruffled his arms. She remembered the Sparrows sweeping down over the mountains of the Scarp. Looking into his sad lifeless eyes, she couldn't imagine being frightened of the Sparrows now.

Then Jemma went back to the Whale, seeing a curious contraption next to the glass, like an old gramophone. She set the needle onto the plate and a sweep of aching song echoed through the dark, the same calling she had heard before when she had dipped her hand into the sea in her dream. Except now the notes were not connected any longer to the being who floated trapped and still. The song had somehow been recorded. It was distant and severed and she knew she couldn't Keep it, even if she had wanted to.

Adeline turned in a circle, following the echoes cascading through the dark. Then her voice came rising and trembling. 'Someone's here,' she said. 'Someone's coming. Quickly, we must go.'

Jemma took off, heading for the sliver of light she had seen earlier, a door across the other side of the chamber. The figure was walking through the dark towards them. *Clop. Clop. Clop.*

'Come on,' Jemma whispered, taking hold of Adeline's arm. 'Open it.'

Adeline took out the key and Jemma helped to settle her shaking hands. A shadow cut across them just as they passed through and locked the other side.

The door had a small hatch. Jemma looked through it to see a thin, wiry man peering into the Sparrow's tank, his hair thick and long and tied back in a slapdash knot. He wore the plain black hessian robes of a student.

He set the lamp ablaze and a sudden brightness shone through the liquid as he adjusted the plate behind. An image of the Sparrow appeared, frozen on the plate.

From a distance, the white Whale appeared like a fading star in the black depths of space.

They were in another passage. Whatever she remembered of Camillo's map would not help her now. Jemma held her finger to her lips as she led Adeline towards the golden gild of another door, showing its muted colours in the warm light of tallow candles in little alcoves above. Jemma tried the handle. It too was locked.

'Who's there?' a faint, dry voice came from behind the door.

Adeline had already stepped away, her face pained, retreating down the corridor.

Jemma listened. She could not be sure if she had heard or imagined the voice.

But then it came again, a voice decrepit and quivering. 'Who's there? Help me. Water...'

Jemma crept to the door and put her ear against it. The panels were of a thick, dark wood. There was a little trap-door above and she stood on her tippy toes up to its ledge and opened the latch, careful not to be seen.

A filthy, bedraggled shape hurled itself at the opening of light. 'Please...let me out. Help me. They have stolen my theory. Mine!'

Jemma hid herself behind the trap door, so only her voice could be heard.

'Tell me more and I may release you.'

The human creature wormed his fingers through the grate.

'Where are you? Let Gassendi see you.'

'Speak first,' Jemma said.

The man who called himself Gassendi thrust his face to the grate, as if to suck in cleaner air.

'They have taken it. Stolen my theory. The Erigena. I found the prophecy. *I found it.*'

A thud inside the cell. She looked through the grate, seeing the small, filthy man writhing in agony on the floor.

'Speak again. What do you know, about this Erigena?'

'She will cause the Shadows to rise...the Sigilli will black out the sun...'

Jemma thumped a fist on the door. 'If you want me to release you – tell me something I don't already know.'

Gassendi let out a wheeze, and when he breathed back in, his tongue made a rasping sound like a thousand clicking insects at dusk.

'She is a Keeper of incredible power...holder of the light...a ravine, an emptiness...a substance they call the Halogaic – that is of the yearning of memory itself.'

Jemma gripped the bars. 'Tell me more about this – ravine.' She had a thousand questions. She couldn't stop herself: 'Why do I feel it inside me? Deeper than the highest mountains of the Scarp? And what is this – *Halogaic*? How will I cause the Shadows to rise? And the Sigilli – how will it blacken the sun?'

But all she could hear were terrible, fizzing cries where Gassendi held his gut, as if some poison was slowly eating him away.

She closed the hatch and ran to Adeline, hearing foot-steps coming towards them from the passage ahead.

'We must hurry away,' Adeline pleaded.

Jemma held her against the wall's dark.

Two men in the same black robes unlocked the door and pulled the wailing, cursing prisoner to his feet, marching him back down the passage away from the girls.

'Let's follow them,' Jemma said. 'Come on.'

'We mustn't.'

Jemma turned and held Adeline's hands. 'Will you let me go. Will you wait here for me, by the door? I promise I'll be back soon. Please.'

Adeline's eyes were wild with fright and confusion, but she nodded.

JEMMA RUSHED DOWN THE PASSAGEWAY UNTIL SHE SAW them up ahead, turning into another chamber, and then the sound of their feet on a stairwell. She went in. The staircase was in the far corner and the footsteps were fading below.

In the centre of the room was a large iron furnace left smouldering beneath a ring of five or six crucibles emitting putrid smells. Jemma covered her mouth and examined the strange apparatus, hanging like a giant candelabra from the ceiling above. Books and papers were strewn on a desk, as if tossed in a state of high passion or rage. Some of them littered the floor, where strange contraptions for measurement lay discarded, some of them scattered in pieces as though they had been violently kicked away.

A book lay open on a stand beside the desk. Could it be...? But it was not the Book of Memory. Its pages were covered in anatomical sketchings of the Whale inside the tank, and the swirling circles of what must have been the attempt to represent the Whale songs.

*The poor, poor Keeper*, she thought. And there was that

word, H-a-l-o-g-a-ic, with arrows connected to the drawings. A series of notes below.

> Halogaic liquid: *conducts and preserves memory*.
> Halogaic glass: *ossified. Impenetrable. Container*.
> Halogaic plate: *captures images*.
> Halogaic light: *the energy of memory, released
> into a filament bulb*.

Jemma went to tear out the page, but thought better of it. She followed the prisoner's cries down the stairs, which seemed to spiral down forever, until she reached a cold, deep cave. There was a thickness and a dampness in the air and great thumping sounds could be heard below. When she finally reached the bottom, she stood at the edge of a vast open cavern of white rock, lit up by candles carved into the walls. The men and the prisoner were gone.

These were the chalk caves Camillo had shown them. *The entrance to the vaults of Ramus must be up ahead*, she thought.

A conveyor belt was suspended above the cavern and sent lines and lines of the chalk rock to be smashed by weights propelled with turning pistons – Camillo's machine. Each thump sent tiny drifts of a pure white powder into the air, falling softly through a sieve, collected in little vials beneath.

But what was powering the machines? Something below. A whirling of strange glowing bulbs painting whizzing lines of light in random patterns of energy that seemed to flow and reach with a sudden brightness towards her.

'So this is where the light comes from,' she said to herself.

She looked up into the caverns, seeing at first only a flicker or two of white passing through the light. Then she could see the very walls of the cave were moving, swarming with White Moths, the same colour as the chalk rock, their wings the size of her hand. They were not interested in her. They were only drawn to the swirling energy.

It was then she heard the whispers. They swept through the light with such intensity that Jemma had to cover her ears.

She rushed to a bridge that spanned the cavern, her eyes splotching with the brightness. The whispers below were made of light and pulsed in the dark. Whenever she closed her eyes, images formed in the afterglow – of the Caravanassi huddled in awful fright, their eyes sunken, their hollow cheeks ghastly and spectral.

She tried to shake the images from her eyes. It was only after the lights had died like a fading current that she could trace out the dark walls of a corridor beyond the bridge, where the last faint cries of Gassendi disappeared.

Jemma followed them until she came to a steep staircase. At the top was a door made of a gleaming, polished night-black marble that seemed to reflect her shadow. She slowly opened it and peered inside.

What she saw astounded her. A vast, airy space lifted from an alabaster floor like a vaulted sky. High above were hanging iron cressets filled with burning asphalt, like giant candles of a thousand tallow flames. They seemed to illuminate the ceiling like stars. Vast pillars projected high into the vaults, casting long shadows on the floor.

Jemma tiptoed across one of these shadows, until she came to a raised, hexagonal platform that looked like an altar, encircled by a crescent of stairs, imposing and garish. Six black marble pillars marked each corner of the geometric points and disappeared into the darkness above, where some of the lights had become extinguished.

She climbed the stairs and hid behind a pillar. The

feeling of something lurking in the shadows. All she could hear was an absolute silence ringing in her ears. When the ringing stopped, she went to the altar. Inside, there was a case of Halogaic glass. And inside the case was the Book of Memory.

Her heart leapt and she wished Edgar was with her. She placed her hands on the glass, searching for an opening, a lock, a lid, anything. But the glass was perfectly sealed, beyond any strength she could imagine.

What was that clinking? Glasses rattling on a tray? She hid herself behind the same black pillar, as Sir Francis Gilbert walked right past the altar and went in to a room on the other side of the hall.

Jemma followed him, hiding in an alcove by the door where two robed guards stood less than a foot away from her.

Inside, she could see a man peering over a sheet of plate glass lit by a lamp below. His black robes were slippery with the light of a Halogaic lamp. He was shorter than Sir Francis, thickset and staunch in limb and frame. Ramus.

He held himself with a bearing that was like the crushing of a question. His hair, cropped around the tip of his shoulders, was not smooth, but rough, suggestive of a brutal indifference to vanity. But when he turned, all she could see was a hardened face. His skin was sickly shiny like leathery stone, cracked and glazed as an ancient pot sent to the furnace over and over again. She could see the pure hatred in his eyes. How many times had the circle turned? How many times had he been devoured by the flames? She could not imagine his torment. She could not imagine the depths of revenge surging in his soul. But she could hear every word.

'So, this is the only Keeper you have?' Ramus said.

'Except, of course, for the Arctic Gull. But most importantly, soon we will have an image of the Erigena.'

Jemma pressed herself against the wall, clasping her hands to steady them.

Ramus came to the Collector and took hold of his throat. 'If you should be lying...' Sir Francis gasped and coughed. Then Ramus released his grip.

Sir Francis rubbed his throat and moved away. He cupped his hands behind his back, walking along the smooth marble floor flecked with gold. He gestured to a lone servant standing in the corner, who came forward with a glass of wine and handed it to Ramus.

'When you find this Erigena, you will give her to me,' Ramus said. 'Then you may have all of Gassendi's contraptions. He promised me the Erigena and gave me nothing but Sparrows.'

'I would advise against such rash abduction.' Sir Francis kept his distance. 'Your methods are, to put it bluntly, too brutal. With my refinements, I will get you what you want. I have my scouts.'

'Don't flatter yourself. Your spies had better watch themselves.'

'My Moths never speak unless spoken to. They flutter silent as the night. Their wings, like their tongues, are made of silver. Though, I will say, my daughter's refinements have cost me more than any Moth. A pure upbringing is very expensive. Treachery, by comparison, comes cheap. But I assure you,' Sir Francis coughed again, 'we will achieve our goal.'

'Our?' Ramus chortled. 'You seek nothing but your own profit.'

'What you destroy, I collect. To preserve the artefacts of this miraculous land has been my honour.'

Ramus laughed, again sipping the wine. 'You are an

insignificant compromise. I care nothing for your "preservation". Still, I like you. You are no "magician with a message". Your conjuring is as harmless as your avarice. You are both the extent and the limit of my tolerance.'

Ramus returned to his chair and Sir Francis followed.

'There are pieces to a puzzle that I feel are somehow connecting,' Sir Francis said. 'We may even have all the pieces themselves. Yet how they fit together still alludes me.'

Ramus stood up from his chair. 'My only wish is that I could be there, to witness Bruno's first execution.'

'Alas, according to Alchemy's principle of balance,' Sir Francis grinned, 'what the light gives, the shadows will take. A fair swap, if I may say. When the wheels of memory turn, Bruno will finally meet the fate that history meant for him.'

'At the very least, I want a scribe to record every pang of pain, every syllable of his suffering. I want a description of how his flesh burns, whether he looks up towards the "heavens", or down to "hell". When he cries as the flames first lick his skin, I want precise recordings of his agonies.'

'Such satisfactions await you in the future,' Sir Francis said. 'And more.'

'Don't flatter me, like one of your obsequious Moths. You better find the Erigena, or else she will hold the Keepers strong.'

Sir Francis spread his fingers again across the chair. 'Even if she does sustain the Keepers, with the unleashing of the Sigilli, we will crush them.'

Ramus began to pace and swirl his glass. 'In any case, I want your experiments with the Whale to cease. I wish to see it dead by tomorrow.'

'The sorry creature awaits his fate, at your command. You are certain it is the Keeper?' Sir Francis said, smiling.

'Quite sure,' Ramus said. 'I have a Cray in my dungeon, confessing to his sightings.'

Ramus held the wine glass to his ample nose, his gold rings glinting in the Halogaic light, and breathed in the delicate fumes. 'A fine vintage,' he pronounced.

'You will not find better,' Sir Francis replied. 'But still, I strive.'

Ramus took a sip and seemed to savour the sweet burning with a wince. 'One last thing. There was a Walrus who was pulverised half to death last night in the wrestling tents. I took the liberty of handing him over to your Dungeon Moth. A rare specimen.'

'A Keeper?' Sir Francis said.

'Alas, no. He would, then, already be dead. He is of some noble origin, I am told. Perhaps you wish to preserve him. A measure of my good will.'

Jemma backed away, knocking the candle-lamp on the wall, spilling hot wax on her hand. 'Ouch!'

'Who's there? Show yourself!'

She flicked off the burning wax and ran along the outer wall, the two guards following after her. There were so many doors, but she could see the one she'd left half open. She rushed down the stairs and crossed the bridge, covering her eyes from the whirling light below, but she could not shut out the whispering. Only the loud thumping of the machines relieved her ears.

The guards were close behind her now. She scrambled up the spiral stairs, slipping occasionally on the stone, holding her hand against the roughened walls as she circled higher and higher. But someone was in the room. Jemma could hear the sound of rustling pages, and then she saw the rim of a black robe beneath the stand where she had looked at the drawings of the Whale.

The guards were right on her heels so she dived under a

desk and hid behind a pile of books. There was only a short gap now to the door.

The two hooded guards stumbled into the room.

'Can I help you?' the man reading looked up from the book. Jemma was glad she hadn't ripped out the page. She could not see his face, only the wild curls of his hair above his folded hood. She recognised him as the one who had been studying the Sparrow preserved in the tank.

'Sorry to disturb you, Tomassi. We saw someone running through the passages. Have you seen anything?'

'I can assure you that I have not. Perhaps it was a Moth looking to steal some chalk. But I will alert you if I do.'

'Thank you. And sorry to disturb.'

The guards turned and descended the stairs.

Tomassi stood almost motionless. He turned another page of the sketchings and continued his fine drawing.

'You may come out now. They are gone.'

Jemma wanted to run, but she made herself stand slowly and go to the door.

'I will not hurt you,' Tomassi said, looking up from the book. 'I wish only to capture with my eyes an image of your pretty face. You are the errand girl of Camillo, are you not?'

'Yes,' she said. 'I'm sorry. I got lost.'

'Of course,' he said, examining every feature of her face.

'I have all that I need. Now run along. Your loyal friend is waiting.'

Jemma rushed down the passage to the door and took hold of Adeline's hand. She was not expecting to feel such a great relief and affection at seeing her new friend. 'I'm sorry I was so long.'

They ran back, past the Whale tank, through the cavernous room.

'This way,' Jemma said. 'Follow the trail of crumbs, remember.'

In the pantry, Adeline still shivered and trembled. The key was shaking in her hands and she could not settle them.

'Here,' Jemma said. 'Let me.'

She took the key and turned it until they heard the click. But as she took it out again, Jemma quietly clicked it back, just enough to be sure the lock did not fully catch.

## CHAPTER 24

## PEACOCK'S PLUME

As soon as he had said goodbye to Jemma, Edgar flew back to the library. With his beak and claw, he prized open the secret door set into the bookshelf. Sir Francis was not there. Curtains of dark maroon velvet hung heavily to the floor. Along the walls were glass cabinets filled with artefacts, precisely arranged.

He flew up to a desk in the corner where the Cray chest had been carefully placed. An array of tools were scattered beside it – a magnifying glass, a fine pointed chisel, a brush and a cloth, a beaker of ointment. In a glass cabinet beside the chest was a beautiful mortar and pestle made of some exotic stone, whose grains and patterns were dazzling in the tallow light. Beside it were chunks of a white, brittle rock that looked like chalk. Some of it had been ground into fine white powder, kept in little vials. The cabinet was locked.

*Where could he have gone?* Edgar thought. He swooped to the floor, searching behind each of the curtains, until he found another door.

It was not closed and he pushed easily against it, seeing at first only darkness within, like the bottomless pit of a well. When his eyes adjusted to the dark, tapered by the odd candle flickering in the wall, he could see the staircase winding below. He glided down, careful not to flap his wings.

At the bottom there were a series of passages. Edgar flew into each one, hearing only silence, until the second last, where he caught a faint footfall. He followed, taking off down the corridor at great speed, flying stealthily in the stagnant air.

Then he saw a movement up ahead, at first no more than a flicker. It was Sir Francis, passing through the candle-light ahead. Edgar slowed, keeping to the shadows. The Collector was a spectral shape moving along the wall – then he seemed to disappear altogether.

Edgar followed cautiously, hovering along the side of the passage until he came to a door, almost invisible in the dark. It was made of an intense black stone. He tapped against it with his beak, but it was as if he had knocked against the face of a cliff. The only feature on its surface was the geometric carving of a hexagon. There was no hole for a key. Edgar paused, considering the door. *How could he...? Ah.* He tested the rocks in the wall alongside until he came to one that was not held by mortar. But he could not shift it with his beak.

He pushed against the door once more with his claw, but there was no way he was ever going to open it.

'Damn,' he said, flapping against the stone in vain. All he could do now was fly back to the study.

THE BLANK PAGES OF THE SCROLL WERE THERE, STILL open, and Edgar began to copy intricate drawings of contraptions and machines.

He was about to dip the quill into the ink when he heard a rustling behind him. In the corner stood a Peacock, raising her plume. Her feathers were not coloured. They were brown and plain, yet the patterns adorning her sweeping tail were beautiful.

The Peacock turned and rattled her fan of feathers, quivering and vibrating in a dance. For a moment Edgar watched, entranced.

'Finally, I have caught your attention,' she said. 'For a Raven, you are not very observant. Have you not seen me watching you from my perch?'

Edgar stood for a moment, silent, thrilled. The Peacock giggled, perhaps sarcastically. It was difficult to tell.

'As a matter of fact, I haven't,' he said. 'I have many more things on my mind.'

'I knew you could hear me,' she said. 'I saw you before. Looking at the book of Ravens. Sneaking around. Whispering into your little friend's ear. Don't worry.' She was still quivering her plume. 'I promise I won't tell.'

'Are you another one of his possessions?'

'I am more than a mere possession,' she said. 'I hold a promise of a very special kind. A possession is merely a desire fulfilled. I am the inkling of desire.'

'What do you mean?'

'Why do you think he has not stuffed me yet?'

'I don't know,' Edgar said, going back to his page and continuing to copy another ingenious machine – a conveyor belt with levers and pistons for crushing rock.

'It's because he suspects that I can change, just as he suspects that you can talk. Do you know why he holds such hope? Because we are exquisitely beautiful – well, I am, anyway. There are no more of me left in this land. For him, uniqueness is beauty. We have all been ravaged. Yes, I think that is the word. Now you are curious, I can see. Do you think I am not an expert at reading desire? My survival has depended on it. Even you desire to see me change. Just as you desire to change yourself.'

Edgar looked up from the page. 'Perhaps you should speak for your own desires,' he said. 'I prefer to keep mine to myself.'

The Peacock flew to the desk, her long feathery tail sweeping all the way down to the floor.

'I saw it in your eyes, when you were reading before. Didn't those pictures of transformation fascinate? Do we give in? Or shall we practise restraint? Tell me, are you afraid to let desire take over your reason?'

'Perhaps you can help me,' Edgar snapped. 'What lies behind that door, that black door in the passage below?'

'It is a risk, isn't it? To decide how much you will reveal, for what I know. And then you must weigh it all up in your clever little mind – is she one of his spies?'

'Well, are you?'

She swept her feathers across the pages of Camillo's book.

'I am not. I have allowed myself to be collected for my own survival. But it is not only my uniqueness that keeps me. I have enticed my collector with possibility. This is what you share with me. You, and the girl. This is why you are still alive.'

The study door swung open and Sir Francis stepped inside.

'It is a door to the vaults of Ramus,' the Peacock whispered, before collapsing her plume and retreating to her surly perch.

'A curious Raven, I thought as much,' Sir Francis said. 'I see you have made an acquaintance. Perhaps you may forge a friendship. But I would not trust her, if I were you. She cares only for herself.'

Edgar made a *kraah*, just as Eugene entered.

'Dinner will be ready soon, Master.'

'Excellent,' Sir Francis replied. 'Please,' he said to Edgar, 'won't you join us? And perhaps you would be so kind as to collect your little friend.'

## CHAPTER 25

# A CHANCE TO TALK

Edgar flew into the drawing room where Jemma was listening to Adeline at the piano and watching a Moth dancing in the light of a candle. Adeline played with a sweetness, perhaps a longing to please.

He came to rest on Jemma's shoulder. 'We need to talk,' he said.

'Not now,' she whispered. 'That butler might come in.'

'This place is very strange,' Edgar said, with an urgency that could not wait.

Jemma took Edgar on her arm and moved to the bay window, pretending to look out onto the garden. He flew up to her shoulder and filled her in on everything that had happened – the black door to the vaults of Ramus, the Peacock watching in the library, the disorientation he had felt in the passages beneath.

'Do not trust your instincts here. If we are to find out what we need, we must learn to feel bewildered.'

'I know...' Jemma said. 'I found them too. Passages and caves where machines crush white chalk into powder. It's being powered by this energy beneath. I don't know why, but it seemed to know I was there – it reached out and I could see all these faces. They were faces of the Cara-vanassi, Edgar, I know they were, except they were all hollow and sad and something terrible is happening to them. And it's somehow making the light. And I found this.'

She opened her bag and showed Edgar the glass plate. It was a photographic image of a girl, her arm raised above her head, beside a white bed, cowering against a wall. 'It looks like Adeline.'

'It is a striking resemblance.'

'It's like they use these tanks, to capture memories. They call it Halogaic. It takes different forms – liquid, glass and light – but I don't understand what it is. And that's not all,' Jemma whispered. 'I found it, Edgar!'

'Found what?'

'The Book. It's in this huge hall, where there's a raised altar, except it's cased in Halogaic glass you could never break.'

'Why didn't you say so before?'

'Because that's not all. There's something else, too, down below. A Whale in a giant tank. It's the Keeper, Edgar. I know it is.'

Another Moth fluttered across the outside of the glass.

'What else did you discover?'

'That Sir Francis plans on collecting all the Keepers, after they're dead. The preserving liquid, it's all cloudy with these strange, clumpy bits floating around. The Whale Keeper's alive – I know he is. They're somehow recording the memory-songs on these plates. You can hear the sounds, but it's all frozen and dead. I don't know how it works, but we have to stop them, or there won't be any Keepers left.'

'That isn't the plan,' Edgar said. 'What about the Book?'

'The plan's changed,' Jemma said. 'I can't leave him there, Edgar. I won't.'

'Keeping the Whale? It could weaken you, and we cannot risk our only chance of taking the Book of Memory.'

'Or it might make me stronger.'

'What does any of this matter if we can't get through this – Halogaic glass.'

'Wait here,' Jemma said. 'Do your *kraa aah aah* if anyone comes.'

'It doesn't sound anything like that, but very well.'

Adeline was lost in the music as Jemma crept out through the door.

Edgar noticed the Moth begin to flutter after her and he flew to the top of the door and swooped down, forcing it back to the light, keeping it still with the threat of his beak.

Jemma nosed into the hallway, then stepped back. The butler was carrying a tray into the dining room. When he was gone, she dashed down the corridor, into the sorting room. She searched for her blade. A sudden flare of feathers sent her stumbling into the book stand, but she turned and caught it before it toppled over, her heart beating with fright. The Peacock eyed her from side to side. Jemma could see the golden blade in the corner where she was perched.

'Do you, talk?' Jemma said.

The Peacock only fluttered her tail.

Jemma slowly stepped around the perch. The bird's eyes followed her every step. Jemma reached out and took the blade and put it inside her vest, slowly backing away.

When she returned, Adeline was still playing, but she smiled at Jemma as she joined Edgar at the window.

'Look.' She showed Edgar. 'Remember what Sir Francis said, it's made of mneumonic gold. It can cut through Halogaic glass.'

'We cannot go tonight,' Edgar said. 'It is far too danger-ous. We will have to wait until morning. I will devise a distraction, and I think I know just how to do it. Be careful what you say tonight. He is watching our every move. I fear that our cover will not last for much longer.'

When Edgar stopped whispering, Jemma noticed the silence.

Adeline rose from the piano and reached out her hand.

'Come,' she said, 'let us go to the dining room.' The Moth followed them into the corridor and fluttered in the light.

~

SIR FRANCIS WAS ALREADY SEATED AT THE TABLE, surrounded by furnishings of gleaming oak. The room was lit by crystal chandeliers, which matched the glasses and decanters on the table. A mirror hung over an elaborate fireplace, where a line of tinctures glistened in the light of candles. He stood to greet his guests, while the cook, tight-lipped, her forearms bulging, lifted a bowl of golden pota-toes onto the table. She had already set down sumptuous salads and meats.

'I am sorry,' he said to Jemma, 'but your Raven has not been set a place. Mrs Hurley here simply would not have it. But he may perch on the back of a chair. And perhaps, later indulge in our scraps?'

Edgar flashed his eyes as Jemma placed him beside her on the chair. The cook, serving the meal, cast a scowl at Edgar. Sir Francis smiled, evidently amused.

'Mrs Hurley please,' he said, 'our guest must be starving. Give her another potato, at the very least.'

When the meal had been served, Adeline recited a prayer and Eugene filled Sir Francis's wine glass.

'At last, we have a chance to talk,' Sir Francis said to Jemma. 'I am utterly intrigued. You must first tell me how it is you came into our city?'

'Oh, it is a sad story, Father,' Adeline said. 'Jemma is an orphan and she has travelled far across the land.'

'How terrible for you,' he said.

Jemma swirled a potato in the delicious gravy. She had never tasted better. It was rich and sweet and full of goodness.

'I had my contacts check your credentials. You have quite a reputation for being a little thief.'

Edgar flared his wings.

'Father!' Adeline said.

'That is a lie,' Jemma said. 'I stole nothing but fish guts to pay the Gulls for digging clams. I earned my own passage to Adocentyn and now I have an honest job with Pico Camillo.'

Sir Francis took another sip of wine. Eugene stepped forward and refilled his glass.

'Indeed, he is fond of employing vagabond Finches – why not an orphan of the Wharf. But how ever did you pay your fare?'

'I was a bet collector.'

'I see.' Sir Francis frowned. 'A very ugly business.'

'Perhaps she can stay here, Father, with us, if she is an orphan.' Adeline's voice was full of hope.

'Charity is indeed a virtue, my Sweet One. But I am sure she is happy in the employment of Camillo. Now, won't you eat your meal before it gets cold. I am afraid Mrs Hurley is not so charitable when her food is left to waste.'

Adeline turned to Jemma, her face sparkling.

'We have so many rooms. You may choose any that you like. I would even give you mine, if you so wished. We will be like sisters.'

'Perhaps, my Darling, let our guest be a guest. She has evidently travelled far. And met all sorts of creatures. Tell me, did you ever take refuge with a Cray?'

Jemma remembered what she had heard below.

'They are not known for their hospitality,' she said, feeling a wave of anger that took the shape of the Gull warriors rising up. If she knew how to wield them as a weapon, she'd strike him down. But she calmed herself.

'Quite,' Sir Francis said. 'Yet I am guessing you have at least passed through the Delphin Caves, judging by your attire. That is Delphin armour, is it not? I have some in my collection, though not as fine a vest as this one. So you were received there, as a guest?'

'Yes, and I had the honour of sitting at a banquet.'

'A banquet, no less. I should love to have acquired even just one of their exquisite stone candles. They are carved from the cave itself, I believe?'

'The caves are beautiful,' Jemma said. 'There's a whole wall of candles, like a huge beehive, except some of them went out.'

Edgar perched on Jemma's shoulder and whispered in the ear opposite Sir Francis. 'Be careful.'

'Do you know what extinguished them?'

'I...couldn't say.'

Sir Francis swirled his glass. 'Well, then, I am sure Camillo's meagre wages only cover your most basic needs. Perhaps you may wish to sell the trinket around your neck. That is a Delphin jewel, is it not?'

'Father!' Adeline said. 'She is not one of your common pedlars. Let us please leave her possessions to herself!'

Sir Francis jolted at this display of defiance. His eyes became harsh.

'You will not command me in such a way, nor will you ever presume to do so in the presence of guests.'

'I am sorry, Father. I was just trying to...'

He took a sip of wine and composed himself by smoothing out his hair. 'Of course, I understand. You are protective of your companion. You are forgiven. Now why don't you run along, my Sweet One.'

Jemma scraped the last of her gravy onto a spoon. She would have licked her plate clean if she'd been sitting at her table in the Wharf. Adeline left half of her plate uneaten. She rose and took Jemma's hand.

'My name is Adeline, by the way.'

'Is it, now?' Sir Francis wiped his mouth. 'And how did we come upon this name?'

'It is one I chose from somewhere in my memory.'

'Very well,' he said, pursing his lips.

Jemma felt his eyes upon her. 'But my affections are a father's right, are they not, my Angel?'

'Of course, Father. You may call me all your cherished names. We will run along now, if we may.'

'Very good. But on your way, put the Raven inside the sorting room, with our precious Peacock. I do prefer the wildlife to sleep in a separate room.'

'Of course.' Adeline curtsied.

Jemma took Edgar to the door and said, 'First thing in the morning, I'm going to the Whale Keeper. If I don't come out to breakfast, you better come and find me.'

'Remember what I told you,' Edgar whispered. 'And for Scarp sake, be careful.'

Jemma threw him up into the sorting room, where the Peacock seemed to sulk in the corner.

'It is done, Father,' Adeline called. 'Come,' she said to Jemma, 'this way.' And they skittled down the hall.

## CHAPTER 26

# LIVING DOLL

The objects in Adeline's room were carefully arranged – a dollhouse and a rocking horse, a fine chest of drawers. There were no mirrors, only a modesty screen with pretty floral patterns, which stood in the corner beside a china basin and a pitcher of water. A long muslin curtain veiled Adeline's bed. In the candlelight, it looked like threads of a web glistening in the moon.

Adeline pulled back the curtain and leapt onto the bed.

'Come,' she said, bouncing on her knees. 'I will teach you a clapping game. You start your hands like this.'

Jemma sat beside her and they began to clap, Adeline teaching her a pattern.

'That's it!' she said. 'Now let's see how fast we can go.'

They clapped together, faster and faster, holding the pattern until their hands began to flutter and smart.

Adeline fell back, laughing on her pillow.

'I'm so glad you are staying,' she said. 'I've never had such happy company before.'

She sat up and held Jemma's hands again.

'You said before, about the scent of the flower, that it reminded you of your mother.'

Jemma released her hands and lay back on the bed.

'I think I have a memory of her. I'm on a beach, playing in the waves and I'm just about to eat some sand and she stops me. Except, I don't know if it's really my memory.'

'How can a memory not be yours?'

'If someone made it, out of other memories, to frighten me.'

For a moment, Jemma wished to hear the woman's voice from the palace again. She needed it to tell her what to do.

'It's like he made what I wanted to see, but I don't know why.'

'And who is "he"?'

'Did I say he? It could have been a she for all I know. I can't say who it was. Perhaps it was only me, after all, just dreaming.'

'Do you dream often?' Adeline said, sitting now with her legs crossed, leaning forward.

'Not really. At least, I don't really remember my dreams.'

'Neither do I, except for one. At least, I think I half remember it. There's a room, and a bed with white sheets. Nothing else. Just these old brick walls. And I'm afraid. I don't want to be in this room with the white bed.'

'And it's always a dream?' Jemma asked. 'It's definitely not a memory?'

'It can't be a memory,' Adeline said, 'because my very first memory was like waking from a sleep, into the garden, where I saw the beautiful flowers.'

'You don't remember anything before?'

'Nothing before this. Just the flowers. And then, looking into the water of the fountain, not knowing who I saw in the reflection. It sounds silly. But I did not seem to know that it was me. I felt so happy to think I had found a friend, but then terrible disappointment to see it was only myself. Now you are here! And I don't have to be on my own.'

Jemma's realisation formed quickly in her mind. She reached into her satchel for the glass plate she had found beside the empty tank.

'I've got something, and I have to tell you what I think it shows,' she said.

'Wait,' Adeline put her finger to her lips. 'Someone might hear us.'

'But there's nobody here.'

Adeline got up from the bed and looked behind the lampshade. Then she reached out and grabbed something.

'A Moth,' she said, and held it in her closed hands, so her fingers formed a prison. 'It's just a plain one. See how it flutters in the middle of my hands to avoid anything touching its wings?'

'Why are you so worried about a Moth?'

'They can hear. My father hires them as spies.'

'So they can talk?'

'Yes, but only when they change. Except they rarely change between forms because they lose too much powder. It also rubs off their wings when you touch them. That's why Moths hate being touched.'

Adeline walked across the room and threw the unfortunate creature out of the window. Jemma saw it flutter for a moment, then fall down to the ground and crawl away into the shadows.

'It is expensive for them, to be caught. He will have to change into his human form so he can grovel to my father and earn more powder. It is what he pays them with, if they want to live and fly.'

'Did he send that Moth to spy on us?' Jemma asked.

'I doubt it. He may have thought he could catch something, to win a favour. But he would never accuse me. Father would know it was lies.'

'Even if it was true?'

'It was you he was listening to. But why? Do you have something to hide? Wait. I see by your face you do.'

Jemma stood up from the bed. She couldn't hold it in any longer. But she needed somewhere to begin.

'I'll tell you about my mother. She's like a Keeper, but I only hear her as a voice, when I need her. At least, that's how I imagine her. I know it can't be real. It must have come from the magic of the Scarp, because I never heard it before I discovered...'

'Discovered what?'

'A palace. With the most beautiful rooms I'd ever seen. As soon as I went inside and stood beside the hearth fire, it felt like I was...home. But then it disappeared, and I've been wandering ever since.'

'There's so much of this land I know nothing about,' Adeline said with a sigh.

'I wish I could tell you.'

'Tell me what?'

'The things I've discovered. But if I did, you'd never be the same.'

Adeline laughed. 'How could I not be the same? Tell me. Please. You must.'

Jemma sat down on the edge of the bed. She felt herself on the precipice of a terrible choice, trembling at the thought of holding another's fate in her hands.

'Alright. I'll tell you one thing. This city was made by a great memory magician. His name was Jiordano Bruno.'

'How do you know?'

'Because I've seen him. And I've seen his book of secrets. But someone made another city – a dark city – and trapped him there as a prisoner. And now that same darkness has come into Adocentyn.'

'How could that be?' Adeline protested. 'It's always so light here, so beautiful. You must have seen it for yourself.'

'That's only on the surface. It's like a glittering sun that's rotten inside. Bruno has these Keepers, they're like protectors of the land. And the ones who've come to Adocentyn from the dark city, they're hunting them down.'

'How do you know?'

'Because I've seen some of them. Right here. And so have you.'

'Where?'

'In the tanks below. That Arctic Gull. She was a Keeper. And before they took her, she gave me all this memory to hold.'

Adeline began to shift uncomfortably. 'That cannot be...'

'And the "creature", that Whale floating in the liquid. He's a Keeper too. And if I don't save this Keeper, all their songs will be gone. And all their memory of the ocean too.'

'It's just my father's collection.'

Jemma climbed from the bed and went to the dollhouse. 'And he doesn't just collect Keepers. He collects people as well. He collects orphans, and he puts them into those tanks, like the empty one we saw beside the Whale. There's a liquid inside – they call it Halogaic – that somehow absorbs memories. It preserves them on these photographic plates.'

'But that's silly,' Adeline said. 'Father wouldn't.'

'I think you're from another land, like me. An orphan too. You were treated with terrible cruelty, so you'd never forget your master, a man called Gaspar Scoppius. A Dark Keeper. When he made the Rupture to Adocentyn, and freed Ramus from the execution fires, I think he brought you with him, and gave you to Sir Francis as a gift. And Sir

Francis has taken your memories, so he could make you into someone else.'

'What are you saying?' Adeline sat up on the bed. 'That can't be true.'

'Then why don't you remember anything before that image of the garden?'

'I don't know.'

Jemma took out the glass plate from the satchel and came back to the bed.

'I found this, near that empty tank in the chamber below.'

Adeline took it in her hands and held it up to the light.

'It's just as you described in your dream,' Jemma said. 'Except it wasn't a dream. It must have been a memory, before they took you away.'

Adeline shook her head. Her hands were trembling.

'It's like he's collected you, the same as everything else, and he's made you into a pretty flower. An ornament. A living doll.'

'Please don't say any more.'

Jemma took a handful of rag dolls that were so lovingly arranged in the little wooden house.

'Where do you think these come from?'

Adeline took one from Jemma and clutched it to her chest.

'They're mine. My father gives them to me.'

'They're not yours, and they're not his either.' Jemma was shouting now. She couldn't help it. 'They belong to people. The Caravanassi people.'

'No, they are discarded. I can assure you,' Adeline said. 'The Harpooners bring them for me. They find them washed up on the shore.'

'That's not true,' Jemma said. 'This one here —' she took the doll from Adeline's grip — 'I recognise it. My friend

Daria, she's a Caravanassi girl, and this belongs to her. I saw her making it with her own hands. She went on this boat, see, and then she disappeared, and I think it's got something to do with the chalk caves below, and how they make the energy and the light. I've seen their faces, all starving and hollow — it's the Caravanassi, and they're doing something horrible to them!'

Adeline fell, crying, on her pillow.

'I'm sorry...' Jemma said. 'I didn't want to tell you. I never wanted this. Any of it. But it's the truth.'

Adeline curled up with her hands over her ears, shuddering.

'I cannot hear this anymore. Please, just leave me alone.'

Jemma reached out, but she was frightened by the violence of Adeline's convulsions. Her hand rested on the downy quilt.

'Alright,' she said, wishing she could take it back, 'just pretend I never told you anything.'

She quietly left the room. As she had wanted, there was the voice again. A lullaby in her ears. And she knew it was a memory of someone singing her to sleep. The voice kept singing, then it whispered like a flutter of wings.

*Follow the Moth.*

Jemma stepped out into the garden.

## CHAPTER 27

# ENTHRALLED

E dgar was astonished. The Peacock, fluttering her plume, turned in a whirl spinning faster and faster, her feathers shaking wildly in a blur of colour. She rose up, changed into another form, and stood before him. Her human self. A glittering green dress clung to her figure, the lashes of her eyes were soft like feathers, her hair, long and streaming down her back. At first, she simply moved, raising her arms and turning, dancing. Her figure was just as she had described – exquisite.

She looked at Edgar, who stood, watching, from his perch.

'Do you know how long it has been since I took this shape?' she said, stretching and spinning around the floor. 'And now you do not satisfy my eyes in that form. Go on, change. I bet you can. Didn't you see it in the book? I was watching you. I saw your desire. If the secret is there, don't you want to find it again?'

'I'm afraid not,' said Edgar.

'What a shame.' She walked up to the perch and stroked

Edgar's wing. 'I would have liked a companion. I am sure you would be quite exquisite too.'

He swooped down to the emerald table, looking into the crucible, at the ashes of his feather. Then he flew over to the door and tried the handle.

'I would not bother,' she said. 'We are locked in for the night. During the day, I am free to roam as I please. But at night Sir Francis shuts me in here. Does it surprise you that he doesn't trust me?'

'Not in the least,' Edgar said.

'Don't worry, that morbid butler will unlock it in the morning. But for now, we are trapped here together. And I have not had company at night for such a long time.'

'Don't you have a Keeper?' Edgar asked.

'My Keeper has long since perished.'

'Then how can you live?'

'The Collector is a kind of Keeper. He can pick and choose. He can Keep only a few. That is why he is so careful with his selections. So willing to dispose of what he does not desire. Why do you think he keeps us in his "sorting room"?'

'What, exactly, do you want from me?' Edgar asked.

'Nothing less than your full attention.'

'I cannot give it to you. I am in the midst of a puzzle.'

'What if I promise to tell you something, in exchange?'

'Tell me what?'

'So now I have your attention, but for how long? As long as I hold my secrets?'

'I'm afraid you quite bore me,' Edgar said, taking a swoop around the room and coming to rest on the emerald table. 'I work on probabilities, and you are not scoring very highly.'

The Peacock moved, hips swaying, and sat down on the

chair, reaching across the table to stroke Edgar's feathers once again.

'What if I told you the Collector is not from this world?'

Edgar turned at once.

'I can almost feel your little heart racing.'

'Where is he from, if not from here?'

'From another place. He discovered a passage, I do not know how. A Rupture, he called it.'

'Where is this passage?'

She stood, then swayed, as if she was drunk.

'It exhausts me, you see, to change,' she said, yawning and catching hold of the velvet chair. 'I am tired. You have literally sapped me dry. Oh, but you've been so very sweet. Now I must let my secret sleep.'

Almost in an instant she had changed again, her plume collapsed. Her energy depleted. She skulked away into the corner of the room and closed her eyes.

Only a single candle burned on the emerald table, flickering and gasping at the end of its wick. Edgar's heart fluttered like the flame. What if he was locked in here all night and all day? What if something happened to Jemma when she went for the Whale, and he couldn't help her?

He tried the door handle one more time. Then he scoured the shelves for a secret room. Nothing. He paced, watching the flame until it died, his mind swirling in the dark. *If I have to distract the Collector*, he thought, *I have to find a way to keep him enthralled.*

## CHAPTER 28

## MAGDEN

J emma crouched behind a hedgerow, watching the Moth Adeline threw out of the window, still crawling in the shadows. In the next instant he changed into human form and gathered himself in a collection of rags, an attire that looked as if it had been patched together with old, dusty Moth wings.

He stumbled through the hedge, clutching various parts of his body until he came to a door leading into the library. She saw Eugene looking through the little trap. Jemma followed, still hiding. Trying not to think of Adeline and the mountain of hurt she had caused. 'Stick to the plan,' Edgar had said.

She listened.

'What do you want, Magden?'

'To see the Collector. I have some information.'

Jemma cursed, trying to remember what exactly she and Adeline had said.

Eugene opened the door and led the bedraggled Moth in. Jemma inched along the outside of the house, peeking in windows, until she found them in the study. She crouched under its slightly open window and peered in.

'Wait here,' Eugene was saying. 'And don't touch anything.'

'I touch only myself. I am in pain, I tell you, pain – great pain.'

As Eugene left, the Moth cast his gaze around the room. He shuffled over to a cabinet on the desk and put his hands up to the glass, staring in.

'I remember in the days a plenty, we would fly as thick as bees in the moonlight, changing as we liked to the dance, back and forth we fluttered in the air like pollen-lubricants of wing. Now we scrape and grovel and spy in porcelain drought, afraid to change, to fly, to be, the Great Moth again.'

A voice came from behind. 'Have you come to mumble lament, or to smudge my glass?' Sir Francis walked over to the armchair and sat down. 'What is your news?'

'I would be worried, Master. The girl could be a corrupting influence.'

'You are a fool to tell me that before I have given you powder.'

'Not a fool, if by telling you give me more.'

Jemma could see a look of loathing on the Collector's face as the Moth stood before him.

'Go on then. What has she said?'

His wretched hand hovered like a twitching wing to receive the powder. Sir Francis, almost in a casual manner, went and unlocked the cabinet, taking out a vial of chalk. The Moth, quivering, poured the chalk-powder into his hand and rubbed it on his face, in his hair, the back of his neck.

'Nothing in particular,' he said, his voice now tingling with pleasure. 'It is more her manner. Probing, you might say. Curious, even. She has asked, for example, about the key.'

'And what did she say?'

'Your daughter? Nothing, of course. A keepsake, she said.'

'Perhaps you now understand true obedience.'

'Oh, I obey you, Master.'

Sir Francis took out one more vial before he locked the cabinet and sat down again, turning the vial around and around in his fingers.

'You obey nothing but powder. She caught you, didn't she? I can tell – you're dry. Either you're making something up or you're hiding something. Either way, it will get you nothing.'

'They spoke of mothers, Master. Mothers and memory. Of a scent that evoked her form.'

Magden fixed his gaze on the twirling vial.

'But that is not only why I come. This may be worth a great deal, Master. We found him before, prowling in the garden.'

'Who?'

'My tongue is a little dry. You know what we say: not to flutter is to suffer.'

Sir Francis threw the vial of chalk to the Moth, who caught it, sending a plume into the air. To Jemma's surprise, he changed back and forth in the cloud of powder.

'Like lubricant nectar. You won't be disappointed, Master: it was a Seal.'

'An ordinary Seal from the wrestling dens?'

'Of the special kind. We caught him prowling in the orchard. Filled his eyes with Moth-dust. Took the liberty of locking him up, in the special cell.'

Jemma felt her knees turn cold in the damp grass. How long had that Seal been watching her? What if he escaped?

'Excellent. You will have more powder for this.' Sir Francis took out another vial from the cabinet.

'May I be so bold as to suggest we interrogate him too?'

'Another fine judgement, but do not ask him trifles. Focus your attention on the creature he holds prisoner. I want to know the secrets of his incantations.'

*The Sigilli*, Jemma thought, *they're talking about releasing the Sigilli*.

'Your wish is powder, Master, powder.'

'Take it,' Sir Francis said, handing him the vial, 'and whatever pleasure that remains, is yours.'

Sir Francis retrieved one more and waved it in front of the dilapidated Moth.

'I assure you, Master, there is nothing less, and nothing more.'

'Then you will have the same. Nothing ventured, nothing gained. Follow her, though. The girl, that is. Do not let her out of your sight. She must not leave this place.'

'I am your favourite spy, am I not? You have my word.'

The Moth, a line of spittle running down his cheek, took a bow, threw up the last of the powder, then changed within it and fluttered out the door.

Jemma scampered back to the other side of the garden. She sneaked inside the guest room, seeing every speck on the wall as a Moth. Every shadow, a place for it to hide.

# CHAPTER 29

## SUBMERGED

As soon as she sensed the dawn, Jemma put the golden blade inside her vest, and the flint box Arlen had given her, just in case. Then she checked the corridor, examining every shadow for a Moth. She walked silently along the hall, scanning the cornices and the skirting boards and the high, dark spaces above.

At the far end of the corridor, someone was leaning against the wall. Waiting. Jemma stopped, not knowing if she should turn back or keep walking. She kept going, straining to see who it was – the butler? The cook?

But it was Adeline, stepping out to block her way. Her eyes were puffy and red, as if she had been crying all night. Her voice was bitter.

'How do you know I won't tell my father?'

'You won't.'

'How do you know?'

'I just know.'

'You *don't*.'

Adeline leaned, hitting her head against the wall. Her voice was surly with hurt.

'I could call out now. The Moths would come and take you, and you'd be gone.'

'Or you could help me,' Jemma said.

'You don't know who I am.'

'Neither do you. But this is your chance. To know who you really are.'

Adeline cast her watery eyes towards the ceiling. Her lips trembled as she spoke. 'You said yourself my memories were stolen.'

'We could find out what happened. I could help you.'

'What if I don't want to know?'

'Then we talk about the future. What you do, from now.'

'How about I do nothing.'

'That's already something.'

Jemma could see the pain in Adeline's face.

'You hurt me.'

'They hurt others. Would you rather be their happy doll?'

'You know I wouldn't. Still, you've made everything unbearable. No matter what I choose. And you made me believe I was your friend.'

Jemma stepped towards her.

'You are my friend! But you have to let me go or another Keeper dies, and all that it Keeps will be wiped out of existence. Ramus and the Collector will take hold of this land and fill it with a black sun. A museum of dead memory. Fossils in your "father's" collection. Just remember, you have a key around your neck. You can open doors. Help us to escape. But if you won't come with me, you have to let me pass.'

Adeline ground her fist into the wall. Her voice was dark and sharp. 'I hate you.'

'I'm sorry,' Jemma said, 'but I don't hate you.'

'Maybe you will –'

'No. I never will.'

Jemma walked past her. Then she turned once more, and took out the Blade of Adocentyn, filling the dark hallway with a strange, pulsing glow.

'I know you see its gold, just like me. Your father didn't, but you see its light. Maybe it chose you too.'

She wound her way down the stairs to the kitchen. She didn't look back.

Mrs Hurley was preparing the breakfast. Jemma hid inside the storeroom. It was freezing on the hard stone floor and she shivered, but it was not only with the cold. She wished Edgar wasn't locked inside the sorting room, so he could scout ahead for Moths.

*I don't hate you Adeline*, she thought. *What I hate is the truth, because it never does anything useful, except to hurt.* Why did she always have to be its messenger? Having to hold forever the memories of faces turned by truth into pale, bewildered ghosts. She thought of the Caravanassi boy's sorrow. And Raddahkin when he told her she was the Erigena, how she had tried to run away. Even Camillo said he was just a recluse concerned with nothing outside his workshop – was he even thinking of them now?

Mrs Hurley wore a tight-lipped scowl. She had already squeezed the oranges. The jug of fresh juice and mint was sitting on the tray, along with pots of tea and jars of condiments.

Jemma stayed hidden until the big burley cook wheeled a trolley of steaming delights past the kitchen table and through the corridor, to the foot of the stairs. This was followed by a shrill shout, 'Eugene! Need a hand with the breakfast trolley, now!' And then, shortly after, the bump of rickety wheels going up the stairs.

Now was her chance. Jemma dashed into the pantry and pushed against the door. It clicked open.

*I can't let it close,* she thought, *or I'll be trapped inside that hall.*

She went to the shelf and heaved a sack of rice across the floor and set it against the doorjamb. Then she slipped into the darkness of the passage.

A Moth, who had been watching her, hiding among the jars of brown sugar and oats high above on the shelf, fluttered down and followed her into the passage, invisible as the dark itself. Silent as the air.

Jemma followed the trail of crumbs they had left on the previous visit. She had not yet grasped the magnitude of what she was about to face, too worried about whether she would even find the same door. She could have sworn it was over to the left, but the crumbs told her otherwise, against her most powerful instincts.

It was a strange feeling, not like being lost. More like knowing your house was ahead, but turning the opposite way instead, only to find the front gate right where it wasn't meant to be.

Eventually the trail led her to the door.

At first, her eyes were woolly with the dark. The tank was a fuzzy glow far off in the distance. Only a tallow candle shone faintly from above, casting a shy, insipid light over the Whale, its white bulk moon-like, its sheer size incredible to behold.

A surge of anguish came over her at the violation of the Whale, at the impossible task ahead of her.

She rushed to the tank. And when she came to it, she threw her hands against the Halogaic glass. The Whale did not move. She thumped against the glass to wake him up. It was hopeless. She leaned her head against the surface, looking at the Keeper's wrinkled eye. It did not even open it now. Perhaps it was already dead.

She slid down the side of the tank and sat, huddled, on the floor. She should have listened to Edgar this time. The simple fact was it was too late. They might have lost their chance to steal the Book.

She did not see the Moth hanging above her in the darkness, fluttering in the silence.

The Whale began to move. At first, there was only a shiver in its tail. But then a long convulsion rippled through its entire frame.

Jemma stood up, seeing the horror of its discomfort and distress. Tapping on the glass, she saw the Whale open its enormous eye and look at her with a desperate plea, as if to say, 'Hurry, I can't hold on much longer.'

There was a chair at the end of the tank and she leaped onto it, climbing up to the top. She took out the golden blade and pressed it into the Halogaic glass. It cut right through, as if she was slicing butter.

She cut a hole in the top. The Whale Keeper rose to the surface, its blowhole making a sound of breathing and suffocating all at once.

Jemma reached in and touched his skin and held him. She could feel it – as she had with the Gulls and the white Porpoise – the memories rushing into her vision.

It was a feeling of being submerged, floating in the sea. Something was moving from very far away, a shape swimming towards her from the other side of the ocean itself. And now they came from all directions, the massive Whales, each of them sounding a song as they passed.

It was as if they were trying to make her hear, remember, until it was just the songs themselves that swirled around and around. They grew louder and louder until Jemma felt that she was going mad, that her ears would burst, the songs almost howling and screaming and consuming the dark. Dizzy and disoriented, she rose to her feet and stumbled to the edge of the tank.

She fell to the floor. Then everything was black.

The Moth fluttered down and rested on the glass. The Whale was sinking to the bottom of the tank, lifeless.

The Moth hovered above Jemma's body, as though tracing out her crumpled figure on the floor. Satisfied that she was not moving, he took off again, fluttering away into the passage, following the crumbs towards the kitchen.

## CHAPTER 30

# CONFESSION

W hen the butler released Edgar, he flew through the darkened hall and into the library, followed by the sauntering Peacock. The Collector came in from the study.

'Good morning, Raven,' he said. 'I see you are up bright and early. I always dine alone for the first meal of the day. Yet had I known you were stalking, I would have saved you some scraps.'

Edgar flew up to the reading table.

'Your friend must be in the breakfast room with my daughter. Perhaps she, too, will have some scraps?'

'I am not hungry,' Edgar said.

The Collector looked at him, enthralled.

'You have dropped your disguise. How very forthcoming.'

Edgar flared his wings.

'I am very pleased indeed,' Sir Francis continued. 'Pretence is tiring, don't you think? But here I am doing all the talking once again. Won't you tell me all about your little friend. Is she really just an orphan?'

'I do not know,' Edgar said. 'And even if I did, I wouldn't tell you.'

Edgar noted the effects of the taunt. The Collector walked towards a shelf.

'You fascinate me, Raven. You delight me, very much. Even so, I would be careful what you say.'

'Perhaps you can tell me, why you surround yourself with the powers you so evidently lack?' Edgar continued. 'If it is true what they say – that collecting is a kind of confession – what do you suppose you confess?'

'There is such a thing as etiquette. Perhaps you have heard of it?'

'I thought you disliked pretence,' Edgar said.

'There is a fine line between etiquette and pretence I would, of course, agree.'

The Collector picked up Camillo's book and began flicking through its pages, taking careful note of Edgar's twitching feathers.

'Very well, then. I will answer your impertinent questions. You want to know why I collect? Put simply, it is divinity. The very act of eternity. For there is, literally, no end. And where an end is threatened, that is merely the beginning of rarity.'

He looked up at Edgar, who raised his wings as if to fly.

'You see, uniqueness is like a circle, a beginning and an end unto itself. Intrinsic being. A value that you might say is "beyond good and evil".'

The Peacock flared her wings in the corner of the room.

'I am a collector, too, of sorts,' said Edgar. 'I collect knowledge. Now tell me, how is it that you made this palace?'

'I built it, brick by brick. My own design, of course. Some parts I conjured myself.'

'Through your "dabbling"?'

'I can assure you, I have discovered much, through my dabblings. But what I wish to discover right now,' Sir Francis leaned over the table, 'is who you really are?'

'Perhaps you can enlighten me first,' Edgar retorted. 'Your daughter, do you Keep her? No, you do not have such powers, do you? Perhaps you only trap her, then, like a Moth in a glass.'

Sir Francis smiled. 'Are you always in the habit of asking and answering your own questions?'

'Where is she from then? Is she a specimen from the old orphanage of Gaspar Scoppius?'

Sir Francis cleared his throat. Edgar flew to the opposite shelf.

The Peacock fluttered her feathers, out of delight or hostility it was impossible to tell.

'Let me warn you, Raven,' he said. 'You would not want any harm to come to your "friend". For you see, knowledge has a price, and so do rarities. When you put the two together, well, then we have something priceless. And what cannot be paid for must be got by other means. Do you follow my drift?'

A knock at the door. Adeline came into the study, her eyes filled with worry.

'What is it, my Angel – have you lost your companion? You look upset.' Sir Francis searched her face.

Adeline glanced up at Edgar.

'No...Father,' she said. 'I am just tired. You know how I cannot sleep when I am so happy. My friend is...in the breakfast room. I came to ask your permission, to explore the orchard. And after, to visit the herbarium. I've told her all about it, and—'

'Very well,' Sir Francis said.

'Thank you, Father. Forgive me for the disturbance.'

Eugene, who had been waiting in the door, took advantage of the opportunity and stepped forward to speak discreetly in his master's ear.

'Your guest has arrived: Deacon Ramus.'

'More interruptions, just when things where getting interesting. Please show him in.'

'Very well.'

Sir Francis turned and looked at Edgar. 'We will speak again, Raven. We will speak again very soon.'

Then, tucking Camillo's book under his arm, he smiled again, and walked out of the library.

# CHAPTER 31

# HALOGAIC

E dgar flew with full speed down the stairs, swooping into the storeroom where Jemma had hidden on the freezing floor. Mrs Hurley was busy at the sink, scraping and clattering pots and trays and pans.

'Damn again,' Edgar said, and waited.

She dunked several tea towels into the water, going into the kitchen yard to hang out the sodden cloths.

Edgar leaped into the air and flew over the table, past the smouldering stove and into the pantry.

'Good thinking,' he whispered, seeing Jemma's sack of rice propping the door open.

Just then, a Moth flew out of the gap in the door, through the pantry and into the kitchen. Edgar sprang into the air, following the Moth, who fluttered erratically, landing among the jars of spices above the fireplace. With a single sweep of his wings, Edgar sent the jars to the floor, but the Moth was nowhere to be seen.

Edgar circled the fireplace, working his way up and down every inch of the shadows above.

'Where have you gone?' he muttered, landing on the table, poised and waiting for the slightest flicker of movement. Now every speck on the wall took the shape of a Moth.

What if he chose the wrong one and the little wings fluttered away? He peered at the shadow beneath the mantelpiece, seeing a tiny hole in the wall. Edgar flew up, and then he saw it, buried tightly in the crack. He pecked at the hole, hitting the brick. The Moth took off again frantically, dropping to the table in a last effort to hide in the grainy wood. Edgar trapped its fluttering wings in his claws. He reached in and took the wilted Moth in his beak, searching for a place to keep it.

Through the window he could see Mrs Hurley coming back. Above the sink was a small glass jar and he darted forward, trapping the unfortunate creature inside. He watched it desperately fluttering to avoid touching the glass. Then it seemed to weaken and keel over.

Seeing Mrs Hurley's hand on the door, Edgar flew low beneath the table and back into the pantry. He could only hope she wouldn't see the helpless Moth and let it go.

He darted through the passage, seeing the trail of crumbs on the floor.

'Very clever,' he said. 'Why didn't I think of that?'

The next door was open and he flew across the dark to the great luminous tank, seeing the dead hulking Whale and Jemma, seemingly lifeless on the floor.

'Oh no,' he said, 'no, no, no,' brushing her face with his feathers.

'Wake up,' he whispered, 'please.'

She stirred.

'Jemma, it's me.'

'Edgar?' came her sleepy voice. She opened her eyes.

'Edgar...'

'Can you stand?' he asked. 'Come on. Let's try. At least see if you can make it behind this curtain.'

He could hear muted voices above, perhaps in the study.

'I think they are coming. If you can, hurry.'

Jemma pulled herself up, her head dizzy and strange. She rose to her feet, swaying and rocking until she had found her balance. Then she walked slowly, with great effort, to the curtain.

Edgar led Jemma to a place behind the tank, where a line of boxes and strange equipment had been stacked in the corner. Jemma leaned against the box.

It was like she was still very far away from land, submerged beneath the sea. Like she had just taken a breath and was now swimming underwater, floating, weightless. She wondered how on earth she was ever going to reach the shore.

'What did you say, Edgar?' Jemma slurred, still dreamy.

'Never mind,' he said. 'I hear them coming. Be very quiet. Do not make a sound.'

'Who is it?' Jemma felt herself returning, just a little, and sat up against the box.

'I can't see. Wait.' Edgar flew to the top of the curtain, then returned.

'Not the Collector, another. Shorter. He is wearing black robes.'

'That's Ramus,' Jemma whispered. Her mind still felt heavy and fuzzy. She took hold of the curtain and peered through a gap at the stocky man, his face a mask in the Halogaic light.

They observed him, examining the Whale tank, frowning at the lifeless hulk before him.

Sir Francis stepped into the room, followed by Tomassi.

'My deepest apologies,' Sir Francis said, walking over to

the tank, and standing beside Ramus. 'Some unexpected visitors.'

'What of this strange equipment?' Ramus said, with a tone of impatience.

Sir Francis ordered Tomassi to step forward. 'Please share the wisdom of your experiments.'

Tomassi leaned in close to the side of the tank, steepling his fingers.

'It was a discovery that I made almost by accident. At first, I had thought the Halogaic liquid only cleansed the memory. But this is not so. It also stores memories in the solution itself.'

Ramus frowned at Tomassi. 'I do not follow. Explain.'

'See here,' Tomassi said, pointing to the tank. 'The solution is almost cloudy where it has absorbed the memory, and is itself highly reactive. Even as we speak, it responds to the sound. The Whale memory is encoded in song, and it seems to seek this channel. By passing a sound wave through the solution, I have managed to capture some of the Whale's song, recorded here on this plate.'

'So it is the Keeper?'

'Undoubtedly. You see the solution is turning almost grey? That is a sign it is thickening. It will grow darker still. The most powerful effects are where there has been some kind of pain or trauma. See these cloudy plumes in the Halogaic solution? They are painful memories, like the scar tissue of the body. Look here, if we pass a conductor through the solution, it lights this lamp. But if we now pass it through a cluster, it burns even brighter.'

Tomassi's eyes twinkled in the bright light the liquid had fired with a strange, almost pulsing luminosity.

Edgar flew to Jemma's shoulder. 'So that's how they're lighting the city. They're somehow draining energy from the Keepers. From the suffering of the Caravanassi.'

The Collector stood again, peering with great pride at the Whale.

'The extraction of the energy must be complete.' Ramus touched the tank again. 'I wish only to see what I desire the most. A dead Keeper.'

'The process is nearly finished.'

'How will you capture the songs?'

'I have set up the plates. Then all we need to do is switch on the machine – as the sound passes through, it will play the songs, and record them.'

'Excellent,' Sir Francis said. 'You will set this up at once.'

Tomassi began to assemble the strange contraption. Then he said, 'The implications, may be profound.'

'Focus on the demonstration,' Sir Francis said irritably. 'We will theorise later.'

'No,' Ramus said, 'I wish to hear this theory now.'

Tomassi spoke with a quiet intensity. 'These memory clusters, once released, are drawn to whatever will contain them, a plate, or a globe. But they seek, first of all, to exist. When a Keeper dies there is a great surge, a force of yearning more powerful than we can imagine, condensed inside the solution itself. But what if the memory clusters are actually seeking a rememberer?'

'I do not follow,' Ramus said.

Tomassi paused for greater effect, seeming to relish the attention.

'You've seen how it can fire a lamp? This is the very path of memory, a movement from the darkness to the light. And through the light it seeks eternity, just as it clings to these plates. What if we could harness this memory of the dying Keepers? Not just to light the city. What if we found a way to Keep it all, together? We would have a source of incredible power. But to contain it, we would need an emptiness, a nothingness, a space as vast as the yearning of memory itself.'

'You are speaking, of course, of the Erigena,' Ramus said. 'So far our search has come to nothing.'

'Let's hope it stays that way,' Edgar whispered.

Tomassi went to the Sparrow boy's tank and returned, holding the glass plate. A look of triumph in his eyes. 'It seems, Master, we have had her all along. One of Gassendi's Sparrows who was sent to search the Wharf reported seeing a girl, running from the Poachers, protected by the Arctic Gulls. I have extracted this image from his memory.'

Sir Francis held the plate up to the light. As soon as he saw Jemma's image, he flung it into the dark. The plate shattered into a thousand shards.

Ramus turned. 'If you should fail me,' he said to Sir Francis, 'think of the fate of Gassendi and his Sparrows.' Then he disappeared up the stairs.

Sir Francis whirled to Tomassi. 'Catch the Raven. And when the Dungeon Moths are finished with the Seal, take him to the special cell.'

'I will do so at once, Sir.'

'Then come back for the girl.'

'The same room?'

'No, the other one. I want them kept apart.'

'It will be done at once.'

Sir Francis stormed upstairs. Tomassi sped off, into the dark.

## CHAPTER 32

# THE GILDED CAGE

'We have to steal the Book and get out of this place, now,' Edgar said. 'And I think I know where we can find a way into the vaults of Ramus.'

He darted through the passage, flying in the shadows, Jemma following behind. When he reached the black stone door, Edgar showed Jemma where to push against the loose mortar in the wall. She released the lock and the door swung open. Edgar swooped inside and up into the dark recesses of a long hallway.

They sped down the passage, hiding several times in the alcoves as footsteps approached and receded into the dark. When they came to the end, Jemma recognised at once the vaults rising up to the crescent lights above. There was the raised platform in the middle of the vault and the altar, shining with the strange black lustre of mica.

Dark robed figures walked to and fro, carrying piles of books or instruments for geometric calculation.

'We have to do it now, before they raise the alarm,' Edgar said.

Jemma slipped into a room filled with crucibles, like the ones she had seen in Gassendi's ransacked chamber. A black robe was slung across the back of a chair. She put the robe on and gathered a pile of books.

'Come on,' she said. 'Follow me.'

They walked across the hall, Edgar hiding in the folds of the cloak. They circled the altar and then climbed the stairs on the other side, hiding behind the black marble pillar.

Jemma took out the golden blade and, crouching in the shadows, cut a line in the glass as she had done before with the Whale tank, surprised again at the ease with which it cut. She made a gap big enough for her to reach in and take hold of the Book. She carefully slid it out and put another bound manuscript in its place. Then she put the Book of Memory at the bottom of the pile she was holding.

'Who'd have thought it would be this easy,' Jemma said. She'd felt the thrill of using the golden blade, of taking one step closer to thwarting Ramus, imagining his face cracking at the news. Returning to the Shadow city to retrieve the tampered copy, only to be banished from Adocentyn forever.

'I wouldn't speak too soon,' Edgar whispered. 'We still have to get out of here. I've counted six doors coming out of this gaudy hall. Which one do we take?'

'I know the one,' Jemma said. 'Follow me.'

They crossed beneath the blazing crescent lights and had nearly reached the door, when a voice came from across the hall.

'You there – where are you going?'

It was too late to run. Two men in black scholars robes approached. Jemma stopped but did not move.

'Show yourself at once.'

She was slowly turning around, as Edgar flew at the

scholars' faces. They stumbled backwards into each other and fell hard on the marble floor.

'Run!' Edgar said.

Jemma dropped all but the Book of Memory and they rushed through the door and down the cavernous stairs.

'This way,' Jemma called, leading Edgar across the bridge under that bright gyrating light and through the whispering that was almost shrieking in her ears. Edgar gripped hold of Jemma's shoulder, 'What is that noise?'

'It's coming from the lights,' Jemma said. She held her ears until they were climbing the spiral staircase into the ransacked room.

When she reached the top, Tomassi was waiting.

She stopped in her tracks.

'You really should find another escape route,' he said. 'But I am feeling warm-hearted and will promise to say nothing to Sir Francis about your escapades, if you give me that Book.'

Jemma looked up at his wild matted hair and his hungry eyes. Tomassi's thin fingers were stretched out and quivering before her. No. They were so close. She was backing away, and then Edgar was flaying his claws into Tomassi's face.

In the scuffle, Tomassi fell against a pile of metal instruments. Jemma took her chance, running into the passage.

Edgar let out a *kraah* and freed his wings, but Tomassi struck a blow, sending him into the hanging crucibles and spiralling into a heap on the floor. Edgar rose immediately and shot across the room. He flew wildly, darting into the passage that lead him to the tanks, piercing the dark with rage at anyone who might harm Jemma. But where was she?

He followed the crumbs through the stagnant air with ferocious thrusts of wing that sent him swerving through the pantry door and into the kitchen.

At first, it was like he had flown into a web of elastic stretching against his face, his eyes, then wound all around his wings. The more he beat against it, the more tangled he became.

Eugene grabbed the top of the net and held it tightly until Edgar stopped thrashing.

'Here is the culprit, I think, Mrs Hurley.'

'That's him alright, wot sent my spice jars flying. To the dungeon with 'im, I say.'

'And so it shall be done, Mrs Hurley, and so it shall be done.' The butler took the tangled bird into the sorting room, where a beautiful gilded cage stood waiting on the emerald table.

'Did you know,' Eugene said as he placed the ball of feathers in the cage, 'my Master had me choose this one, especially – "Nothing but the finest will do".'

The Peacock, standing on the perch, raised up her plume.

'Please help us,' Edgar called to her, as the cage was carried away, and out of the door.

## CHAPTER 33

# A CREATURE IN THE DARK

Jemma lay huddled on the stone floor shivering in the cold wind that blew inside her – her mind full of visions of an icy plain on the edges of a sea. The feeling of being submerged under the waves, a distant Whale song echoing in the deep, came over her, and for a moment she could not tell if she was in air or water. All she remembered was a putrid hand covering her mouth and being dragged backwards through the dark. But worst of all, they had taken the Book of Memory.

A surge of useless anger went through her. She had kicked and stamped and struggled to get free, but there were three of them, three hulking Moths that bundled her in their grip and threw her headlong into the cell, where she now lay.

'What should I do?' She didn't know if it was her own voice that answered.

*Strike a light.*

'How?'

*The flintstone...*

'Is that what a Keeper is? Light in the dark? Warmth in the cold?'

*I am with you. Remember.*

She could feel the life of the Wharf inside her, the smells of roasting corn cakes, the Gull kids brawling over a fish head, the tar-fires on the Tern ships glittering upon the sea. Raddahkin kneeling, holding her shoulders – *I have my faith in you girl.*

She pulled herself up and reached inside her vest for the flint box. Fumbling in the dark, she set a small bundle of wick grass on the floor and struck the flint until it flared and then died away. It was enough for her to see an empty lamp hanging above.

She struck the flint again, quickly taking hold of a longer piece of grass and reaching up. The lamp's tallow wick had nearly burned to the end and so she turned it down to a faint, radial glow.

Then she blanched.

A creature moved in the dark. A sad, groaning sound.

At first she dare not move any closer. Her cell mate looked half dead, except it was moving of its own free will.

The light barely reached it and she did not want to exhaust the wick, so she approached cautiously. In the flickering light she caught glimpses of ugly flesh, wounded and torn. It groaned again and rolled towards her. She jolted back.

Then a force of wild emotion swept through her.

She leapt forward, seeing the Walrus clearly now, his tusks gleaming and bloody in the light. She threw herself down and took Soren's head in her lap, feeling the pain rippling through his body.

'What have they done to you?' she said, clearing the mucus away from his eyes. He looked up at her.

'Jemma,' he said. 'Is that you?'

He let out a cough, spitting muck out of his mouth. The convulsions grew stronger as he began to change.

'I do not want you to see me, like this.'

'No,' she said, 'don't waste your energy. Stay still.'

She turned away, unable to watch the surging skin stretching with agony. Soren's groans were almost unbearable. The shocking wounds began to tear and bleed.

She had no sea-fennel. No aniseed spirit. There was nothing she could do. But then she saw the tank against the wall of the cell, the Halogaic liquid glowing faintly in the light.

'They're waiting for you to half-change and die like the Arctic Gull so they can put you in that tank. Another relic in his sick collection.'

Jemma stormed forward with the golden blade and cut the glass. A thick, gelatinous substance oozed to the floor.

Soren had now fully changed and lay, barely moving on the freezing stone. If the Halogaic preserved memory, then maybe...

She scooped it in her hands and rubbed it on the wounds. It seemed to work. It seemed to stop the blood.

'Still, I cannot die,' he said. 'Still, she Keeps me.'

'No,' Jemma said. 'I'm your Keeper now. You Keep in me.'

'Release me then,' he said.

'I never could.'

'When you told me, that night about my fate, you already set me free. I came into the city to fight my final fight.'

'Who did this to you?' Jemma said. 'If I find them...'

'It has nothing to do with him,' Soren breathed heavily, wincing with the pain. 'The Delphin Prince. He is a fine fighter. Fair, fierce, brave. If you had only seen it. I could have won. I chose not to. Why – why do you Keep me? When all I want is to fade, like Sharmenai?'

'There are no rules for that,' she said. 'I don't have a choice.'

'Please try,' he said. 'Release me.'

With all her strength she lifted him so he leaned against the wall. He raised his head, and in his eyes there was an anguish she could not bear to see.

'I need you,' she said. 'I need your help. These people, they've trapped me. And I have to get out of here. So you see, I need you more than ever.'

The old wrestler, a light flaring in his eyes, stirred with a fierce convulsion of anger.

'If anyone ever touches you,' he said, 'I'll—' But the pain shot through him. He fought against it. 'It seems I spoke too soon. So that was not my final fight – this is.'

'I'm sorry,' Jemma said. 'I know you're ready to go.'

He reached out and brushed her cheek.

'I remember when I found you in that bundle of cane-fleece. You weren't a baby. You could walk and talk. It was like you'd just woken up from an ordinary sleep. You sat up, wide-eyed, looking all around the Wharf. Some traders started hollering, "A child! A child's in that basket of cane-fleece!"

'I came running over, and soon's I took one look at you, I knew you were mine for taking care of. But you were stubborn, even then. Every day you'd go missing, and I'd find you, right where the basket lay, looking out to sea. It was like you knew exactly what you were looking for.

'No doubt, you still remembered your father back then. Whoever he was. I only caught a glimpse of him, looking back from the stern of a Navigator. There was no one else with him that I could see. But you were too young to remember now what you remembered then.'

Jemma felt a surge of sadness and love, pain and emptiness all at once.

'How come you never told me before?'

'Because after that, you were too busy getting into mischief on the Wharf to worry about him coming back again. Except I always knew you had it in your heart to search for other places, other worlds. To hunt for ruins. That is what the loss of love demands.

'You gave me something to live for. And you gave me truth. And you set me free. And if any would dare to harm you, they will have to face the wroth of Soren!'

He gripped his hands and flexed his arms. The wounds, still raw, were no longer bleeding.

'You are all I live for then,' he said. 'Let them come. Let them try to harm you.'

He pulled himself onto his knees, then pushing forward with his battered arms, raised himself up. He stumbled and Jemma held him, until he stood, alone and trembling in the flickering light.

'If you are my Keeper, then I will Keep you too. That is my vow.'

He seemed to peer through the dark, into a vision of the night.

'You asked me once what I remember of my past. There is one image that has always remained,' he said. 'The star of my people – it is my only true memory.'

'What is it called?' Jemma looked at him.

'It is the source of my name. Sorenstar.'

The light went out.

# CHAPTER 34

## THE WHITE MOTH

The gilded cage hung from a chain. Edgar searched the darkness all around him. All he could see was a shaft of light cast under the door and a shape bundled in the corner.

'Jemma, is that you?'

At first there was only a deep silence. It moved around him like a substance in the stagnant air. He could feel it in his lungs and he coughed and wheezed at the foulness of its taste.

Then he heard the sound of a clinking chain against the stone.

'Who are you?' Edgar called, gripping the bars of the cage with his claws. 'Who's there?'

'Here we are, together in the dark,' came the voice from the corner. Edgar was startled by its tone – gentle, learned, humble.

The flame of a lamp above suddenly flickered into life. The Seal sat in the corner, leaning into the wall, his arms chained at either end. A hood had been pulled over his eyes.

'How did you do that?' Edgar asked.

'I conjured it,' he said, 'from what is within.'

'Just like you did in the Scarp, destroying the palace?' Edgar pecked at the cage door. 'You have been hunting us – why? Tell me what you would have done, if you had caught us?'

'Killed you,' he said.

'For a prophecy?'

'I cannot say.'

'Was that your intention, when you destroyed the palace?'

'It would have been better for her that she had perished then.'

Edgar clawed at the bars.

'If I did not have these chains, I probably still would,' the Seal said, 'though I have nothing against you.'

'If you touch her, I will kill you.' Edgar leaped to the highest part of the cage, his eyes ferocious.

The Seal smiled. 'With your beak and claws?'

'I would, at least, peck out your eyes.'

'And still, I would see.'

His voice had now changed, crackling with pain.

The Seal heaved intermittently, but Edgar could perceive his immense powers of control. It was as if he gathered the agony to himself, then released it like a breath.

'Take the hood off your face, at least, so I can see you.'

The Seal, unable to reach that far, shook the cloth from his face. Edgar saw the white scar above his lip, emerald-eyes peering with a strange calm that unsettled him.

Then the Seal closed his eyes, holding out his arms against the chain. The lock on Edgar's cage fell away. The door swung open. Edgar flew out, swooping into the freedom of the cell, landing on the stone. Suspicious. Grateful.

'Water,' said the Seal. 'Pass me water.'

Edgar stood near the bowl, obviously positioned to torment the prisoner more. It was just out of reach.

'Why should I?' Edgar said. 'Why shouldn't I let you die?'

'I will unlatch the door.'

'Why can't you remove your chains?'

'They are made of star-iron, coated in a resin the Moth make from their wing dust. That I cannot break. But the latch I can.'

'And how do I know you'll do it?'

'You don't,' he said. 'You can only take my word.'

The Seal gasped. It was evident that whatever control he had before was slipping away. He writhed for longer than the Raven could bear, then slumped forward, hanging by the chains.

Edgar slid the bowl to him. The Seal reached out and took the rim to his lips and drank it all with a madness. Then he heaved forward again, retching away all that he had drunk.

Only an immense effort of will could have contained the surging pain. Edgar remembered the Seal chanting incantations outside of the cave when he had followed him into the forest. He tried to imagine the discipline of a mind that must constantly work to imprison such a horrendous beast.

The Seal raised his head as though to test his will against an enemy that he no longer conquered. That had now defeated him.

'You will have to give me a moment,' the Seal said. 'They have given me poison.'

'Why do you want to hurt her when she is protecting the Keepers?'

'How can she protect them, when she is the prophecy herself? Foolish Raven. You should have listened to your

Council and put her in a tomb. Instead, you have put before her a fate even worse than this.'

'How?'

'You let her fulfil the foretelling. And still, you do not see. I am dying. *The Sigilli will be unleashed.*'

Edgar felt a fear greater than he had ever known.

'What do you hold prisoner?' he said. 'What is it, that is going to escape?'

'She is a creature worse than fate. Why do you think they keep me only half alive? So she can nourish herself with every ounce of my being. Extracting my life will give her only a little pleasure.'

'Who is she?' Edgar said.

'Nothing like these putrid dungeon spies. She is the Queen of the White Moth. She will spawn an army from terrible light and rise like a shadow over the land and black out the sun.'

The Seal was silent. He closed his eyes, whether from the pain, or the battle that raged with the creature escaping him, Edgar could not tell. Then he raised his head.

'There is nothing more I can say.' He spoke now without the slightest trace of pain. 'Without my incantations, they knew the chains would not hold her for long. They have already set her free. Taken her to the chalk caves, where she is feeding on the memory of the Caravanassi. She is growing an army of White Moth and once she has succeeded, you will never defeat her.'

'There must be something we can do,' Edgar stood still.

'Her spawn will cover the skies. They are not like these decrepit Dungeon Moth. They will glow with her light and, when they change into their warrior forms, they will become an ever-replenishing army who will march over the land and never stop fighting, until they die.'

'There must be a way,' Edgar said. 'A fail safe?'

The Seal laughed. 'If you knew what I know, you would not be saying such things.'

'This land has mysteries that neither you nor I can fathom.'

The Seal, slumped forward on his chains, raised himself once more.

'You know as well as I that they have opened up a Rupture to a dark city. Once the White Moth have cleansed the land of all that lives in the light of a Keeper, the *Shadows will rise again*. You know this to be true.'

'I will believe it when I see it.'

'Oh yes,' said the Seal, 'you will see it. And then you will believe it.'

He focused on the door. Released the latch.

'I made my oaths,' he said, 'oaths I never intended to break. But hear this. If you ever escape from here, get her out. Out of this land and far, far away. She is in danger here, more danger than you can imagine. It is not only Ramus and his army. The other Seals will hunt her, too. Now go,' he said, 'while you still can. They are coming.'

Edgar flew into the passage, then turned.

'Where will I find her?'

'A door encased with a metal plating, not gold, but brass,' the Seal murmured, his voice suddenly weakened. He fell against the chains, at first barely moving, then still. Edgar could not tell if he was dead or alive. But he knew there would not be life in him for long.

## CHAPTER 35

# I GIVE YOU MY NAME

'A brass door? That really narrows it down,' Edgar said, swooping through the dark. He searched wherever his wings took him, frantic in his flight, until he heard a voice.

He flew into the high spaces of the passage, from where he could see two Dungeon Moths standing guard outside a door. The voice was Adeline's. She was dressed in a black cloak and Edgar could see her pouring white powder from a little vial into her outstretched hand.

'My father sent me here to give you this. It is a gift for your patience.'

She blew the powder into a cloud. The two Moths changed forms back and forth in delight, fluttering to her pale hand as she poured out more of the white powder.

When they had settled in her palm, she gently closed her fingers and held them shut. She took out her key and opened the door, throwing the stupefied Moths into the far corner of the cell.

Jemma came out.

'Thank the Scarp,' Edgar said, and flew to her shoulder as Adeline removed her black hood.

Soren followed and looked at Edgar. 'I am pleased to see you, Raven,' he said. 'Who would have thought you would be a *good* omen.'

'And I'm pleased to hear you no longer believe in ridiculous superstitions,' Edgar said. 'But I think we have someone else to thank.'

Jemma went to Adeline. 'I knew you'd come,' she said.

Soren held out his hand. 'I am a wrestler from the Wharf. I have known Jemma since she were a child. A friend of hers, is a friend of mine.'

'It is a great honour to meet you.' Adeline raised her hood. 'But we mustn't linger here. Come this way.'

Jemma had never seen Adeline before without her fine dresses, her hair tied up in knots and curls. In the black hessian cloak her eyes were an even deeper green.

Soren walked behind the others, scouring the shadows.

'We must be quiet. Stay close,' Adeline said.

She led them through a dark winding passage and then to a grey door. Taking out her key, she opened the lock and pushed against the stone.

'This way,' she pointed, 'to the garden – then through the olive grove, to the outer wall. The Moths will be on their way.'

Edgar flew on, scouting ahead.

As they followed, Adeline took Jemma's hand. 'I'm sorry. For what I said before.'

Jemma paused. She wanted to say something, but she couldn't find the words.

'I know it now,' Adeline said. 'All of it. The truth. Thanks to you. And I think I know why "Father" gave me the key. In case he ended up locked in a cell, like that other poor wretch we found. He must have thought that my love would save him. That is how he bred me. Well, now it has. I am going with you.'

Soren came rushing through the door, swiping his face. 'A cloud of Moths are coming. Watch out for their dust – it stings your eyes.'

Adeline turned and locked the door. 'We must hurry. This won't hold them for long.'

They ran into the garden where they had first picked the yellow flowers, passing the fountain, and on through the orchard until they came to the boundary wall.

Soren was trying to climb it, but there was nothing to take hold of and he fell back to the ground.

Edgar flew above and saw the Moths gathering at the top of the grove, their numbers overwhelming, changing into their human forms. Jemma recognised the one she had seen in Sir Francis's study. Magden. His face was dusted with powder and spittle dripped from his mouth.

'I will have the Raven,' Magden called. 'He crippled my son. Now he will never change again. Never fly.'

Soren paced the line of Moths, facing them as if he was back in the wresting tents when the crowd cheered as he splayed his strength.

Edgar flew to Jemma and Adeline. 'There must be a way to climb over.'

'You will never get away from here.'

A sweet, mocking voice came from above them in the trees.

'At least, not without my help.'

The Peacock landed before them in a flurry of feathers. Then she changed into the same exquisite human form revealed to Edgar the night before.

'I have been watching you, Erigena. And I think you will be needing this.'

She held out the Book of Memory.

Jemma took it in her hands, feeling the blade of Adocentyn glowing warm against her chest. 'I never thought I'd see this again,' she said. 'But why? The Collector...he'll finish you off for this.'

'I would rather be stuffed and displayed in a cabinet than be dead already, as a living relic. Besides, I know that you will never forget me. He never took my name. And now I give it to you.'

Magden came forward. He threw a plume of powder into the air and a thousand Dungeon Moths changed into a swarming cloud.

The Peacock changed again and flew full speed towards them, her eyes fixed on Magden.

'Wait,' Jemma cried, 'I don't know what it is – your name?'

'Leorah!'

She disappeared into the cloud of Moths, beating against them with her beautiful wings.

Edgar followed but he could not hold himself in flight and was quickly overwhelmed, falling to the ground.

Jemma called out to him, but he was already lost in the cloud of Moths.

Soren ran to protect Jemma, but the Moths were already upon her, filling her every sense with silky dust. She coughed and choked and then she could not breathe. She fell to the base of the wall, madly swiping at her eyes to clear the sickly fluttering Moths.

She felt the same grip of filthy arms dragging her back into an even thicker swarm, except she could not see or hear or smell a thing. Her senses were stuffed with Moth dust.

There was a wind swirling around her and she imagined it was the Scarp-palace dissolving into oblivion. She cried out for Edgar. A shadow engulfed her, towering above.

The Moths, who were in their human form, hugged their rags about their frames and changed in fear, joining the swarm flying towards the olive grove.

The wind was like a tornado that ripped their wings.

Jemma wiped the dust out of her eyes and ran to Adeline, who was slashing at the Moths clinging to her face, her hair and hands.

It was a machine! The one she had seen in Camillo's workshop, but now all the parts were folded out, a magnificent assemblage of pulleys and wheels that turned huge canvass blades. Camillo landed.

'Come on, get in!' he called over the deafening noise of the rotating blades.

Sorenstar lifted each of them into the contraption, then jumped on board.

Camillo thrust the lever up so the blades spun ferociously, the powerful winds blasting the Moths again, scattering them like pollen into the trees.

They rose into the air.

Edgar, recovering himself, dived onto the platform and scuttled against the sides. But Camillo had not perfected the flight. They lurched first to one side, then to the other, the very weight of the propellers keeping them so low they barely cleared the wall.

'Quickly,' Camillo said, pointing to a barrel of water. 'You must wash away the Moth dust before it sets into a resin and blinds you.'

Jemma splashed the water onto her eyes and nose and mouth, even her ears. Her face felt like it was on fire and she was unable to wash away the foulness of the taste no matter how much water she used. She poured some onto Soren's face, who lay exhausted on the deck.

Adeline washed the dust from her face, while Edgar

submerged himself completely, preening his feathers, shaking himself free of the sludge coating his wings.

'I am so terribly sorry,' Camillo said, heaving a large windmill-like rudder, propelling them forward. 'I have been wracked with guilt for sending you there. I should have known better.'

'Where are we going?' Jemma said, clutching the Book with one hand and the side of the flying machine with the other as they lurched again, only just clearing the buildings.

Ahead of them in the West, in the setting sun, were the spires of an enormous wrestling tent along the edges of Adocentyn's harbour, and the crimson sea. Behind them lay the shadow of the Moth swarm, the Collector's palace at the top of the hill, its hexagonal spire casting a long shadow upon the grove. The tower of lights rose above it all, sweeping its beams over the city.

Below, to the East, a valley of forest and mist and a road beyond, where lines of travellers – was it the Caravanassi? – wandered with carts and wagons.

The city itself descended to the sea in walls of sandstone glowing golden in the setting sun.

'Night is coming,' Camillo said. 'We must go to the wrestling tents at once and find the Delphin Prince. Do you still have the letter?'

Jemma felt inside her vest, beside the golden blade. But her voice was shaking, thinking of Leorah lost forever in the shadows of the grove.

'Yes, it's here.'

'If it contains what I think it does, the Delphin Prince will have to join us. And we will need his help.'

A wind behind sent them hurtling through the air. Camillo swerved and plunged the lever down.

'Brace yourselves!'

The landing was even worse than the flight. They crashed into a cushion of dark foliage and tumbled out before the wrestling tent, the blades tearing themselves apart in the trees.

Camillo lay in the grass, a little dazed. 'Not as bad as I thought,' he said, pulling himself up.

'I am Pico Camillo, by the way. And you are?'

'Adeline.'

'And I am Soren.'

'I have heard of you,' Camillo said. 'A great wrestler.'

'Not so great, I'm afraid.'

Camillo looked towards the tent. 'That remains to be seen. Our fight has only just begun.'

Jemma untangled herself from the bushes and peered at the enormous wrestling tent.

'You will have to go inside and wait. Give the letter to the Delphin Prince,' Camillo said. 'The rest of us will find a boat. I will signal with a light. We do not have much time.'

'She will not go alone.' Soren folded his arms. 'I know all of the ways inside and out. I will go with her.'

'Very well,' Camillo said, 'but I will need the Raven to scout for a boat.'

'My name is Edgar, actually.'

Edgar perched on Jemma's shoulder and then flew up to a high branch, looking out over the harbour.

'In any case, I can see plenty of boats already,' he called down to Camillo.

'Yes, but who is inside, Raven? We don't want to set off the alarm before we even begin.'

Jemma was clutching the Book of Memory to her chest. She held it out to Camillo. 'Here, you better take this.'

'I'll keep it safe,' he said. 'You have my word.'

'Be careful,' Adeline said, hugging Jemma. She turned up her hood and followed Camillo and Edgar.

Jemma watched them disappearing through the trees,

feeling the same, sudden loss as when she had parted from Edgar on the Cray boat. It was the sense of something slipping and falling forever inside her ravine. She had once believed that to be an orphan was to take what you needed, only for yourself. She had felt the burden of the Erigena, and the guilt of knowing the truth. But to Keep is to hold another and to never let them go – it had to be.

She took Soren's hand.

'Let's go.'

# PART V
# WHITE NIGHT

# CHAPTER 36

## THE DELPHIN PRINCE

Soren lifted the heavy canvas side of the wrestling tent.

'You first,' he said.

Jemma rolled herself under and Soren followed. They were inside a dressing room. She peered through the door, seeing at once two enormous tanks.

It was like nothing she had seen in the Wharf. The tanks were over twenty feet high with a wide fighting platform running between.

The match had begun and the two contestants were clashing on the platform, sliding past each other and into the tanks.

Jemma saw the Delphin Prince change from his human form as he dived into the tank, swimming magnificently, turning and spinning in the crystal water. Whenever the fighters leaped out again onto the platform, they changed into human form, then back to Seal or Dolphin in the tanks.

The Prince struck the wrestling Seal, who fell tumbling into the opposite tank, a streak of blood like an arrow trailing behind. The Seal then emerged on the platform, stronger and angrier, smashing against the Prince and sending them both tumbling into the tank.

Clouds of red billowed around them and it was difficult to see. The Delphin swam and hit the Seal hard in the side, appearing only for a moment on the platform before diving again into the opposite tank. The crowd was roaring so loud Jemma could hardly feel her own heart.

Now he swam all the way down to the bottom – the crowd still cheering wildly. And with the pure indulgence of performance, the Delphin sprang from his tail and launched himself up through the water, changing and striking the Seal in mid-air, where they spun interlocked, then thumped down to the platform together.

The Seal had fallen harder and the Delphin Prince, taking hold of his weakened frame, pinned him to the ground. In the tradition of the defeated, the Seal changed, recoiling in pain.

But then he writhed in agony. An arrow had struck him out of nowhere.

Panic shot through the crowd. Jemma looked up to the tops of the stalls and saw Poachers in their black robes, arrows reigning down.

There were people falling in front of her, others running, screaming, trampling on whoever was in their way.

Soren hoisted Jemma onto a ladder at the back of the tanks.

The Delphin, dodging an arrow, dived into the pool. The archers had seen Jemma and were walking over the crowd, light-footed, using fallen bodies as steppingstones. An arrow whizzed past her, ricocheting off the tank.

*That must be Halogaic glass*, she thought. Then she had an idea. She banged on the tank until she had caught the attention of the Prince and signalled for him to swim higher up. Then she turned to Soren.

'You've got to climb up to that other tank and swim to the top,' she said. 'Wait for my signal.'

Soren shot up the stairs, dived in and changed into his Walrus form. Then Jemma cut two long slashes in the glass, one in each tank, and pulled herself up to the platform.

At first the water only trickled from the cuts, but then a great cracking noise released two enormous waves. Soren and the Delphin swam through the wave and reached the highest stalls where they swept through a line of archers, and then changed, sending the archers flying into the surging tide. The people below, no longer crushed, rose to the surface, gasping.

The Prince grabbed hold of a bow and flung arrows at the hooded archers who were now clinging to the sides of the tent.

Sorenstar dived back into the water and leaped onto the platform where Jemma stood. One of the archers, with his bow fully strung, held her in his sights. He must have been ordered to keep her alive and in his confusion he turned to Soren. But Jemma charged at the archer and pushed him to the edge where he stumbled and fell into the muddy swamp below.

'This way!' Soren pointed below.

They scrambled down to the Delphin Prince, who was holding up a side of canvas leading to his dressing room.

'Who are you?' he said, as they stepped into the room. 'Wait, you're that Walrus from the Wharf. I gave you the thrashing of your life.'

'And I'll give you one now if you don't shut up and follow us.'

The Prince was taking swigs from an aniseed flask. 'I

follow no one but myself,' he said. 'But those archers weren't after me. They were after the girl. Who is she?'

Jemma handed him the scroll.

He took another swig as he unrolled it. But almost immediately his expression changed. A look of disbelief, almost horror, came over him.

'Oh no,' he said, 'no, no, no, not an Oath!'

He flung the letter away.

'Anything but an Oath!'

'What is it?' Jemma said. 'What does it say?'

The Delphin Prince kept muttering over and over, cursing and drinking and cursing until a familiar voice sounded from the edges of the tent.

'It is an Oath to follow the Erigena, to protect you, Jemma, till the ends of memory, forever and for all of time.' Camillo pushed himself through the canvas, 'And you know what that means, my young Prince Aspar.'

'What right has she to slap an Oath on me?' The Delphin Prince flung the empty flask against a barrel so it smashed into pieces.

'Still having your tantrums, I see,' Camillo said. 'Why don't you ask her yourself. We are going to the Delphin Caves right now – unless you wish to break your Oath before it has even begun?'

He turned to Jemma. 'We have found passage, with a good friend of yours, I do believe.'

## CHAPTER 37

# WHO YOU ARE

It was already dark when they reached the outskirts of the harbour. The boat was hidden between the landing shacks, a figure standing at the stern.

Jemma recognised the piles of craypots at once.

'Arlen!'

He stood taller than she remembered him.

'I kn-knew I'd s-see you again.'

She leaped on board and hugged him. He did not look away shyly this time. Now it was Arlen standing at the engines, reading the patterns of stars in the sky.

'G-got to hurry,' he said. 'H-Harpooners will be coming soon.'

'I'm not getting on *that*.' Prince Aspar folded his arms.

'Transport not fit for a Prince?' Camillo said sharply. 'Go on then, back to your mud bath, where you can swim in the muck of your broken Oath.' He stepped onto the boat. 'Let us move.'

Arlen turned the engines low and they drifted out, the Delphin Prince leaping on board only at the last minute. He stormed past Camillo and into the cabin below.

'I will keep watch from the front,' Soren said, scrambling through the craypots, 'and keep my eye on him.'

Jemma turned to Arlen.

'Edgar told me – they stole your things,' she said. 'All your treasures.'

'S-s alright,' he said. 'W-weren't mine anyway. S-still g-got the Whale-lines.'

'But your father...'

His eyes turned away, gazing up watery into the stars. Jemma might have disliked the old Cray, but she never meant for this to happen. That he would be made to suffer for her, in a cell. He held his word, after all.

'Th-that was his honour,' Arlen said.

They drifted without lights through the harbour walls, until the engines fired and they followed a Whale-line towards the Delphin Caves.

Jemma took Adeline to the cabins below and showed her where the clawed spear was still mounted in the boat and told her all about their escape from the Harpooners, and the Delphin Queen with their magnificent hall, where they would be given a sumptuous banquet and have their own warm pools of mineral springs and see the most amazing acrobatics.

'I warn you now,' Prince Aspar stepped forward and took a swig from an aniseed flask he had found in the Cray's cabin, 'there will be no such welcome for me. They'll cast me out again. You wait and see.'

'A self-fulfilling prophecy, is it not?' Camillo appeared at the hatch. He climbed down into the cabin and sat at the table. 'Or perhaps merely a case of self-pity.'

'You know nothing, old man.' The Delphin waved the flask in his face.

'I know who you are,' Camillo said.

'And who is that?'

'I'll leave that up to you to find out for yourself.'

The Prince, tightening his grip on the bottle, stared hard at Camillo and then disappeared through the hatch and onto the deck.

'Why is he like that?' Adeline said, looking out after him.

'He is still the brooding boy who left all those who loved him,' Camillo said. 'Full of the pride and rebelliousness of his heart. Never admitting the great fear of his responsibility. To return home is to begin again where you left off. All that has been since then, all that you think you have become, is folly and illusion. We must let him be. And besides, he is very nearly drunk and he will be looking for a fight.'

'With who?'

'Himself, projected onto an enemy the shape of which he does not care. He has been hiding all his life from this very night.'

'Then I will watch him,' Adeline said, 'I know he will not strike me.' She raised her hood and went out into the night.

Jemma ground some powder from the flintstone, striking swiftly to make a spark. She lit a candle and a fire inside the peat stove, and then she made them a pot of black leaf tea. Edgar flew in from patrolling the skies.

'I can see you have done this before,' Camillo said. 'It is quite a skill, is it not?'

Jemma cupped the warm mug of tea in her cold hands. She did not answer. This was no time for small talk. It was time for answers.

Camillo took a sip from his tea.

'When you first arrived, your presence set a cloud over me,' he said. 'A heaviness. Memories returned that I thought I had conquered. And when I awoke from my delirium, I realised what I had done, and I was very nearly too late.'

'What was too late?' Jemma said.

Camillo shifted in the hard wooden chair. 'It seems that it is worse than I had ever imagined.'

He placed the Book of Memory on the table and opened it. Jemma could see the word that made her heart leap. *Sigilli.* Edgar came to her side.

'I know they caught the Seal,' she said. 'I heard them talking. The Collector and the Moth they called Magden.'

'That treacherous spy,' Camillo said. 'Both he and the Collector will suffer for our escape. Ramus does not forgive as much as he does not forget. He no longer needs them, now that he has finally spawned an army.'

'What do you mean?' Jemma said.

Edgar turned the page to an image of a creature of pale beauty, with dark eyes and black lips, her wings glowing with the same bright phosphorous Jemma had seen emanating from the chalk caves. Above her outstretched wings, a swarming cloud blacked out the sun.

'I was put into the same cell as the Seal,' Edgar said. 'He is the one who helped me to escape.'

'Why would he do that?' Jemma said. 'I thought he was supposed to be hunting me.'

'I do not know,' Edgar took a sip of tea. 'Perhaps he thought it was hopeless, anyway. When I left the cell, he did not have many breaths left.' He pointed to the picture. 'This is what he released. The Queen of the White Moth.'

They all looked at the page, their tea growing cold.

'It says here, the White Moth feed off the memory of sorrow,' Edgar said. 'If that is what they are somehow creating with these loops of the Caravanassi...if she is feeding off the energy that is released from their suffering, the skies may soon be swarming.'

Even now Jemma could hear that whispering. It was full of energy and anguish and it sounded like the fluttering wings of a million Moths.

'Does it say how we defeat her?' Jemma held the candle over the page.

'All that is written here are the incantations, and the practices of meditation for the Seals to imprison the Sigilli entrusted to them,' Camillo said. 'Now that she is released, there is nothing here that can tell us what to do.'

'Then what was the use of stealing the Book?' Jemma said. 'What was the use of giving Bruno the map, and saving the Keepers' memory – any of it – if we can't do *anything*?'

'We go to Raddahkin,' Camillo said. 'We have no choice but to prepare for war. And, most importantly, he will know how to train our most important weapon.'

'And what is that?' Jemma asked.

'It is you.'

～

CAMILLO'S LONG GREY HAIR SHIMMERED LIKE A WEB IN the candlelight.

'Do you think it is a coincidence that all the powers of this land are seeking you? What are they so afraid of, do you suppose? What do they desire? These are the questions I asked myself. And on the morning you left with that little thieving Finch, I set off in search of some answers for myself. Raddahkin knew much about you, but not all. He said that if I wished to discover the rest of the story, I would have to find a housekeeper who lived in the palace with Bruno, and who fled when the Seal destroyed it. And he wanted me to tell you about your parents before I brought you to him.'

'I know her,' Jemma said. 'When we first went into the

Scarp-palace, I heard that housekeeper talking about a girl. Now I know it was me. She told Bruno I was safe. That she'd been watching me. That the Terns would never let a hair be harmed on my head. So Raddahkin knew about my parents before, and he didn't say anything in case it got in the way of us bringing back this Book. Well, now I have, and I know what you're going to tell me. You're going to say, "Jiordano Bruno is your father". Why else would he have cared at all? That's what you're going to tell me, isn't it?'

'If only it were that simple.' Camillo paused, and sipped his lukewarm tea. 'He is, in part.'

'What do you mean, "in part"?'

'You were already born when your mother and Bruno first met. He had grown obsessed with the prophecy of the Erigena, not least because it threatened his own powers.'

Camillo turned to the last page of the Book. Drawn across the page was the line of a passage from Adocentyn to another point on a map, where a second sun radiated in circles and strange symbols. At the centre was the golden blade and an image of a girl surrounded by a vast shadow, in which three Sigilli were etched. There were numbers scribbled in the margins, and swirling lines running all over the page, as if to connect or to decipher, it was impossible to say.

'These are the co-ordinates that he discovered. You were from the world Bruno left behind, but of another time and another place. This is where his calculations led him. For many years, he laboured to make a Rupture in reverse, so he could find you.'

'I don't understand,' Jemma said. 'How can I be from another world?'

'Your parents were both scholars of the ancient Arts of Memory. They worked together at a university, deciphering forgotten texts, and this first passion lead to another, but it did not last. Your father was more ambitious than your mother, but she was more brilliant. He refused to let anything get in the way of his work, including the burdens of being a parent.'

'You mean he left us?'

'Not completely. They still laboured together on the manuscripts that were both of their life's work. When Bruno finally succeeded in crafting this passage, he walked easily into their world, being a Magus himself. It was not difficult for him to pose as a visiting professor. It was like he was a key that did not merely open doors, but whole universes of mystery that had for years alluded them. But Bruno was not expecting to fall in love with your mother. As you can imagine, your father became jealous, but not only because of their growing affection for each other. The thought that Bruno was giving more secrets to her fuelled him with anger. He had been growing obsessed with the idea of travelling between worlds, into the realms of memory that he had only read about. His actions grew increasingly erratic. He threatened to expose Bruno, to expose him as a fraud, but who would have believed his story of memory-lands? Instead, he used the knowledge Bruno had revealed to find the Rupture. He must have over-head him telling your mother of his fears about the Erigena. When he walked through the passage, he brought you with him. You were not yet three years old.'

'Why?'

'Perhaps to punish your mother. Or else to satisfy his yearning to understand our land's mysteries. He secured the use of a Navigator and travelled first to the Raven Halls that lay beyond Adocentyn in the South, on the edges of the unformed lands, where he told them of the prophecy. Edgar will have to tell you if he remembers an explorer coming into the court.'

'The Raven have long been hospitable to travellers, explorers, navigators of all sorts,' Edgar said, 'who have opened the beginnings of paths, so long as they agreed to share their discoveries, or extend our Scrolls. Although, I never met such a one as you describe.'

'In any case,' Camillo continued, 'this began the Raven's search through the records, for any mention of a prophecy. It must have become apparent to your father that you were in danger, Jemma. Why would he be travelling with a small child and seeking such knowledge? He fled the Raven Court and scoured the shores until he came to the smallest, most insignificant place in the lands of Adocentyn. Soren was known for his honour and his warm heart. Most importantly, your father must have recognised the pattern of the loop in which he was caught. And that is where he left you, wrapped in a bundle of cane-fleece on the edge of the Wharf, before disappearing.'

'Where did he go?'

'No one knows. That was the last sighting of him, the day he left you and sailed away in a Navigator, one of the explorer's ships. There are many unstable regions beyond Adocentyn, unshaped, untamed by a memory Magus. Perhaps he went away in shame of what he had done. Who knows?'

Jemma felt a thousand different emotions crowding inside her, each as incomprehensible as the next. She wanted to take off and search for him at once, but then a wave of anger washed in and her breathing felt strange. A yearning for him, love and release and bitterness came next.

'If he worked out Soren was caught in that loop, he must have known that as long as he was a prisoner, I would be safe. He left him to suffer, all that time, for me?'

'Had he been given the choice, Sorenstar would have suffered twice as much to protect you. But when Bruno discovered what your father had done, he was furious. He stormed back through the Rupture and sealed it before your mother could follow. At first, she fell into a deep despair. But she was just as wilful. Bruno had revealed many secrets, enough for her to find another Rupture, to a place somewhere in the unformed lands, where the Seals could not find her, but from where she could try to find you. Perhaps a place you both remember.'

How could something make sense, but be impossible to comprehend? It was a wild feeling that came over her, swirling like the pulses of pure energy she had seen in the chalk caves, containing all the hope and all the answers she had ever dreamed. Yet still the anger seethed inside her until she couldn't tell the difference between sadness and love.

'I can feel that she's here,' Jemma said. 'She's like my Keeper, isn't she? That's why I can hear her voice, in the lights.' And she knew the flickering images of the film she'd seen so long ago in the Scarp-palace were real. Her playing in the shallows. The woman telling her she'd speak to her in the whispers of the lights. It was real, the memory dissolved and melted on the bulb of that old projector.

'There is one last thing you should know,' Camillo said. 'Your father did not come here only with you. He told another about the passage. An acquaintance of his. Of course, you know him, only too well. Sir Francis Gilbert travelled with your father as far as the Raven Halls. That is where they parted. Sir Francis found his way to Adocentyn, where he made that fateful partnership with Ramus, who had already made his passage into the city. Sir Francis is the one who told Ramus of the prophecy of the Erigena. And you know the rest of the story, from there. But not how it will end.'

Jemma was bristling, nauseated, wishing the Collector a

fate worse than Gassendi's when she had seen his fingers worming through the grate. Edgar pecked gently at her shoulder.

'I can see the effect this has had on you,' Camillo said. 'I am sorry that you have such little time to comprehend it. But we must hurry and ask for the protection of the Delphin. These waters are far too dangerous to travel alone.'

He turned to Edgar, who was looking again at the image of the Erigena. 'That is a dangerous book for those who do not know how to use it.' Edgar bowed and stepped back as Camillo closed it.

'We must return the Book of Memory to the one who created it. Kept from the hands of charlatans who seek to exploit its magic.'

The light from the candle, which had been flickering, turned steady. Something had changed. Jemma registered it, even through the sick feeling in her stomach. All three looked to the hatch.

'Why are we stopped, in the middle of the ocean?'

## CHAPTER 38

# THE MEMORY SEED

'Where are they?' Prince Aspar whirled, stumbling, shouting into the darkness. 'I'll fight them. I'll fight them all!'

'Qu-quiet now,' Arlen said. He had stalled the engines in case the Prince fell overboard.

Adeline stood away from Aspar as he brought the bottle of aniseed to his lips. Finishing the bottle, he threw it over his shoulder, where it smashed into the engine case.

'Fool!' Camillo said.

Edgar helped Jemma pick up the broken glass and drop it in a craypot.

Aspar was about to dive into the water when Soren grabbed him, fighting the drunk and thrashing throws.

'This is how I could have beat you,' Soren said, 'so now you know, eh? The grip of Sorenstar.'

When he stopped struggling, Soren released him.

'What are you all looking at?' Aspar said, retreating to the cabin, as Arlen fired the engines.

'It's alright,' Adeline said, following after the Prince. 'I think it is because he is so close to home.'

There were no guards swimming in their wake as they approached the Delphin Caves. And when they entered the gates, no torches blazed on the landing. All was empty and quiet but for the constant dripping from deep inside the caves and the occasional sound of rock crumbling and falling into the pools.

Jemma led the way.

'Hello?' she called out into the caves.

No one answered.

She felt the awful silence and the stagnant air and she knew something horrible must have happened. As they wandered through the empty halls, there was not even the hope of someone hiding, survivors or soldiers. There was only a dread emptiness.

Jemma pushed through the heavy curtains into the Great Hall. There was nothing. No candles glowing in the honeycomb walls. No tumbling acrobats. The banquet table had been smashed and looted.

'So now you have your candles, Sir Francis Gilbert,' she scorned.

It was only then the extent of the desecration − the annihilation − struck home. Her body grew numb as she went into the passages beyond. She came to the Keeper's chamber. The pool was still and black, where she remembered the white Porpoise leaping out, slumped forward, touching her temples.

Aspar had followed her. He struck a line of flint and set the wall lamps ablaze. Then he fell to his knees at the edge of the pool.

'I'm sorry,' Jemma said. Tears welled in her eyes. 'I should have saved them.'

'Why didn't you!' The Prince gripped his hands into fists of rage.

'Why didn't *you*?' Jemma retorted. 'You were meant to return, to be the Keeper. Amara waited for *you*.'

The Prince cried out into the empty caves. 'Then why haven't I perished too? Why am I still here?'

It was only then she realised what the gift of the white Porpoise was. A memory seed.

She took off the jewel from around her neck. It was as if she had always known what to do.

At that moment, Adeline came into the chamber, and stood beside the pool.

'You've got to come here,' Jemma said to Aspar. 'I need to give you this.'

She threw the jewel into the dark water. At first, it sank right down into the invisible deep. But then a point of light appeared and it grew and dispersed the darkness so the pool glowed turquoise again and seemed alive.

The Prince stood, looking in. 'What...what am I supposed to do?'

'Look,' Jemma said. 'What do you see?'

An image began to appear. The memory seed opened to the picture of a boy standing alone in the Great Hall, looking up at the Delphin warriors carved into the walls. Aspar could not take his eyes away.

Adeline gently took hold of his arm. 'He will be here for some time, I can see. I cannot remember what I have lost, but I will wait with him, for as long as it takes, for him to recover his people's memory. But you must go, Jemma,' she said. 'They will be sending an army soon. When I went to find you in my father's palace, I saw them – the White Moth – breeding in the caves. They looked so fierce and hungry, feeding on the light. It will be a terrible swarm washing over the land. You must warn the other Keepers. The ones you told me were still alive.'

The two girls looked at each other, as if for the last time. Jemma went to go, but then she stopped. 'What you said to me, that time I saw you in the hall. It was true,' she said. 'I did hurt you. I made everything unbearable. No matter what you chose.'

Adeline held the shaking Prince by the edge of the pool. She steadied him so he wouldn't fall. 'Not anymore,' she said. 'I choose this.'

A rush of wings descended into the chamber.

'I have flown to the lookout,' Edgar said. 'The Harpooners are heading straight for the caves.'

Jemma followed him through the passages. Edgar flew ahead, stealing seconds in the air, flying into the Delphin hall, trying to imagine the banquet coming alive.

'I wish I could have set my eyes on all of this,' he said, 'all its colour and life. Will you paint me a picture of how it looked, so that I may one day tell of its splendour in the words of a scroll.'

'I can't,' Jemma said. 'Not here. Not now.' She felt the loss itself pulling her in. The terrible fear she had felt alone in the dungeon. The memory of the Delphin Caves – it was seeking to live. She must not disturb its path as it drew towards the pool of the Keeper.

'And I'm so afraid...of what I could do.'

Her anger boiled as she passed the banquet table. As it peaked, the form of a Gull came swooping through the cave and changed into its human form, a warrior, fierce and striking with vengeance, then disappearing again into the dark.

'What on earth was that?' Edgar said. 'How ever did you do it?'

'I don't know.' She looked into the empty hall. 'It just comes when I feel the anger.'

'Then you must learn to use it,' Edgar said. 'You have powers at your disposal, that you do not even yet know that you possess. Raddahkin will help you to wield them, as weapons. And we will need them, if we are to have any chance at all of defeating the White Moth.'

## CHAPTER 39

# THE WEAPONS INSIDE

They travelled through the night, leaving Adeline and Aspar behind. Jemma watched the Harpooner's lights flashing in the distance. Arlen's eyes were fixed on the stars.

'Those thugs are on our tail,' Camillo said. 'But they would not dare to enter the waters of the Terns. Even so, we must keep an eye on them. They will throw everything at us when the time comes.'

Steely shapes glistened ahead. Soon they were close enough to smell the boiling pots of the great fire stoves on the barges of the Terns.

Jemma stood beside Camillo looking at the cliffs. The ridges seemed to be etched by starlight, the walls of shale a black monolith hidden in the dark. Already, in the distance, she could see the shape of the wrestling tent at the Wharf, the camps filled with Caravanassi and the jetty where she had first dived for sea-fennel. The fleet of Tern ships were anchored opposite, floating like an island. It was a strange feeling, returning home – seeing yourself as you were before, but no longer who you are. Now she understood why Aspar wanted to escape it.

She went down into the cabin.

Soren lay on a bench near the table, sleeping. There were no candles burning in the cabin and in the starlight, in the pale glow filtering through the window, she could see his wounds, still raw. She remembered all the nights when she had seen his scars and eaten the bitter soup and she almost wanted them to return. As she drifted into the memory, she barely noticed Sharmenai sitting in the corner.

'Why did you take him from me?' Sharmenai said just like before, except now she was even closer to being a Shadow.

'Give him to me,' she said, her gaze fixed upon the wounds. 'Give him back.'

'You know I...can't,' Jemma said. For a moment, she didn't believe that anything had happened since the time she had first set foot in the Scarp. The Shadow city. The Delphin Caves. The Collector's Palace. Arlen and Adeline. The story Camillo had told. They were fading on the very edges of her mind.

'I wouldn't even know how.'

Sharmenai lunged at Jemma, who stumbled back into the corner of the cabin and screamed for Edgar as she held out the golden blade. Its piercing light cast a shroud of blackness at its edges. Sharmenai was gone.

'What is it?' Camillo rushed down as fast as his body would let him and Edgar darted into the room, scouring every corner, half expecting a Moth to appear.

'It was her, again,' Jemma said. 'Sharmenai.'

Camillo helped Jemma to the table. 'Raddahkin told me the story of how you freed Soren, cut the loop, but you had also taken her memory. He said that as we travel closer to the Wharf, she may come for you.'

'I didn't mean to take him from her...' Jemma huddled into her chair. 'It was her memory and I took it away. The only thing she had.'

'And yet, could you have left Soren enslaved in that loop?' Camillo said. 'Come, girl, I think fresh air will help.'

❧

THE DAWN WAS A MISTY RED THAT JEMMA IMAGINED appearing only in the dreams of Crays.

'This is a colour I have not seen for a long time,' Camillo said.

Black smoke rose in coils from the Tern ships.

'The smell of tar,' Jemma said.

'That can mean only one thing,' Camillo sniffed the air. 'The Terns are preparing for war.'

Arlen steered them through the passages of a vast flotilla of ships sitting opposite the Wharf. Jemma could smell the broth pots. The Terns were sitting along the railings in their human form, eating from their bowls, peering at her through the rising steam. Some had changed and flew high in circles above.

They followed the maze of ship paths, taking them in ever smaller circles until they reached the very centre of the spiral. Arlen secured their ropes against the dark and ancient wood of the Tern Keeper's ship.

Edgar flew up to see, but the flying Terns keeping guard above swooped around him and he thought better of it.

'Patience, Raven,' Camillo said. 'She must go alone.'

Arlen nodded as Jemma climbed up a ladder and on to the ship.

The deck creaked under her feet. Everything else was completely quiet, her steps the fixed point of all attention.

At the end of the running planks she recognised the

doorway and stairs leading down and, as she had done before, she went into the dark passages below and to Raddahkin's door.

No one had followed her. She could hear the silence in her ears, the pulse of her heart. For a moment, she did not want to enter. All she could feel was the dread of what was to come.

Thinking of the Wharf, she remembered what Camillo had said of the Delphin Prince: 'To return home is to begin again where you left off. All that has been since then, all that you think you have become, is mere folly and illusion.' She felt like the biggest fool of all. Everything the prophecy said had come true. She'd seen the Shadows with her own eyes. The White Moth would rise again and soon blot out the sun. They had saved Bruno – she hoped – ruined the Book in the city of Shadows and recovered the last copy in Adocentyn. But it didn't matter. Thanks to Sir Francis, Ramus had used the prophecy against them. The biggest folly of all was the idea that she could save anything. Wasn't this what the Erigena was supposed to do? She had not felt the full weight of it until now. All she had really done was to travel in a circle, where nothing seemed to begin or end, except the knowledge she had gained and the fact that she still knew nothing.

The truth was she felt more afraid now than any time she had been in the Shadow city, in the dungeons of the vaults of Ramus. She couldn't see any possible way to defeat the Queen of the Moth, the Sigilli. And if she could, that must mean she had something just as vast and terrible within herself. It was like the image of the girl she had seen on the final page of the Book of Memory, surrounded by the coil of darkness. She had always had the sense that she was standing on the edge of a bottomless ravine. This is why she needed to fill her mind with the mountains of the

Scarp. To seek the paths of the old treasure hunters. To keep going and never stop. It was always so she could fill this ravine. To push the emptiness away. She remembered the dreams of falling in, when Soren would soothe her night-terrors. She would fall and fall. She would clutch the sides but the walls of the ravine would suddenly become like sheets of ice and she'd slip again into the darkness. Falling. Grabbing hold. Slipping again. Jemma knew that whatever Raddahkin was going to tell her would take her back to the edge.

A wave of tiredness came over her and she sank to the floor outside his door. She didn't even know if they'd succeeded, if Bruno had escaped or returned. But why did it even matter if he was so weak? That must only mean she was the one to save them. And this was the cold fear that gripped her bones – that, somehow, she would have to Keep everything. What if she never found another place to take hold? What if it was like the Delphin Queen had said – that it would send her blind and drive her mad? Either way, she couldn't escape what was coming. Up until now she had always had a place to watch things from afar. She had kept part of herself separate in that distant place high up in the Scarp. But now she felt so many belonging to her.

Jemma picked herself up and went into Raddahkin's chamber. An oil lamp burned on the table. He was standing at the coal stove, tending a pot of black leaf tea.

'I want to know first how I'm supposed to defeat this creature they call the Sigilli – the White Moth. Because all the rest means nothing if I can't.'

'What you have said is true,' he fanned the stove-flames and shut the grate. 'To face this creature, you have to learn to use the powers of the Erigena.'

'Why didn't you show me back then? Before you sent us into all that darkness?'

'Because you were not ready to understand it.'

'You mean because it didn't suit your mission. What about mine?'

Raddahkin took the pot from the stove and poured the steaming tea. He sat down at the table. Jemma stood where she was. She did not take her cup.

'There may be a chance, once you hear what I have to say, that you'll take a different path. Let us be clear from the beginning. The choice will be yours. And when I answer your first question – how can you defeat this creature – I would not blame you, if you chose to walk away.'

'What does it matter anyway, if the prophecy is fate?'

'It matters a great deal,' Raddahkin said. 'Fate is only a set of conditions, a series of potential endings you form and shape and alter with the power of your own will. There is no outcome yet. There is no final sentence. That is what you have to write. And this is not like rolling a dice. What you choose means something. Those who you hold and refuse to let go. Those who do not deserve to suffer. Those who you love. The voices that you hear, alive, and those that call to you and you alone.'

'I don't even know what this Erigena is supposed to be.'

Raddahkin leaned into the light and put out his hand.

'This wood. Feel it,' he said. 'This is my substance. It is the basic material of all the remembrance of the Terns. It is the structure that holds all the other forms, images, life. Our memory. From it comes every nuance, every smell, every texture.'

'Why are you telling me this?' Jemma said.

'For all Keepers there is something basic, elemental, from which all else is built.'

'Like the Delphin Caves – it's the rock itself.'

'And for the great Whales, it is the sea. But you do not hold only one substance, do you?'

'What do you mean?'

'You already know,' Raddahkin said. 'You have felt it, all along, even if you could not say it. Haven't you.'

'You know nothing of how I feel,' Jemma said.

'Perhaps not. But this is what I can say. There is a substance that is of memory itself, out of which all the elements in their simple forms exist. The Keepers have only one of these elements. You have them all – wood, sea, rock, wind. And those that you Keep already, like the Arctic Gulls whose memory you can wield.'

Jemma remembered the Gull warrior in the Delphin hall, who had taken the form of her anger.

Raddahkin refilled his cup.

'It is the power not only to hold, but to use and shape the matter of memory as part of your will, intentions, feelings, actions. The Gulls are a part of you, as much as they exist in this land. As are the Whales, and everything else that you Keep. We have been watching you since the day your father first brought you to the land of Adocentyn and left you on the Wharf. We knew that one day it would be time for us to play our part. And that time is now.'

He stood and went to the door beside the stove, where she and Edgar had first set out for the Shadow city.

'You have much to learn if you wish to channel and control what you may ignite inside you. For in this land, what is inside of you can be outside too. There is no separation. It is one. And the memories interweave and make the forms of this land. You will have to use your powers if you wish to destroy the lights that feed the White Moth.'

'How?'

'Follow me.'

He led her through the door, and it was as if they had just stepped outside onto the edges of the sea, yet they were still inside the chambers.

'You have already learned how to cover images with the blanket of the dark – I saw you when you smothered the Shadow of Sharmenai with the golden blade. You will have to learn to go the other way around without the power overwhelming you.'

He called one of the Terns from high in the sky, striking it down towards her.

'Quickly,' he said. 'Defend yourself.'

Jemma drew out the blade but the Tern easily swerved to the side.

'A shroud will not work with a nimble flying Tern. What will you do this time?'

The Tern swooped and Jemma released a Gull, their wings locking, sending them spiralling down where they changed into their human forms and clashed. The Tern pinned the Gull to the ground. Jemma winced with the Gull's pain.

'I can't do it!'

'Don't underestimate what you can do. There are other weapons you possess,' Raddahkin said. 'Try again. Control. You must learn control. It is no different to holding the weapon in your hands. Learn to strike with precision.'

This time, Jemma sent a radiant form to strike the Tern, her spear pinning his shoulder to the ground. Leorah stood above the broken Tern, fierce, devoted. Smiling at her Keeper.

'I am guessing she must have given you her name,' Raddahkin said. 'That is a great honour to give. So now she is part of you. In time, you will learn to see through her eyes too. But please, release the Tern. I feel it as my own pain.'

Jemma let him go and the Tern recoiled. Leorah changed into her Peacock form and flew into the sky.

'You see,' Raddahkin said, 'what you hold seeks to live. You are its light, its energy, its very means of existence.

That is what your enemies have tried to create by artificial means. That is why they want you weak and defenceless, but full of the potential they will harness and use to destroy the Keepers.

'But you have weapons. You have seen that you can strike with the warriors of the Gulls, with Leorah too. And then, there are the elements of memory, the wind, the sea and the ice. The great forms of the Whale Keepers. For the next test, I will let you choose. I wish to see what you can create with your own devices.'

Jemma tried to raise the sea by taking the image before her and imagining the surface whipping into waves. But the water remained still and she saw her grimaced face in its reflection, as if it was mocking her.

'It's hopeless!' she said. 'I can't feel anything.'

'That is because you are not drawing on what is inside you. Try again. Use your own memories.'

Jemma closed her eyes and remembered the great trade winds. She had seen them funnelling through the valley. The gales of the East that kept even the Navigators docked for days. And the moon winds that shifted with the tide and sent ships ploughing into rocks. She called up all of the winds at once and set them against each other so the water rose up in a crest and hovered like a still and beautiful wave, in perfect balance. Then she released it and turned to her memories of winter in the Scarp, the snow drifts and ice fields on the high plateaux, broken only by the dark stalks of flax trees and the spikes of thistle-weed. She blew this winter breath upon the surface of the sea, calling on the memories of the arctic Whales whose songs of ice froze the sea from beneath. Then she held out the blade, and with the image of the sun, she melted back the ocean, leaving it calm and still as a pond on a summer night.

For at least a minute, Raddahkin did not speak. Jemma

stood, gazing upon the stillness, feeling the forms wild within her, equally as amazed as her teacher.

He stepped back inside the chamber. Jemma followed.

'You already have many resources to draw on, it is plainly evident.'

'But how will I defeat her?' Jemma said. 'You still haven't told me.'

Raddahkin sat down at the table and gestured for Jemma to do the same.

'You must walk the memory-path of the Caravanassi. That is the only way.'

## CHAPTER 40

# TO WALK THE PATH OF SORROW

They were still sitting in Raddahkin's chamber, when Camillo and Edgar joined them.

'It is too much to ask,' Camillo said, on hearing the plan.

'What choice do we have?' Raddahkin snapped.

'I have word from one of your scouts,' Camillo said. 'The Delphin Prince Aspar is rising again. He will soon have a Delphin army to join us.'

Raddahkin scoffed at the inadequacy.

'And I have sent Soren and the Cray boy to call upon the Whales − giants of the sea. They will change and walk the shores again. They will rise for their Keeper.' Camillo stood over the table, his robes and his silver hair flowing in the light.

'Don't you see?' Raddahkin said. 'To defeat the White Moth, we must go to the very source that fuels them. There are none who could walk the path of the Caravanassi and not be consumed by their sorrow. There are none who could hold this memory, to release it from Ramus − none, but the Erigena.'

Jemma stood up, skittling Edgar across the room.

'I'll do it,' she said. 'I have to.'

Camillo turned to her. 'It could very well destroy you,' he said. 'It is too great a woe to bear. Do you understand? This memory will seep into you, the kind of anguish you have never known. Tell her, Raddahkin, what you discovered.'

Raddahkin sat down at the table. 'When I went to see the Raven, they would not speak of what had happened to the Caravanassi. The loop contains memories of unspeakable things that a child should never have seen. Even though the Caravanassi Keeper is an old woman, what she Keeps in the loop are her memories of when she was a girl. I think you have met her – Daria.'

'I don't understand,' Jemma said. 'Daria?'

'She is the girl who lived the old woman's memory – it is Daria's story that is told in the loop, remembered by her older self. The Caravanassi Keeper resides in a chamber deep inside the gambling tents.'

'That's why Daria forgets what happens to her, when she comes back to the Wharf – it's the beginning of the loop?'

Raddahkin nodded. 'And the place where it returns, to play over and over again.'

Jemma thought of Daria's dolls that Arlen had found in his cray-pots. 'What happens to her? To the Caravanassi when they board the ships?'

Edgar settled on Jemma's shoulder.

'To bear such a burden, none should ask,' Camillo said.

'And what if they succeed?' Jemma moved to the fire stove. 'How much more will it grow, when they find other scars, other loops? The unformed lands are vast, you said it yourself. They will become unstoppable, and then what?'

Edgar flew to the table. 'Then I will go with you.'

Jemma held herself back from going to him.

'You can't, Edgar. Not this time. You've got to let me go on my own.'

'I won't hear of it.'

'You've got to stay with the fight, Edgar,' Jemma pleaded. 'You've got to watch and tell them what to do. Every army needs a commander and unless we have one, we won't be an army at all.'

'I can't leave you,' he said. 'I am sworn to protect you.'

'And what happens if they win? Do you think I'll be protected then?'

'The girl is right,' Raddahkin said. 'If she goes, then she must go alone. Listen to her. We will need you to read the battle, to be our eyes from the air.'

Edgar flew to Jemma. He whispered something in her ear, then flew again to the table.

'Very well,' he said. 'But I insist that we at least see a map. We cannot have a plan unless we have something to go by.'

Raddahkin unrolled a canvas scroll on the table. 'Here, you may have your map. This is what we have managed to trace.'

They could see the outline of a circle that went from the Wharf and out to sea, past the shale cliffs and the Delphin Caves and beyond the harbour of Adocentyn. The loop continued to a hidden port. From there, a long road stretched to the tunnels of the chalk mines, leading to the pulsing lights beneath the vaults of Ramus, where Jemma had seen a million White Moths fluttering in the caverns. The loop went on through the mines and out into a forest, until the final road, which lead back to the Wharf.

'We do not know what happens along this journey,' Raddahkin said. 'None have seen the path of the Cara-vanassi except the Keeper herself, and those who live her memory. Only you can see the power of the loop and cut it

with the Blade of Adocentyn, just like you did with Sharmenai's memory.'

Jemma felt for the blade inside her vest.

'She will have to invite you into the loop to travel the
path,' Raddahkin said. 'The White Moth are coming. We
will hold them off for as long as we can. But you must go
quickly to the Caravanassi. The boy will show you the way.
You must go into the chamber of the Keeper – she will tell
you what to do next. Listen, but be careful of her words.
They will not always mean what they seem.'

JEMMA WENT INTO THE PASSAGE OUTSIDE RADDAHKIN'S
door. The Caravanassi boy stepped out of the shadows and
held up a lamp. He had been waiting.

'Hello again,' she said.

'He-llo.'

Jemma smiled at him. 'When did you start talking,
then?'

'After I...' he stopped.

'After you shared your memory with me?'

The boy nodded, his eyes jittery.

She held her satchel close. 'I lost mine that day the
Sparrows came to the Wharf. I never would've escaped the
Delphin Caves without this one.'

'I'm – glad it helped – you.'

'So, can you tell me your name?'

'Yos-ka,' he said.

'I'll always Keep it safe,' she said. 'Yoska...do you know
where to find the way, to your Keeper?'

The boy lowered the lamp and shook his head. 'Too
much – sorrow. Can't – hold it inside. Never be the same.
Might – drown you.'

Jemma went closer to him.

'I know,' she said. 'It must be a terrible pain that feeds the White Moth. I've seen the chalk caves beneath the city, flashes of hollow cheeks and vacant eyes – I can't imagine what they've seen. But I have to walk that path if we've got any chance of breaking the loop.'

Yoska shuddered. She gripped his arms and after a time she felt the nervous anguish in his heart releasing. She could see his memory forming inside her, his face floating under water, his final breath releasing. She tried to breathe for him but she was drowning and she fell to the deck, gasping. The boy helped her up. Once she was back on her feet, she took his hand. The image was gone.

'You see, I can hold what you've seen. I can Keep it. There's a voice that's always with me, see. It won't let me drown. If I can follow the path and release you from the loop, then I might be able to find it too.'

The light brightened in Yoska's eyes. 'Then you will see – what happens to me. We go this way,' he said. 'Follow me.'

# CHAPTER 41

# WHITE NIGHT

The approaching cloud held them in awe – its dark centre, the bright sunlight glittering on the fringe and rippling back and forth, in waves of radiance. As the first swarms of the White Moth passed the sun, a great shadow spread across the lines of the Caravanassi. It swept over the smoke-house and the wrestling tents, penetrating the depths of the ocean, and enveloped the barges of the Terns whose fires boiled even brighter, the tar smoke dissolving in the dark. The Caravanassi were cowering, hiding as best they could.

Luminous lines of Moth in the distance claimed the horizon and all the sky.

'So it has begun,' Raddahkin said. 'If Bruno was ever going to return and fight, now would be the time...'

Camillo shook his head. 'Even if he did, the Shadow city will have sapped his strength. Our hope lies elsewhere.'

'I wouldn't underestimate Jiordano Bruno,' Raddahkin said. 'Even if we do defeat these creatures, we still have Ramus to contend with.'

Edgar flew towards the cloud in a vain attempt to gauge

its size. Then he circled back, looking at the wrestling tent from the Tern ship. The lines of ropes pegged into the ground gave him an idea.

He landed on Jemma's shoulder. The Caravanassi boy stood beside her. They could not take their eyes from the mass of wings.

'If we somehow get out of this,' she said to Edgar, 'you said you'd tell me about Arlia. The one you left behind.'

'I promise I'll tell you,' Edgar said. 'I will even take you to the Raven Court, not as a criminal to be thrown into a Raven tomb, but as the Erigena who saved the land. Then, together, we will write the scroll – the Chronicles of the Memory-Lands.'

'You can scribe,' Jemma said.

'And you can explore the Black Gorge. You'll need a new frontier, now that you are the greatest treasure hunter of the Scarp.'

Jemma stroked his wings and Edgar nuzzled into her hair.

'Remember what I whispered in your ear,' Edgar said. Then he turned to the Caravanassi boy. 'We will at least make a swipe at the first wave of Moth. But you must get her to the Keeper, while you still can. Good luck.'

～

JEMMA AND YOSKA TOOK OFF, JUMPING ALONG THE smelting barges, the tar pots lighting their way, until they reached the shore and followed the roasting fires through the Caravanassi camps. No children danced around the flames. All those who could hold a weapon now stood waiting, gazing awestruck into the approaching swarm. Except for the Trade Masters, who had filled a cargo ship with their ledgers and sailed away.

Jemma looked into the white night. There was Edgar, commanding the Terns. They had unfurled the ropes of the wrestling tent. Like a huge inverted parachute, it rose into the air with fifty carriers, sweeping across the first attack of flying Moths. Those it touched were forced to change into their warrior form as the tent hurtled to the ground, catching more Moths underneath as they fell. Their weight sent them smashing through a line of wagons, landing in a heap of twisted bodies. The Gulls, swooping over them, changed into their human forms and struck down those who escaped.

In their warrior forms, the children of the Sigilli – fully changed – were both exquisite and horrendous, pure white except for the dark lines running from their eyes to the points of their cheeks, as if they wore a mask. Their slender limbs made them eight feet tall, and their spears were coated in Moth dust.

High above, the Terns streaked the sky with boiling tar, igniting the flying Moths like brilliant phosphorous. But one of the Tern carriers, picked out and surrounded, fell blinded from the sky into the sea, the tar-fire exploding into steam.

At the Caravanassi tent Jemma turned to find Camillo had followed them. He held her shoulders.

'You must hear this before you go,' he said. 'A messenger has returned from the caves. The Delphin Prince Aspar – he has become the Keeper, and the girl, Adeline, she has drunk of the emerald pool. She is one of the Delphin now and it is said the Delphin soldiers kneel to her as their Queen.'

Even through her marvelling at the thought of Adeline being Queen, Jemma's voice wavered. 'He'll grow old and blind in that pool, just like the Delphin Keeper before him.

I never asked for that. I never asked him to sacrifice himself.'

'You only gave him the seed,' Camillo said. 'You did not force him into that pool. He chose himself. But you gave him the greatest gift of all – the chance to redeem himself.'

Jemma turned, hiding away her glistening eyes.

'I have no words to give you other than the truth,' Camillo said. 'We can hold off the White Moth for just long enough. It is up to you now. Look out for the Seals, they are hunting you. If you alter the Caravanassi memory, they will know where you are. The Shadows will sense it, too. No matter how strong the temptation, you must complete the memory-path, so you can cut the loop. When the sorrow comes it will take away your will to hold and Keep what you see. If the sorrow takes over, then you will fail. Remember – you are the Erigena.' Camillo hugged her for one last time. 'Now go.'

Yoska took Jemma's hand and stepped through the folds of the Caravanassi tent. Inside there were no players at the tables, only figures huddling in the dark corners, their faces lit up by the glow of smoke weed. They looked at her, afraid. Some had doubt in their eyes, some maintained their natural scorn, but none stood in her way.

Yoska took hold of a lamp and beckoned her through a curtain. The walls of the passageways were hung with thick patterned fabric. In the flickering light, the colours were still bright reds and maroons, though the fabrics were old. They circled through the passages, passing many times through heavy curtains, where guards stood ready and expectant.

It was only then that Jemma realised she was inside a vast memory palace that was made of woven cloth instead of stone and wood.

She followed, knowing that without her guide she would

have become helplessly lost. So many openings passed them by, passages leading to who knows where.

And then she noticed the silence. It hung heavy in the passages, where even the sound of their feet was absorbed by a lush material.

What was happening outside? She both wanted and didn't want to know. In here, the white night seemed like a dream. It was as silent as the air she breathed, with such a heaviness it hurt her lungs and slowed her steps.

Finally, they came to an attendant who stood before a finely patterned, woven door. He had a solemn face but his eyes were frightened. His look was one of disbelief, as if to say, 'What? All our hopes rest with *her*?'

Yoska turned to Jemma at the entrance. A clear bright hope was in his eyes where the sorrow had fled. He held her hand once more.

'I – am – with – you,' he said.

'Can't you come with me?'

He shook his head. 'You will – see me on the path.'

'But I thought you escaped? Raddahkin saved you...'

'I must return – so you – see all of it,' he said.

'Then I'll see you, soon,' Jemma said.

She stepped inside the chamber.

THE CARAVANASSI KEEPER WAS AN OLD WOMAN WITH withered hands. Her tattered dress, once brightly coloured, was faded grey and hole-filled. Her hair was draped with a loose-fitting scarf that covered her mouth but not the rest of her weather-wrinkled face. Her eyes, like the Gull Keepers, were cloudy-blind. It was hard to believe that she was Daria as an old woman, but the longer Jemma looked, the more she could see the resemblance.

I know you, she wanted to say. But did she? Jemma's eyes were drawn to the light of a lamp hanging on the canvas wall. An acrid smell of kerosene filled the tapering dark.

'Come. Sit,' the old woman said. She sat on a woven rug, hunched over by the flame.

'Are you the Caravanassi Keeper, then?' Jemma asked, sitting down.

'Here...let me see your face,' the old woman said, her long fingers touching the bones of Jemma's cheeks, just like the Gull Keeper before her.

'Yes,' she said, 'that is good. I was about your age. You will walk in my steps, with my feet. You will see with my eyes, feel with my heart...release me.'

'Release you from what?' Jemma said.

'Cannot speak of what I see. You will see.'

Inside the folds of the chamber there was an even deeper silence. 'How will I know when I see it?'

'When you float away from your eyes. When you have no voice. When the ache begins.'

'Of what,' Jemma said. 'I want to know.'

'Then go...' the Caravanassi Keeper reached out, pulled apart a fold in the canvas tent. Through it, Jemma could see Daria with her parents and Besh, sitting in the back of their wagon, waiting to board the ships.

'You will follow me. Stand where I stood. See with my eyes. Witness what I have witnessed. It will alter you. I was just a girl, just your age. Walk away, do not see what I've seen...have to...have to...'

She reached out and touched Jemma's cheek, and in her other hand, she held the woven doll, frayed, but unmistakeable.

'I know I have to,' Jemma said. 'But what if I don't make it? What then?'

The Keeper lifted a brass urn, exquisitely carved in the shape of a peacock.

'Leorah,' Jemma whispered, and as she said her name, Leorah came brushing her tail feathers through the door of the tent.

'I am here,' she said. 'Tell me, how is that impossible Raven?'

'Being brave,' Jemma said. 'He's fighting the White Moth.'

'I am with you, too,' Leorah said. 'I am your weapon, remember.'

'There is the path...' Daria said. 'Follow it...if you will...'

'Go,' Leorah said. 'She will close the curtain soon. Then the path will be lost.'

Jemma stood.

'If you need me,' Leorah said. 'Just call my name.'

## CHAPTER 42

# WHEN THE SHADOWS RISE
# AGAIN

E dgar flew in circles, rising above the swarm. He could see the skirmishes below where the Terns and Gulls fought off the last of the first wave of Moth. He pitied them – soon they would look up to see the next wave, and the next, an impossible force before them.

'Think,' he said, 'think, Raven, think,' but the magnitude brought nothing but a feeling of the infinite helplessness.

How long would the fire pots burn on the Tern ships before they were smothered? No. That could not happen. There must be a way. But no sooner had he allowed this glimmer of hope, the Moths began to change into their warrior forms in vast numbers upon the lower ridges of the Scarp, marching down into the valley, where they halted and formed a battalion stretching back in waves, an endless field of wheat as far as the eye could see.

Only the lines of the Caravanassi cut through. 'They're protecting the memory loop,' he said. And then he thought of Jemma – how will she ever break it?

Edgar hovered in the air. To his left, the skies above the

forest were clear but he knew it was filled with Shadows and fog. Ahead, the Moths began their advance, the absolute silence more excruciating than any war cry.

'We must, at least, strike from the air.' He ordered the Arctic Gulls to form their ranks.

From the barges, fireballs of tar began to rain like falling comets over the marching Moths. They had as little effect as an ember in an ocean.

Above, a new line of flying Moths blacked out the sun once more. Streaks of fire in the sky the only light. At the sea, Edgar could only just make out the lines of waves tumbling to the shore.

Edgar commanded the Gulls to fly low and change their forms to strike the marching Moths, and change again in succession. Flying, striking, flying again, the Gulls clashed with the White Moth spears, sparks flashing. The Moths fell ten to one, but still this didn't matter. Even if it was a thousand to one, their numbers were overwhelming.

He looked again at the waves surging towards the Wharf, perfect breakers, the white spray of the sea rushing forth. But they were not waves at all. They were the lines of the Delphin. As they struck the shore, they changed into their human forms, the new Delphin Queen leading the first rank into battle.

Edgar swooped down towards Adeline, a rush of joy in his heart. But then he lost sight of her. He was surrounded by a cloud of flying Moths, thick as the air.

He flew desperately but he could not shake them off. He beat his wings to no effect. Diving down, he tried to free a line to the sea but instead he flew into the marching Moths. A spear struck the tips of his wings.

He pushed through and up again, straight back into the cloud.

*The forest*, he thought, *that's my only hope.*

He set a course and clamped his eyes shut, powering through the mass of flying Moths, his wings heavy with powder, until he broke through and felt the brush of leaves in the canopy of the trees. But the Moths had followed and circled him in a clearing, forming a fluttering dome from the canopy to the very roots twisting in the earth.

Edgar flew in one direction, then another, trapped. There was not a single gap. The bright dome began closing in. He circled in a panic. As the first Moth went for him, he plunged to the ground.

~

THE WOODEN SHIP HAD TWO LEVELS — A HOLD BENEATH and an open deck above. Soldiers herded the Caravanassi on board across a bridge of planks, ignoring the White Moths filling the sky. Jemma recognised the soldiers' black boots and long grey coats that reached to their knees and bell-shaped hats. They were whacking animals that came too close to the edge of the planks.

Jemma followed the lines of Caravanassi going into the hold, keeping to the middle of the bridge to avoid the soldiers' sticks and looking up for Edgar in the skies.

Inside the hold, she could smell the manure of chickens and mules, hear the bleating of goats and the clanging of pots as the caravans came to a halt. It was dark in the ship's hold and occasionally she would see the sudden flair of a match as a Caravanassi lit a pipe, reminding her of the hollow flashing faces in the chalk caves.

Soon the ship was so packed it was difficult to move. The smoky air made her eyes water. She couldn't see Daria but she caught a glimpse of Yoska climbing the stairs to the upper deck. She followed him.

The Caravanassi were gathered in a kind of holding pen

on the deck. Some took shelter under a makeshift awning, while others were huddled and exposed – whole families were bundled together in blankets. No one talked. About half a dozen soldiers stood watch outside the pen, in the bow of the ship. They seemed indifferent to the crowds of Caravanassi behind them, to the battle raging at the Wharf. Some were jostling and joking, others leaning over the rails, looking bored.

Jemma heard a *Yoy! Yoy! Yoy!* and the ship was moving. A murmur swept through the Caravanassi. The soldiers walked the perimeter of the pen. They wanted silence and they struck the deck with their long sticks, *thwack thwack thwack*, pointing at any who made a noise. Satisfied the cargo was settled, they returned to leaning on the rail.

Jammed in the pen, Jemma couldn't see the Wharf, only the White Moth's shadow as it washed over them and retreated. When they passed the shale cliffs she thought of Arlen, how calm he had been when they were being chased by the Harpooners. How shy and kind he was. How much she missed him. Where was he now?

Yoska was sitting by himself cross-legged at the front of the pen. He was playing with a handful of dice, like the ones she had seen in Arlen's chest, carved by the Caravanassi out of bone. He rolled them, counted to himself, picked up the dice and rolled again. Jemma was desperate to ask him to teach her how to play the game, but she didn't. She watched him. The boy rolled, and rolled again, this time too far. One of the dice skittled outside the pen and a passing soldier unwittingly kicked it across the deck where it came to rest at the feet of another soldier who was leaning on the rail.

*Don't!* Jemma almost called. Yoska crawled out from under the pen, following the edge of the ship where it was dark under the shadow of the rails. The soldiers were looking out to sea. Jemma stopped breathing. The boy kept crawling, closer and closer to the high black boots. When he was close enough he reached and clutched the dice. His hand slowly retreated over the toe of a boot, just as the soldier looked down.

'Who do we have here?' The soldier picked him up by the scruff of the neck – Yoska's legs were kicking above the deck. 'What should we do with this one?'

'Let's see if he can swim!' Another soldier grabbed his feet as the others chanted. 'One! Two! Three!' and let out a raucous cheer as they tossed the screaming boy over the side.

Jemma rushed to the rail within the perimeter of the pen, agony inside her. She wanted to dive after him, swim to the bottom of the sea and give him bulbs of sea-fennel. Daria came up to the rail beside Jemma. She saw the Cara-vanassi boy and hollered: 'Hey! Hey! Over there! Hey!'

A soldier pointed his stick – 'Keep her quiet or she'll be next.'

Daria's father rushed over and covered her mouth – her shouts muffled in his hand. She tried to wriggle free and she was wailing. Her mother took her sobs to her chest and Besh held her hand, looking wearily over his shoulder, out to sea.

Jemma watched helplessly as Yoska was getting smaller and smaller in the waves. And then he went under. She gripped the rail, feeling the Gulls rising up in their warrior forms, ready to strike.

*Do not alter the memory.*

'It's too hard.'

She turned away and slid to the deck and huddled her knees, losing breath in the boy's memory as he drifted under the sea. Her lungs restricted as if filled with water and she coughed, sea sick. She heaved over the side.

The other Caravanassi, one by one, cast objects into the

sea, tributes to the vanished boy. One woman threw in her scarf. Another, her special tea set that she had carried up to the deck. A Caravanassi man dangled a bag of dice over the rail, then let go. Daria broke away from her mother's arms and tossed her doll over the side, watching it floating in the waves.

Jemma imagined them sinking to the bottom of the sea, washed into Arlen's craypots.

'He'll Keep them for you,' she whispered. 'He'll hold them in a wooden box. And one day, I promise – we'll give them back.'

They arrived at a landing beyond the Delphin Caves and the harbour of Adocentyn. The Caravanassi were ordered to leave their belongings in the hold and walk on a road that lead to the side of a mountain far off in the distance.

*That must be the beginning of the chalk tunnels*, Jemma thought. She heard murmurs – why must they leave their things behind? A Caravanassi man protested, pointing to his wagon, but he was struck to the ground. Jemma flinched at his pain – she sent the earth rumbling and cracking beneath the soldier's feet and he jumped back in fright.

*Stop*, the voice whispered.

'I know I can't alter the memory, but I want to, so much...'

She followed the walking Caravanassi on a road that lead to the side of mountains far off in the distance. The soldiers on horseback behind were wielding sticks to any stragglers. Where was Daria? Jemma joined a train of children running between the adults like it was a game, but after a kilometre in the heat of the sun, they slowed and held their parents' hands – if they had parents – or fell behind. An old man stopped and gripped a stitch. He waved his family ahead. 'Go...go,' he said.

The road was dusty underfoot. The sun was high and

sweltering in the sky. Some, too exhausted to continue, were left where they fell.

'Come on,' Jemma said, 'keep going.' What else could she do?

She saw Daria about twenty metres ahead of her, holding her father's hand, looking behind at a mother kneeling on the side of the road rocking her crying infant. The road rose steadily towards the mountains, the lines of Caravanassi feet sending up clouds of dust into her face.

Jemma did not try to exert herself. Whatever was to happen, had to happen, and she had merely to stumble into its path. The sun was hot and white-shining in the specs of rocks and pebbles on the worn out tracks. She grew thirsty, but did not expect to drink, for this was all part of the memory she gathered into herself.

Breaths that were not supposed to be, were hers. And she grew more and more conscious that the pain in her feet and the ache in her throat were what Daria had to suffer, and she suffered them too.

The weary Caravanassi trudged on. Jemma recognised the woman who had pulled her into the wagon when the Seal had followed them through the Scarp.

She stopped to question her. 'What happens to you?' But the woman didn't answer. Jemma saw the hungry eyes of children who were squatting on the side of the road picking seeds out of weeds. What awaited her pressed upon her terribly. She walked and walked until she was almost crying with thirst.

*Wait!* she wanted to shout to Daria, but no voice escaped the parchedness of her throat. When she reached the entrance to the chalk caves, soldiers with sticks stood at the entrance striking any who paused or refused to enter. The dark engulfed her.

~

Edgar covered himself with his wings waiting for the Moth to take him. A memory of Jemma filled his mind, when he first saw her digging in the Scarp – she was heaving clods of soil from the ancient moss-covered rocks with an iron spike.

'You can come out now,' she'd said without stopping. 'I know you're hiding over there.'

He flew to her. 'Have you found any treasure?'

'Not yet.' She kept digging.

'I'm Edgar by the way.'

'I'm Jemma. Can you do me a favour?'

'What is it?'

'Fly up over the ridge and tell me if you see any ruins, just like these.'

He flew up and back. 'I think there might be.'

'Come on then,' she said. 'I'm the only treasure hunter left in the Scarp. You can join me, if you want to.'

'I would be delighted,' Edgar said, and settled on her shoulder.

When he opened his eyes, he saw something extraordinary. Shadows, reaching for the flying Moths, feeding on their light. The Moths fluttered away in desperate fright, some of them changing into their warrior forms and trying to run, only to be devoured. The Shadows streamed in from almost every direction, like a rushing wind through the trees.

Edgar took off into the air. 'Well, who would have thought?' It had given him an idea.

He flew over the canopy of the trees, making sure a cloud of Moths were following. The Shadows, hungry and clamouring over each other, fed in a frenzy, swiping the air, their touch dissolving the Moths into plumes of bright dust.

Edgar collected more, plunging into the forest again and again, each time feeding the Shadows with Moths.

Below him, the Harpooners had attacked the barges and spilled the tar pots. Huge flames lit up the sky and the ocean. He saw the chaos with clarity – it was completely hopeless now. The attack was never-ending. He could see Adeline and the Delphin cutting down the white battalion, holding their line against the entrance to the Caravanassi tent.

Edgar called the Terns to abandon the flaming ships and fuel the remaining tar-fires on the barges close to the shore. So many had fallen. Edgar could feel the weakening of his heart, an anguish beyond any he had ever felt. Something fixed and whole was being torn into pieces, scattered and burning in the sea.

But the sinking Tern ship had opened a way. Edgar could see all of it now: the Cray boat charging through the tar flames with Arlen steering and Sorenstar standing at the bough. They tore through the wreckage and struck the shore, leading a great line of Whales who rose up as giants from the sea and changed, towering as tall as the trees. They inflicted terrible damage on the White Moth, sweeping them back from the edge of the Wharf.

Adeline ran to the shoreline, greeting Arlen and Soren while Edgar hovered above.

'You must go to the Caravanassi tents,' she said to Arlen. 'We cannot hold them for much longer. You must not let them find the Keeper while she holds open the path.'

'You l-look like a Qu-queen,' Arlen said.

'And a fierce one at that,' Soren said.

'Then here,' she handed them armour and weapons, 'I give you these.'

Soren took hold of a Delphin sword. Arlen chose a bow and put on the armour.

'Take this too,' Adeline said, handing him a Delphin mask. 'It will protect you from the Moth powder. Now come.'

Edgar watched her lead them to the Caravanassi tents.

'We will take the Scarp ridge, but you must stay here,' she said. 'They are trying to capture the Keeper.'

'None will get through this door while I am here.' Soren turned to Arlen. 'Now take my hand and get up on the roof. You can't shoot a bow from down here.'

Arlen scuttled to the top of the Caravanassi tent, the canvas giving way beneath his feet. If the Whales had struck a blow, the Moths were coming back in waves. Arlen could see one of the giants swiping in the air. He stumbled and fell, clutching his eyes, opening a path below.

Arlen took a shot at the approaching line but the arrow went far off its mark.

'Learn to shoot straight,' Soren called. 'And quickly!'

Arlen knelt and strung his bow. This time he hit his mark.

'G-good enough for you?' he called, but his satisfaction did not last for long.

Edgar swooped above the tent and saw the look of disbelief in Arlen's eyes when he took in the scale of the White Moth army, the clouds of flying Moths in the air, the unfathomable numbers of marching warriors stretching into the valley.

Arlen peered past them, trying to perceive an end, looking for an opening from beyond the horizon itself.

'Jemma.' He whispered her name, just in case she could hear it, stringing his bow, shooting arrow after arrow.

'How many more?' Soren called from below.

'A f-few,' Arlen called.

He struck a White warrior, seeing it flay into powder, shielding his eyes from the dust.

Adeline had given him a hundred arrows and already he had used half of them against the never-ending swarm.

Still hovering above, Edgar saw one of the warrior Moths make its way to the Caravanassi tent. It was taller than the others, its eyes and chest streaked with marks of charcoal black.

'Soren,' Edgar called. 'Down there!'

Soren faced the creature, standing in the entrance to the Caravanassi tent. The White Moth threw down its weapon and Soren did the same. Then it lunged and they were locked in battle.

THE TEMPERATURE HAD SHIFTED FROM UNBEARABLY HOT to freezing in the dark. Jemma huddled herself and rubbed her arms, shivering as she walked, hearing crying children and the moans of the Caravanassi who had endured exposure, heat, thirst, abandonment and cold – what next?

The soldiers did not follow them into the cave. The long march through the tunnels came to an end in an open chamber, where Jemma recognised the wardens from the Black Moat. They were sorting the Caravanassi, separating husbands from wives, parents from their children, who were put together with the sick and the elderly.

Daria screamed, 'No – Mama!' and a warden whipped her neck. As she cowered, Besh stepped in to take the final blow. Jemma rushed to comfort her and was struck hard on her back – her blood blazed and the rock cracked in the caves above, sending a fissure into the dark. A great plume of chalk dust filled the cavern. The wardens, suddenly afraid the caves might collapse, began to move the separated groups of wailing Caravanassi.

Those able to work in the chalk caves were given

shovels and picks and herded into a passage on the left. Jemma took cover in the dust cloud and waited so she could follow behind the wardens, who sent the others to a passage on the right. Covered in dust, they looked like ghosts suddenly brightened by the light as they exited the tunnel.

Daria's group were walking towards a dark forest. Jemma remembered it from Raddahkin's map – the path went through the forest, then came out on the other side where the Caravanassi walked the final road back to the Wharf. Thick swathes of fog hung in the canopies of the trees and Jemma could hear the moaning of people inside the forest. She saw Daria disappear into the trees.

'Leorah,' she said.

'I am here.' Leorah appeared in her human form, holding a spear, the blade shaped like a peacock feather.

'I'm afraid,' Jemma said.

'Then let me go first. We will take the path along the cliff and see what's on the other side of the forest, before we enter.'

Jemma followed Leorah, walking between the edge of the forest and the chalk cliffs, hearing the constant moaning rise and fall as the fog thickened and receded in the canopies of the trees. Ahead of them a narrow channel of water ran from the forest to another entrance in the cliff.

Jemma knelt and dipped her hand in the channel. 'It's not water,' she said. The liquid was thick and gelatinous. 'This is Halogaic.'

From deep inside the cliffs Jemma heard a loud hammering of machines pummelling the chalk.

'Let's take a look,' Jemma said.

They followed the channel through the entrance in the cliff. Inside the cave, lines of Caravanassi were striking the white rock. Others collected the powder and poured it into buckets rising on a conveyor belt, sending them high into the caves, where sickly White Moth, only just spawned, were fluttering and feeding in a frenzy. At the very centre, the White Queen seemed to float in the pool where Jemma had first seen the wild light on her way to Ramus's vault. The light, fuelled by the Halogaic substance, passed through the Queen and radiated all around. She glowed like the brightest star Jemma had ever seen, the younglings fluttering and hovering about her.

Jemma felt a sickly hollow inside her, the image of the Moth Queen too powerful for her to shape into anything other than its own terrible splendour.

'Leorah, what should I do?' She tucked herself up as small as she could against the cave wall.

'We must go,' Leorah said, 'and see what happens in the trees.' She took Jemma's hand.

They crossed the channel and continued along the cliff edge until they came to the other side of the forest – the exit. At the beginning of the road leading to the Wharf, Jemma recognised the same lines of the Caravanassi that she had seen from the Scarp. It was as if they were reborn outside the forest, where their wagons and carts and belongings from the ship were waiting.

The forest was dark and thick with trees and a coolness breathed through it. Jemma yearned for water. A sudden movement of the earth beneath her feet, a writhing in the dirt. She scuttled back, terrified, expecting awful creatures to fly up and attack. Leorah stood ready with her spear. But what emerged were hands, then arms, heads and shoulders. It was people she saw, crawling out of the ground. The Caravanassi.

Some were brushing the dirt from their clothes, bewildered. A fog now surrounded them and, almost invariably, they sat down at the base of a tree and huddled their knees up to their chins. Some had watery eyes, some were weeping. A woman looked at Jemma, as if to accuse her of something, but then she only shook her head and fell into her own world of grief, as if to say, 'So what, then.'

But the fog seemed to be affecting them. After a while some began to stand and look behind them, as if half expecting someone to appear. Others simply gathered up their things and walked through the fog and onto the road.

'What's happened?' Jemma asked. 'Why did you just crawl out of the dirt?'

They ignored her, too preoccupied with the journey ahead. On the road outside the forest, the lines of the Caravanassi took form. Wagons were hitched to horses. Donkeys loaded with sacks. She heard the clanging of pots, the calling to animals.

Jemma turned away from them. Part of her desired to know. Part of her resisted, yet there was nothing she could do to stop what lay ahead.

As the group of Caravanassi travelled on the road, Jemma went the opposite way into the forest. Something echoed through the trees. She found herself shivering as the fog surrounded her and little icicles formed in the smaller branches of the trees and gathered on the leaves. She was shaking with cold. There was no snow, yet the ground was frozen and her feet were turning numb.

'Leorah – I don't want to see.'

'Then follow me,' Leorah said.

~

SOREN LANDED A HEAVY BLOW AND EDGAR SAW THE White Moth keel. But the Moth struck back into Soren's chest. As he fell, the creature flung a plume of dust into the air.

'Look out!' Edgar called. He fluttered helplessly above

but already the effects of the blinding dust took hold. Soren stumbled and another Moth thrust a spear into his chest. Arlen cried out, unable to stop shooting his bow at the ceaseless onslaught.

'Soren!' Arlen called.

Now a line of Moths began to follow their leader towards the tent, but Soren would not have it. He got to his feet. Another spear went into his side and Arlen let out another sickening cry. He stood ready to jump, but Edgar had already flown to one of the Whale Giants, who swept the Moths away and stood guard, a look of mourning in its sad, drooping eyes.

Arlen could hear it, a song like those he had heard along the Whale-lines in the dead of night, when a stillness had settled on the sea. A song of sorrow and loss as deep as the ocean itself. All the Whales were leaning up, arching into the sky, each sounding an aching note into the swirling, smoking white night.

It was the most beautiful sound he had ever heard.

'Soren!' Arlen called his name once more, but the great Walrus did not move. His body was curled around the spear like a half-moon, pale and calm and lifeless.

Edgar heard the dirge of the Whales sweep across the battlefield. He whirred in circles around Soren, *aah aah aaaah – aah aah aaaah* – sounding the mourning call of the Raven – *aah aah aaaah*.

Then all he could do was thank the light of Soren's star that the Caravanassi Keeper was protected again.

He flew back towards the forest. By now the feeding Shadows had brought in the fog. He hovered above it, unable to enter the forest, afraid of the emptiness that touching the fog would bring. What use would he be if it blanked out his mind?

The fog hung all around the canopy and soon it was

impenetrable. He circled above, looking for a break. Anything.

*If I cannot bring the Moth into the forest,* Edgar thought, *then I'll bring the Shadows to the Moth.*

It would only take one of them to follow – then it would be like opening a dam. A river of Shadows would flow.

Then he saw a contraption rising into the air from one of the barges, across the flaming sea. It was Camillo's flying machine. He steered above the fire, the machine unsteady until momentum took hold. He flew into the cloud of Moths – protected from their dust by the wind of the blades – and on to the edge of the forest. Edgar landed on the helm.

'I need you to clear the fog,' he said, 'so I can fly into the forest. Follow me.'

'Lead the way, Raven.'

Camillo cut through the plumes of wings and powder, propelling the blade even faster as he swept over the canopy. Already the Moths had flown into the spinning blades until they were choked and rattled into a deadly stillness, but it had been enough to blast a clean hole in the fog. Edgar caught one last glimpse of Camillo's machine before he dived through the canopy and into the trees.

He took a single Moth in his beak and darted through the forest until the Shadows began to chase him. Now he had no choice. There was no escape, except to fly through a thick band of fog at the edge of the trees. To fly and hope the Scarp he wouldn't lose his mind.

'Here goes...'

And then he was in the fog. He grew disoriented, forgetting what he was doing and where he was going, flying aimlessly into a sea of blankness. The Moth was still in his beak. He was so very cold. Ahead there was a glow.

He flew towards it – he didn't know why. It was the fire

from the sea lighting through the fog. He flew, a torrent of Shadows trailing behind, until he was in open space again, clear of the fog. And then he lost consciousness altogether.

Edgar fell to the road, his body nothing but a tangle of feathers swept onto the hillside.

## CHAPTER 43

# ANOTHER WAY

Jemma closed her eyes. *The image of a single star shimmering over the ice wastes of the North, far beyond the Scarp. A Whale song sounds across the empty plains, and when the star falls, it plummets into the Southern Ocean and disappears into that fathomless ravine within.*

She let out a cry, a savage burst of fury and pain that startled Leorah, who cowered back. Jemma knew that Soren was dead and she had done nothing to help him. It sent her running into the forest, Leorah behind her.

In the distance, they could hear shovels digging in the frozen ground, a rhythm of thuds and the clanging of metal and stone. The wind in the leaves, or a woman's voice, wailing.

They came to a clearing where the fog drifted higher into the branches. There was a line of trees. Before them, twisted up in the roots of every trunk, were Caravanassi, shivering, eyes gaping, pointing in front of them to the pits dug into the earth. A veiled woman sat on the edge of the first pit, swaying and weeping. Further along, the diggers struck the earth, *thud thud thud.*

Jemma looked at the figures caught in the trees. She recognised her at once.

'Daria,' she said, rushing to her. 'Daria, it's me, Jemma – remember? Talk to me.'

Her mouth was open but she could not speak. Jemma recalled the words of the Keeper: *When you float away from your eyes. When you have no voice. When the ache begins...*

Leorah knelt beside her. 'Careful,' she said. 'It's like the tree is growing around her. It's somehow releasing the fog. This is how they make the Halogaic.'

'This is what they do to them!' Jemma took out the golden blade from her vest and began hacking at the roots. As soon as she had cut Daria free, the fog disappeared from the canopy. It seemed to be a system where the Caravanassi's suffering turned to fog and was captured above, condensed in the leaves, and collected as Halogaic liquid into the channel below, running into the caves.

Daria fell to the ground and Jemma held her, but she was still pointing to the pit.

'B...Be...'

'Besh,' Jemma said. 'Where is he?'

Leorah rushed to the edge. 'Do not come any closer,' she said. 'Do not come down here.'

'But I see it through your eyes,' Jemma said. 'What they do before they crawl out of the graves –'

Jemma jumped down into the pit, digging with her hands. The veiled woman who kneeled on the edge began clutching the earth.

'No,' Leorah said. 'We cannot alter the memory, you know that.'

'I can't leave him here,' Jemma said. 'I won't. He's still alive.'

'If you altar the memory, you cannot break the loop,' Leorah said. 'The Shadows will come.'

'Then I'll find another way to break the loop!' Jemma thumped the pit. 'I can't let this happen – not now. Not ever. I'm going to get Ramus.'

She dug into the stony earth, like the ruins in the Scarp, until her nails began to bleed, until she felt a limb, then another, a hand, a rough of hair. She dug around the body with all her strength and then she hauled the boy out of the pit.

'Besh,' she said. 'Please...wake up.'

At first, his head fell limply to his chest. Then he jolted forward and coughed, gasping at the freezing air.

Besh shook the dirt from his eyes and crawled towards his sister. He made a sound like nothing Jemma had ever heard, neither joy nor sorrow, neither animal nor human. Then his body shook with cold and fear and pain. Together, they lifted Besh to his feet and Daria held his weight.

'I'm sorry,' Jemma said. 'I changed the memory – I know I wasn't meant to, but...'

Daria hugged her brother and Jemma felt the sobs in her chest.

'Thank you,' she said.

Jemma pointed. 'Go that way, through the trees, follow the road. The wagons are up ahead. They will take you home.'

Daria nodded and led her brother away, still dazed, still shaking the earth from his hair, still wiping his eyes, still numb at the offence.

~

THE VEILED WOMAN WAS WEEPING BY THE PIT. IN THE distance, the diggers had paused. Now they resumed their work.

'Stop!' Jemma screamed at them, her hands gripping her hair, 'Why don't you stop!'

The woman began to rise.

'Why didn't you?' she said.

The veil fell from her face and Jemma saw it was Sharmenai.

'Where is he?' Sharmenai said. 'Give him back.'

'I lost him,' Jemma said. 'They've killed him – he's never coming back.'

Sharmenai howled into the woods and Jemma could hear the crackling of sticks and leaves. Then she saw Shadows gathering at the edges of the clearing.

'Take her!'

'Run,' Leorah said. 'Now!'

Jemma sprinted through the trees, past the line of pits and the Caravanassi reaching out their arms through the roots. Another mourner, kneeling just in front of her, stood and turned, blocking her way. Jemma saw the veil of black hessian fall. She saw the green eyes of a Seal, with long fire-red hair.

The Seal held up a wooden staff and gathered the Shadows to herself, leaving Sharmenai defeated and screaming on the edge of the pit, 'Give him back!'

'Keep going,' Leorah said. 'I will hold her off.'

Leorah struck against the staff. The Seal stumbled, falling. Leorah pinned her by the throat to the ground.

The Seal closed her eyes and seemed to fall into a trance. Jemma could feel it now, as the Seal took hold of Leorah's arms, slowly guiding the point away from her throat.

Jemma struggled against her but felt the force of the Seal's superior will. It was as if a part of her was being torn across a threshold, into a space of nothingness. Into the ravine. She refused to let go.

A fierce anger took hold of her. She put her will against the Seal, giving Leorah the strength to pull herself away. But this was Jemma's very weakness. Whatever dark emotion she held within, this was the Seal's power, opening the ravine inside Jemma. A Rupture. It was the same force Jemma had felt in the Scarp, obliterating the palace.

The Seal held Leorah over the ravine. Then let go. Leorah tore off into the dark, but not without striking the Seal with her spear first. The Seal fell forward, clutching her stomach.

Jemma felt an abyss inside of her, a gaping hole of loss.

The Seal, folded double and holding her wound, picked up her staff and released the Shadows.

Jemma ran through the clearing, past the pits, striking the tree roots as she went with the golden blade, releasing the Caravanassi. The Shadows were gaining but she sprinted out of the forest into the sun, hearing their screeches echo from the trees, against the chalk cliffs.

Arrows reigned down from the cliff-tops, fired by the Poachers she had seen in the wrestling tents of Adocentyn. Jemma dived into the hollow of a cave and peered through a gap at the Poachers. There were five of them. She called up five Gulls, guiding them through the sky, where they changed forms in mid-air and struck the archers, changing again and flying off into the clouds.

She ran to the base of the cliff. One of the archers had dropped his bow. She picked it up and collected the fallen arrows, then followed the cliff line to the channel of Halogaic that lead into the chalk cave.

Inside the cave, two Moths were standing guard, their figures towering above the Caravanassi workers, who were barely able to lift their picks. They were broken and exhausted. The sight of them stirred her again. Jemma crouched behind the wall, and took aim. The first Moth burst into powder. Before the other could turn, she shot again, but not without seeing the dark streaks of its hateful eyes strike at her with vengeance before it too vanished into a cloud of dust.

The Caravanassi, too tired even to notice, kept working, until Jemma called to them.

'Come on,' she said. 'You've gotta get out of here. You've got to come with me.'

When recognition took hold, they threw down their picks and hammers and cast their buckets into the dust. She led them out of the caves.

'Go,' she said. 'Follow that road. Don't stop for anything. Just keep walking, you hear?'

They nodded wearily. A woman kissed her hand – it was Daria's mother – her face white with chalk dust, the bones of her face showing through.

Only when she had seen them reach the road did Jemma go back into the caves, treading carefully through the discarded hammers and picks, the machine still blindly clanging.

She used the pick marks to climb, refusing the temptation to look at the radiant light, until she found a small tunnel burrowed into the chalk. It led to a passage and she recognised it at once. There were the barred doors of the dungeons and, up ahead, the bridge running over the caves, where she had first seen the Halogaic light. This would take her to the vaults of Ramus.

Further along, voices. She crept forward, then leaned into one of the dungeon grates, hiding in the shadows. But something reached through the bar and held a filthy grip over her mouth. She heard a cracked whispering close to her ear. Smelled foul breath.

'I implore you,' Magden said, 'not to move or make a sound. Listen to the humble whimpering of a faithful

Dungeon Moth. I tell you because I tell you, nothing more. Take my words, or leave them. My Master, the Collector, is banished. He has fled back through the Rupture, from whence he came. You must retreat from this place. There's nowhere left for us in this new world. We'll dry and die, this I plainly see. Oh, the error of my ways. What use for powder then? When nothing left to spy. Help us escape. We'll serve you, Master, Keeper of all the memory-lands, the true Moth of chalk. Erigena. Let us rise again, in porcelain bliss, to dance by the light of the moon...'

Jemma flung his putrid hand from her mouth, but now he held her by the shoulder.

'Never,' she said, struggling against him. 'Not after what you've done.'

'Then at least I'll earn a vial of chalk for this. "Here"!' Magden hollered into the caves. 'I have her, here! The Erigena! The Daughter of Memory, no less, no more. I have her...powder...give me powder...'

## CHAPTER 44

# THE MEMORY OF THE SEA

Two robbed scholars dragged her up the stairs to the vaults of Ramus, where she saw once again the black altar – a raised platform in the centre of the hall surrounded by pillars of alabaster rising into the darkness.

Where the glass case had once held the Book of Memory, there was now a large tank filled with the Halogaic substance. Ramus was standing on the platform waiting for her. His expression was of a malice-hardened stone, yet she could see the satisfaction in his eyes.

'You are a foolish girl if you thought you could defeat the White Moth,' he said, his voice deep and severe, echoing in the vaults. 'And yet, they fulfilled their ultimate purpose. For you have returned of your own free will. The Keepers will soon be destroyed. And the Erigena, yes, indeed, she will Keep us all.'

He came up close. Peered into her eyes.

Jemma tried to squirm away, but a guard held her face in the lock of his grip.

'It is terrible, is it not, to be alone with one's own judge and avenger. You will be like a star thrown forth into empty space and into the waters of infinite solitude – have I explained it correctly, Tomassi? I wish her to know the details of her fate before we throw her into the tank. After all the trouble she has caused.'

Tomassi stepped forward, touching the sides of the glass as Jemma had seen him do once before when the Whale had floated lifeless and immense before him. Yet she saw that he was nervous – his arms shook. He steadied himself before he spoke.

'Of course, you are correct, in essence. Though may I add some detail to the noble theory you have so eloquently suppositioned?'

'Indeed you may,' Ramus said.

Tomassi walked back and forth as he spoke.

'To be set adrift in the Halogaic substance? For the Erigena it is like a living death. I mean, it is the inverse of life, yet life will not be extinguished. She will be, inside of herself, an implosion, a black hole, where memory splinters into light, contained within the vortex, a dispersal into luminous matter where you are all at once each moment of existence.'

He turned to her, only for a moment daring to meet her eyes. She remembered her fear inside the Delphin Caves when she thought she was trapped forever in the dark. But that helpless moment was nothing compared to now.

'You must prepare yourself for this final transformation. I say this for your own good. You must release and enter it tranquilly or else it will feel like you are being dragged screaming into the darkness, clawing at the sides of noth-ingness. Then you will be more darkness than you will be light. But you yourself, you will be the worst enemy you encounter. You yourself lie in wait inside this vast empti-ness. All your chambers of fear, your ravines and forests and shadows. To stare into the world as it is, formless, black and empty, yet full of power, swirling invisibly, wanting no more than to form yourself from your own cesspit of whirling. Has not all of memory demanded such a consciousness?'

'And tell us of the song she will sing.' Ramus spoke with an almost childlike relish. 'I wish to hear of it again.'

Tomassi cleared his throat. 'Surely, your Grace, the girl has heard enough. This is cruelty beyond measure.'

'Nonsense,' Ramus said, 'continue at once. To the end. Unless you wish to join her.'

'Very well.' Tomassi continued to pace. 'The...sheer terror of the abyss will...release a song. A dirge, one could say. More like a howl that otherwise must never be heard, must never be uttered, for the terror and rage and anguish could unleash even blacker holes than the one she had created, imploding all within. Eating a world or creating Ruptures that we could not know to where. But without it, we could not release the – the pure opening of...potential.'

Ramus took her face in his hand, gripping her cheeks so it hurt.

'I will take what Frater Jiordano has so long denied my great teacher, Scoppius. The sweetest revenge of all – to witness your eternal fate, Daughter of Memory, as the death of the Keepers of Adocentyn, and the source of a new world shaped by *my* will.'

'That will *never* happen.' Jemma squirmed and kicked against the scholar's grip. 'You've got to stop him!' She glowered at Tomassi, who cowered back.

Ramus's face cracked with laughter. He waved his gold-ringed fingers in the air.

'Throw her into the tank.'

At first, it was like she was falling through an endless sky until a substance cushioned her and she felt the memory releasing, dispersing, a billion photons of light. She wanted to reach out and grab hold of the images but now they were islands and she was a raft drifting away, until she found herself washed up on the shore. It was the same memory she had seen in the Scarp-palace, at the beginning of the film that she had so long ago fed onto the reel: a child, playing in the shallows of the waves. Only now it continued.

Jemma looked up, into her mother's eyes. She was smiling down at her.

'I knew I would find you again,' her mother said.

Jemma marvelled at her loving face, at the devotion in her eyes. It was a caressing force like nothing she had ever seen or felt or known. A power so gentle it seemed to hum with the sweetness of bees.

'Where are we?' Jemma heard her own words as the child's voice.

'Where we need to be,' her mother said. 'Where I can hold you for a while longer.'

She brushed the sand from her daughter's hands and the sides of her eyes. Jemma felt her salty touch. She could hear the gentle waves, feel the coolness of the water on her toes, the warmth of the sun on her back.

'They want to hurt me,' Jemma said.

'They cannot hurt you here.' Her mother held her closer, kissed her.

'You're the voice, aren't you? The voice I could hear, all along. You've been waiting.'

She felt the nodding on her cheek.

'But I cannot stay for long,' she said. 'Forgive me.'

Her voice was as soothing as the waves.

'What will I do? I'm stuck, and I can't feel my arms any more. I can't move.'

'You can move with this memory.'

Jemma felt herself release into the little limbs that must

have once belonged to her. She felt a sudden joy, as if she had only just learned to walk.

'But how will I get out?'

Her mother was stroking her hair.

'Look before you. What do you see?'

'Nothing but the ocean.'

'Then use the ocean.' She said.

Jemma reached out and touched the water.

'Wait. Mother...'

'I must go, my darling one.'

'Can't you stay? Just a bit more?'

'Time is running out...'

'Wait...'

'I have to leave your memory now, so another may come. I will search for you.'

She turned and smiled and walked over the sand, further and further away, until she disappeared into a line of trees.

Stabbing sadness washed over Jemma like a wave. All at once, she felt a sharp, awakening pain. A sudden jolt. She saw Ramus through the glass, and Tomassi, peering in as if looking at a specimen, writing and recording all of his observations in a book.

She looked into the memory again. A man was walking towards her, with dark hair, wearing a plain white tunic.

'I recognise you,' he said.

'I'm Jemma...'

'Just as I remember, when you were three years old. Do you know where we are?'

'In my memory – the one I share with my mother.'

'And the one you share with me. Show me what you are holding...'

Jemma held up her little sword.

'How can that be? It's the Blade of Adocentyn.'

'I took it from your palace in the Scarp. I'm sorry.'

'Don't be,' he said, kneeling. 'Look how it glows at your touch – the first rays of the sun. The blade will only glow for the Erigena. Tell me, what must we do?'

'Hold my hand,' Jemma said. 'If you want to come with me.'

Bruno took her hand. With her other she reached out, her arm floating, the blade slicing through the Halogaic glass. Blurry faces on the other side formed the most grotesque expressions of fear, as she released the memory of the sea.

~

A MASS OF WATER SWIRLED AROUND THE ALTAR, CAUSING a whirlpool to spiral down beneath them. It was a Rupture, an opening to the Shadow city. Jemma held on to a pillar, her head dizzy from the Halogaic. She looked over the edge to the bottom of the whirlpool, where she could see the spire of the Black Moat, the putrid canals, the pyre swarming with Shadows awaiting the execution.

Ramus pushed against Tomassi to keep himself from falling in. Tomassi lost his balance, grabbing the two scholars beside him but they were all sucked into the swirl, their faces frayed with terror, screaming into the city of Shadows.

Bruno faced Ramus in the centre of the altar. They were the same height. The same build. They had the same dark hair, except Bruno had far-gazing loving eyes, while Ramus's were as cold as marble.

'You know the two worlds must balance,' Bruno said. 'One of us will be drawn into the Rupture.'

Ramus lunged at Bruno, grabbing his arms, wrestling him towards the edge, Bruno slipping on the black shiny stone.

'I will not burn in your place for eternity,' Ramus said.

'Neither will I.' Bruno pushed and Ramus lost ground. But his stony grip was stronger and he wrestled Bruno back.

'You have no powers here anymore do you, "great Magus". You are weak. You have no Keepers at the call of your will.'

'No,' Bruno said. His feet were sliding closer to the edge. 'But she does.'

Jemma let go of the pillar, a fuzziness still clouded her mind but she focused on the Scarp, the place inside her she would always return to. She summoned the great North wind, which blew against Ramus, his hair streaming, his face grimacing. Bruno pushed him to the opposite edge.

Jemma thought of Adeline and Camillo and the memory of Leorah. Of Raddahkin and the Terns – did they make it through the Moth swarm? Of the lost Gull Keeper and the Caravanassi boy Yoska drowning in the sea. Of the songs of the Whales. Of Arlen, and his father who was killed in a cell. Her dearest Soren falling as the brightest star from the icy Northern skies. Of the Queen Amara and the memory seed. The terrible pits and the weeping trees. And Edgar – Edgar – where could he be? She looked at Ramus and held the wind against him.

'You've got two choices now,' she said. 'Return to the Shadow city by your own free will, or I'll blast you over the edge.'

Ramus looked over his shoulder to the bottom of the whirlpool. Only his grip on Bruno stopped him falling. But Ramus leaned with all his weight, his cracked face smiling as he pulled Bruno with him into the Rupture.

'No!' Jemma slid across the altar, peering over the edge. The Shadow city disappeared as the walls of the whirlpool broke like thundering dams, crashing into the Rupture. It had swallowed one of them, but it left the other swirling in the waves that rose and crashed against the walls of the vault. Jemma grabbed hold of the pillar and then she saw him sweeping past in the swell. She took his arm. Bruno held on as the water peaked and suddenly receded, draining with incredible force into the caverns below, extinguishing the lights, drowning the piercing screams of the Moth Queen and her spawn – the great wave gushing out of the caves and smashing through the forest.

## CHAPTER 45

## RETURN

P iera gathered up the bundle of black feathers and scrambled up the hill of the Scarp.

'Foolish Raven,' she said.

Several times she lost her footing.

'Foolish Raven,' she said again, as she walked across the rocky path, through the palace door, and into the study, where a fire crackled gently in the grate.

She placed him on the soft cushions of the divan where Jemma had once helped herself to a fresh almond cake, and stoked the fire, sending little embers rising into the hearth.

Edgar's eyes were still closed, but his chest was rising and falling with breath.

The housekeeper took out an iron plate and set the kettle to boil on the flames until the tea-steam drifted around the room like a tonic. Still, he did not stir.

From a little glass vial, she dripped water into his beak. Then she sighed and gently stroked his wing.

'All the trouble that came the minute you two set foot inside that door. Trouble indeed.'

She puffed the remaining cushions and stoked the fire once more.

'Now just you wait here,' she said gently. 'We have guests in the kitchen. We are preparing a feast for Miss Jemma. You'll wake up for her, I dare say, if you'll wake up for any.'

～

'PLEASE...MERCY,' WAS THE ONLY VOICE JEMMA AND Bruno heard in the silence and the blackness in the caverns.

'Go then,' Jemma said, and let Magden out of the cell.

'I bow to you...Erigena...Daughter of Memory. Never will I forget...'

He changed and fluttered into the dark. Where once the lights swirled with the White Moth, the cavern was now black and empty, emitting a putrid vapour that filled the air.

Jemma and Bruno walked in silence out of the cave, along the cliff and through the trees, which had been uprooted with the force of the vast Halogaic wave. All the pits were filled with mud and debris floating in from the forest. Now the earth was a black sludge. Each step was slow and heavy. The smell of the ash coals of ancient trees mingled with the salt of the sea.

There was no fog any longer in the canopies, and on the road ahead of them the last line of the Caravanassi, broken free of the loop, trudged through the mud and the wreckage, abandoning their wagons as they walked. An old blind woman in a black veil turned, holding the hand of a little girl who guided her along the path. She seemed to look at Jemma and nodded because she knew. She knew.

Jemma's eyes were filled with the bleakness of the ruined valley, her mind wandering in the lingering memory seeping into the night.

A hand took hold of hers. She did not resist its guidance as Bruno pulled her up the steep ridge, where she once used to scramble seeking treasure.

'Climbing the Scarp,' Bruno said. 'Just like you've done a million times before.'

When they reached the palace, lovely smells greeted them in the stairway, stirring up feelings of melancholy that seemed to ache and long for its own dwelling place in the dark.

'I can't believe I didn't see you that day,' Bruno said, 'hiding behind the curtain. If only I'd known you were there.'

'What did you expect?' Jemma said. 'I'm a Scarp hunter.'

Bruno smiled. 'Piera must be cooking up a feast.'

'Where did she come from?'

'When I was a boy, she was more than a housekeeper. She was like a mother to me – I could never forget her. You should go to the kitchen,' Bruno said. 'I think your friends are waiting. I know you still have questions – I will see you later in the study.'

JEMMA LINGERED OUTSIDE THE KITCHEN. SHE HEARD Adeline speaking.

'Mrs Hurley may have been mean, but she knew how to make the best potatoes. She never taught me, but I used to watch her. She would boil them first so they were soft in the middle, and then coat them in butter before she put them in the oven so the skins were crisp and golden.'

'J – just like these,' Arlen said.

She went in.

'Jemma!' Adeline came forward and took her hands. 'You *have* to try my potatoes.'

'And my ragout,' Piera said. 'But not yet – someone needs to set the table, and that's not going to be me.'

'I w-will,' Arlen said. 'But first – g-good to see you.'

Jemma hugged him. Tears gathered in his eyes. 'I'm s-sorry about Soren. I c-couldn't save him.'

'It wasn't your fault,' Jemma said. Her eyes filled too.

'He was the b-bravest wrestler I ever saw.'

Adeline hugged them both. 'I long to hear your story one day,' she said to Jemma.

'And I want to hear yours – Queen of the Delphin.'

Adeline still wore her armour. 'You will always have a place at our banquet table, in the Great Delphin Hall. The caves have come to life again, thanks to you.'

'I'm s-sure you'll want to know,' Arlen said. 'Camillo is helping Raddahkin s-salvage all the Tern ships they can.'

'Where is Edgar?' Jemma said. She had been scanning the kitchen expecting him to fly in at any moment.

'Oh, you should have seen him,' Piera said, 'when he come out of the forest, through the fog, leading all those Shadows that were chasing after him. They set upon the White Moth like the darkness to the light, and then it was like they were all devoured. Like they all cancelled each other out. A pure obliteration. It was him who done it. It was him who took them down, just when all was lost, *when the Shadows rise again.*'

'But where is he?' Jemma said.

'Upstairs in the study. He is – sleeping.'

Jemma ran up the stairs and down the corridor, until she came into the study. Bruno was sitting at his desk, the Book of Memory open before him.

'He is there, nestled in the cushions by the fire.'

She knelt down and stroked Edgar's feathers. The pot of tea beside him was still warm and she filled the vial with cinnamon-scented tea, sending little drops into

Edgar's beak. He moved and received it, but did not open his eyes.

'I heard what you did,' she said. Her tears spilled down her cheeks. 'Brave Raven.'

Bruno stood beside her.

'He will regain his mind and his memory,' Bruno said. 'But it will be a long recovery. Indeed what courage, to have flown through a forest of fog.'

Jemma watched Edgar's breaths rise and fall – but she already knew how a Raven sleeps.

'I once feared the Erigena and the prophecy that has come to pass,' Bruno said. 'That's why I searched for you all those years ago.'

'Were you going to kill me too?'

'I thought that I would make a Rupture, to a place far away on the edges of the unformed lands.'

'Banish me – like you were banished?'

'Yes, I suppose. But when I met your mother, everything changed. You know the story. As soon as I set my eyes on you, I knew that I could never harm you. That I would love you – dare I say more so than your own father, who brought you into all of this danger for his own selfish ends.'

'You were watching me, all this time?'

'I charged the Terns with protecting you. In the end, you were the one who protected us all, and the land itself. But we cannot stay here.'

'Why?'

'The Seals will not give up. There are two Sigilli left, and the Seals will hunt you down to fight against the prophecy.'

'But you created them, didn't you?'

'Yes, with one purpose – to eliminate what most threatens this land. I cannot alter that mission.'

'How can I threaten Adocentyn when I'm the one who Keeps it?'

'Because you already Keep too much – and as your powers grow, in the hands of our enemies, you would be the key to a new world. A new order. For you have not yet learned to master your powers, even though you have learned to use them. And so long as you are still *potential*, you are the greatest threat of all.'

Jemma stood beside the fire. 'Where would we go?'

'To the world where you were born. It will give us time. A place to hide. Thanks to you, I had the Book of Memory to make our passage. From there, we will search for a way to find your mother.'

'Where is she?' Jemma said.

'The Rupture I spoke of earlier – your mother used it to enter the unformed lands. She thought, from there, she could find her way to Adocentyn.'

'But she did find me...'

'Only in the memory we created, together.' Bruno took Jemma to the projector.

'You've fixed it,' she said, running her fingers over the newly spliced film.

'It was me behind the camera,' Bruno said. 'We made this memory so we could always find you, if we needed to. I must warn you, though.'

'About what?'

'To return to your world, through the Rupture – you will forget this land. It will haunt you, and yet you will hold it inside you, and feel its effects. That is how you will Keep the land safe, until you have to return.'

'How will I know?'

'Adocentyn will call you, if it needs you.'

'I won't leave Edgar,' Jemma said. 'Who will look after him?'

'Piera,' Bruno said. 'I trust her completely. She may eventually grow irritated with his infinite curiosity –'

Jemma went and stroked his feathers again. 'He can drive you mad alright.'

'But she will never let any harm come to him. I promise you that.'

Bruno pulled back the curtain. 'We must go now. The Seals will already know you are here, just as they will sense that you are gone from the land. If you want to protect the Raven, and all that you have fought for, we must go.'

Bruno pressed on the wooden panel. He opened the door.

Jemma kissed Edgar's beak. She nuzzled her face in his wings. She whispered to him through her tears – 'Didn't I tell you, Edgar – we'd find something big this time.'

~

Keep in the loop about Jemma and Edgar's next adventures in the memory-lands by visiting: www.bdreeves.com or signing up to my reader's list: www.bdreeves.com/contact

If you would like to help other readers discover *Jemma and the Raven*, please consider leaving a review at your book retailer of choice. Thank you and happy reading!

# AUTHOR'S NOTE

The Renaissance memory magic of Giordano Bruno (1548-1600) and his rebellion against the authorities of the Inquisition provided historical inspiration for the broader narrative behind *Jemma and the Raven*. Bruno, like me, was fascinated by the ancient Greek practice known as the 'art of memory'. People would construct elaborate fictional palaces in their minds to hold memories – often represented as objects and symbols placed inside rooms in special combinations. To remember something, you would picture yourself walking through your palace, in and out of the rooms. The furnishings and objects you had placed inside would spark the corresponding memories. (Jemma and Edgar, of course, discover a memory palace in the Scarp in Chapter 1). Bruno developed the Greek art into an even more elaborate system of the mind, where the imagery of memory could be used, manipulated and configured in magical ways to channel powers and open up innumerable possible worlds. The name for such a figure was a *memory Magus (magician)*.

Giordano Bruno was known as a passionate, intensely

curious, temperamental, creative and original thinker who dared to challenge authority with his imagination. He was also considered a heretic for his books and beliefs about memory magic, and was eventually burned at the stake. Apart from these broad facts, the Jiordano Bruno in *Jemma and the Raven* is a fictional character. In the novel, I play with the purely fantastical idea – what if he was never actually executed, but used his powers as a Magus to forge a passage to the memory-lands, and escape?

The City of Adocentyn took inspiration from a magical utopian memory city. It was originally described in what Giordano Bruno and other Renaissance mystic-philosophers believed was an ancient text, called the *Picatrix*. Adocentyn is credited with being the first depiction of a utopian city in Western literature.

The 'Shadows' is a term used in Bruno's philosophical ideas about memory images. However, in the novel, I use Shadows to depict memories that die without the love of a Keeper, as well as a type of memory born from suffering and despair. Likewise, the term 'Sigilli' is borrowed from Bruno's actual writings, but used differently in the novel, where it provides a general name for the 'monsters of memory'.

The practitioners of Renaissance memory-magic were fond of using animals and forms of matter as symbolic or talismanic totems. I use this idea for the Keepers, who have the power to transform between animal and human forms, and whose memory is also grounded in a special type of substance – such as wood, rock or water.

The Caravanassi are completely fictional and do not depict any particular historical period or people. I have cherry picked a number of historical names for other characters, borrowed from the cultural milieu surrounding Bruno's life and times. Pico Camillo is an amalgam of Pico Mirandola and Giulio Camillo, both creative and inventive practitioners of the art of memory, who came before Bruno. The terms 'Erigena' and 'Halogaic' are also wholly made up. They are pronounced 'Er-i-jeen-a' and 'Hal-o-jay-ic' respectively.

As far as the bad guys go, I chose names that had a ring of harsh consonants about them, and who might have stood on the side of the authority. The name Ramus was drawn from Peter Ramus, a rather stern reformer who tried to abolish the use of imagination in the art of memory. Of course, Peter Ramus was not evil, compared to the Ramus in the novel, who is. Gaspar Scoppius was actually quite a nasty character of the time, as well as in the novel. He is believed to have attended Giordano Bruno's execution, and was known to be a man of "malignant and contentious spirit" who stood on the side of the Inquisition. Mocenigo was a real historical figure who did betray Bruno to the Venetian Inquisition while he was staying at Mocenigo's house as a tutor and guest. I have used these basic facts to create the obsequious character of Mocenigo in the Shadow city. Sir Francis Gilbert is a purely fictional name and character with no origins in the history of memory.

# ACKNOWLEDGMENTS

While the act of writing is solitary, the journey of bringing a book to life is filled with many acts of generosity and support. I would firstly like to thank my family for putting up with my retreats into solitude, for listening to almost every update on the plot, and for believing in me and the story. A great debt of gratitude is owed to my readers of early drafts – Natasha Allen, Eva Mills and Emily Gale – your responses, comments and feedback were invaluable. To the editors who contributed to the book – Alison Arnold and Lu Sexton – I cannot thank you enough for your queries, challenges, encouragements and meticulous scrutiny of every word. Many sources were consulted for historical inspiration. The most significant by far were the works of the late, renowned Renaissance memory scholar, Francis Yates. In particular, *The Art of Memory* gave wonderful insights into the history of memory from ancient Greece to the end of the Renaissance; *Giordano Bruno and the Hermetic Tradition* provided the most illuminating foray into the origins of memory magic.

www.bdreeves.com